THE VERY INSIDE

An Anthology of Writing by

Asian and Pacific Islander

Lesbian and Bisexual Women

EDITED BY

Sharon Lim-Hing

ISBN 0-920813-97-6

1994 copyright Sharon Lim-Hing

Individual selections copyright © by their respective author(s)

Acknowledgement of permission to reprint material will be found
at the end of the book.

Canadian Cataloguing in Publication Data

Main entry under title:

The Very Inside: An Anthology of Writing by Lesbian and Bisexual
Asian and Pacific Islander Women

ISBN 0-920813-97-6

1. Lesbians' writings, American.
2. Lesbians'writings, Canadian (English).*
3. American literature — Asian American authors.
4. Canadian literature (English) — Asian—Canadian authors.*
5. American literature — Pacific Islander Americanauthors.
6. Canadian literature (English) — PacificIslander — Canadian authors.*
7. American literature — Women authors.
8. Canadian literature (English) — Women authors.*
9. Bisexuality —Literary collections.
10. Lesbianism — Literary collections.
11. American literature — 20th century.
12. Canadian literature (English) —20th century.*
I. Lim-Hing, Sharon

PS508.L47V4 1994   810.8'0353   C94—930680—0

Cover Art: Shelter/Wedding piece 1992 Debi Ray-Chaudhuri
Production: Leela Acharya
Managing Editor: Makeda Silvera
Cover & Book Design: Stephanie Martin
Typesetting/layout: Jacqueline Rabazo Lopez
Printed and bound in Canada by union labour

Published by **Sister Vision Press**
P. O. Box 217, Station E
Toronto, Ontario
M6H 4E2   Canada

Sister Vision
Black Women and Women of Colour Press

THE VERY INSIDE

An Anthology of Writing by

Asian and Pacific Islander

Lesbian and Bisexual Women

EDITED BY

Sharon Lim-Hing

Acknowledgements

SINCE THERE ARE MANY WHOSE NAMES I DON'T KNOW, I can't thank everyone who has helped in the long process of making this anthology. However, I would like to name a few people whose belief in this anthology has sustained me and developed the book. For their part in getting out the call for submissions, I would like to thank V.K. Aruna, Mi Ok Bruining, Susan Y.F. Chen, Siong Huat Chua, Anna Fang, Gayatri Gopinath, Joyoti Grech, Naomi Guilbert, Darlena Bird Jimenes, Donna Tanigawa, Nellie Wong, and many others.

Thanks to the ad hoc committee that prepared the terrain for more work by Pacific Islander women: Peou Lakhana, Trinity A. Ordona, Kris Lee (AKA Lee Sauw Wah), Carol U. Song, Ann Mei Chang, Caroline Jean Lee, Jee Yuen Lee, Ann Y. Uyeda, Eveline Shen, Lisa Kahaleole Chang Hall, Haejung Shin, and J. Kehaulani Kauanui. Thanks to the New England War Tax Resistance for early financial support. Thanks to Indigo Som for lending the title of one of her poems to this anthology. To Leela Acharya, thanks for her flair for detail throughout the production process. I would like to express my gratitude to Jacquelyn Ching Black, Larissa Heinrich and Makeda Silvera for their support in all phases of the anthology; Makeda's guidance and experience have been invaluable. Finally, I would like to thank my mother for her support and love.

Table of Contents

Introduction Sharon Lim-Hing

ORIGINS, DEPARTURES

Shrapnel Shards on Blue Water Lê Thi Diem Thúy	2
The Polite Question Svati Shah	5
New Mexico Asian Pacific Lesbian Tze-Hei Yong	7
I Am a Story Ami R. Mattison	12
Manahambre Road Shani Mootoo	16
Re-Entry Lisa Kahaleole Chang Hall	18
Who Am I? Anu	19
24 Frames Jacquelyn Ching Black	22
Scorched Willy♀ Chang Snow Wilkinson	23
White Rice: Searching for Identity Juliana Pegues/Pei Lu Fung	25
2632 Then and Now C. Allyson Lee	37
Who Am I? Peou Lakhana	40
Heart Murmur Mi Ok Song Bruining	42
Ancestor Teresa Tan	44
Owed to Grandmother C. Allyson Lee	45
What is Between Us? Teresa Tan	49
For Naan Shani Mootoo	50
Putih V.K. Aruna	52
True Confessions of a Queer Banana Midi Onodera	64
Lost Pictures Sharon Lim-Hing	70

FINDING/FOUNDING COMMUNITY

Family Reunion: The Longing Elsa E'der	74
A Recognition Shani Mootoo	76
An Asian Pacific Lesbian's Alphabet Alice Y. Hom	78
Slowly, But Surely, My Search for Family Acceptance and Community Continues Susan Y.F. Chen	79
Tita Talk Zelie Duvauchelle, J. Kehaulani Kauanui, Leolani M., and Desiree Thompson	85

All At Once, All Together   Ann Yuri Uyeda   109

Lunch Vignettes   Svati Shah   122

Something We Both Know   Svati Shah   124

distractions   Vanessa Marzan Deza   126

We Three: X, Y, and Z   Rini Das   128

Solitary Bravo   Darlena Bird Jimenes   129

Gold Gate (Gam Moen)   Brenda Joy Lem   143

Rice Dreams   Linda Fong   144

My Mother's Mother   Amy A. Zukeran   147

Anita and Auntie   Kitty Tsui   149

A Chinese Banquet   Kitty Tsui   154

Tha Phi Neah Yeung The...? (Only the Two of Us...?)   Peou Lakhana   156

A Letter to Female Homosexuals   Patrice Leung   162

WAKING FROM A DREAM OF LOVE

AT&T   V.K. Aruna   166

Yoo Hoo   Susan Ito   167

this hunger in my hips   Vanessa Marzan Deza   184

Making Love to You   Little Earthquake   187

the very inside   Indigo Chih-Lien Som   188

Summer, Manhattan, 1991   Minal Hajratwala   189

Jeannie   Mina Kumar   191

Foresee   Le Thi Diem Thuy   212

Island Dream   Ana Bantigue Fajardo   215

warm weather thoughts   Vanessa Marzan Deza   217

Brewing Secrets   Minal Hajratwala   219

Misplacing Alissa   Ami R. Mattison   221

Amita and Vinita   Ka Yin Fong   233

Dusk to Dawn   Neesha Dosanjh   234

in my sleep   Indigo Chih-Lien Som   237

Enchanting Forest   Brenda Joy Lem   239

Love Poem   Little Earthquake   240

Letter from Bali   Naomi Guilbert   241

Untitled Linda C. Parece   242

When My Love Lay Sleeping... Suniti Namjoshi   243

Swirling Tales, and the Concept of Tea Lisa Asagi   244

Stork Cools Wings Mona Oikawa   249

Rati Little Earthquake   255

Ode to a Fierce Butch Lani Ka'ahumanu   256

Akairo (The Color Red) Tomiye Ishida   258

Just once before I die I want someone to make love to me in Cantonese   260
    Indigo Chih-Lien Som

Your Love Has Undone Me Nila Gupta   262

LIFE STRUGGLE

A Litany for Our Survival Vanessa Marzan Deza   266

Identification Card Nila Gupta   270

In the Mind of An/Other Alice Y. Hom   272

internalization Indigo Chih-Lien Som   276

Ashes Lisa Kahaleole Chang Hall   277

Suddenly, You Realize... Margaret Mihee Choe   279

Often It Is a Stilted Eye Which Contains One Woman's Love for Another Heidi Li   284

A Visit Home Heidi Li   286

Olelo Kupuna O Hapa Kanaka Maoli Wahine J. Kehaulani Kauanui   292

Little Girl Blue Neesha Dosanjh   293

Invitation Canyon Sam   296

December 1989 Patrice Leung   307

Who Will Remember Me When I Return to America Elsa E'der   312

Custody Lynne Yamaguchi Fletcher   317

Recurring Dreams Lynne Yamaguchi Fletcher   319

Junks Inside Me Donna Tsuyuko Tanigawa   321

Butterflies Lihbin Shiao   326

Recipe C. Allyson Lee   333

OUT OF FIRE, GRACE

Yellow Woman Speaks Merle Woo		342
Oh Canada Nila Gupta		343
Mini Liu, Long-time Activist Linda Wong		345
Love Letters From the Movement Ann Yuri Uyeda		352
Debi Ray-Chaudhuri: Working towards a new language Joyoti Grech		363
Leolani M., Native Hawaiian Islander Joyoti Grech		369
The Myth of One Closet V.K. Aruna		373
"Asian Pacific Islander:" Issues of Representation and Responsibility		
J. Kehaulani Kauanui and Ju Hui "Judy" Han		376
In Search of a More Complete Definition of Activism Eveline Shen		380
The Challenges Facing Asian and Pacific Islander Lesbian		
and Bisexual Women in the U.S. Trinity A. Ordona		384
Cross-Racial Hostility and Inter-Racial Conflict Trinity A. Ordona		391
Response to "Room of One's Own" Anu		398
Untitled Sharon Fernandez		403
Representations of Indian Lesbianism Mina Kumar		404
The Politics of Breast Cancer Merle Woo		416
I Like Beef Wit' Words Donna Tsuyuko Tanigawa		426
Untitled Anuja Mendiratta		428
Hapa Haole Wahine Lani Ka'ahumanu		432
Contributors' Notes		454

Introduction

O N THE DAY I FIRST HAD THE IDEA TO START THIS ANTHOLOGY, my reasons were somewhat different from what they are now. It was the summer of 1990 in Somerville, Massachusetts, whose streets I walked in fearful, defiant anticipation of clusters of teenagers wielding the word "Chink." Heat was entering the triple-decker apartment building like a steam press riding the hood of a Mack truck, and the neighbors' dog, tied up outside my window, was barking incessantly. In that uncomfortable moment, it became clear to me that Asian and Pacific Islander lesbians should have our own book, apart from just a few of us representing all of us in the larger spectrum of women of color anthologies, apart from appearing furtively in collections of works by predominantly straight Asian women, and apart from helping to provide diversity for white-dominated anthologies. I wanted a book of our own that would speak to us about our lives as lesbians and bisexual women and our experiences in the many racist, homophobic communities that we inhabit. When reading anthologies by Asian women in general, for example, I often felt left out, since the overall themes did not address issues specific to lesbians and bisexual women.

At that time, we did have *Between the Lines: An Anthology of Pacific/Asian Lesbians of Santa Cruz*, (eds. C. Chung, A. Kim, A.K. Lemeshewsky, Dancing Bird Press, 1987). It was thrilling to see pictures and poems and stories of women with whom I could readily identify, but it was an out-of-print book that was hard to find. Also, as the subtitle stated, it set out to offer a pioneering but limited sample — of six contributors. For our issues, thoughts, dreams and rage, we deserved a large book along the lines of collections such as *This Bridge Called My Back: Writings by Radical Women of Color* (eds. Cherríe Moraga and Gloria Anzaldúa, Kitchen Table Press, 1981) and *Nice Jewish Girls: A Lesbian Anthology* (ed. Evelyn Torton Beck, Beacon Press, 1982).

I liked the format of an anthology; a successful anthology presents, in an intelligent and engaging way, an array of visions and voices. Some are sure, experienced artists to whom we readily surrender. Others are rough cut and raw, hesitant yet insistent, or idiosyncratic and even quirky: new voices to add to the polyphonic richness of the whole. The Asian Pacific Lesbian (APL) community, as it was called then and is still sometimes called now, certainly had its established writers, and as my four-year odyssey confirmed, more than its share of undiscovered, gifted creators.

Early on, I expanded the idea of the book to include bisexual women. My experience in Boston-based groups like the Alliance of Massachusetts Asian Lesbians and Gay Men (AMALGM) and Asian Sisters in Action (ASIA) showed that a considerable number of Asian women identify as bisexual, for reasons yet to be determined. I wanted to include these women, queer companions and sister resisters to compulsory heterosex. And it was important to do so, I felt, in light of persistent biphobia. If it is true that bisexuals bring ambiguity to our midst, let us welcome this questioning in all of us, for rigidity often results in sickness or death.

The dream of the anthology progressed from conceptualization to a first call for submissions in 1991. The original call solicited writing and art work by Asian Pacific Islander lesbians and bisexual women. Although a number of publishers expressed an interest in the project in its early stages, in 1992 I decided to ask Makeda Silvera if Sister Vision Press would be interested in taking on this anthology. I admired how Makeda had constructed the generous, beautiful and far-reaching collection, *Piece of my Heart: A Lesbian of Colour Anthology* (ed. Makeda Silvera, Sister Vision Press, 1991). It was a successful collaboration between Canadian and U.S. lesbian writers, which I also wished to achieve. Another compelling reason to work with Sister Vision was that it is a woman of color press. Makeda answered enthusiastically, and Sister Vision and I began to coordinate outreach efforts.

We put notices and ads in journals, magazines, and newspapers and sent stacks of flyers to conferences, events, bookstores, publishers, schools, community centers, writers' groups, and all sorts of organizations. We also called or wrote to women and encouraged them to send in their work or to create something new for the anthology. Many people pitched in, distributing and posting flyers locally. Word of mouth also helped get the call out.

It was during this second call for submissions (extended three times in 1993) — more like a campaign — that questions about some essential terms arose. More than one potential South Asian contributor asked if "Asian" in this context included South Asians. Given the many anecdotes I've heard and read of South Asians who were told that they did not belong to established, primarily East Asian groups operating under the rubric of Asian or Asian-American, this was not surprising. But it saddened me.

Intellectually I knew that the reciprocal claiming of and exclusion to "Asian" has historic roots. Immigration patterns bear a close relation to colonialism; the metropole extends or denies entry to denizens of its (former) colonies and territories according to its current labor needs, political climate, and level of condescension. At the same time, conditions in our countries of origin encourage us or our ancestors to stay or to leave. Because of entry restrictions that have allowed in more East than South Asians, in the U.S. "Asian" refers to people, things and ideas of East Asian ethnicities, most often Chinese and Japanese, even though Indians have been coming to the U.S. since the nineteenth century. Conversely, in the U.K., "Asian" refers to people and cultures of the South Asian subcontinent, including but not limited to India, Bangladesh, Pakistan, Sri Lanka, and Nepal. In Canada, "Asian" has come to mean East Asian, and South Asians must struggle against invisibility. The struggle has been fruitful, however; the term "South Asian" is gaining more recognition. Furthermore, perhaps due in part to the unifying effects of severe classism and racism, the South Asian lesbian and bisexual women's community is one of the most vital and active in Canada. In the U.S., South Asian lesbians and bisexual women's energetic participation and leadership have led to greater respect for their concerns.

Yet it seems that many people continue to cling to a truncated version of "Asian" and think only of East Asians. It is true that the one word may be too confining for such a vast range of cultures and people. Are there enough reasons for "Asians" in the North American context to come together as one heterogeneous group? Do these reasons hold for lesbians and bisexual women, and are there additional reasons?

For the purposes of this anthology, "Asian" is used by women who identify some part of their heritage or origins in Asia, from South Asia to Southeast Asia (including Cambodia, Vietnam, Laos, Thailand, Malaysia,

Singapore, Indonesia, and the Philippines) to East Asia. Some of us were born in Asia, others' connection to that part of the earth dates back four or more generations. Some of us have dual or multiple heritages. Some of us were adopted, often by white parents. Some arrived in the U.S. or Canada via other places, like myself, third-generation Jamaican-born. For most of us, any heritage is much more complicated than simply pointing to a map.

Because ethnicity is often perceived visually, wherever I go people try to speak to me in Chinese, Japanese, or Korean. I suppose I have a homegirl look about me. But I'd be better able to respond if someone spoke to me in Jamaican English. Within this rhythmic mix of African, European, and Asian words and inflections, I grew up believing that all kinds of people can live, love, and work together. Generations earlier, East and South Asians settled in many parts of the Caribbean, where they joined a palette of peoples. It is the island of Jamaica, inhabited by people of all colors, that comes closest to any definition of home for me.

Different relationships to a real or imagined Asia do not illustrate atypical ways of relating to one's "heritage" (because there is no one model), but rather point to the wide range and potential of any definition. It also indicates the choice we each have between conforming to available identities or challenging and extending the content and boundaries of those identities to suit ourselves.

One example of using this choice is illustrated by the term "Asian and Pacific Islander," which clumps together Asians and Pacific Islanders (indigenous Samoans, Fijians, Hawaiians, Guamanians, Polynesians, and so on). In 1990 the phrase was used by the U.S. Census Bureau as one of the four major racial categories (the three others being white, African-American and Native North American). In the U.S., many groups had already adopted this terminology, probably with the best of intentions. Yet from West to East Coast, many "API" organizations had few or no members of Pacific Islander heritage and missions that ignored Pacific Islander issues. In their essay "'Asian Pacific Islander:' Issues of Representation and Responsibility," J. Kehaulani Kauanui and Ju Hui "Judy" Han discuss the "engulfing" of Pacific Islanders by Asian-Americans and the differences between the two groups that this inclusion glosses over. For example, the types of racist stereotypes that Pacific Islander women face are different from those facing East Asian women; these and other specifically Pacific Islander issues have never been addressed by an API agenda.

The lesbian and bisexual women's community also reflected this inclusion/marginalization of Pacific Islander women. But at the West Coast Regional Asian/Pacific Lesbian and Bisexual Network (APLBN) retreat, which took place in California in October 1993, women of Native Hawaiian heritage spoke out against the presumptions behind the term API. It was high time for a thorough examination of the status quo. Out of the pain and self-examination of that conference, a committee formed in San Francisco in order to generate texts by women of Pacific Islander heritage specifically for this anthology. With input from Pacific Islander women, Asian women took responsibility for creating conditions within which Pacific Islander women might feel that their name was not being stolen and their issues suppressed. It was through this committee that most Pacific Islander contributors sent in their work.

Previously, I had been wavering in regard to Pacific Islander women's work. Few had responded to the call for submissions, undoubtedly wary of further cooptation. I did not want to tokenize the women who had responded. Nor did I want to close them out, since they wanted to be a part of the anthology. So the implosion of "API" at the retreat was a timely opportunity for this anthology and the movement to reconsider what this coalition might mean and what it can bring about.

I don't claim that this anthology resolves the issues around the terms Asian, Pacific Islander, or Asian and Pacific Islander. In fact, this book may raise more questions than it pretends to answer. Any ensuing exploration of these terms I can only view as healthy. Self-definitions are in flux, as we create and discuss them. I have done my best to ensure that everyone feels welcome to participate in such a conversation.

Part of what I originally envisioned for this work was to include visual art. My one regret about this anthology is that it contains only a few examples of art. This is probably due to the fact that I am a writer, and did outreach as a writer, with a writer's connections. I am very proud, however, that the art is of a very high quality.

The Very Inside is arranged in five sections. "Origins, Departures" discusses the seeming imperatives, the construction, and the choices around identities. "Finding/Founding Community" explores the painful groping involved with finding or staying in a group in which one might be accepted and find the warmth and joys of comradeship. "Waking from a Dream of Love" contains work on desire, love, the relation between the two, and the ways that we dream and live out these elements. "Life Struggle" speaks of the hard part of surviving, the daily fight against racism, sexism, homophobia, violence, madness. In "Out of Fire, Grace," contributors write of organizing, activism, creativity, art: necessary, inspiring pieces for all of us.

During the four years of anthology gestation, folders and later cardboard boxes of manuscripts, letters and discs have been ferried from Somerville to Paris, Paris to Miami, and Miami to my kitchen in the Boston-area once again. Now the anthology is about to take off with the power of its strong and visionary contributions. As I look back on these four years, many of the reasons for which I originally ventured out on this long project still apply. However, celebrating the enormous variation and richness within this one, large group is now more important to me than defining Asian and Pacific Islander lesbians and bisexual women in opposition to other groups. In four years, I have come to a better understanding of the complex, perhaps impossible promise of such a grouping.

We are not a blip on the graph at an intersection of "race" and sexual preference, nor at the hub of triple oppressions (sexism, racism, homophobia). Yes, this book speaks of our many oppressions, but it also speaks of our strength, our beauty, our dynamism, and our creativity. We are escaping and resisting, extending and enriching what it means to be Pacific Islander and Asian, bisexual and lesbian, what it means to be alive, what it means to create. Here are different genres and different subjects by women who have taken their difference and channelled it into art. The work in this collection will challenge, perplex, entertain, and enlighten.

Sharon Lim-Hing
February, 1994

ORIGINS, DEPARTURES

Lê Thi Diem Thúy

to my sister lê thi diem trinh

shrapnel shards on blue water

every day i beat a path to run to you
beaten into the melting snow/the telephone poles
which separate us like so many signals of slipping time
and signposts marked in another language
my path winds and unwinds, hurls itself toward you
until it unfurls before you
all my stories at your feet
rocking against each other like marbles
down a dirt incline
listen

ma took the train every morning
sunrise
from phan thiet to saigon
she arrived
carrying food to sell at the markets
past sunset
late every evening she carried her empty baskets
home
on the train which runs in the opposite direction
away from the capital
towards the still waters of the south china sea

once ba bought an inflatable raft
yellow and black
he pushed it out onto a restricted part of the water
in southern california
after midnight
to catch fish in the dark
it crashed against the rocks
he dragged it back to the van
small and wet
he drove us home
our backs turned in shame
from the pacific ocean

our lives have been marked by the tide
everyday it surges forward
hits the rocks
strokes the sand
turns back into itself again
a fisted hand

know this about us
we have lived our lives
on the edge of oceans
in anticipation of
sailing into the sunrise

i tell you all this
to tear apart the silence
of our days and nights here

i tell you all this
to fill the void of absence
in our history here

we are fragmented shards
blown here by a war no one wants to remember

in a foreign land
with an achingly familiar wound
our survival is dependent upon
never forgetting that vietnam is not
a word
a world
a love
a family
a fear
to bury

let people know
VIETNAM IS NOT A WAR

let people know
VIETNAM IS NOT A WAR

but a piece
of
us,
sister
and
we are
so much

more

Svati Shah

The Polite Question

When they ask me where I'm from
they want described
an exotichappyspiritual Limbo Land
A nowhere place in brochures
and Funky Camp catalogues.

With my pen and a profound lack of social grace
I answer

that I am Actually from a house in the suburbs where we eat rice
and dal and talk about going to Disneyworld.

I am from a room upstairs that becomes a temple on weekend
mornings. As we hear the same sermon on Ma's mono tape
recorder, I listen to the Hindi cadences, the voice so familiar, and
watch my sister's face for an indication of the man's profundity. She
blinks rarely.

I am from the pillow in front of the T.V. where American culture
blared out hour after hour after hour. I am from the light box itself,
where I learned to love Julia Child's hands, the difference between
Kansas City and Topeka, and the virtues of smelling and tasting
like aerosol sprays.

I am from the driveway where we taught each other how to roller
skate and I faked an Indian accent to justify my brown skin.

I am from a small, beloved college town, where I discovered razor
blades, therapy, girl love, and the meaning of solitude.

I am from weekend retreats and conferences where we believe in our powers to change laws, attitudes, policies, ignorance. I am from circles of friends who teach me the phrase Woman-of-Color and concepts like "race management."

I am from bookstores and bookshelves which have seen my disappointed back when I realized that volumes full of childhood friends had never known an Indian heart.

AND
I am *from* the arms of the few who know
that I can talk like a Yankee and eat like a Gujarati, too.

Tze-Hei Yong

New Mexico APL

Y ES! THERE REALLY ARE LEFT-HANDED, ASIAN DYKES IN NEW MEXICO! I'm proof that we can and do exist out here in this Hispanic/Native American/Anglo state. Although I may be the only one...

Every few years, it seems, I meet a new relative that I haven't seen since I was very young. Inevitably at these encounters, usually when we all sit down to dinner, the new relative notices my sinistral tendencies and exclaims (in Cantonese, mind you), "Gosh! You're left-handed!" And then they ("they" being all my fluently-speaking-Cantonese, older-generation relatives) jabber away, talking of so-and-so, "who's also left-handed," and "Cousin M —she's left-handed too, you know," as if they were discussing who in the family had claimed to have seen spaceships or something. Apparently, left-handedness is a much rarer event among Asians than among Anglos.

At any rate, that's how I came to know of my Cousin M (on my mother's side): I kept hearing her name whenever my relatives got on the subject of my left-handedness. Since I was a kid, I've always thought maybe Cousin M was a dyke too. I mean, she was left-handed, wasn't she? Already a point in her favor for being different. In the pictures my parents had of her as a teen, she had short hair, was thin and kind of boyish, plus she had that certain *quality*, that I can only describe as "absence-of-trying-to-attract-the-opposite-gender." I did finally meet M in person a few years ago, but I'm afraid I couldn't tell if she was a womon-loving-womon or not. My "gaydar" (gay radar) doesn't seem to work cross-culturally very well, and M was raised in Hong Kong. She is in her early thirties now, and unmarried — perhaps she intends to emulate two aunts (on my mother's side), who have chosen to follow the honorable tradition of spinsterhood. Of course, that always leaves open to question whether my two aunts were indeed really spinsters. Ah, but I dare not ask them THAT.

Now, I have been to Hong Kong twice in my life, and when I was there for the second time a few years ago, I stayed with one of my cousins (on my mother's side) and his family. He's quite a few years older than I, and he told me a story that my mom told him many years ago about how my two brothers and I were named. As the story goes, my parents wanted to have two sons — and two sons only. In ancient Chinese history there were supposedly two kings who were brothers, and my parents were going to name their two sons for these two kings. Sure enough, their first child was a son, and so they named him after the first king. Then they had their second child — and that was me. Oops. Well, my cousin says there's a tradition that if you want a son but get a daughter, you give the daughter a male name and then the next child will be a son. So they named me after some other king, and left it at that. Sure enough, the number-three child was a son, whom they named after the second/king/brother like they'd planned. My cousin made it a point to add that girls who are given male names in fact often grow up to be rather masculine.

Now with that kind of a history, you'd think that my parents wouldn't have had such a hard time dealing with me being a lesbian, wouldn't you? Oh, well. Not so.

I can remember having dreams about holding other girls' hands and kissing them when I was fifteen. I never did anything about it, though. Just dreamed. When I got to college, I knew right away that we had a Gay and Lesbian Student Union group — because it was listed right there in the list of chartered student organizations, complete with a phone number and (ohmygoddess!) people's names! I kept that knowledge tight to me, like a secret treasure — always looking for the GLSU's name when the new list came out; looking for their meeting notices in the campus newspaper; and never talking to anybody about it.

It took me two years before I got up the courage to walk through the door into one of their meetings. During those two years, I went through the usual period of:

"Well, maybe I am... Well, maybe I'm not...

Am I?... No, I'm not!...

I'm not?... Yes, I am!"

I even tried to "play straight" for a semester. For me that meant growing my hair long and wearing sweaters that showed off my breasts instead of my usual androgynous flannel and T-shirts. I also tried to be interested in guys (that's a rather important requirement, you know). It was really quite amazing. In quick succession, I was asked out on dates by two different men — just one was a record in itself. I took one fellow up on his offer, and quickly came to the conclusion that chin stubble and French-kissing a man were pretty gross. Then that summer I went to Hong Kong for the first time with my mother, staying with my aunts (her sisters). From Hong Kong, my mother, my aunts, and I took a guided tour to Thailand. And among the other people in the tour group, there were these two young wimyn in their twenties who were travelling together... I didn't understand 90 percent of what was going on on that trip because the tour guide spoke in Cantonese, but for those seven days I was nevertheless having the time of my life! In hindsight, I'd say that those two were a typical lesbian butch-femme pair, personality-wise, and I had this intense wonderful crush on the more femme one. I spent most of my time on that trip thinking about her, trying to figure out if she and her friend were lovers, and gasping inwardly whenever she looked at me or smiled.

So after all that, I figured I was hopeless — wimyn seemed to be in my blood. Back at school the next semester, it took only a few weeks before I managed to walk into a GLSU meeting. It was "tell your coming-out story" night. When it was my turn, I announced to the room that that meeting was my very first instance of coming-out. For more than three years, I had questioned my sexual orientation, and never said a word to anyone about it. Now I was finally announcing my lesbianism to the world. Everybody in the room applauded!

A few months later I told my parents that I was going to GLSU meetings. They actually reacted pretty well at the time. The way that I explained it to them, they interpreted it as that I was "just going through a phase." (Sound familiar?) I think that it was only as this "phase" seemed to drag on, and they couldn't see an end to it anytime soon, that they started to get a little more upset about it. But if being a lesbian is just a phase, then I'm quite happy to be in arrested development!

Let's see. Shall I tell you about when my mom disowned me? Ugh. It's a gory story — as all such stories are. Suffice it to say, my dad is a great peacemaker, and for this Asian family, the integrity of the family unit is very important. By the next summer, my mom was inviting me to lunches with the family again. In fact, a few years ago my parents (and most of my family) met my second lover, Ann, and my mom even took a liking to her. I tell you, after what I've been through with my mom, it was a distinct pleasure to see her sitting on the couch, chatting amiably with my lover about teaching (they're both teachers), ghosts, and other things.

For total acceptance by my family, though, I think Ann would have had to learn Cantonese. Plus, of course, she'd have to somehow metamorphose into a Chinese person. They might accept that she and I are lovers, but that still doesn't stop my mom from making snide comments in Cantonese (when we're all, including Ann, sitting at the dinner table) about "that white one!" (Oh Goddess. Do you ever get the feeling sometimes that your parents are just crazy?!?)

Yes, I admit it. Ann was white. Not just white, but Scandinavian white — red hair, blue eyes, freckles, the works. My first girlfriend was a six-foot tall pink Amazon. It's kind of tough to be PC (politically correct) when you don't even know one other Asian dyke in a city of 50,000+.

Ah, but back to New Mexico. Don't get me wrong. I really love this place — after fourteen years here, the deserts and mountains and open spaces have become a part of my being. Not to mention our unique mix of different peoples and cultures. Unfortunately, what New Mexico *doesn't* have, is a lot of Asian queers. I could count us all on two hands, and still not use all the fingers. I'm always looking around at dances or queer events, so I can recognize two or three Asian-looking wimyn by sight now. About a year ago I finally got up the courage to introduce myself to one of these wimyn at a dance. Now she and I and a couple of other (non-Asian) dykes get together regularly to play the Chinese "game of four winds," mahjong. It is good to have an Asian friend, but S is third generation, and pretty Americanized. I am still searching.

I am a second-generation Chinese-American. Thirty years ago, my parents met on the proverbial boat coming over to America. They have always spoken Cantonese at home, but they also both work and so as children we had a white babysitter. I can understand simple Cantonese like "it's time for dinner," but I cannot speak it. I love to hear the occasional Cantonese on TV or in movies, or even rarely people on the street or in a store. I can feel the language in my blood, feel the recognition from buried synapses formed long ago in my brain. Cantonese is my native language as much as any other, for it was the first language I heard. It was the language around which my neurons first structured themselves. They say that language shapes how we perceive our world. And so in that way, at least, a part of me — some of the most basic parts of who I am —will be forever Cantonese. I like that.

And so I continue to search. For a Chinese dyke who can teach me the Cantonese word for lesbian, and help me open up that buried Cantonese part of me. For more Asian queers, who can understand what it is to be slanty-eyed and short, to love someone of your own gender, and to have a crazy family that you love. Until then, I guess I'll just have to be the resident left-handed Asian dyke in New Mexico!

Ami R. Mattison

I Am A Story

*The original draft of this essay was written in March 1992
for a feminist event entitled "Difficult Dialogues" that is held
annually in Atlanta, Georgia. The purpose of these panel
discussions was "to explore gateways and barriers to
communication and collective action among women of
different cultures." For the third annual session, "Telling Our
Stories: Connecting Herstories," I was asked to tell a story,
as outlined by a memo from the organizers: "Think about a
time when you could remember: yourself as different from
others, yourself as different from what was expected of you
by others, yourself experiencing privilege and/or being
discounted and/or being made invisible." At the time of this
event, I felt that the explicit parameters and focus of these
"dialogues" further illustrated the structural impossibility of
my existence and my experiences, as a culturally-displaced
Pacific Islander Lesbian, within preconceived notions of
identity. Also, I thought that the composition of the panel
and the format for discussion exemplified the ineffectual modes
of interaction that we, as feminists, continue to invoke. At the
same time, I felt that my active participation was crucial to
the significant political gesture that this event represents.
Thus, I wrote this essay in order to illuminate the problems of
reducing identities to easy categorizations of social difference.*

I HAVE APPRECIATED THE STORIES THAT OTHER WOMEN HAVE TOLD TODAY.
I share with them similar experiences of otherness, isolation, and
invisibility, as well as experiences of social privilege. However, I want to
tell a different story, and I want to tell it in a different way:

A month ago, I sat down to write my story. I wanted to write a
story that might begin to convey my understanding of the multiple

differences that I represent. Specifically, I wanted to focus on my sense of a culturally-displaced racial identity and to relate those experiences with growing up as a colored child in the late 60s and early 70s in Montgomery, Alabama. (I use the term "colored" here because in the South at that time, one was either white or colored.) I wanted to tell my story to you today and to begin to talk about why it's a difficult story to tell. However, my story provokes pain and anger and fear in me, even now. More important, as I wrote my story, I realized that to fit my experiences into the limiting framework of today's agenda required an undue violence against my sense of self, like some rending of flesh and splintering of bone.

Thus, I'm not going to tell my story the way I originally wrote it. I'm not going to tell you the details of my victimization; nor will I indulge the personal anxieties that are related to my experiences of social privilege. I'm not going to tell you some easy, conventional formula of my existence and the most convenient social categories to put me in. My silence today may seem in contradiction to the purpose of our coming together — to dialogue, to begin to articulate our differences in narrative forms. However, I've spent a lifetime learning, trial by error, to deal with and to understand the ways in which the experience of my differences connects to everyone else, to social structures and relations, to politics and life. I don't want to parcel out my struggle and give it away to you within a non-reciprocal framework.

At the same time, however, I want to tell you that my stories (and there are many) continue to provoke discomfort and anxiety in me. I'm often asked by friends and strangers alike, by feminists and non-feminists, by white women and women of color: *What are you?* By now, I know that by this question most people are asking about my race. Four years ago, I participated in a social/political organization for women of color. After two years of active membership and after pushing for more commitment from the group as a whole, I spent one meeting disclosing my experiences of racial identity. When I finished talking, a woman asked: *Are you a woman of color, or not?* The issue was inclusion. The lack of understanding was familiar.

Race seems so natural for most people, like a given assumed by everyone else. For most people, race is more than skin color and hair texture and other physical features. It's about language and family and social structures, about shared history, traditions, and common cultural assumptions. For most people race is the culmination of these social and individual experiences. We gather them to us, make sense of them, attempt to place them into pre-existing social forms and structures. We lend them coherence and ignore the blurred edges. However, my experiences are difficult to contain and to shape in this fashion.

Are you a woman of color or not? My parents are white, my brothers are Native American, and I have been called many things: *chink, jap, nigger, faggot, dyke, injun, half-breed, po' white trash*. I know the destructive power of words. I know their constructive power, as well. The first time I defined myself I was very young. I pressed myself into a corner of my room because it was the only place safe enough to be. I am a dark thing, I said to myself. By the simplicity of those words, I found comfort then in the darkness of an inexplicable existence that was unreflected by the people and the racially-dualistic culture that surrounded me. Since that moment, I've outgrown any sense of safety from such an inadequate life sentence. Now, I know that to occupy such purposeful darkness, to stand with self-imposed silence is a dangerous and lonely position. However, this position is familiar for me, and choice is a limited notion here.

A silence surrounds me and my words today, not because I don't want people to understand me, but because I don't have time to fill in that void, to even begin to address years of the confusion and pain associated with my identity. Nor can I offer in such a short space the complexity of my experiences, the ways in which their meanings both contradict and coalesce with one another. Finally, I stand with this silence because I haven't yet found a language to describe the sense of loss I feel, to articulate my fury towards the social circumstances and the system of politics that conspire to withhold from me the privilege and power of a culturally-specific and singular racial identity.

Still, others ask me: *What are you?* They want to know. They need to know. They take bets on it, discuss it among themselves. I could easily tell you the pat definitions I take on when circumstances demand them, like the time another woman of color spoke to me as though I were a white woman who was speaking out of bounds. When politics turn to angry didactics, when the banners go up and numbers must be counted, I can easily pull out my "card of authentic membership." I know who I am then and who I must become: Call me Pacific Islander. Call me Working Class. Call me Lesbian. Call me Your Worst Fucking Nightmare.

Today, I don't want to reduce myself to these bite-size morsels, free for your consumption. I don't want my differences to be so easily resolvable for you because they're not so easily resolvable for me as I move through the very complex political situation of my everyday life. I don't want you to be comfortable about me and my differences because I must live in a world where I cannot be comfortable with them myself. For the moment, hopefully, you will share this discomfort and anxiety with me. Listen: I'm not telling you what you want to hear today because I don't want us to dissolve the most radical potential I think my experiences offer, a potential that represents infinite possibilities for self-meanings.

I am the impossible and the possible, the continual doing and undoing of self. I am an experience of self that continues to explode the very categories of race, class, gender, and sexuality, an experience that offers the potential to rewrite the determinations of that constellation of identities and to expand their connections. I am a story I cannot tell today, though I have lived it many times. I am a dark thing. I lurk somewhere in the lonely excesses of your experiences, at the most dangerous edges of your imagination, where shadow meets light, where thought meets language, where silence beats against the sound barrier.

Shani Mootoo

Manahambre Road

Herstory I bring with me
A handful of photographs
shuffled like a deck of cards
fanned out   I pick one   An Ace!
MANAHAMBRE ROAD

Princess town to the left,
San Fernando, Mon Repos, to the right
Nadia somewhere in between
Looking at me
Singing "as the sun slips behind the sea"
Checkerboard acres of arrowed cane fields
Sway to her singing
The jagged horizon — Trinity Hills
Range beyond range, alizarin crimson, navy blue
Ageing Kodacolour does that to mountains, you know

Road side mango trees — *I keep the memory of their smell*
                    from the corner store downstairs
                    with their Fiji mango imports
                    plentiful in the cool spring air
                    but not quite so authentic as our
                    Trinidadian julies, doodose, cutlass

But Nadia's smell — gone gone gone she's been gone so long
                    I sniff at the photo, and smell
                    the camphor balls from the
                    box that safeguards the past

Her eyes, grey. No! light brown — no...
Well, they were unusual anyway
She is married now and has two children
Happy, they say
I wonder if she still sings
"As the sun slips behind the sea"
Or even thinks sometimes of me.

Lisa Kahaleole Chang Hall

Re-Entry

Approaching the sea   too wary
to believe warm welcome
I've served twenty years
in water that bites hard   no caresses
from rocky shores   polluted bays floating
garbage and dead bodies —
an angry or indifferent mother
turned away
Here, purple and blue and
green are the colors that dance
out my enduring love   warm pacific
water of peace   the water that
I love
The sand slaps kisses
along my feet   the land pulls deep
a solid current that flows
into one   belly blood bone
My heart expands   kicks off
its shoes   I leap
into the ocean   diving deep
chanting low
Salt tears celebrate
our meeting

Anu

Who Am I?

WHO AM I?
I am Uncivilized, Barbaric, Heathen,
      Primitive, Oriental
I am Passive, Submissive, Self-Sacrificing,
      Obedient, Sati Savitri
I am Dyke, Deviant, Queer, Assimilated —
      Bitch-From-Hell

STOP IT, STOP IT
Stop it you Europeans, you Safed-Chamris,
      you White folk
Stop telling me to speak English the "right" way
Add the preposition, use the noun,
say comment not comment
It's all your colonizing language
And I am slow to learn!
Stop telling me you are "civilization"
Because you know how to eat with a knife and fork
and drink tea from bone China with the little pinkie up
And if you are liberal
Stop telling me I am beautiful
You only see my exoticism
WHO AM I?
I am not your little Indian doll
to be hung in living rooms to soothe your white guilt
or transplanted onto your T-shirts to mark your possession

STOP IT, STOP IT
Stop it you men, you Indian men
Stop telling me to dress in a sari because
      you like traditional women
while you preen in a Western suit
Stop telling me to be quiet, to quit screaming
      because you obviously know more
and good girls do not shout
Stop telling me I am not Indian, just queer
      that I don't deserve my rich culture —
this time I have gone too far
My mother already told me that
And stop telling me to love you,
      my God-Husband, my Pati-Parmeshwar
while you crush me to the ground with
         your ton of good Hindu beliefs

WHO AM I?
I am not your little Indian doll, your guriya
      to shove, beat
      idolize, pedestalize
and then stick your prick into.

STOP IT, STOP
Stop telling me to COME OUT, you White lesbians
For how else are you to know I am ONE too?
I would never be seen as YOU, a DYKE
Unless I cut my hair, give up the salwaar kameez
and pour a bag of flour on myself
Stop telling me to give up my sexist culture
How dare you tell me what Sexism *really* means to me?
Stop asking me to go out to dinner
      to India House of course
      to discuss what it really feels like to be an Indian Lesbian
      If you really want to know — Pray for reincarnation

WHO AM I?
I am not your oh-so-oppressed little Indian doll
              wound up to sing and dance
and add color to your ranks.

STOP IT, STOP IT
Stop it you straight folks,
Stop asking me when I will have an arranged marriage
like all the other 800 million Indians do
It hurts to know my commitment
              will not be recognized,
be honored in a shaadi
And goddammit, I told you I was Lesbian
And stop that ridiculous shocked expression
              when you see me wearing a pink triangle
or kissing another woman full on the mouth
I am not on Display
WHO AM I?
I am not your little Indian doll to
              be given away to the first gudda
who comes with a huge festive baraat

WHO AM I?
I AM INDIAN
I AM WOMAN
I AM LESBIAN
I am not your plastic doll

Jacquelyn Ching Black

24 Frames

Willy ♀ Chang Snow Wilkinson

Scorched

heat of august in arizona or utah or something
bryce canyon a big white overgrowth
jagged and rough
not like the smooth black burning car seat
of our air-conditioned dodge dart
i am sticking to the vinyl not made for little legs in shorts
head over the edge
the edge of the front seat
like a puppy panting, tongue out
searching for that blast
of artificial cool
in my face
mom and dad and guidebooks
and me
where is everybody
no sisters no brothers no lines
marking back seat territory
they are gone
they grew up
and too cool for this
i am alone
alone in this thick white heat
heavy over darkened asphalt

another diner USA
and mom's got another waitress flustered
over her request for soyu sauce
after they tear up the kitchen finding only worcestershire
which doesn't come close and sure ain't chinese
she realizes she happens to have a small bottle in her purse
just checking
just making sure
a few more folks
can dance
for us
i am holding on
hanging on to the over-shellacked table
dying for something standard
regular and all-american
a treat only gotten
in special circumstances
cheeseburger, the child's plate
root beer, carbonated and foreign, its taste overdone
i am hanging on
hanging onto another red-checked tablecloth
plastic menu/smile
i wanna know
i wanna know
does the waitress
do these people
what do they think
what does it look like
do i look like anybody
do they wonder
do they think
i'm adopted?

Juliana Pegues/Pei Lu Fung

White Rice: Searching for Identity

I NEED TO REMEMBER. HOT, MUGGY NIGHTS, WHITE T-SHIRTS, SANDALS. The street vendors: sit-down-and-eat, mashed sweet bean on ice, all the bicycles in the street. Offering food at all the temples, incense in giant animal holders, grains of shiny white rice inside of them and huge white candles. Eating oranges, cracking open lichees from the branch until hands are red from the juice. Huge rolling hills, monuments to Chiang Kaishek, ponds with lilies, arched stone bridges, carp that swim up, begging for food. Huge thunderstorms: quick, everyone, get out of the lake or pool or stream (and I remember how I thought the bathtub too for a while). My memories are a blend of the four-year-old's trip, the twelve-year-old's movies, old photos, and wishful thinking.

     I worry about my mother. Chinese woman in Alaska, surrounded by her white husband and acculturated bi-racial children. I am still not sure what she thinks of us.

     Her eyes grow black when my younger brother says, "You talk dumb, I don't understand."

     She flashes back, "Then maybe you are dumb one, huh?"

     I watch my brother. He's ignoring her, shrugging off the exchange. What can I tell him? How can I tell him, this Chinese boy who eats his rice with ketchup and a spoon?

For Tom
My thirteen year old brother
> Do you know you are Chinese?
> You dress white
> talk white
> your friends are white.
> Do you know you can never be white?
> I didn't.
> Does it hurt to see you
> because I remember I was too?
> I feel like I have lost so much
> Do you have to go through the same process
>   the same pain?

> I want to yell at you
>> You are like me
>> you are me
>> You are not like them
>> you are not them
> I feel your embarrassment
>> your shame.
> How can I be mad, struggle with you
> when I don't want to blame you.
> I'm just scared I will soon see a stranger.
> What kind of world is this
>> that turns blood into other
>> flesh into enemy?

My thirteen-year-old brother
> You are Chinese
> that is something that can never be taken away,
> no matter how hard you try.
> Listen,
> Chinese is not Hong Kong Fuey
>> Long Duck Dong
>> fortune cookies
>> buck teeth

Charlie Chan
Fu Manchu
It is not "oriental studies" and it is not model minority.
Chinese is the Middle Earth
Boxer Rebellion
lichee nuts
jasmine tea
red envelopes
paper lanterns
It is pride and humbleness and
knowing there is no contradiction in being both.
Chinese is you and Chinese is me.
Come with me. We will be fierce
and we will shout it out
WE ARE CHINESE!
unwilling to be anything else.
My thirteen-year-old brother
come with me.

My father was a pilot for Pan-American Airlines (how utterly appropriate). And while he was working in Taipei, Taiwan, fell in love with my mom, his secretary. And, likewise, the secretary fell in love with the boss. Though, sometimes, late at night, sitting on the green shag carpeting in the living room, cracking watermelon seeds, my mother tells a different story. How pompous she first thought he was, how she fought a lot with the boss.

But eventually he won her over, they married, and moved to the States where they raised their hapa children to be commendable citizens, or at least in the case of their oldest daughter — making a living without asking to move home, visiting without bringing home girlfriends.

Oh, they had such hopes for me. Sent me off to college a straight A student, voted "most likely to succeed." And I barely made it through two years.

College is where my anthropology professor pointed out to everyone in the class that I was in fact not white, not at all, but brown. I started skipping class.

And college was where I found my first Asian friend.

Karen

Why did you say you couldn't speak Chinese?
Why did you lie?

The school put us together as roommates
because we were both Chinese
Hadn't thought to check OTHER
or just to leave the boxes blank

We lived together for almost a year
and we never talked about being Asian
School, politics, boys... even girls
but never about being Asian

Are you sorry you took me home to meet your mom?

She spoke Chinese
You spoke Chinese
'course I couldn't tell
if it was Mandarin or Cantonese
She took us out for dim sum
and was happy that I tried
All the foods you wouldn't
The afternoon was hot and muggy
Two Chinese chicks hanging out in Rosemead
You said you couldn't speak Chinese
And I was too scared to ask you why you lied.

Like many women, queer or straight, I have been abused by men. The worst was my first boyfriend — we dated for two years in high school. It was a slow progression from jealousy and obsession to full-blown possessive violence and sexual abuse.

And before it got bad, you know, *really* bad, I questioned a lot. I wondered how this person who was my friend before we became lovers was still my friend, but also a lover I was starting to hate. And how what I wanted then was so simple.

> I didn't want to
> > but I didn't say no
> I cried afterwards
> And you held me
> > asking what was wrong
>
> But you never thought
> > to ask me
> If I wanted to
> > the next time

In identifying my first long-term sexual relationship with a man as abusive, I have come to see a continuum with the subsequent relationships/flings/friendships I have had with straight white men.

And how even while I was denying my identity as an Asian woman, it was always me, always there.

I Am No One's Lotus Flower

When we were first dating
He said
You look more Asian
With your hair up

I couldn't figure out
If that meant I should
Wear my hair up
Or down

Then there was the lover
Who said
You look more Chinese
When you cry

I tried not to cry
After that
Biting my lip
When we argued

He called me his little Mao
That's how political he was
Too busy talking to listen
Hear me now

I am not *your* anything
My heritage is not a turn-on
It is my own to claim and love
I am no one's lotus flower
No one's

While I think it is important to break the silence of physical and sexual abuse, I am more than tired of people who think, when I come out as a lesbian, "Ah, that's why. Because men have been so bad to her. Now it makes sense."

I can't speculate what would have happened in a perfect world, only that we do not live in a perfect world, and to the core of my being, I love women. I love being with women, touching them, tasting them, and having the same done for me. *That's* what makes me a lesbian.

> I want to say and have people listen:
> I loved women before I disliked men.

My best friend Lisa and I practiced kissing inside that broken down clubhouse
       her brother had made
when we weren't pretending we were Wonder Woman or riding
our invisible horses

I spent the night at Stephanie King's, who tells me dating boys isn't as fun
       as having girls sleep over
       "Have you ever felt fingers inside of you?"

I danced for the first time with a boy to "Crimson and Clover"
       pretending it was really Joan Jett

> I kissed, and ran, and wrestled, and loved girls
> Before I even knew what the word lesbian meant

> I want to say and have people listen:
> I loved women before I disliked men

> I loved myself before I learned self-hate
> And I loved women before I disliked men

"Nobody I know can keep it up," she tells me, "you can try but it eats you up inside." I know, or at least I think I know, that Maria means passing for straight, assimilating.

But maybe she means passing, really passing. We're both hapa and have spent our adolescence with hair lighteners, perms, lots of eye-liner, she even did green colored contacts once. We're also both lesbians. When we hang out sometimes there's this automatic, unspoken sisterhood. And sometimes an automatic, unspoken pain.

"Nobody I know can keep it up — you can try to pretend but it eats you up inside."

I had put on a dress and lipstick today, and someone presumed I was white. A thought on passing:

When I dress up to look more feminine, does it also make me look more white? Is passing for me passing both as straight and white?

But then, too, when I'm in my kinda lesbo identified arty clothes, do I not also look white? Not passing het, but "assimilating" into the "lesbian culture," as if such a thing existed.

I do not have a strong sense of my own culture, what it is as an Asian lesbian. Is that passing? What's left then?

Why is it some people assume I'm white and others know I'm not? What does it mean in terms of race, racism, assimilation, internalized racism (sexism, homophobia), being hapa?

Am I really too white to be Asian? What does other mean when you're half and half?

Mixed Blood

No sensible person will suppose that love or affection has anything to do
with blood.
To require such, would mean, in turn, that biology is indeed destiny,
That even the noncommittal have roots.

But the pounding is within. The blood flows.

The blood of a freshly hacked chicken, hanging in the marketplace.
Let it bleed, let it bleed, or the meat will turn tough.

The blood from three generations, torn apart by coups, revolution,
drought, flood,
        and now assimilation.
The eldest daughter, dead on the operating table,
        a hemophiliac never to make it to Gold Mountain
        where the streets are paved, or was it the railroads?
The blood yearns for sticky white rice (no, brown rice is not more nutritious,
        it is the tradition that sustains)
        and fish eyes plucked out with chopsticks begin each meal.

The blood pounds and mixes. It is not pure.

The blood that courses from two centuries of work and exploration
        we now know as colonization
A family tree that reads PLANTATION IN THE CHERAWS
without mentioning the slaves.
A bloodline pure because slaves were never given the family name
        now tainted a lighter brown.

The blood fouled pounds stronger, stronger.

New day, same story. Shoot-em-up adventure movie.
Big muscled white man shoots hundreds of brown people
        smashing through their huts
        burning their food, yet
        loving "their women."

The pounding beats on my brain. Over and over.

The blood spills off the screen.
The crowds cheer as it flows, sticky hot beneath their feet.
I scoop it up and take it home for me and all the other children
Who are Asian, but not Asian
White, but not White.

We will bathe in it.
The blood that pounds in us
And soaking our bodies
the same.

No sensible person will suppose that love or affection has anything
to do with blood.
But the nonsensical cry for reconciliation.

Mom called last night and said she loved me and supported me 100
percent. Said I don't have to worry about how she feels about it. Instead she
worries about the obstacles I will face around closed-minded people. What
else? We talked about who in the family and from my past knew.

She asked if she could tell Aunt Teresina because I guess Teresina did
my charts this new year and asked Mom whether I was studying the I Ching
or Buddhism. Did I want to become a Buddhist nun? When Mom replied no,
not that she knew of, Teresina explained that my charts showed that I would
never get married and that there was not going to be a man in my life in my
next cycle of the rooster (twelve years). Now I know, Mom said. I think it's so
funny, a Buddhist nun! Like there wasn't a more obvious answer. But I guess I
can no longer doubt the words of Chinese astrology, just the interpretation.

Mom said she didn't think it was genetic in my case, said that maybe I chose who I was more attracted to. She said at this time she really didn't have any personal questions and wanted me to know that she didn't ever want me to divulge anything I didn't want to. I could sense that part of that was fear.

I did tell her I had a crush on someone. She wanted to know 1) if she was a lesbian ("I don't want you to waste your time on someone who's not.") and 2) if she was single ("She doesn't already have a 'friend,' does she?"). Still Mom.

Before my father buys my mother a house for the new larger family with the birth of my brother Tom, an unsuspected pregnancy when my mother goes off birth control at age 36. Before my Aunt Teresina marries an old flame from Taiwan to get citizenship in the U.S., and talks, sometimes yells, in Mandarin with my mother every night on the telephone. Before my mother considers herself an American, as much as a transplant from mainland China, then Hong Kong, then Macao, then Taiwan, can.

She calls this her country now, but just see how she bristles when my Aunt Elizabeth, Dad's brother Jack's second wife, tries to tell her American feminists' impact around the globe.

"Silly woman, what can she know?" she whispers to me and to the delight of my cousins, Elizabeth's stepchildren, in the kitchen, over frying wontons at the annual family get-together.

Slamming cupboards, sighing loudly, especially when my father asks her where his shoes or wallet is, she moves noisily, angrily, through the house, sometimes coming to a stop late at night at the kitchen table, eyes dull, head on her hands.

"Is something wrong, Ma?"

"No, no, you wouldn't understand."

Before my mother began her life in these States, where after more than twenty years she is still called a foreigner, she lived in a big stone house, surrounded by a garden with bananas and mangoes, three generations under one roof, and gave birth to a red, wrinkled, screaming baby: me.

She gave me a Chinese name first, though I wasn't able to remember it until later and just recently have come to claim it as my own. I'm still not sure if I have the inflection right.

Pei Lu Fung
Like a peacock it means
Proud
Asian
Woman
Lesbian

Proud
Like a peacock
Lu Fung

C. Allyson Lee

2632 *Then and Now*

TREES FLANK BOTH SIDES OF THE ROAD AND MEET IN THE CENTRE, forming a lush canopy on this Kitsilano street. The trees are taller now than they were thirty years ago when I came to Vancouver each summer with my family.

Driving slowly past 2632 today, I see a house so changed that nothing of the present structure reminds me of how it used to look when I was ten, visiting my grandmother. The house looks cold, distant and uninviting, a dull beige with brown trim. Gone are the moss-green shingles and candy-apple red steps which led up to a porch where we'd idle on that old fabric swing, whiling away the summer evenings. The house seemed enormously tall to me then, and I would run off to its side, in the shadow of the neighbouring house, to catch a forbidden smoke.

The house was a busy thoroughfare back then, with friends and family going in and out so often that it was rare for me to listen alone to the chimes of the grandfather clock. Sometimes we'd sit in the living room, resplendent in old burgundy corduroy furniture covered in linen and doilies. There was a big, soft armchair that my grandmother used to sit in when she'd cradle me and comfort me after I'd had a bad dream. Alongside the glass French doors was a decorous black lacquer couch, its back carved with mighty, fiery dragons so impossibly hard that no one ever sat in it. To its side on the floor was the old brass gong, stippled and resonant, never used.

Family dinners with twenty or more people were common, everyone cozying up to each other, diving into mountains of steaming rice, succulent barbecued pork and sweet greens. The decibel level at such gatherings was joyously cacophonous — all that noise and commotion — so much life. The dining room was, between family dinners, a disaster. All kinds of paper, books and tacky paraphernalia would be piled at random on top of the solid oak table which served as a catch-all for whatever junk was brought into the house.

Off to the side of the dining room was my grandmother's bedroom, only large enough to accommodate a tiny dresser and diminutive bed. The sun would pour into the little room and reflect my grandmother's smiles and laughter.

But the real heart of the house was the kitchen, where everyone laughed, argued, and cried. This is where my grandmother spent most of her time catering to all of her visitors, dishing out endless amounts of food, making sure we didn't leave the house hungry, even on our way out for a meal. Getting her to sit down with us at the table was impossible. She preferred instead to perch on the red stool just off to the side so that she could leap up to fetch another bowl, pour some tea or cut another apple for someone.

Just off the back of the kitchen was a small glassed-in porch which smelled of ripe fruit and salty fish. That's where we'd store the pears, apples, and peaches that we'd pick off the old tree in the backyard. From this porch we could see the yard which contained all sorts of little treasures such as dead mice that the cats would abandon — my grandfather would order me gruffly not to look at them because they were dirty — or little brown crabs which I'd find at the beach and project off the top step. It was on this porch that my mother would routinely leave out saucers of milk and call out "Here, Kitty, Kitty..." managing to feed not only our cats but also all the other ones in the neighbourhood — she claimed that she didn't know which ones were ours.

The real adventure was sneaking up the creaky carpeted stairs to explore the rooms of my uncles. The front one belonged to my Great Uncle Kew, and it always smelled musty from the piles of dog-eared books he had lying around, everything from animal encyclopedias to Quotations from Mao. The middle room was occupied by my Uncle Jing, who suspended from the ceiling his prized model airplanes with wings made out of balsa wood and thin parchment-like paper, so delicate to the touch. They looked like giant mosquitoes hanging from the ceiling, and gave the room an eerie jungle-like feeling when the lights went out. You could switch the naked lightbulb on and off by pulling a string with a tiny plastic cat tied onto it. The smallest room belonged to my Uncle Dunne, the artist, whose talent was reflected in the way he meticulously arranged his personal things on the dresser, and modestly displayed little painted eggs and unfinished drawings for critics not yet old enough to criticize. Everything smelled of oils and Tiger Balm. Each morning he would set out three little plastic dishes filled with treats of chips, candy, and toys, knock softly on the wall and wait for us little people to come in. His face, like his room, was full of sunshine and peace.

As I drive by the house now, I am not compelled to go inside with the porch gone, the windows reduced to thin, unrevealing slats. I do not want to know how the new owners have changed things inside, destroying all that was my grandmother's. And all the while I am looking at this unacceptable transformation, I am reminded that my grandmother is no longer here. A chill runs up my spine, and suddenly I am lonely, longing for the warmth and joy that this house brought to me so many decades ago.

Peou Lakhana

Who Am I?

who am i
i am khmer and i am lesbian

i am from a country so far away
a country most people cannot point to on a map
a country rich in natural resources
precious stones and metals lie hidden beneath the earth
fertile earth allowing for farming on land and water
pure waters teeming with fish
a country whose people are rich
in culture, history, religion and myth
a country that is still being ravaged
a people who are still being raped

i am the lucky one   i think
i left cambodia safely
while most of my friends and relatives were butchered
along with one-third of the population
butchered by our own kin
installed by the government of this country
because of the red scare
but i know the only scare is the brown scare
someday i want to go home
one day i will go home

but i am here now
fighting a different war
i am fighting an ex-lover
who sees me as the "exotic oriental"
i am fighting an uncle who
sexually abused my youngest sister
and tried to abuse me
i am fighting a sister who
tries very hard to be anything but cambodian
i am fighting my parents for acceptance
i am fighting men who objectify me
i am fighting women who judge me
i am fighting whites who oppress me
but most of all i am fighting myself
a battle between optimism and cynicism
a battle i fear   i am losing

i am here   naked before you all
with my spectrum of emotions
yes i hurt, i feel, i bleed
and yes i laugh, i love and i live

the next time you look into a mirror
the person you will see
contains   pieces   of   me

Mi Ok Song Bruining

Heart Murmur

When I was a child,
I was told
that my heart beats differently —

it's not like a normal one.
Something like it skips
or echoes — something

like that. Tell me
what does
a normal heart sound

like: What does
it hear
in the cold, blackness

of cryptic, bleak nights?
How does it respond
when my heart once knew

and listened
for nine liquid months
in a muffled, fetal sac?

And for three instinctive
post-natal months,
nestled next to the milky warmth

of her swollen breast?
But, does not remember
her futile, featureless face?

How does a heart respond
and beat to the aching
memories of the profound

murmurs of my wretched
difference and others'
numbing indifference —

of the wrenching separation
between a mother
and her child, and I wonder —

does she have a heart
murmur, too?

Teresa Tan

Ancestor

my bloodline is there on the shelf
where fetal pigs and pickled salamanders
throw glassy-eyed stares from gleaming quart jars,
where kindred spirits bobble up in aldehyde marinade.

blood is an inside river, red replica to ancient sea,
but the tide is swelling in my blue veins
and moon is a jellyfish caught on the cloud.

I was amphibian once, and small, hardly higher
than the song of a frog and like a frog
I drifted in a world no one could fathom
prune-shriveled pink, blind, my legs wound
tight as clocksprings.

is every mother an ocean, every child tethered
like soundless submarines deep in the amber harbor?

blood is an inside river, running red to the age-old sea,
but the tide is swelling in my blue veins
and moon is a jellyfish caught on the cloud.

C. Allyson Lee

Owed to Grandmother

My PO PO,
            such warm, comforting arms you had,
                      encircling me
                and holding me gently
        while I cried,
singing a theme on t.v. which I found to be sad.

You protected me
        as much as you could.
                You told us that night
                        the dinosaurs in the Calgary Zoo
                            come alive.
And I would crawl into your arms, pretending to be scared,
                but wanting to go to the park to see it come true.

Even when I was older,
                you didn't want me to be led astray.
You told me that you thought a big ticket lineup
                at the Hollywood Theatre
                      meant
                that it was a good movie.
So you went in, alone, and were so shocked
                by what you saw
                that you sat through it TWICE
                to make sure you'd seen it correctly
                      the first time.
That movie was "The Graduate."
You left the theatre bent over,
                hiding,

trying to make sure that the neighbours
wouldn't see you coming out.

Your next movie was "Emmanuelle,"
and you warned me that it was
"not a nice movie for young girls,"
as you laughed hoarsely to yourself.

We went together into Gorilla Records in
North Beach, San Francisco,
because I wanted to buy a poster of
John and Yoko
nude.
You didn't even bat an eyelash, but leaned your
elbows on the counter and stared wide-eyed at
the coveted item, saying softly in feigned disgust:
"The Japanese government should DO something
about her!"
And then Dad came storming in, yanked us out of there
before I could buy it,
saying:
"This is NOT a place for a nice Christian family."
You and I both knew that if he thought of me as
being a nice Christian girl,
he was sadly mistaken.

You gave me your unconditional love,
and never once did I ever hear you utter an unkind word
about anyone.
You were the only one in the family who didn't issue
caustic criticism
or unsolicited advice.
I never felt judged by you, only encouraged and supported.
Remember the money you sent to me for those guitar lessons?
And the little present you gave me: a little wooden man

with a scruffy beard and a guitar...
It was as though you might have wished that you could be
doing all those things I was doing then;
you would have made such a great hippie.

But, like Mum, you had to keep up appearances,
  and so, you would pretend to be shocked by anything
    associated with the sixties:
      nudity, profanity and lasciviousness.

  Mum would take particular delight in suggesting to me
    that I play a song for you
      from the Woodstock album,
        you know,
  the one that starts with "Give me an F..."
    and you would enjoy it immensely.
Playing "Goddamn the Pusher Man" for you
  would send you into fits of giggling.

    We got a lot of mileage
      out of that one.

No one will know how much you did for everyone,
  because you did it all quietly
    and with dignity.
All I ever saw was everyone, including Grandpa,
  shouting orders at you,
    telling you to do this and that,
      to get that and this...
no one ever asked you what you would like for yourself.
Would you have known what to answer?

You kept all your little knick-knacks and curios
  neatly bundled up and tied with bows and ribbons,
   labelled so carefully,
    everything organized and in its place.

I never saw you do anything else, PO PO,
    other than serve everyone else.

You taught me humility and dignity,
  and you taught me how to laugh at life's absurdities.
And posthumously, you taught me
  about the selfless act of standing up
   for someone else's rights.

   My PO PO,
   at 81
   a piece of me
   died with you.

Teresa Tan

What is Between us
(for grandmother Kam Go)

you are wrinkled like a river
and shuffle when you walk

I cannot speak your language
those inky, cryptic characters
would not lie on my tongue
or slide from that brush

so mark an "x" for your name
and the mystery of you

I wonder what is China
if not the bone white
brittle cup in your hand
or a gold tooth winking
the charm of old Fukien

sometimes the ocean comes between us
other days I drown
in a sea of odd sound

still your soul
comes laughing beyond
dark eyes dancing and darting
two bass fingerlings in the brook

Shani Mootoo

For Naan

who made the incredible journey from Nepal to Trinidad to be a bride,
and never, in all her years there, spoke a word of English.

The requested moment precisely,
the alarm clock radio blurts out, CBC Vancouver,
fluorescent red glow pries me awake to hear read
a letter from two flight attendants from New West
      ON HOLIDAY
Pawing the foothills of the Nepalese Himalayas
enamoured of the simple primitive lives of the Nepalese
of beautiful smiles white teeth
of brass bells tinkling tinkling
on beasts of burden as they trek over
this pass that summit—
how they wished to remain as long as they could
before returning to civilization—
if you're planning a trip keep in mind it costs only 10 rupees,
or 30 cents, for a bed per night. What a deal!

They brought back trophies of authentic Kulu Valley topi.

Images I have hoarded jealously
from National Geographic's favourite topic
span panoramic across my mind.
But how it irks me to know the colour of the hills
before the snow blues everything
to know of pebbly faces creviced as the hills around
to know of Naan's girlhood clothing swirling
dusty red dandelion saffron
sequins iridescent and beads of glass
to know of yaks, yak butter, remote mountain culture

to know of these, how it irks me
from travelogues, adventure journals and PBS TV.

How it berserks me
that I have exoticised
my greatgrandmother's land
by my yearnings.
That someone else continues to relentlessly
tame conquer colonize gaze objectify leave paw marks
where I can only dream of an embrace

but this is how I know the look and lay of Naan's land.

If I were to do the white thing and pilgrimage there
would my cousins, I wonder, gladly see Naan in me?
and I, Naan in them?
Do I dare wear a Topi?
It's been so long that I who have mineable traces
of authentic Nepalese swirling in the heritage river,
Surely I appropriate if I dare to wear
a topi from the Kulu Valley.
Let me suggest something.
When my presence in this land irks you
when your eyes froth spit curse because of me
brown as I am
other as I am
ancestor of the pebbly face
Remember how you love to haughtily climb all over
my greatgrandmother's mountains, this pass that summit
simple primitive lives beautiful smiles white teeth
brass bells tinkling tinkling beasts of burden trek
remember how you are charmed by my Naan's quaint ways
(as long as she stays in her place)
And remember how you love to photograph all of this
in another land.

V.K. Aruna

Putih

Shaken by the hot afternoon breeze, ripe red cherries fell on dry sand and exploded, their sticky seeds spilling through cracked tender skins in the sprawling shade of the old cherry tree. In the shade of that tree were traces of a hopscotch game left from when children played after school. And there were also tears. From a boy whose mother lashed him with a cane for disobeying her. Whose curses shook the quiet afternoon and scattered frightened sparrows. Yet, the boy never made a sound. Even afterwards, when she made him kneel for an hour under the tree, and neighbors stood by watching the sun burn his shoulders. This is a story I recall of a time and place so far in the past that I am no longer a part of it. A memory with no past before or after it.

PUTIH SQUATTED BAREFOOT IN THE BATHROOM, HER HANDS GLIDING BACK and forth over the the wooden washboard, scuffing and scrubbing clothes for my family. As always, she half hummed, half sang a love song from an old P. Ramlee movie, breaking off every now and then to wring out a blouse or sarong.

The night before Putih moved in, Mum asked, "Geeta, did you finish your arithmetic homework?" I said yes.

"Did you color your geography map?" I said yes again. "Have you done your Malay grammar?"

I rolled my eyes and whined, "Amma, I've done it already. I always do my homework!"

Then Dad said, "Well, read the next chapter. Why should you wait for your teacher to give you the homework?"

I left the kitchen where we were all sitting and went out front. Whenever Mum and Dad wanted me to leave the room, they always gave me something to do, even if I had already done it. So, I waited for them to start talking, tiptoed down the passageway, and huddled next to the wall where I could hear what they were saying.

"...had the baby and went home for two months."

"What did Maniam do?"

"Went through the agency and got a new servant."

"So what did she do?"

"Showed up this morning and cried and cried, asking them to take her back. Said she had complications during delivery."

"What did Maniam say?"

"Well, he couldn't fire the new one because the deposit was paid up. And they couldn't afford to lose the two hundred dollars."

"Don't blame them. She shouldn't have left like that."

"That's what Maniam said. Anyway, he gave her thirty-five dollars and told her to reapply with the agency. Then he heard we were having servant problems and immediately recommended her."

"So where did she stay last night?"

"Central bus stop."

"What? Alone?"

"Yah, she had no place to go."

"Well, I suppose we could try her. The principal has already told me not to take any more leave. We can't leave Geeta by herself."

"And I've run out of sick leave so I can't stay home either."

A long silence followed.

"Is she trustworthy?"

"Extremely. That Maniam definitely guaranteed. And she's good with children. If not for this pregnancy thing she would have been with them over four years."

"Well... it's hard to find servants who'll stay these days."

"That's what I said. But anyway, there is one problem."

Dad dropped his voice so low that even when I held my breath I could not hear what he was saying. Then mum burst out,

"Four?"

"Yah. First two divorced her. Third husband died.
Fourth chap is an army private."
"What about children?"
"Six. All with her parents in Kuantan."
Mum sighed a long sigh.
"As long as she worked for Maniam she behaved properly.
So, I don't think there'll be problems regarding that."
Mum sighed again. She did that when she was nervous
or irritated.
"At least she speaks English so we'll be able to give
her instructions."
Another sigh came through our thin cardboard walls.
"Well, we don't have a choice. We might as well try her then."

Unlike the other servants who worked for us, Putih did not hide in
her room. She surprised us with all kinds of desserts, joked with my father,
and had a gold front tooth. Within a few weeks, Dad boasted to a neighbor,
"She's quite good. Doesn't complain about anything, no strange men in the
house when we're not around, and on top of that, no stealing." Mum took
longer to respond. Putih won her over by criticizing the servant next door.
"Achee, she waters the condensed milk when she feeds the children and
puts tons of it in her own tea. She lets flies sit on the baby's face. I've seen it
with my own eyes. And you know, Achee, she doesn't send money back to
her children." Mum was satisfied. Putih's outrage signalled that she would
take even better care of me.

I liked Putih too. She never tried to pinch my cheeks to say how
chubby I was. She did not have betel nut breath. She did not spy on me and
tell Mum and Dad about everything I did. Best of all, she knew stories about
pontianaks — ghosts of women who died at childbirth and came back to
haunt the living, particularly men. Such stories were forbidden in our house.
Putih would have got the sack if Mum and Dad ever found out she was
filling my head with her un-Christian tales. The stories became our secret.

———————

The love song in the bathroom ended. Putih got up slowly, sighing like always, thumping her spinal cord to get the cricks out of her back. Sitting behind her, trying not to make a sound, I watched as she turned the tap on full force and waited for the bright orange pail to fill up.

A fly buzzed in my direction. I tried to sit still so it would go away, instead it zipped past my ear and landed on my face. I wiggled my shoulder, shook my head but it stayed there. So, I smacked the air, and the wooden stool I was sitting on, creaked. Putih turned.

"Allah, i'llaha, illa 'lah... how long you duduk sana?" she demanded.

"Just now only," I mumbled.

"Your amma said, you must go to sleep. Pergi!"

I hated sleeping in the afternoon. Besides, I had the measles. The sheets scratched and my rash itched. "There's no fan in my room, Putih, it's too hot to sleep," I tried to win her sympathy.

But she remained adamant. "You budak jahat, go to sleep."

I used a different tactic. "Tell me a pontianak story."

Putih laughed. "No, no. I busy," she shook her head and resumed rinsing clothes.

I inched into the bathroom. "Come on-lah Putih, tell me cerita. I can't sleep now."

"Oi, budak jahat. You jatuh sakit nanti, your amma scold me," and she pushed me out of the bathroom. Putih believed if children stood in water too long they caught colds. I refused to budge.

Putih glanced over her shoulder, clucked loudly, and heaved herself up. "You sick!" she grabbed my arm. "You sleep now!"

I wriggled free. "Okay, okay, I'll read pantun for you."

"No, no pantun," and she dashed over to the kitchen cupboard to get the cane that Dad kept on the top shelf. I ran to the other side of the table.

"Come on, Putih, I will sleep early tonight. Let me read pantun," I coaxed as her fingers groped busily along the shelf for the rotan. Empty-handed, she came after me. Putih never hit me. This was her way of getting me to do what she said. I giggled and scampered out of her reach. We circled the table a few times, bumping chairs and table legs, until she gave up. Then she dragged in a long breath, let out an even longer sigh, and glared at me.

"Pantun?" I persisted as she clopped noisily back to the bathroom in wet wooden clogs.

Putih threw me a dirty look. "Dah, bawa buku," she snorted.

Pantun were poems with four or six-line stanzas. If there were four lines, the rhyming pattern was first and third, second and fourth. If there were six lines, it was first and fourth, second and fifth, third and sixth.

Putih's book of pantun was old. The binding was torn. A once-green cloth cover was stained brown. On several dog-eared pages were water marks, noticeably over those poems that were her favorites. Although I read the poems again and again, most of the words were beyond my nine-year-old vocabulary. But I knew they were about love, heartbreak, and missing someone far away.

Putih's arms dunked and pulled shirts and socks. I stood outside the bathroom, coughed a few times to clear my throat, and then let my voice rise and fall the way she had taught me to read.

"Ikan belanak bilir berenang,
Burung dara membuat sarang;
Makan tak enak tidur tak senang,
Hanya teringat dinda seorang."[1]

Putih smiled. Soap splashed around her ankles, soaking her long tunic. I flipped the pages and began the next poem. "Hujan panas ribut berdengung..."

Suddenly, screams came from across our house. "Hai-yah, dead dog's head, I'll beat you till your life goes out of you." It was the pig farmer's wife berating Teck Seng, her thirteen-year-old son, fourteenth child in a family of fifteen.

I raised my voice to drown her out. "...*Jatuh berderai di tengah kota...*"[2]

The yelling increased. "You good-for-nothing son of a dog! You want to die?"

I stopped reading. I could not concentrate. Putih stepped out into the backyard to spread our clothes on the line. I leaned on the window sill and watched her, listening to the fight going on at Teck Seng's house.

"I have homework. Ask Mei Cheng," Teck Seng argued back, his voice crackly like other boys his age.

"Hai-yah! You do what I say and don't argue with me," his mother shrieked back.

Something clattered on their cement floor and Teck Seng's sister, Mei Cheng, screeched, "She told you to do it!"

At that instant, Putih interrupted, "Geeta, bring me some clothes clips."

Suddenly there was a loud crash followed by Teck Seng shouting the worst Chinese curse one can ever use, "Fuck your mother's cunt!" The moment he said it, I knew what would happen. The air was filled with sounds of a cane lashing against a body. The more Teck Seng argued, the harder his mother whipped him, calling on all the Chinese devils to strike her wicked son. The beating grew fiercer, the shouting, louder.

"Oi! Geeta, where are the clothes clips?" Putih yelled from the backyard. I ignored her and ran out front to look into Teck Seng's house. As I got there, the front door flew open and the pig farmer's wife dragged Teck Seng out into the middle of the village and forced him to kneel under the cherry tree. "Move and you die. You dead dog's head!" she spat. Then she stormed back into the house and slammed the door.

I watched Teck Seng under the tree, his head bent over his chest to hide the tears. "Eh, berapa lama I have to wait for you?" Putih's voice broke the silence.

I rushed to her with the clothes clips. "Teck Seng's mother beat him. She made him sit under the tree," I said, still hearing the screams and the slash of the cane.

"Tcheh! Those people don't know how to raise children," Putih grumbled in Malay. "God will punish her," she said and slung the last towel on the clothes line.

The run on Miss Jinak's stocking went up all the way from her right shoe to her calf. She was the only teacher in my school who wore stockings and dresses, short dresses with high heel shoes. Dad said it was because she was a Eurasian. He said they were a loose breed. One of mum's close friends was a Eurasian too and Dad liked her a lot. She didn't wear stockings and her dresses came below the knee. She brought us cakes and biscuits for Christmas and Mum got recipes for chiffon pies. She also called Dad, Uncle. Maybe that's why *she* wasn't a loose breed.

"Geeta! Are you dreaming again? Bring me your book!" Miss Jinak had spotted me. I took my exercise book with the unfinished math problems and walked to the front of the class.

"Not doing your work as usual? Is this why your mother sends you to school? To sit around and waste time?" her voice was smooth and cold like the iced rose syrup the tuck-shop sold on extra hot days.

Most of the girls liked Miss Jinak. I did not. She never called on me when I had the answer to a question. She never held my paper up and said, "Geeta got the best marks in class," although she did for others who were her favorites. And she made Chandrika, Ramabai, and Maimunah stand outside a lot when they did not do their homework. She made them cry when she scolded them for putting safety pins in their shoes where the buckles used to be. She told them, "If your mother can't buy you proper shoes, stay at home and tap rubber."[3]

I heard Miss Jinak's pencil tapping the table top as she waited for an answer. She did not like me, I knew that. But she was a Eurasian and Dad said they did not even have a country.[4] So I looked Miss Jinak in the eye. I acted like I was not afraid of her.

"Well, Geeta, since you don't like to work like the rest of the class, you can model for us in the corridor," Miss Jinak continued coldly. I did not move.

"Did you hear what I said? Just because your mother is a teacher in this school, don't think you can pull any monkey tricks on me. Stand outside."

I stood in the corridor, math book in my hand. Some of the girls snickered. I scowled at them and vowed to get them after school. I also plotted to get even with Miss Jinak.

Mrs. Lim was our school taxi driver. Every morning and afternoon, seven of us in blue-and-white uniforms packed like sardines into her old Morris Minor with bad brakes. One morning, Mrs. Lim was sick, so Dad drove me to school. When we reached the main intersection, our car broke down, and we had to wait for the mechanic. I was an hour late. Dad scribbled a note for Miss Jinak. She read the letter and excused me without comment.

When Dad came home from work that day, I told him a different story. I said, Miss Jinak tore up the letter and made me stand in the corridor for one hour. Dad ranted all night. He was furious. I was thrilled.

The next morning, Mrs. Lim was still sick, so Dad took me to school again. Just as we arrived, the school bell rang. Suddenly, Dad announced, "I'm going to give that bitch a piece of my mind."

Miss Jinak and Dad talked in the corridor for a long time. I squirmed in my seat, pretending to read *Androcles and the Lion*, trying to see if Dad's face seemed real angry or slightly angry. I never got a chance, Miss Jinak kept blocking my view. Finally, Miss Jinak came inside and stood before the class. "Girls," she said, "this is Geeta's father. He wants to know if Geeta was punished yesterday for being late to school." My stomach turned upside down. My legs felt weak.

The class chorused, "No!" I had a terrible urge to go to the bathroom.

"Thank you, class. Go back to work." Dad and Miss Jinak conversed a little longer. Then he left and Miss Jinak came back in.

"Class, I want you to hear this. Geeta told a lie yesterday. She told her father that I made her stand outside for coming late." A quiet murmur spread around the room. Miss Jinak looked at me, then turned to the blackboard, and began writing out comprehension questions for *Androcles and the Lion*.

That afternoon, Dad took time off work. He waited to pick me up from school. Mum left school a little early too because Dad telephoned and told her what happened. We all rode back together in complete silence.

At the house, Mum went into the room to change out of her sari. I went into the room to pray. Dad parked the car. Meanwhile, Putih kept asking me why my parents had come home. I was too terrified to talk to her. Then Dad strode in.

Unlike the other times he did not go to the kitchen cupboard to get the cane. Instead, he went to the backyard and picked up the dog leash. The first thing he said was, "Why did you tell a lie?" and I felt a stinging pain cut through my left arm. Again he asked, "Why did you tell a lie?" I did not look up. I tried not to cry.

"Answer me!" his voice shook the house. "You shamed your mother and me in front of your whole class, in front of your teacher." Another lash ripped through my arm.

"Apa 'dah jadi? What happened?" Putih asked, her tone sharp. Dad ignored her and continued yelling.

"Did the devil get into you? Why did you lie?" He hit me again. I did not say a word. I had nothing to say.

The leash landed on my back and legs. It broke the skin on my arms which caught most of the blows. Dad raised his hand to strike again. Mum rushed in front of him. "Stop it! She's not a dog, you can't be hitting her like that," she intervened, pushing me out of Dad's way.

He turned on her. "You stay out of this! She made a bloody fool of me."

Mum stood firm. "Well, then use a proper cane. Don't hit her with that."

Dad raged on. "If she can't act like a child, she must be treated like a dog. I've told her a thousand times, if I catch you lying, I'll skin you alive." He shoved Mum aside and grabbed my school uniform blouse.

The beating did not seem to stop. Neither did Dad's constant demanding, "Why did you lie?" Mum held on to Dad's arm but he was stronger. The leash kept coming. Finally, in a shrill, quivering voice, she yelled, "All right, go ahead, kill her. If that's what you want, kill your own daughter because of what *that* teacher said."

"Either you discipline her or I do," Dad spun around and screamed at Mum.

Mum screamed back, "She's already learned her lesson. What more do you want?" To me, she ordered, "Tell Dad you are sorry."

Tears and mucus flowed into my mouth. "I am sorry, Appa, I won't do it again."

My father did not seem to hear me. "Didn't I tell you, never ever lie to me?"

This time, before I could answer, there was an ear-shattering "Oi!" Putih marched up to my father, flung her blue plastic suitcase on the ground, and railed in Malay. "I'm not going to work for people who beat their children. You find yourself another servant. I leave. Now!"

Dad was stunned. He stared at Putih. Then he threw the leash on the table and stalked off into the bedroom, slamming the door so hard, the cardboard walls trembled.

Mum told me to wash my face, and picked up Putih's bag. In a voice still shaking from the encounter with Dad, she told Putih, "Don't be crazy, we don't want you to leave. He was just disciplining her," and disappeared into the bedroom.

I stood in the bathroom, choking because the sobs could not come out fast enough. Pain throbbed all over my body where the leash had made contact. I hated my father, hated Miss Jinak. Putih wiped my face and made me blow my nose. She changed my clothes, swearing under her breath when she saw the blood streaks on my uniform blouse.

Dad did not come out of the room until later that evening. When he emerged, he smelled of Axe-brand Chinese medicated oil which Mum had rubbed on him to ease his tension headache.

No one spoke much for the rest of the day. Putih listened to Malay pop songs on her portable transistor radio. Mum graded exercise books. I sat in my room and tried to finish my homework but could not stay awake. As I drifted into a dream, I heard Dad say to Mum, "I think we should move Geeta to another class. That damn teacher of hers will use this incident to penalize her for the rest of the year. And I didn't like the way she spoke to me." From across our house, a pig squealed in its sleep, a dog barked. As the day's events danced like ghosts behind my eyelids, I thought, "I did get even with Miss Jinak after all."

Under the cherry tree, everything was quiet. The afternoon sun had turned zinc roofs into sheets of searing metal. Chickens drooped as they scratched for food. From my bedroom window, I watched a family of ducks waddle to the hyacinth pond outside the pig farmer's house and plow into the crusted green layer of stagnant water, hurriedly gobbling whatever they found.

Before Putih came looking for me, I reached under the bed. My secret box sat at the furthest corner, covered in dust and cobwebs. Inside lay unpermitted treasures — movie star cards, lipstick from Mum's old handbag, ballpoint pens, a marble that I found in the school drain, dried up invisible ink that used to glow in the night, a comic book that wasn't about Jesus, and my last two balls of cherry-flavored bubble gum. Cecilia Ling Li Fung had given me eight of these bright red chewy delights, sent all the way to her from America, in exchange for a book that my aunt in England sent me about King Arthur and his Knights of the Round Table.

I grabbed the bubble gum and sneaked outdoors. Teck Seng was still kneeling in the sand. Making sure no one saw us, I circled the tree, then dropped the gum on the ground. Teck Seng did not move.

At that instant, Putih's voice sailed through the front door. I rushed back, slid the latch on the gate and stole one last look at Teck Seng. His head was still bent over his chest. His hunched shoulders still formed a shield. But the gum was gone.

From behind me, Putih scolded, "You naughty girl, belum tidur lagi?" as she squeezed water from the sleeves of her kurung.[5] I grinned. "Okay-lah, now I will sleep. But first you must tell me a story. A pontianak story."

As always Putih exclaimed, "Allah, i'llaha, illa 'lah," while outside, a commotion erupted among the ducks. I rushed to the window and saw the ducks, a flurry of brown bodies, webbed feet and flapping bills, jostling and quacking lustily. They had found crumpled yellow gum wrappers in the hyacinth pond.

1 This poem was borrowed from "An Introduction to Malay Pantuns," hlm. 15, in *Kumpulan Pantun Melayu*, Dewan Bahasa Dan Pustaka, 1983. My translation of t h e pantun is:

The gray mullet swims downstream,
The dove is building a nest;
I have no appetite, I don't sleep well,
All I do is think about you.

2 Taken from "Pantun Bunga Rampai," hlm. 80, in *KPM*, 1983. The half completed pantun should read:

"Hujan panas ribut berdengung,
Jatuh berderai di tengah kota;
Hari petang duduk termenung,
Hanyut di dalam lautan cinta."

Translated, the poem means:

Hot rain, howling wind,
Splashing in the city/town;
When evening comes I sit musing,
Floating away on the ocean of love.

3 Poor South Asian children in urban areas are frequently put down for being rubber tappers' children while poor Malay students are frequently put down for being padi planters' children. While people from these communities still carry out the work on rubber plantations and padi fields, these put-downs are clearly prompted by racial and classist stereotypes. British colonizers brought Tamils from India to work the rubber plantations of pre-independence Malaya. Since then, this job has been carried on predominantly by Tamils. While today, Tamils on rubber estates also hold mid- and upper-management positions as well as union-organizer positions with reasonable salaries and benefits, the tappers themselves are among the most economically and politically disenfranchised people in Malaysia.

4 The term Eurasian refers to people of mixed heritage where one parent is white. However, the term is also used for people with dual Asian heritages — Chinese/South Asian, Malay/South Asian, Malay/ Chinese. In Malaysia, as in many other countries, people of mixed blood/heritage are viewed with suspicion and subjected to derision. However, with time, as inter-racial communities have become "more Asian" and "less Euro-Asian" the antagonisms against Eurasians, particularly those perpetuated by people of my parents' and grandparents' generation, appear to have been subsumed by the fact that Eurasians are no longer "people without a country."

5 Kurung or baju kurung is a two-piece outfit comprising a sarong tied under a tunic that reaches below the knee. Both pieces are usually of matching fabric. The garment is traditionally worn by Malay women and still is part of Malay(sian) fashion.

Midi Onodera

True Confessions of a Queer Banana

B ANANA. BANANA BREAD. BANANA SPLIT. BANANA CREAM PIE.
It wasn't that she didn't like them.
She had just never acquired a taste for them.

During a school break, when she was eleven-and-a-half-years-old she became a contestant on a local game show. It wasn't the "Price Is Right" or the "Wheel." It was a show about perception. What we see and what we think we see — it was about the movies. The object of the game was simple. View a short movie clip. Answer the question. For instance, the clip might be the famous scene from *Singing In The Rain* where Gene Kelly performed the title number. The question: was the dancer wearing a raincoat?

For weeks prior to her television debut she sat glued to the set watching the adult version of the show. For the most part she answered correctly. She was amazed that so many adults had difficulty with the answers. But then she thought that adults never really saw what was in front of them.

She chose her wardrobe carefully. Red looked good on her. Dickies were back in style. Jeans and of course her good luck sneakers. They piled into the car, Mom, Dad and her two brothers. They drove and drove. Out to the suburbs. Out to the television station. Her palms started to sweat, she rubbed them on her pants. Her brothers joked and said she didn't have a chance — she wore glasses. She told them that since she had glasses she had doubled her chances at success. She hated wearing glasses.

There was a studio audience. The lights were brighter than she had imagined. She was sweating. She worried that her glasses would fog up and she wouldn't be able to see the movie clips. The host was the weatherman from the local news. He had dyed black hair. She met the other contestants. They all wore glasses. That cancelled out her advantage. They seemed older than she was, or at least taller and certainly smarter.

"Five, four, three, two, one... we're on the air."

Applause. Her family sat in the fourth row, but she couldn't see anything because of the bright lights. She was really sweating. She somehow managed to get through the stupid interview session with the weatherman/host. The game began. The first question was so easy she thought she had misheard it. All the contestants were correct. The game progressed, but the questions did not become more difficult. She couldn't believe it. How could the questions be so easy and why were her opponents consistently wrong? She had scored a perfect game.

"After a message from our sponsor, the final question."

Applause. "We're back."

The movie clip. The big and final question. Watch closely. Look carefully. Search the screen. Anticipate the question. It had to be a difficult question to make up for all the easy ones. Use your eyes.

A group of three men. All strangely dressed. One wore a long black coat, formal wear, a tuxedo with tails, glasses, big eyebrows, big moustache, too big to be real, a cigar in his right hand. Another man in a trenchcoat and a hat, he carried a horn, also in his right hand, his hair was large, curly. The third man in a regular suit, maybe a size too small for him, a hat with a feather stuck in it. They stood in a hotel lobby, talking, having fun. A bellboy walked by. He carried a tray of fruit in his left hand. Apples, oranges, bananas, pineapple, grapefruit. The man with the horn reached over to the passing tray and took a piece of fruit, a banana. He began to peel it. End of clip. The lights came back on. The audience silent.

"What did one of the men take from the tray?"

The ticking clock. Her black marker and her blank card lay in front of her. She peeked over at the other two contestants, they struggled with the answer, their markers poised. She knew the answer, that was obvious. What she couldn't remember (or maybe she never knew) was how to spell the name of the fruit. When did she ever have a reason to spell it. Her mind was a blank. She tried to remember a commercial she had seen. It was for the Bic banana pens — a hot seller. Even though she didn't own one.

B. That was a good start. A. Okay keep going. N. She was doing well. A. That had to be right.

She stared at the card. The letters marked in black.

BANA

It didn't look quite right, but she didn't know what came after that. She tried to conceal her sweat. The ticking clock. Time was up.

The weatherman/host picked the other contestants first. The girl, maybe her name was Mary, said grapefruit. How could she have been so wrong? The boy, she thought his name was Tim, or at least she thought he looked like a Tim, said apple. Were these people blind? She knew she was right. But would they accept her answer?

She held up her card. Applause. Laughter.

"Bana. Well, that sure doesn't look like orange... that's right, it's banana. And you're our new winner!!!"

Her victory was mixed with embarrassment. She won a brown plastic "modern" watch — a timepiece. A Timex. It broke two weeks later.

Banana. Bananas, jam and peanut butter — the Elvis special.

She had eaten them. It's just that she didn't crave them.

She knew it. She reluctantly admitted it. She had looked in the mirror enough times to see that it was so. She was a banana. Yellow on the outside. White on the inside. If that was not enough, soon after her game show experience came the other revelation in her life.

It was during the rehearsals for her school pageant. She and two of her girlfriends decided to perform the song "Born To Be Wild." Weeks of rehearsal, choreography, selection of costumes. She would be the main singer and her girlfriends, two blondes would dance around her in a circle. She had the microphone. She practised at home. In her bedroom, in the shower, lying in bed.

During one of the after school sessions, she began to notice a change in the way she related to her two girlfriends. She began to notice that the words of the song started to make sense to her in a way that she had never thought possible.

"Looking for adventure and whatever comes our way. We were born, born to be wild..."

From her chair, she looked down on her two friends dancing around her. She thought, she imagined. They were wild. They wanted adventure. She began to think of herself as the real singer, the male singer.

She thought of her friends as groupies, girl groupies. She wanted to be a rock star. She wanted to head down the highway. But most of all, she wanted a girlfriend. A real one. So they could both be ready for whatever came their way.

Banana. Banana cake, banana fritters, banana daiquiris.

It wasn't that she actively lobbied against them. It's just that the thought had never crossed her mind.

Names, the identities we give ourselves.

Over the years, due to direct political action, social and economic shifts, the words that we use to describe ourselves have been rescued from the derogatory usage of the mainstream. We are dykes. We are queers. We are fags. Many of us have found strength, support and love through our sexual identity. But we are by no means a homogeneous community. We are split by sexual practice, gender, politics, race, culture, class, food preferences.

Leaving behind the baggage and the pressure to be politically correct, I want to ask, how do we reclaim parts of our identity which were never fully ours to begin with?

When I was growing up, my grandmother lived with us. To say that we were close is an understatement. She spoke only Japanese and I only English, but we found our own form of communication which was based on trust, love, and companionship. To me, my grandmother was my link to Japan. She showed me how to make Japanese pickles, appreciate the cherry blossoms and made sure I took my shoes off before entering the house. All of these things and many more made up my sense of Japan. In her presence, I felt Japanese. My grandmother died last year, she was almost 102 years old. Suddenly I had lost the one person in my life who had personified my cultural heart.

My grandmother spent over 80 years in Canada and yet up until the day she died she spoke and wrote Japanese. It was a form of Japanese that no longer exists. Like everything, language evolves and her Japanese did not keep pace with the fast-paced Ginza district of today. Hers was a Japan of the 1920s.

I am a Sansei. I have never been to Japan. The distance between my North American perceptions and Japanese culture are as vast as the sea that separates the two countries. I am not proud of the fact that I cannot speak Japanese, nor am I comfortable with the idea that I would be hopelessly lost in a Tokyo train station. And yet to the person on the street in Anytown, NA, I could be from any number of foreign "exotic" countries. Can I claim these countries, these geographic markers as my own? If I choose to do so, how will I be "read" by others in this Japan-bashing, anti-Asian climate? How do I define myself inrelation to the country I was born in?

I cannot claim to be Japanese. To do so would be a lie. It's a presumption that I am somehow linked to a country that I do not even know. My Japan lies somewhere else, not to be found on a map, not to be conquered and not to be pinpointed as the economic enemy. My Japan is something I will never visit because it is always with me.

But how do I define myself? How do I acknowledge all the parts of who I am? How do I define my identity without false implications?

I am a queer banana. I say this with a need to reclaim a definition which has haunted me since childhood. An insult, an accusation that one is in disguise, a traitor — yellow on the outside and white on the inside. I don't see how watching the Brady Bunch or going to an Osmond Brothers concert could make me a traitor. I am of Japanese descent but I am third generation Canadian.

Many of my Asian-American friends have other terms to define themselves. Nip-anese. Chink-ese. OY-IN (Outwardly Yellow, Inwardly Neutral). But somehow the term "queer banana" (or bana) is one that I feel most at home with. It is simple, direct and visually striking.

How we decide to name ourselves and what term we end up feeling comfortable with is not without its problems. In a world of constant change and evolutionary word play, the real intent and meaning of these self-described names is sometimes lost. I call myself a "queer banana" but I know how this can be used against me. I know how this term can be misinterpreted and how by naming my identity I am still open to misunderstanding. The context and history of this term is personal and I would never use "queer banana" to describe someone else. I believe it is important to encourage the continual process of self-examination and self-definition. Today I may be a "queer banana" but tomorrow I may not be. But whichever way I decide to describe myself, the meaning will be one of my choosing and my design.

Sharon Lim-Hing

Lost Pictures

O PENING A POPSICKLE, I CUT MY THUMB WITH THE KITCHEN KNIFE. A week later, my father took a picture of my guinea pig, whom I imaginatively called Guinea. The guinea pig dragged out its days in the darkness of a large wooden crate in a corner of the garage. Its pen was carpeted with moist droppings on which carrots and grass were thrown. In his isolation, Guinea would sometimes emit forceful, high-pitched screams, "Eeeee, eeeee!" But usually he was silent in his boring, lonely, shadowy, shit-filled box. Occasionally, I took my pet out, and he wandered around the tiled house, his feet pink and padded with innocuous claws. He had smooth hair and was white except for a black patch on his bottom and over his left ear.

In the photograph, Guinea's entire body is featured three-quarters, and my hand hovers in the background, ready to clutch him should he make a dash for the door, the couch, or anywhere I didn't want him to go. My left hand, the thumb with a straight line, a cut, still a flap slightly open (but not bleeding).

"Look," said my father, "Your cut wasn't healed yet." And it was true, the real thumb, my thumb in the then-present had healed yet still wore a thin sliver of dried skin and scab that would soon fall off, or be picked off. Now when I look, I can't find any vertical cicatrice. All I can find are thin horizonal creases that deepen into wrinkles when I bend my thumbs. Where has it gone to? I know it was there. The evidence: the photograph. If I could just find the photograph. But where is the picture? Is it just in my mind? Was it one of those photographs that my father chose to leave behind when we migrated, piecemeal, one or two family members at a time?

My father had his own darkroom. Sometimes we were allowed to go in while he developed his photographs. That was his hobby. Under the red light and the yellow light, between periods of complete darkness, I would sit on the cool tile floor looking at photo albums. This is when we lived downtown, with Popo and Gunggung, before you were born. This is Janice and Frankie when they were babies. This is the house in Mona Heights. This is when we went to Montego Bay. Yes, you went too, you were inside Mommy. The voice that explains this is my mother's.

My father would work silently. Out of nothingness, on a blank sheet of paper, a gesture was swished, became a quarter ghost, then a half ghost. Then took on the fullness of a person, or a fish, or a statue that my father had looked at through a black box. Sometimes, as the image lay in a tray under the running tap, as we breathed the sour chemical odor that originated from a brown glass bottle or an amber and red Kodak package, the light was turned on to reveal that it was too dark. When the pictures dried, curling obstinantly, my dad would cross his legs, take up his pencil, and cover the dust spots or white scratches with a thin layer of graphite. I never understood why he took pictures of things other than people, these photographs seemed dull to me. Stupid common goldfish. A tree's shadow moving across a gravel path. A smiling Buddha three inches tall on his desk, gathering a cloak of dust.

"Why you leave all the pictures of the children? You can't replace them!" my mother shouted at my father, years later, years from now, once we had all left and couldn't go back. I can't even imagine those abandoned photographs slowly disintegrating at the bottom of a garbage dump in Jamaica. The goldfish and the family lonely and maybe afraid but frozen in their poses. The black and white contrast, a balance so carefully achieved, now fading, reverting to a ghost life. Or turning sepia. Or perhaps disappearing behind a curtain of grey fungus. No. It's as if they never existed on this earth.

My parents began having shouting arguments about whether or not to migrate to America. After a while, my mother did not want her picture taken. Her hair was not right, she wasn't made up, she said. There is a whole series of photographs of the side of her head, swiftly averted and blurry, or her arm out warding off the glance that could be preserved and displayed, or of her whole body darting out of the frame, again blurry. My father took to astuce. He purchased a long, heavy telephoto lens. Through the louvers of their bedroom window, he aimed it at my mother as she was working in the garden. The result of my father's espionage is a grainy but also slightly hazy picture. Hair pulled back in a bun, jaws clenched in determination, eyes set on a goal unseen by the viewer of the photograph, my mother lifts heavy shears with both hands and attacks the prickly hedge along the fence. In the background is the foot of the giant who fell asleep and became covered by caves, forests, birds, villages, Blue Mountains. Drops of sweat slipped down her face into the grasshopper-filled universe and were not captured by the camera. In a corner of the garden, water from the hose tasted of green plastic and was warm from the sun.

It was this stubborn streak in my mother, her strength, exposed by the telephoto lens, that insisted on bringing us to the vast potential of America and succeeded in depositing us in the barrenness of Miami.

When people ask me why my parents moved from Jamaica to Miami, I tell them what feels like personal cliches. They wanted a better life. People were afraid Jamaica was turning communist. There was too much violence. Or, smiling, my mother wanted a better place to shop. How much this covers, and covers up, like a dark, velvet film of fungus growing across an abandoned photograph.

FINDING
/FOUNDING
COMMUNITY

Elsa E'der

Family Reunion: The Longing

Be strong Sisters/my heart
is on fire wanting more
than security/complacency/esoteric ideology
I reach
with your faith in me
over the abyss
between love and desire

Be strong Sisters
too much turning
each I from Our Eyes
old fears/unspent tears
as weakness struts
as power
as pride
as goddamned color-of-the-year

these days/my test
boxing and bleeding
cornered as indifference
among you

we be gallows and guillotine
rope and tree
too much thrusting his/story
all carnal aggression/screwed visionary

who has dreams
to cross when the waters part
who believes
in walking 'tween walls
falling on both sides

Be strong Sisters
my back bends alone
unknown without you
my eyes stoop to nightmare
to demons
to sorrow
to anger and hatred
unknown without you

Sisters
help me be strong

Shani Mootoo

A Recognition

"You're Trinidadian"
I blurt out proudly, smugly,
accusation not, of course, intended.

"I recognize the accent!"
Mine suddenly dips deep and curves — like a kite,
thickens like sugar browning in oil for a stew.

>*I am aware that*
>*Our paths*
>*Would likely not have crossed*
>*Back there*
>*So why is it, now,*
>*I throw myself upon her over here?*

Before I can ask
"So where you come from?"
"So what's your name?"
"So who is your father?"
she has turned away, but I hear her say,
"I am Canadian." The reply
dropped flat and mercilessly terse.
I understand.
There is no room to negotiate.

I feel ashamed
to have been excited
To have exposed
a yearning.

Something I understand —
Anonymity. Autonomy.
Freedom to self define.
To forget.
To come out.
To escape.

Or else suffocate.

Sometimes there is, necessarily,
something I understand,
no room to negotiate.

Alice Y. Hom

An APL's Alphabet

A is for Asian Pacific lesbian
B is for butch women who turn me on
C is for calamari which I eat with shoyu
D is for dildo that is lavender in color
E is for elegant when I wear my plaid shirt
F is for femme women who turn me on
G is for going down, farther than before
H is for hurrah when I make her come
I is for intense when she pulls me close
J is for joss sticks that I toss in the air
K is for Kulintang music that makes my heart race
L is for latex that feels smooth against the skin
M is for money that comes in red envelopes
N is for nipples that are always perky
O is for oops when I poked the wrong opening
P is for please when I want to have sex
Q is for queer, you know what I mean
R is for rice which I like sticky and wet
S is for safer sex which everyone should do
T is for tits which go in my mouth
U is for ugh when they have not showered
V is for vulva that gets slick with sweat
W is for whoa when she goes too fast
X is for X-rated films of gay boys that I watch with API dykes
Y is for yodel because I can't sing
Z is for zoom when I can't slow down.

Susan Y. F. Chen

Slowly but Surely,
My Search for Family Acceptance
and Community Continues

September 1991

IT IS TUESDAY NIGHT. MOM HAS JUST TOLD ME THAT WE ARE GOING *to have a meeting in the kitchen, just the three of us: Mom, Dad, and me. I think "Oh no, I really, really dread these confrontations. I don't have enough strength to go through with this." This meeting has come as a result of recent months of friction between us over issues such as my going to too many "useless" meetings, receiving what they perceive as too many phone calls (from the wrong people) and, at the center of all the "problems," homosexuality...*

I was living at home again after college graduation. I initially came out to Mom and Dad three summers ago in 1988 when I was a sophomore. I had formally started telling others about myself only six months earlier. By then, the loneliness and frustration of not being able to confide in anyone had grown to an unbearable level; I thought I would explode at any moment from the isolation. Since seventh grade, I had had crushes on other girls but did not have a clue as to what to do... so I did nothing, and kept all my feelings to myself. After joining a support group in college, I was happier than I had ever been in my life. That was the first time the *real* me was able to function (at least part of the time), and I was better able to express myself. I was no longer just quiet, polite, friendly Susan, as others may have seen me; another part of me was allowed to emerge.

As a result, I wanted to share the "good news" with my parents — that I was so happy as a result of being in my first relationship with a wonderful woman. The ideal coming out scenario turned out to be a personal disaster because they found out by accident, before I could even formulate a plan to tell them. Soon after, my father said in Mandarin Chinese (the language we speak at home), "You step on my heart," and that was very painful to hear. After months of bickering, alternating with periods of noncommunication about the subject, I concluded that they just did not understand. Mom continued to say from time to time, "Every girl needs a boy to do things for her." And ever since then, she had the attitude that I would change and that I was at the stage in life of being "lost."

To make the coming out process even more difficult, I was afraid to say the "L-word" (lesbian) in front of them, out of embarrassment. I imagined that they would only think of the sexual aspect, but "lesbian" meant so much more to me — it was sharing my life with a woman I loved. Although all references to homosexuality were made indirectly, we always knew what we were talking about. Actually, sometimes my mom would discuss the topic of homosexuality in a roundabout way, and I would pretend that I didn't know what she was talking about, just to be annoying. As the months passed, the arguments continued. I began to lose hope that they would ever accept me as who I was. However, an occasional bout of optimism made me feel confident that one day they would understand. I did not know if that day would be months from now or many years away. So, I went into my own coping mode by not discussing the topic unless they brought it up. And, at the same time, I did not go out of my way to hide who I was. I thought this would be the easiest route for both me and my parents.

I grew up feeling pressure to measure up to my ChineseAmerican peers. There were frequent comparisons with "so-and-so's daughter or son," who won the piano competition or got near-perfect SAT scores. I wanted to make my parents proud too, but I seemed to fall short. While some of my peers grew up to become mainstream "successes," I did not automatically admire them, because in my eyes such success seemed superficial. I realized that it was unhealthy to judge my selfworth by comparing myself to others, but I found it a difficult habit to break. And being a lesbian often made me feel a greater compulsion to achieve. Although I once longed to be like some of my peers, I started to identify with another group of people — those who were active in areas of social justice, who did not promote progress at the expense of human suffering or define success only in monetary terms.

There was a significant gap between what my parents and I considered important in life. They wanted me to go to school, get a good job, be comfortable ... but not get involved with anything resembling "political" activity. At that time, learning about activism was *all* I was interested in. What a conflict of interest! I wanted to transform my formal education into skills that I could use to improve the wellbeing of people. Of course, that included the struggle for lesbian and gay rights, as well as other social justice issues. My sole purpose in life was not to make lots of money, although I knew that money is necessary for survival in this country. I wanted to make a difference in my own way. I didn't expect honors or recognition from others; I just wanted my parents' "blessings." It depressed me — the idea that I could go through life doing my best to fulfill my goals, but my parents would never "see" or appreciate it. For example, something very important to me was often labelled "a waste of time" by my parents. As much as I worked on improving my selfconfidence and independence, I suspected that I would always feel a loss unless my parents shared in that sense of pride.

I was lucky that my parents would never disown me or refuse to assist me financially, if necessary. That was comforting in a lot of ways, but I also lived with constant guilt because I was aware that being a lesbian was a source of difficulty for my parents. Their continued feelings of hurt and shame worried me. Some of my nonAsian friends suggested that I just respond with, "Forget it; if they don't accept me it's not my problem. I'll just continue with my life as I please, and ignore them." Even during difficult periods, I could only maintain that attitude for a short period of time. Then the guilt returned. Besides, I loved them very much. Despite feelings of bitterness, I tried to find ways to retreat or compromise in order to soften the situation, especially since deep down, I knew that everything I had came from my parents. They had done so much for me and I "owed" much to them in return.

When I discussed the complexities of family acceptance with other Asian friends, I would inevitably bring up the topic of PFLAG (Parents and Friends of Lesbians and Gays). I was fascinated with PFLAG because it represented a phenomenon to me —parents as activists and advocates for their children on the issue of gay rights. One of my dreams was to see my parents become PFLAG parents, for them to hold signs (such as, Proud Parents of a Lesbian Daughter) and march in a huge gay and lesbian parade.

A friend of mine once said that Asian parents just didn't become PFLAG parents. In my case, I thought he could be right. My mom thought they had been "brainwashed" in the same way that I had been.

I feel tense as I take a seat at the kitchen table with my parents. My younger sister (who is supportive) is standing by the door, and I motion for her to go away. I think about my new-found identity as a Chinese lesbian and my efforts to become more "independent." But I question whether I can continue to live at home where my mail and phone calls are screened and where Mom is often still waiting up for me when I come home late at night from the club. In order to improve our relationship, we must create a new understanding between us. I know this can only be settled in a long, meaningful discussion with my parents, but I also dread the thought. Now, here is my chance to honestly discuss the issues that have been on my mind...

My parents' problem with homosexuality probably revolved around a number of issues: the lack of discussion of it in the local Chinese community, the shame and fear of their friends finding out, and the disappointment that their daughter was not going to travel the "standard route." A most important aspect, I realized, was the issue of happiness. My parents had always spoken of the importance of me being happy. I believed they had this image of "homosexuals" living extremely isolated and shadowy lives. They did not know that I now had the ability to be extremely happy, especially when I could be open as a lesbian, or at least partially open, as most situations allowed. I felt fortunate to be "out" as a lesbian in spite of the added burdens of societal discrimination and ignorance about homosexuality. However, it was ironic that my parents were the ones who were contributing to much of my current level of unhappiness. How did I communicate my feelings to them, though? I was lucky that my parents cared about me, but they smothered me with their constant worrying and attempts to influence my direction in life.

Throughout our discussion, my parents remain patient; Mom asks questions and raises different points, while Dad mostly listens. By comparison, I am like a child who is throwing a tantrum. Their patience only makes me feel more exasperated and emotional; I find it difficult to explain my point of view in a rational way. I think pessimistically, will everything I try to tell them drift away, become a wasted effort?

I tell them — face it, the reality is I will not marry a man, but a woman. There is nothing wrong with me and even though discrimination exists, that is a fact of life and I will have to deal with it, but I can't deny who I am. Near the end of our meeting, my dad finally says, "OK, but maybe you can find a Chinese woman." I look at him in disbelief — I have had this goal in mind for the past year, ever since I discovered what a wonderful feeling it was to finally talk to another woman who was both Chinese and lesbian, and feeling like we could really identify with some of our similar experiences. Before that, I had come across too few Asian lesbians to understand the concept of such sisterhood. I realize that I should introduce my parents to other Asian lesbians. It may just make a difference. But, that is not an easy task...

When I first came out in college, I was the only Asian gay or lesbian person consistently present in the "gay" community at school. I did see one or two other gay Asians, but not often enough to become acquainted. Over the years, the experiences of meeting first, Asian feminists and then, Asian lesbians were truly lifechanging for me.

At a conference in 1990, for the *first* time, I met a handful of Asian lesbians who were politically and socially active. It was a significant event for me because, up to that time, I did not have the privilege of getting to know other Asian and Pacific Islander lesbian and bisexual (APL&B) women. As a token of friendship, one ChineseAmerican lesbian put her arm around me while we listened to a speaker and I felt so happy. We became friends and I was able to "really" talk to her and the other Asian women. She was the one who called me her "sister." I had heard that term many times before, especially when my first partner spoke specifically about her "AfricanAmerican sisters and brothers." But, it took me awhile to get used to the word. I never felt that I could be someone else's sister without knowing that person for a long period of time (or without being related). I had always wanted a big sister, anyway.

As I met more APL&Bs the following year, I somehow expected a similar type of acceptance and warm interaction as I had with the first ChineseAmerican "sister." I was naive in thinking that, and felt dejected for many months, when it finally hit me that it didn't always happen that way. APL&Bs, along with other women of color *were* my sisters, but it made sense in the real world that we would not all get along, become friends and share a magical bond. I felt I had a responsibility, though. The ChineseAmerican lesbian who reached out and called me her sister made an impression on me. There were many APL&Bs still in the closet and alone, to a certain extent. I wanted to reach out to them and offer some support as others had given me.

The past hour has been emotionally draining. Our meeting is coming to a close. I am eager to respond to Dad's request because deep down, that is one of my hopes — to form a family with another APL or B. I realize that my wish may not come true... But, I tell my father, immediately, "Of course, that is exactly what I have intended." He is funny — without changing his serious expression, he raises his hand up in a fist and says "Yay," and does a rah rah motion. I can tell at this point that there is much hope, even though it is my father speaking and my mother still looks very much unconvinced with the acceptance issue. I go on to say that one day I hope that they will not have so much fear in terms of my telling others of my orientation. (My mother frequently implores, "Ok, you are who you are but you don't need to tell anyone.") They say that perhaps there may be a day, not now, where they can talk about this openly with their friends.

I am eager for the day when we can speak up. I already want to be open about myself, but I can understand their situation and realize that they should be allowed some time to "come out" too. In our Asian and Pacific Islander communities, there are, no doubt, many families going through similar struggles. If one family comes out and is not ashamed of it, it leads the way for others to come together to talk, share, and show the local community that homosexuality is truly here and that it is healthy. Well, if only life were so simple...

I consider this another small milestone in the long process of obtaining my parents' acceptance and understanding. With a sigh, I feel a tired happiness and large burden lifted. We have become much closer since my coming out. It was never like this before — we rarely had serious discussions and I did not talk to them about my hopes, fears, or concerns. There are still many problems ahead, but I believe they now accept the fact that I am not going to "change." It's scary to think that I've gotten to this specific point. Sometimes, I think about my "innocent" days of just coming out. Back then, life did not seem as complicated. To see all that I have to fight for before me is overwhelming, but as it is often said, "I can't go back."

Tita[1] *Talk*
A Cross-Talk with

Zelie Duvauchelle, J. Kehaulani Kauanui, Leolani M., Desiree Thompson

In the tradition of talk story,[2] *four Kānaka Maoli*[3] *women got together to share our histories and ideas. Except for Leolani and Desiree, we only recently met each other. At this point in our lives we are all in the San Francisco Bay Area. Our experiences are varied: Kehaulani grew up in Southern California and will soon be off to New Zealand to begin Polynesian Studies on a Fulbright Fellowship. Zelie, a recent transplant from the rural island of Moloka`i, is pursuing a career in music. Leolani grew up in Nanakuli, Hawaiian homestead land, on O`ahu and has been in San Francisco for more than twenty years. She works in the trades. And Desiree, from downtown Honolulu, is a letter carrier.*

Much of our conversation was in pidgin English, and we have chosen to present this to you in that form with minimal editing into "proper" English.

Introductions

KEHAULINI: My name is Kehaulani Kauanui. My *baole* (white) name is Josette, and I've been going by my Hawaiian name for three years. (Yea!) I'm 25 years old, born and raised in Southern California. I've been in the Bay Area for four years, and my mother is *baole* and my dad is Hawaiian.

He identifies only as Hawaiian because both his parents are Hawaiian. My Hawaiian side — everybody's lucky enough to be a homesteader. Mostly on Anahola homesteads[4] on Kaua`i. But we have extended 'ohana (family) spread all over on the island. So I feel like Kaua`i is home away from home for me, even though my genealogy is from Moloka`i on my grandfather's side and Maui on my grandmother's side. My grandmother was born in Kaua`i and I always think of Kaua`i as home. I'm bicultural in that sense, travelling back and forth. I always spent all my summers with my grandparents, was sent home every summer, so I feel that split has a lot to with what I'm about.

DESIREE: I am Desiree Thompson. My Hawaiian name is 'Ānela, and I used to ask my parents why they gave me such a simple name. I kind of wanted a more long, fancy Hawaiian name. My mother is Japanese; she's third-generation American, and my father's Chinese-Hawaiian-German, and he identifies as Hawaiian. So it's kind of strange that we have the Thompson name. My great-grandfather married a Hawaiian-Chinese woman who had land in Maui. And my grandfather, the oldest son, moved to Kona, on the Big Island, so that's where my family's from. My mom and dad are both from Kona.

LEOLANI: You've tried to do your roots?

DESIREE: No I haven't. My brother has done more than I have. There's a little bit of family history but it all comes down from the *baole* side. There's a *baole* man who marries this Hawaiian woman, who's only got a first name and no last name. Then some other *baole* man comes in and marries this other Hawaiian woman, and the whole family history is based on these *baoles* who came to Hawaii. I went to Kamehameha Schools[5] and graduated in '73. That was before the "renaissance" (the re-awakening of Native Hawaiian pride). So my idea of getting ahead was to go to college to be something. It had nothing to do with being Hawaiian. I felt really funny going to Kamehameha because I felt like I was taking someone else's place. Someone who could benefit from being there, whereas I could go to another school and still be "successful." I have mixed feelings about being Hawaiian, because I don't look Hawaiian, and so when people see me, they don't treat me as Hawaiian. I don't know how to explain that.

LEOLANI: Because you look more Japanese, is that what they say?

DESIREE: I look more Japanese, yes, so I get treated that way and when I'm here in the Bay Area, everyone thinks I'm Filipino. So it's kind of confusing. And then when I say I'm from Hawai`i, then they all say, "Oh. oh, okay," but I don't think they really get it. I'm 38, and I moved here to San Francisco six and a half years ago, mainly to be with Trinity, so there's no job motivation or school motivation, just love.

ZELIE: My name is Zelie Kuliaikanu'u Duvauchelle and I was born and raised on Moloka`i. My family has been there for three generations, and very similarly to you, baole men married Hawaiian women. I grew up in a community that was very small; when I was a child, there was barely any cars on the island. We had dirt roads and we played in the roads all the time, and a car would come every once in awhile and they'd just kind of go around us. It was really nice. I fished a lot, learned a lot of those kinds of skills and things growing up because that was a way of life.

Moloka`i has the largest percentage of Hawaiians, still, in the state. So the culture and customs are very much alive. I remember I used to go to Honolulu quite a bit as a child and as a youngster, and people would ask me the strangest questions on O`ahu. They'd say, "Oh, do you folks have cars?" "Yes." "TV?" It was really amazing that they really didn't know. They think it's the leper colony. I think the leper colony just really saved us from tourism.

Being separated in the islands, too, I really noticed that people would talk down to me, would think that I was unintelligent or uneducated because I was from there. It made me angry a lot of times. I was lucky enough to travel quite a bit when I was young. I was raised by my grandparents, which is typically Hawaiian, for the grandparents to bānai (adopt) the eldest child. So I was raised by them, and they had enough time and enough money to take me with them. That made me be more open-minded as far as different cultures and different people, and knowing that there was more out there than this little island that I was on. I am 34 years old. Just came out as a lesbian seven months ago.

I came to California to be with my girlfriend. She wanted to go to school here, and we thought this would be a good place for community, so we have a deal about living here for awhile and then going home. I'm really getting to like it here, so I think we're going to do a back-and-forth kind of thing.

LEOLANI: My turn! I'm Leolani and I moved here in 1968. I was 18 years old. Now I'm 45. I'm German, Chinese, English, and Hawaiian. I'm around 65 percent Hawaiian and you can figure out the rest. My mother was born in Kalamaula on Moloka`i. My dad was born and raised on the island of O`ahu, but his mother died so they became orphans, and there was eight in the family. We did a study on my father's Hawaiian side, but it led to a woman where it was dead end, so we don't know too much about the Hawaiian side. The *baole* on my father's side was a person that came from England to teach in Hawai`i. We were closer to my mother's side of the family. We often went to my grandmother's house on Moloka`i. So I can relate dirt roads, coconut trees, mango trees, and playing in Grandma's yard and stuff.

So yeah. I came here because I wanted to go to college. Where I come from we were always being put down. That's why people can't get ahead in Hawai`i and come to the mainland — to try to get ahead. It's just luck I've come this far without a college education. When I asked one of my high school advisers if I could go to college, she said "no" right away. She didn't even give me a chance by saying you can work your way through college. Right away she says no, you have no chance. So I came here through the Job Corps. Otherwise, I probably would have ended up with eight or ten babies at home.

So I came here for an education to work my way home and here I am after twenty something years! My mom said to stay here because the job situation at home wasn't very good. I think another reason why I stayed here was that I wasn't out. I knew there was something in me was telling me I'm gay. I guess because I was attracted to women since I was in the fifth grade.

Coming Out

LEOLANI: I felt funny kine feelings, right? Maybe not until you come over here and you experience it so, I didn't come out till almost ten or twelve years after I'd lived here. I knew there was a strong gay community. I keep watching it on TV. You know you have all these marchers, and um, who's that guy who got shot? Harvey Milk, how strong he was pushing the issues for issues for the gay community, but I actually didn't come out until I went to APS, Asian Pacifica Sisters. And I worked for five years with them, and I still felt like a part of them after 5 years. I used to be active in racquetball, baseball, and volleyball but now, I just coach. All for lesbians, bisexual, or straight. Doesn't matter.

DESIREE: I came out in college in Hawai'i. I was working in women's studies at the University of Hawai'i. And there I was — I guess I was "straight" working with all these lesbians whom I had no idea were lesbians. And they're all talking about me being a baby dyke. I didn't know that. I heard later that someone was encouraging this other woman in the office to "bring me out," and she said, "No, I don't want to be the first!" This was in '77, sixteen years ago. I guess the thing that's really interesting for me is when I talk to other people, they have really big issues about coming out, not knowing whether they should do this, or what's going to happen to them. Well, I was like fish to water! There was no turning back. After I started to meet people from the local community in Hawai'i, I really separated myself from that white women's studies community. I felt I fit into the local community better, even though when I first came out I always wondered how come all these local women were so butch-femme? I think that's a statement about our culture — how sometimes the feminist ideals don't fit in with people of color.

LEOLANI: The women at home, are they closeted? Or are they open?

DESIREE: I would say most of them (locals) are closeted, or if they are out, it's only to their family and not to the world. They're not out at work. They may have told their mom, but their dad might not know.

ZELIE: I thought it was interesting, when I was growing up, my grandparents had a furniture and appliance store, and the woman that worked there as the secretary for them for fifteen, twenty years, was — is — a lesbian. I grew up with her, and her girlfriend came to all our parties and they were invited as a couple, and I never gave it a thought! I never even thought about oh, they're couple — I mean, everybody knew they were a couple, but nobody ever said they're lesbians. They were just them, they were a couple, they lived together, it was just regular.

It's still like that at home, on Moloka'i. I mean, there's quite a few lesbian couples that live together and they go to all the baby lū'aus, and all the things, they're invited as a couple. That's just the way it is. But there's no men like that. There's no men couples that go to events together.

KEHAULINI: No? I have two gay uncles; they're my dad's brothers. They both dated baole men, and at one time, all four of the men lived with my grandma. My grandma just referred to them as Uncle So-and-so's friend. They went to all the weddings and baby showers and cousin's birthday parties. But I don't know of any women couples in my family at all.

DESIREE: Interesting. Well, I have a couple of gay cousins on each side. A male cousin came back from Vietnam with a baole man. And when they broke up, the baole guy and his new lover get invited to family functions, so they're like part of the family. No one ever really talks about it although everyone knows about it. And then on my mom's side, I have a younger cousin who's a real butch. She's living with her girlfriend, a Hawaiian woman.

LEOLANI: I guess I had one uncle on my mom's side. So my grandmother's sister and another woman — two aunties were living together. They wanted to hānai a boy. They took him in, and as the years had gone by, he never married. So I think he's gay. I like him because of his love for the family and care. Keeps track of birthdays and stuff. Even though he's alone now. Still, I never caught him with a guy. Even though all his functions were with guys.

KEHAULINI: I've been thinking about this a lot. It's something I'm trying to write, about how coming out has been really different on each side of my family, because my mom is baole and my dad is Hawaiian. I think the reason it's been so different is because of race. So to me, my sexuality is really bound up in how I identify racially and they're really connected for me. I've been out for four years, and I came out to my mom first. She was horrified. She's also Catholic, so she really had a hard time, but she's come to accept it. I came out as bisexual and I identify really strongly with bi. So to her, it was like it wasn't just that I was queer, but it was that if I'm with a woman I'm not with a man, and the man that she had in mind for me would be a white man. So to her, being gay means not going white. She's been really supportive of me, and she's met my partner and really likes her now.

DESIREE: So she wouldn't accept you marrying a Hawaiian man?

KEHAULINI: She'd be disappointed, to be honest. She'll say "I loved your father and everything, but..." I really try and challenge her on that, whereas my dad — I've waited to come out to him. I've only been out to him for two years. I came out to them in really different ways. Because with my mother I wasn't with anybody. I came out and said, "I am bisexual and you have to accept it." To my dad, it seemed ridiculous to come out and say, "I am this."

But to my dad I didn't feel the need to come out and name an identity, but when I fell in love, I wanted to tell him right away. For me, coming out on the Hawaiian side means more about talking about what I'm doing, not who I am. Whereas on the *baole* side I feel like I would say "I am this," and it's an identity. But on the Hawaiian side, to say I am this would be seen as really *baole*. They wouldn't see being gay as being *baole*, but they would see saying "I am a this," naming an individual identity would be really *baole*. I struggle with that in my family anyway because I am so *baole*-raised. Going back, I'm always the one that's different. So to my dad, I want to declare what I'm about and what I'm doing, not "I am a this."

I came out to my dad on the phone. (He's still in Southern California. That's how I was born here; he's the only son that left home, so all his family's still there.) I talked to him on the phone one night, and he said, "So what's going on?" and he never asks me that. I think because he noticed in my voice. "Well, I'm in love." And he says, "With a boy or a girl?" And I said, "A woman." And he says, "Black or white?" And I said, "Korean." And he says, "Oh." I said, "You knew, huh?" He says, "I didn't know what. I didn't know one way or another." I said, "Come on, you knew," because they had been baiting me for a couple of years. I didn't feel closeted as much as I just wasn't talking about it. And so he says, "Oh well. I have two gay brothers, so if my daughter's gay, oh well. That's how it goes." And then he met my girlfriend and really liked her. Since then, I've been trying to come out to as much family in Hawaiʻi as possible, and it's been pretty easy and delightful. But my mom has almost forbidden me to come out on the *baole* side, and she hasn't told anybody. She doesn't want to talk about it. I can talk to her about it, and I can talk about what's going on in my life, but she doesn't want it to go beyond her.

I came out to my grandma pretty recently after that, because after my college graduation pictures, I had all these pictures of my girlfriend, and she's got her arms around me in all of them. My grandma's all, "Who's that?" So "Oh, that's my girlfriend." And that somebody else had asked, "Who's that?" and I said, "Oh, that's *meaaloha*" so that they'd know when I said girlfriend, I meant love. "Really? What's her name?" And now they ask, "And how's your friend?" I recently asked my grandma if I could stay with her for a few weeks. And she wrote me back, "You can stay as long as you want, and you can bring your friend, too." I actually care more about the acceptance on the Hawaiian side than on the *baole* side. Because I know there's bound to be more rejection on the *baole* side than on the Hawaiian side.

LEOLANI: My parents are so old. My father's 81; my mom's 69. Sometimes, you don't need to say, in our family. So my aunties and uncles they can see, that's not to be said. So I'm not really out to them. Except for one of my aunts. She asked me, "Are you a lesbian?" I said yes, I had many lovers and I brought them all home. So of course, islanders bring home mainlanders. They never thought they were my lovers. So I had to point out to her, "Remember this girl?" "Oh, yeah, yeah." "Uh-huh, six-year relationship. You remember that girl?" "Oh, yeah, yeah, yeah." "Okay, four-year relationship." She was stunned, no, more like shocked, but she did recall the individuals I brought home.

Being Hawaiian, Growing Up

LEOLANI: Hey, Zelie, where'd you learn writing and singing?

ZELIE: I learned to play music from my first husband, who was pure Hawaiian. That's how I learned. Actually, words to songs and Hawaiian songs I've known. As a child, I really loved to hang around the adults at parties and listen to all their songs. Oh my God, I loved it! They used to always be chasing me away, "Go play, go play!" And I'd be listening to the music and they'd sing all these naughty hulas and my aunties would dance these naughty hulas, and I'd be hiding out and watching my grandma. A lot of the older songs are from memory. I just remember them from sitting around at parties and hearing them over and over and over again.

KEHAULINI: There's something about the music that brings out the sexuality, too. I remember always seeing my grandmother and my aunties and the women in our family as sexual women. Not oversexed, as the tourism market wants them to look, but not as repressed as it has been on the *haole* Catholic side. Because when you see your grandma singing some of those songs, remember the one on the Postbox song, yeah? You know, there's more acceptance about that kind of thing.

ZELIE: There's so much sexuality in the music.

LEOLANI: The songs I learned from my family, the songs they played while they were drinking beer, were Hawaiian songs that originally came from the church.

KEHAULINI: Is most of your Hawaiian-side Christian?

LEOLANI: Yeah, my father and mother, Catholic.

DESIREE: My grandmother was Catholic. My grandfather was Mormon. My father was Episcopalian. We went to Episcopalian church for a couple of years because my parents felt we needed to be baptized to be saved, so us kids would go to heaven. Except for that, I'd say we weren't very religious.

KEHAULINI: All my Hawaiian side is Mormon. But there's all these contradictions, you know. My grandmother's now going back more strongly to it. And it's strange because it's through the Mormon side that most of our genealogy has come through. Strange to learn about Hawaiian lineage kind of through that back door.

ZELIE: The Mormons are incredible. Oh my God, the history, the Hawaiian history that they have, it's incredible. So many people go to do their family trees through the Mormon church.

KEHAULINI: Even if you're not Mormon.

ZELIE: Yeah, amazing. That's wonderful. They have a purpose.

LEOLANI: I'm really happy to see more Hawaiian language being taught here. Was anyone here taught Hawaiian in school?

ZELIE: Mm-mm (no).

DESIREE: Not too many people speak Hawaiian nowadays. Starting with people from my father's generation, the language got taken away from them.

LEOLANI: Wow, I feel like it wasn't taken away. It's just not exercised enough to put it in a house as a number one language. Christians were pounding English into us. That's why we all have English names. To be written on records; that's what I understand.

KEHAULINI: But it was banned, against the law.

DESIREE: My father went to Kamehameha, *the* school for native Hawaiians. They were forbidden to speak Hawaiian.

KEHAULINI: It's the breakdown of an entire culture.

LEOLANI: But why? It's because of Christians, too, right? You have a population collapse, and that's going to affect your language. And only in 1983 was the law taken off the books. 1983!

ZELIE: That's so amazing.

KEHAULINI: You couldn't teach Hawaiian in a public space. It was against the law. The immersion program, Punana Leo, is a way the language is coming back. Hawaiian wasn't even a second language until 1983. More people speak Hawaiian now than in the past three generations.

LEOLANI: It's funny, about speaking Hawaiian, because the last I heard all-Hawaiian speaking was my grandmother and my uncle's wife's mother, speaking fluently. It was like amazing to hear how they could converse with each other, and this is like what, I'm the third generation.

DESIREE: I think that's pretty typical, that we the third generation don't speak, and our grandparents spoke it fluently. See, that's where they killed our parents' ability to speak.

KEHAULINI: Then I'm the fourth generation, because my grandparents weren't allowed.

LEOLANI: But I still feel that — even though we were on the grip of British law, I feel they could have still carried on the language, no matter what they say. It's just like religion, taking the religion away.

DESIREE: I had an opportunity to take it because it was being taught at Kamehameha. But since I was intending to go to college, I had to choose between Spanish and French, because those are the languages they accepted as a foreign language requirement.

LEOLANI: Guess I was pretty fortunate. In '65 and '66 there was Hawaiian language being taught at Wai`anae. I had a teacher who spoke fluent Hawaiian. Of course we had to take English because it was one of the mandatories, and Hawaiian wasn't. I was happy because I learned a lot.

DESIREE: Having known you all this time, Leolani, you're so Hawaiian, and I don't know how you keep it, because the people you hang out with aren't necessarily Hawaiian. You just have this Hawaiian spirit about you and I don't know how you keep it because it's really hard. And you're not an angry person; I don't see you get upset about stuff.

I get really angry that people don't know what I am and just don't want to explain. I feel like I'm an immigrant, and I'm not! I speak English, and that's the only language I speak. I thought I was American in Hawai`i. Don't talk to me if you don't know. But I don't see that in you. I don't see that kind of anger. Maybe you just aren't that kind of person.

LEOLANI: When I was in Job Corps they called us pineapples. You had the blacks, you had the Mexicans — there was hardly any whites. Whenever we sang in the hallway, because there was always curfew, they would say, "Oh, the natives are restless." We're singing because we can't sleep.

I guess that along the way, I just accepted people for what they are, even if they don't have the feelings. I mean being rude to you. It's their problem. My auntie told me, tolerate. Put up with them.

ZELIE: I know what you mean though. I've only been here four months. Oh my God, some people are so *baole*! Some Hawaiians over here are — I mean it's weird. I look at them and I think oh my God, go home for a little while! Please. Go there and get barefooted and get in the dirt or something. I don't know what. But they so *baole* it's unreal.

LEOLANI: When you say so *baole*, what are you expressing?

ZELIE: Their spirit! Their spirit!

DESIREE: Are you talking about people born here or just moved here?

ZELIE: Well they've been here like long time, years and years. They just seemed to have lost something. I can't exactly put my finger on it. I know what you're saying, that Leolani is very Hawaiian still, and she's been here for so long. So it's amazing, it really is. That makes me nervous, when I see people and how much they've changed, I'm like how long have you been here? How long do I have before I gotta go back? Before this being *haole* starts infiltrating my Hawaiian-ness.

Gender and Sexuality in Hawaiian Culture

KEHAULINI: Do you know of or do you make up your own word for loving women or being lesbian or bi in Hawaiian? Because we don't have one for the women, but we have *aikane* for the men, you know? And I also wanted to ask if when you grew up if anybody in your family referred to anybody in your family as *mābū* or if they made the distinction between being *mābū* and being gay but not "crossing over" the genders?

LEOLANI: Back home, we call it butch, that's all. That's all I hear for women.

DESIREE: I think my family called everyone *mābū*. But I don't think there was any word for women.

LEOLANI: Just lesbian.

DESIREE: No, that's not a word they would use.

KEHAULINI: So you say *mābū* is just gay. See because my two uncles, one is *haole*, one is just gay. The *mābū* in my family, he protects our things, he protects our genealogy, he nurtures my grandmother, he's does those family things.

LEOLANI: When I was growing up, my Nanakuli side, and we see *mābū* they're dressed up as women, and they're strong players in volleyball.

KEHAULINI: But you wouldn't call the physical ones *mābū*, right?

LEOLANI: No, no. Most of them dressed up as women, but...

KEHAULINI: Crossing over.

DESIREE: They're transvestite.

KEHAULINI: So one uncle that's gay doesn't cross over, he's just gay.

LEOLANI: Yeah, he's just male, but gay.

KEHAULINI: My other uncle's really femme. Big difference.

LEOLANI: It was a thing where I come from, an evening event, you go down to the park where all the *mābūs* were going to play volleyball, because they're not just playing, the way how they talked, and hit, and expressed themselves was like an evening show.

ZELIE: The *mābūs* for me were always men in drag. Never women.

We never referred to women as *māhū*. That's just something recent that I've heard here. One woman in particular who's Hawaiian, asked me, "Oh, is she *haole?*" I knew what she meant, but it sounded really wierd to me, I was like, "Well, yeah." But I never heard that before. But she's from here. She was raised here.

KEHAULINI: My dad asked me once if I was *māhū* before I came out to him. But what he said was, "You're probably going to go to law school, you're going to do these things, you're going to be independent. Do you think you're *māhū*." And I said, "No, I don't want to be a man." I guess he really did want to know if I was gay. But he didn't ask me if I was gay, he asked me if I was *māhū*. Because a lot of the male *māhū* I know, they don't necessarily sleep with men. They just cross over. And so I told my dad, "Oh, I wouldn't be a man for a million zillion dollars. I'm very happy being a woman." I was waiting to see if he was going to ask me more questions. This was before I came out to him. He said, "You're really masculine" (because at that time I wasn't as femme as I am now). I said, "Dad, look at the women in our family. We've got a lot of *titas* in our family. I am no *tita*. I told him, "Look at the women around me! They're butch!" (But they identify as straight.)

LEOLANI: So you call them *titas*. But *titas* is also known as sisters.

KEHAULINI: No, they're *titas*, they're not necessarily dykes. So I'm saying look at all the straight women around me, look at how butch they look. They're *titas*; they're not necessarily gay, I said. And I'm gay but I'm not a *tita*. So do you create words or how would you want to say it? What would you want?

ZELIE: It seems to me that *māhū* would be a gentler. Like if I was to tell somebody in my family I was *māhū*, they would much rather hear that than lesbian. They would say like oh! They could relate to that. But if I said lesbian, it would be like oh my God, what do you mean? Lesbian, yeah, it's so *haole*. But *māhū* would be like "Oh, oh," immediately they could relate.

KEHAULINI: I've still never used any of those words for myself in my Hawaiian family.

ZELIE: Me neither.

KEHAULINI: I just say I have a partner. And then if I see a cute guy, "Grandma, I like him, I think he's cute," she says "Oh, he's too young for you." She never says, "But you said you liked her." She just says, "Oh, you think he's cute?" She doesn't say "Oh, I thought you were 'da kine.'"

What do you think it is? I think that Hawaiian women before Christianity and colonialism could love whomever they wanted. Why do you think there's no word?

ZELIE: I don't know. That's interesting. Maybe we can call ourselves *aiwahine*.

KEHAULINI: How about *aihine*? Let's drop the *"wa."*

ZELIE: It would be neat to have a term, but it would also be neat to know if there was one. I've never heard one.

LEOLANI: Only because the guys were more out than the girls.

DESIREE: Probably so.

ZELIE: It could have been too that it wasn't even a deal for women to be lovers with each other.

KEHAULINI: So maybe that's why, because the *aikane* term I heard is more of a new term. But it seems like *māhū* is really different than just being gay. Than maybe it was just more of a given that people are gay.

LEOLANI: It's a made up word. It's probably like what she said *māhū* means. Men dressed up as women. But not knowing the definition more, I come here in San Francisco, I didn't know bisexual, there was such a thing. I didn't know transsexual, I didn't know transvestite, I didn't know all that till I come here and I learned. So what category is this? Being that I'm from the countryside, I don't realize that there's just not one, there's like four of them, maybe more. Five. Who knows. It's kind of interesting.

DESIREE: Maybe like you say, it wasn't an issue.

KEHAULINI: But if Hawaiians had 34 different words for time of the day, you'd think that there'd be some words for sexuality, wouldn't you?

LEOLANI: Probably there was, but it wasn't spoken about.

DESIREE: Maybe it didn't get passed on.

KEHAULINI: I don't necessarily buy the explanation that sexuality wasn't talked about, because so much other sexuality is totally talked about. I mean, some of the chants are so sexual. So I don't necessarily want to explain it away by saying that people were more quiet about sexuality.

DESIREE: But the songs are sexual in a poetic way, they use...

KEHAULINI: Some of them are pretty blatant.

LEOLANI: Some of them are hidden secrets, also. It was never really talked about. It depends. History.

ZELIE: I'm very interested to know, if anybody finds out anything please.

LEOLANI: I think a lot of things are hushed because of how Christians had turned our language around to become English. A lot was hidden. Because a lot of it was taboo also. I wish I could go more into it. My cousins are always talking about it.

KEHAULINI: There's a Native American, she's part Laguna Pueblo, Paula Gunn Allen,[6] and she talks about when whites colonized the Southwest, that they actually used more violent tactics on tribes that had more gay people within them, and that there was a violent repression of tribes that were led by women and tribes where the *berdache*, which is similar to *mahu*, where they had a prominent position within the culture, that it was suppressed really violently, really devastated. Part of what I wonder is that with the Calvinists, who were pretty violent Christians, coming, they might have tried to extinguish that just like they extinguished a lot of the incestuous mating. I read this article just a couple months ago saying how Hawaiians had many different partners, how the Calvinists made that illegal, and would imprison you if you committed "adultery." I just want to talk more about the link between colonization and Christianization. And suppressing the sexual...

DESIREE: If Hawaiian history was oral and it wasn't written until the Christians came, of course they left out a lot of sexuality, and then, the first thing they brought was the Bible, right? I mean they didn't write down Hawaiians' histories in the Hawaiian language. Their main purpose was to learn the language so they could translate the Bible into the language and teach Hawaiians to read the Bible, so obviously lots of things got left out.

LEOLANI: The sexual part for sure.

ZELIE: I think a lot of the answers would be found in chants. Just because of the oral history thing, and I know for me, I've learned a lot through chants about our history. A lot of things that you could never find out other than simply by those chants. And there are people, very gifted people, that are getting messages from our ancestors through dreams and through direct contacts through meditations. And I've met a couple of them and it's just wonderful, and they're real spooky. I mean I just say spooky, like whoa, this is very powerful, *chicken skin kine*, you know. One of them is a *kumu* (teacher) that comes to Moloka`i. I would very much be interested in asking him the next time I'm back in Hawai`i.

LEOLANI: I agree with what you've been saying about chants and studies. When the *kumu hula*, studies through the oral tradition sometimes history was reinterpreted. Oftentimes, this led to conflicts between the *kumu hula* and they would go off to teach their own interpretation.

ZELIE: How about stories of people actually being visited by ancient ones, just people who hold that part in our culture, you know, people who were passing things on. It's very necessary, obviously, for them to come back and come into our lives in spirit because it's been lost. So it's really wonderful and beautiful that it's happening on that level, and that there are sensitive people to be handling that. It's hard to be those people.

Same Sex Marriage in Hawai`i

KEHAULINI: What do you folks think about the gay marriage proposals in Hawai`i?

LEOLANI: Awesome. (laughter)

DESIREE: I think it's kind of interesting that it's coming up in Hawai`i of all places.

LEOLANI: I would think California would be first, but it's over there.

DESIREE: I think one of the interesting things is the state constitution is questionable in this line. But on the other hand, the *haoles* over here don't even know what they're thinking, in terms of, "Oh, yeah, we can go to Hawai`i and get married and have honeymoons and blah blah blah." Fine. That's what they've been doing all this time anyway. Straight couples, now it'd just make it easier for gay white people to go over to Hawai`i.

KEHAULINI: That's one of my questions about it too.

DESIREE: Whenever I get to talk to local people on the phone,

I always ask about what's happening over there, and they don't really say much. I think it doesn't concern them as much as it does people up here.

KEHAULINI: I'm really leery of it, I feel like, people tend to stereotype our Pacific sexualities as being really simple and open, and I feel like they're almost banking on that to get what they want, as far as the right to marry. I think that there's a tendency for people in the Bay Area and the West Coast, in general, to appropriate our Hawaiian culture, because they say, oh, it's part of their tradition, and so they're taking on part of our culture, what they understand to be our cultural acceptance of being gay and then going with their own agenda, but without any concern of helping us preserve our own cultural traditions and maintain land rights.

And so I feel that people here should make same-sex marriage a reality in this state (California). I think that they should be working just as hard to make it a reality here so that it isn't just another excuse for another honeymoon. And also I feel, like of anything in Hawai'i right now, the priority is the sovereignty movement. I think that they should be asking more Hawaiians how they feel about it, in general. If this goes through, it's really going to benefit the state of Hawai'i, and I think it should be benefiting the potential Hawaiian nation. I was talking with another Hawaiian lesbian here in the Bay Area. We were dreaming up a way that if it passed, and if gay couples here go to Hawai'i, they could support the sovereignty movement, and don't just go check into a hotel for a week and then leave, leaving their garbage behind. When they get a civil right, they should support a Native right. Because gay marriage in Hawai'i is a civil right for anybody else that's there, but for Hawaiians, it's a sovereign right. It's that Hawaiians should be making these laws for our own nation, our own people. Anybody that's trying to push through an agenda for civil rights has to support our sovereign rights. Civil rights are to be included within the laws that already exist, and sovereign rights are to get our own laws so that we can govern ourselves. So I want the sovereignty activists to come out in support of it, and have us talk about it as Hawaiians.[7]

DESIREE: Yes, it's a really difficult thing, because in English, Hawaiians are the same as Californians and Arizonans and all that. Mainland people don't know that Native Hawaiians, *Kānaka Maoli*, exist.

ZELIE: When I first heard and read about it, I had all kinds of things running through my head. Mostly I was concerned that typical of Hawai`i state government it's so rinky-dink and corrupt, and oh my God, so lame. And those stupid heads are thinking we can get more tourists. That's so typical. All they're thinking about is money. So that was my first thought, and then, I'm thinking it would be neat to be able to be married to my partner legally. For me, in my family, if it was legal, my relationship would be more accepted. If it's legal, then it must be okay. And I wonder, who is going to benefit, and what is it really for? Can it be turned into something that is beneficial to the Hawaiian people? If it comes from that kind of thinking, then great, but just to do it, just because we're gonna get more tourists for Hawai`i seems so awful to me. The same thing happening all over again. The money thing...

KEHAULINI: And it's crazy 'cause they always talk about it as the first state that's gonna get it. That's how it's being talked about: Hawai`i will be the first state to get this marriage law, and it's like, wait, who says Hawai`i needs to be a state, you know? I'm still in the mode where I want to question statehood. I want to question why Hawai`i is a state of the United States of America in the first place?

Hawaiian Sovereignty

LEOLANI: With all that rent the government owes Hawaiian homelands, there should be back pay from the government so Hawaiian people can build homes.

KEHAULINI: And the Hawaiian Home Lands are just a small part of our trust lands. We have ceded lands, over a million acres. They're all over, ceded lands. Homestead land is only 200,000 acres, and that's nothing compared to the rest of the state. We have more title to a lot of land.

LEOLANI: And still a lot of it is not developed yet, especially where I'm from, Nanakuli; the whole hillside filled with trees. There's a lot of land that can be cleared. I don't know where the money is going to come from.

ZELIE: The perfect land for Hawaiians to be in would be the valleys because there's water. And the valleys are all the choice lands and those lands are all privately owned.

KEHAULINI: *The Wall Street Journal* had an exposé by Susan Faludi (author of *Backlash*) about the abuse of the Hawaiian Home Lands trust and all the money and where it's been going. The federal government has paid a lot of back rent to the Department of Hawaiian Home Lands. How everybody got homestead land but Hawaiians. And it shows how they sold it to people within the state government. You can't sell homestead land, it's only supposed to be leased. So why is it that the military and different people in government can buy homestead land and lease it and here we have to show all our *palapala*[8] for genealogy and prove this and that Hawaiian blood quantum, when the military can lease it for a dollar a year per acre?

LEOLANI: It's a trip. Plus in Nanakuli right in front of the elementary school, that should be all homestead land.

KEHAULINI: But also in Wai'anae all that beach front land, it's all R & R...

LEOLANI: Yeah, that's true. Seems so out in the boondocks where they have the rest camps. They should be like in Pearl Harbor or Hickham airfield. (laughter)

KEHAULINI: In Hawai`i, a lot of people still can't even say my name. And when I call home to Hawai`i to get something or materials from the library, and I say, I'm calling here from UC Berkeley, I'm doing research, blah blah blah, and I can talk the talk. They'll say, what's your name; then as soon as I give them my name they'll start talking to me like I'm a child. And those are local people that don't respect Hawaiians. And so I have so much anger about the local people that come here, and call themselves a Hawaiian, 'cause most of them do, and they don't even know what the word *kānaka* means. And then they start talking really heavy pidgin. They went to Punahou, they're rich, they come here and they don't give the Hawaiians that were born and raised here the time of day. There's a relationship between them being on our land and us not being able to be on our land, these things are connected. I think that local people who refer to themselves as Hawaiian really trivialize the struggle of our people and blood quantum issues, because we are defined differently as "Hawaiian" and "Part Hawaiian" by the U.S. Federal Government depending on our proof of Hawaiian "blood."

LEOLANI: You correct them.

KEHAULINI: No, they gotta watch out. (laughter) I always get so angry.

LEOLANI: If you want people to know what is needed to be known, you got to correct them right away. Hey, you say my name (Leolani) wrong, it's pronounced Lay-Oh-La-Nee, not, Lee-oh-Lan-Eee.

KEHAULINI: I went to a barbecue after the gay pride march and it was an APS barbecue and my T-shirt said *Kānaka Maoli*. And they said, is that your name? (laughter) They said what's your name, I said, Kehaulani Kauanui. One Asian woman said, "Oh that's nice, is that English?" And I'm wearing a tag that says "half-breed queer," you know, so it's obvious that I'm mixed race, it's obvious that I'm gay, and they still say, oh, is that English?

LEOLANI: It's only because the people here don't really understand our nature. So it's really up to you to correct them. That's how I feel. You gotta make them learn and know how, what we are. Okay, you're the teacher.

KEHAULINI: I don't mind if pepole mispronounce my name. I'd correct them. But, I'm talking about identity issues where people would rather ignore the Hawaiians that are alive and living and call themselves a Hawaiian, and yet they might learn hula, they might learn singing, but they don't care about our survival issues. They want it for the show and the dance and to look "different." There are a lot of locals here and I feel like they have to take responsibility, it can't always be put on the Hawaiians to do the work.

LEOLANI: From back home or over here?

KEHAULINI: Either; I'd rather put my energy when I know there's gonna be something reciprocal.

ZELIE: I'm sitting here thinking about education and just seems to me that the way that the educational system is set up, it's not set up to be Hawaiian.

KEHAULINI: It's almost antithetical to what you want.

ZELIE: Yes. So you know we say, oh yeah, if we get Hawaiians educated, then it's like... look where they have to go to BE educated, and then what happens to them...

KEHAULINI: De-Hawaiianize them...

ZELIE: De-Hawaiianize them to be educated, so it has to do a lot to me with the spirit of the person.

KEHAULINI: Just surviving, come out alive.

ZELIE: That's right, and to come out still Hawaiian. To be educated and still Hawaiian, I am a survivor (laughter). And be educated and Hawaiian at the same time. It is, it's so true.

KEHAULINI: I like that point, yeah. I wouldn't be able to even go through school if my family weren't in some way backing me, even though they don't have any idea what I'm doing. They've told me keep doing what you're doing. I'm the first in my family to go to college. I probably wouldn't be in college if I hadn't grown up here. Because I'm not only the first one who's gone; I'm the only one who's in college. It's just really an unfamiliar process. When I moved from Southern California to Northern California, my dad asked, "Can't you stay at the community college?" So it's really weird because now it'll be okay if I'm the writer, but like don't talk about it. Beause it's still really *baole*. It's kind of strange to go home in the summers and have people only see a certain part of you and then for them to not want to know about the other parts.

I'm really critical of education as *the* solution. It's just one of many paths. In my family, I won't be a dancer, I'll be a writer. Everybody has their own role in the family and I'm gonna be the writer.

DESIREE: See I think that that's how you use the educational system to educate other people about being Hawaiian, as opposed to using your education to make the big bucks. You're getting an education so you can work within the system so that the people who ARE in the system may be able to understand where you're coming from. By being a writer, you'll get the word out, the stuff that other people wouldn't be doing.

KEHAULINI: Yeah, when I was back for the Hawai`i Peoples' Tribunal, a lot of the women who put together the Tribunal on Kaua`i said, "Girl, come home with your Ph.D. and do some damage." They were telling me that "I don't wanna get it, you get it, and then you come back 'cause you have a responsibility to us"; You know, I don't need college to be with Hawaiians. I need college so that I can go deal with that person who talked to me like I'm five years old. My grandmother doesn't like to hear about college. I leave that here when I go back home to Hawai`i. But to deal in Honolulu, you bet, I have it right there with me. Because as light as I may be, the second they see my name, I'm a five-year-old. And they associate that with being Hawaiian.

LEOLANI: It's just people recognizing people who has background of know-how. They always put the Hawaiians down because they don't have college degrees, they've never been given a chance to get a college degree. Like I asked can I go to college, right away she looked at my grades, no. So that kind of puts a downfall right there, makes you don't wanna try it. Where can I go from there, she's telling me I can't go to college, not knowing if a person can. How did that affect you?

DESIREE: Well, both my parents were not highly educated. They came from very poor families, and so the only way they thought that we could survive was to educate us. We didn't have a lot; we lived in apartments; we never had a brand new car, but the kids, my brother and I, went to private schools. And they made a conscious choice to only have two children because they had plans for us. So that was ingrained in us, and I had to go to college. You know when I got into college, I wasn't really happy in what I was pursuing, so I just did it to do it.

KEHAULINI: My family never really encouraged me to go to college. On either side.

ZELIE: I didn't go to college. I went to a community college for a while, and played, you know, went to beach, and stuff like that, much to the disappointment of my family. The plan for me was definitely to board at either at Punahou or Kamehameha which is what my other family members did. Then go to college, come to college on the mainland. And I was a rebel. I just refused. I wanted to stay on Moloka`i first of all, and definitely in Hawai`i. Took my girlfriend to get me to the mainland (laughter). You know it's amazing, all those years of fighting my parents, or grandparents. I should say, not really fighting them but disappointing them. I always felt like I disappointed them because I didn't come to the mainland and go to college; that was their plan for me. Their daughter came to the mainland and went to college. I was the next generation, of course that's what I was gonna do too, you know. And I just did not want to leave Hawai`i.

KEHAULINI: I did it on my own, and they just now realized, oh yeah, she graduated (laughter). Now they see that I'm going to keep going on the path, it's like, oh, you've come this far, okay, keep going. It's just a really unfamiliar process to them. I went to a community college for three years before I could get to transfer to University of California, Berkeley, because I wasn't tracked for college either, at all. I just kept figuring out how to get myself there.

LEOLANI: I like what you have to say about you going to college, and family. I thought your parents always supported you.

KEHAULINI: Morally, saying "Keep going, keep going." My dad never expected me to marry. My mom has always been the one, "You're gonna marry," but my dad never said that to me. I've never felt that pressure to do the wife and kid thing, on the Hawaiian side. In the family, it's like, she's just going to be different no matter what she does. She's the different one.

---

1 Tita: a pidgin English term derived from the word sister-sistah-tita; a "butch" woman who is not necessarily lesbian.

2 Talk story: to converse, but in an informal way.

3 Kānaka Maoli: Hawaiian word for indigenous people, literally means true people.

4 Congress established the Hawaiian Homes Commission in 1920, which sets aside public lands at $1 a year for long-term leases to persons with at least one-half Hawaiian blood.

5 Kamehameha Schools for Hawaiian and part-Hawaiian children, established in 1887 by Bernice Pauahi Bishop, great-granddaughter of King Kamehameha I.

6 The Sacred Loop: recovering the Feminine in American Indian Traditions

7 Native Hawaiian lesbians, gays and bisexuals in Hawai`i have begun this process by becoming more visible as gays within various Hawaiian organizations. Groups such as Na Mamo o Manoa formed themselves in order to support each other and to call upon Hawaiian sovereignty leaders to address the issue of equal rights within their vision of a Hawaiian nation. Native gays have also been instrumental in building coalitions between predominantly *baole* gay, lesbian, and bisexual organizations and Hawaiian sovereignty groups. Native Hawaiians involved in the Hawai`i Equal Rights Marriage Project have also encouraged gay and lesbian

solidarity for Hawaiian sovereignty. See *Island Lifestyle*, January 1994, P.O. Box 240515, Honolulu, Hawai`i 96824-0515. To contact the Hawai`i Equal Rights Marriage Project of the Gay and Lesbian Community Center write to 1820 University Ave. Suite 208, Honolulu, Hawai`i 96822. Na Mamo o Manoa can be reached c/o Ku`umeaaloha Gomes, P.O. Box 12035, Honolulu, Hawai`i 96828.

8 Palapala: papers, documents

Ann Yuri Uyeda

All At Once, All Together:
One Asian American Lesbian's Account
of the 1989 Asian Pacific Lesbian Network Retreat

Note: I recognize some of the potential problems in using the acronym "API" to refer to Asian and Pacific Islander women, two groups of women with different and distinctive experiences. One of the problems is that these differences and distinctions may not be given full respect by use of the acronym. Thus, when reading "API" in this piece, please keep in mind that "API" is intended to read "Asian and Pacific Islander." Where "Asian American" is used instead of "Asian and Pacific Islander," this is a conscious decision and refers specifically to something about the Asian American experience. "Asian" is used instead of "Asian American" to refer specifically to race and not personal identity.

AT 8:25 P.M. ON FRIDAY, 1 SEPTEMBER 1989, CLOSE TO 100 ASIAN and Pacific Islander (API) lesbians and bisexual women sat in a classroom on the University of California, Santa Cruz campus, listening to the opening remarks of the first national/international Asian Pacifica Lesbian Network (APLN) retreat. Seventy more women were expected to join us by the official start of the retreat at 9 a.m. the next morning. Expectancy filled the room as we slowly reached a critical mass of queer API women. For many of us who didn't live in San Francisco, this would be our first time with so many API women who shared a common sexuality.

Suddenly, an inflated latex condom shot into the air, kept afloat by playful hands reaching out to keep it going. A mini safe sex workshop had just finished, and the presenter tossed out foil-wrapped condoms to women who wanted them. Someone had ripped open one of the "freebies" and had transformed the contents into a spontaneous toy. Condom demand, while rowdy, remained limited.

As I watched the condom make its way around the room, I thought about the six-hour drive I'd just completed from Southern California to Santa Cruz, a drive I'd made by myself because I was unable to share a ride with two women from Los Angeles who were driving up. And because I'd just come to terms with being an Asian American lesbian, I hadn't yet met any other Asian American lesbians who also lived in the general Los Angeles-Orange County metro area. Earlier in the evening, I had watched other women arrive with their friends or meet friends at the retreat. In my loneliness I felt uncomfortable and noticeable. To add to these feelings, I didn't have a roommate to share the double room I'd been assigned to in the student dorms. At this point, I was heavily doubting my social skills, feeling like both the social dork and wallflower. Would I be able to meet any new friends?

I had other anxieties, too.

All week, as I had prepared for this trip, I wondered what I expected to get out of this retreat. Most importantly, I tried to explain to myself why I would pay $150 for my retreat registration and drive 200 plus miles to spend my Labor Day weekend with a bunch of API women. I knew part of the answer had to do with my hopes of momentarily escaping my recent ex-lover who I was still living with, to process through our relationship and mutual breakup. But my escape to Santa Cruz constituted only a small part of the answer. What, then, was the real answer?

My uncertainty about the retreat and my inability to answer these basic questions can be traced to the ambivalence I've always had about identifying as Asian.

I grew up in Orange County, California, a fact which almost always prompts comments like, "Hey, it's really conservative there!" In fact, some of the more rabid fundamentalists and right-wing politicians on the local and national level have come from Orange County, their thinking and politics similar to that of Jesse Helms, U.S. Senator from North Carolina.

But there is something of greater, personal importance than the type of politics practiced in Orange County, something which has managed to leave its marks for life on me: during the time when I lived in Orange County, there weren't a lot of Asians. Being Asian, I was always different, could be readily identified as the visible minority, had people use me to validate the model minority myth. While not as bad a situation as it is elsewhere, I had suffered through the angst-producing spiral of isolation-alienation-shame-denial that unfortunately has characterized so much of the Asian American experience, including my own.

As a result, I've grown up learning/yearning to be white. For a long time, I told everyone that Asian was only something I looked like — everything else (really) about me was American (i.e., white). I distanced myself from everything Asian and Japanese, including my heritage and my parents. This strategy worked — for the most part, I was "accepted" as being like everyone else, "accepted" as being white. Yeah, I was a "banana," a "twinkie": yellow on the outside but white inside (really) just to survive.

Now I see how, in this void, my own internalized racism and ignorance made me want to believe the stereotypes of Asians being too quiet, passive, apathetic, reluctant to stand up for what they believed in. The Orange County I had grown up in practically guaranteed that Asians would adhere to these stereotypes. After all, in this environment, who would want, who could dare to be assertive and outspoken if they weren't really white? Consequently, if that's how Asians were (and the media continued to assure me that we were), I didn't want any part of it.

The more energy I put into upholding the stereotypes, the more I thought I could prove I was like everyone else, that I was (really) white. I didn't know any better to debunk the model minority myth on my own, and I didn't know any Asians who could show me truths and strengths about the Asian American experience.

In college, fresh from my first Asian American studies class, I finally came to grips with my indelible Asian American identity.

Yet, when it came to my own "coming out," I stayed in the closet for a long time, knowing the truth about my sexuality but never speaking it because I just didn't think there *were* any queer Asian Americans — while I knew gay men and lesbians, everyone was white. My fear was that I didn't know what it would be like to be an Asian lesbian. It wasn't until May 1987 when I finally saw two Asian lesbians kissing at my first gay pride festival in Long Beach. Seeing these women proved to me that there were, somewhere, queer Asian women. I knew then that I could also be one.

But as far as I knew, I remained the only Asian lesbian, at least in Orange County. I continued to think other Asians, even if they were queer women, would still be like the stereotypes I had grown up with and learned to hate. I could not yet find the truths and strengths about being an Asian American lesbian within my own new and fragile identity as a lesbian. Ironically, while "out" as a lesbian, I became a closeted Asian American. This dual identity was reinforced by the gay and lesbian community in Orange County which was (then and still now) predominantly white. This community took me on face value, that I looked Asian, but they expected me to *act* white. I'd done this charade before to gain acceptance, and I continued to do this for several years after I came out. But this time, because I'd previously lived a life as a self-identified Asian American, I couldn't go back to pretending I was white. So, in frustration, I finally just gave up and separated myself from the community, preferring to live a quiet life and teaching myself how to be Asian and lesbian in the same moment.

On top of all this confusion and collusion, there was no way I could fathom, let alone actualize, being an outspoken, activist Asian American lesbian. That final bit of integration would come several years later.

Thus my uncertainty and ambivalence in 1989.

I had these feelings even before I left Southern California on Friday morning to begin the long drive to Santa Cruz. On the Monday of the retreat weekend, I'd called Trinity, a contact for APLN, to let her know I hadn't yet received any information about the weekend. Being an anal-retentive Asian American Virgo, not knowing anything about the retreat just added to my overall anxieties.

As Trinity patiently addressed my various concerns, she also confirmed my spot among 150 other queer API women. "150?!" I asked with surprise, "You mean there's really that many of us?" There would even be as many as 170 by Saturday morning, Trinity added.

Wow. What would it be like to sit in a room with 170 of us?

I expected it to be like raps I'd been to, sponsored by a local interracial Asian/Pacific gay group — bodies sitting in chairs, exchanging few ideas or personal experiences, reluctant to open up to others, most people wanting to be somewhere else. The stereotypes of Asian Americans played again in my mind. Great: I could hardly wait to sit with these 170 women and feel myself slowly succumb to the stereotypes.

Thus, when my friends asked if I was excited to go to the retreat, I couldn't truthfully reply with an enthusiastic "YES!" I simply wasn't sure what I would be getting into. In the end, my curiosity overcame the stereotypes and unanswered questions. If things got too bad or too boring at the retreat, I promised myself, I could simply head up to San Francisco or hang out in Santa Cruz for a few days.

I did expect to be the only Asian American lesbian attending from Orange County, so as I prepared for the retreat, I also spent much of my time contacting various queer community groups to pick up their promotional material to bring with me. If interpersonal contacts would be minimal, I was determined to at least spread the news that "2, 4, 6, 8: Orange County ain't so straight!" a slogan shouted by the Orange County contingency at the 1987 March on Washington. We weren't San Francisco, but conservative Orange County had its own distinct, visible, and active (although white dominated) queer community.

Now, six hours later, I was here in Santa Cruz.

And beginning to get *excited*.

After the orientation finished and women got their fill of condoms, everyone slowly filed out of the classroom. Some took off to their rooms to finish unpacking or sleep. Others immediately left to check out Santa Cruz. However, many of us remained on the landing outside of the classroom, watching the other women and occasionally talking with those women we knew or wanted to get to know.

For a long while, I could only silently watch everyone, carefully committing to memory the sight of all these queer Asian and Pacific Islander women. Never before could I see so many API women and safely assume that they, too, were queer. What a sight! What a relief it was to finally blend in with the group instead of sticking out because I looked different. In a way, I had come home. Others seemed to share my feelings, for no one really wanted to leave this crowd.

Later, I went down to Santa Cruz for a quick dessert with the two women from Los Angeles. When we returned to campus, I hated to see them drift off to their rooms. After saying goodnight, I was left again with my loneliness.

By the time I was in bed, it was close to midnight of a very long day, but I still couldn't sleep. On my dorm floor, I could hear the Hawaiian women sitting in the hallway and discussing their entertainment plans for the talent show on Saturday night. They softly performed Hawaiian music and commented on the austere living conditions ("What dis? No private shower, phone, or stereo in my room?"). I remembered my own student days when I had lived in the dorms at UC Irvine, always reminded of the constant presence of other people around me by their sights and sounds. Sometimes I miss that communal lifestyle, the accessibility of knocking on someone's door and chatting for a while. I left my door open in hopes that someone would drop by and talk. Old, comforting habits die hard.

The next morning, everyone assembled in a small lecture hall to officially begin the retreat. Overnight, we had grown so we now occupied almost two-thirds of the seats. I was amazed by our numbers and turned around frequently to look at all of us.

The retreat opened with the sharing of some of our common experiences as queer API women, experiences that would form the themes and issues developed over the weekend.

We were told the story of a Korean adoptee raised by Caucasian parents in Holland, who had entered the United States via Minnesota to reach UC Santa Cruz so she could attend the retreat. However, she was denied entrance into the U.S. and returned to Holland.

I had a personal interest in this woman's journey, since Trinity had called me late Thursday night to ask if I could write a letter of invitation asking this woman to visit Orange County and Los Angeles. APLN was trying to build a legitimate cause for the woman to come back to the U.S. as an observer and reporter for an international lesbian group. After Trinity and I had hung up, I combed through my calendar, looking for meeting dates to create an itinerary to cover a two-week visit to Southern California.

When I had checked in on Friday evening, I met Trinity and had immediately asked if the woman had been successful in returning to the United States. Trinity shook her head, explaining the full story would be told the next morning.

Briefly, upon her arrival in Minneapolis, Immigration and Naturalization Services (INS) had picked the woman out of the crowd to ask why she was visiting the United States. She replied that she was here to visit friends. INS then inspected her luggage and found her diary which was written in Dutch. INS went so far as to translate entries into English. Allegedly, based on these entries, INS accused the woman of being unemployed and seeking employment in the United States, with no intention of returning to Holland. INS also allegedly accused her of being a drug user and a prostitute. INS gave the woman two options: return to Holland on the next flight out, or try to fight the INS decision while waiting in jail, a process that could take between two to three weeks. She wanted to fight the decision but decided to return to Holland.

Back in Holland, the woman planned to return to the United States, this time openly as a lesbian. APLN tried to do as much as it could to assist her. The international lesbian group also agreed to help. Letters of invitation addressed to the woman were collected and the embassy contacted.

Everything was going smoothly, except that INS would not release the necessary paperwork to the embassy as requested. This delay, coupled with the time difference between the two countries and the Labor Day weekend in the United States, prevented the woman from returning in time for the retreat.

Later, another woman, who had worked closely on this matter, read the presentation that the woman would have read to us if she had been able to return to the U.S. The Korean woman spoke of living in an isolated, alienating environment that first refused her to be Asian and then, later, refused to recognize her lesbian identity. Many of us, listening to the woman's story, cried as we found versions of our own experiences within her words. We were familiar with much of the pain, separation, loneliness, and confusion she described in her own life. But we also identified with her fierce strength, her pride of survival, the desire to reach out to others and share her story.

Her absence was magnified further by her intense desire and need to join us, to meet other adoptees and queer API women, to return to Koreatown in Los Angeles, a place of importance for her because it represented a community of Koreans also living abroad.

Her absence pointed to something else, too. For all 170 of us present at the retreat, how many other lesbian and bisexual API women were not at UC Santa Cruz? How many other women wanted to come to Santa Cruz from their homes abroad but could not get past INS and so gave up quietly? How many API women were not yet out or comfortable enough with their sexualities to be with other queer women? How many could not afford to come to Santa Cruz due to limited finances? How many women didn't know something like APLN or the retreat existed?

We were the lucky ones: we were here.

At Santa Cruz, I found the usual retreat activities — icebreakers, introductions, caucus meetings, name tags, new and familiar faces, networking, sharing our resources and information, and last-minute workshop changes. But the retreat was also marked by small yet very important differences because our retreat was only for API women — Hawaiian and Filipino time jokes (similar to "gay time"), an update on the 7 a.m. tai chi session, many requests for group photos, an announcement about the afternoon softball game, caucuses based on ethnicity, opening comments spoken in different Asian and Pacific Islander languages (although phrases like "Santa Cruz," "lesbian and bisexual," and "APLN retreat" didn't translate very well).

Perhaps the one over-riding difference of this retreat was the constant reminder of our incredible diversity and our struggle to support this same diversity. As queer API women, we represented different regions, cultures, generations, languages, and sexualities; we held different beliefs about our relationships (celibacy, monogamy, and open relationships), our futures (beginning careers, doing non-traditional work, or rethinking our careers), and our reasons for coming to the retreat (to satisfy a curiosity, a need to be with other queer API women, to meet others, or "just scamming, thank you"); we were at different stages of being "out," ranging from one year to many years. Women came from San Diego, Los Angeles, and throughout Northern California; from Hawaii, New York, and every place in between; from London, Malaysia, the Philippines; and all across Canada, from Vancouver, Toronto, and Montreal.

Yet for all our differences, I think we all understood that diversity is not divisive (an insightful comment offered by one woman).

And, based on that understanding, I began to see that there were special things we shared in common as queer API women, especially as queer Asian American women, no matter what our differences might be.

All too often, we have felt isolated from others because of our ethnicity and then later on because of our sexualities. No matter where we were — with our family, friends, other Asian Americans, the queer community, or the straight white world — we always had to choose what we were: we were either Asian American or we were queer, but never (seemingly) would the two meet in the same breath. Of course, the lack of other choices only managed to fuel our growing senses of alienation. This situation reminds me of the infamous loyalty question posed to the Japanese Americans interned during World War II: If you had to choose your loyalty between the United States or Japan, which would you pick? When asked this question, my mentor's mother replied, "It is as if you were asking me to choose between my mother or my father, and I cannot for I love them both equally."

But until we could recognize our identities and then fight for the right to love them all equally, we would continue to face off hopelessly between the meager choices offered to us, choices made by others about the acceptable ways we had to identify ourselves. Only through resistance (and probably stubbornness) could we break through the isolation we lived in to integrate our various identities. I firmly believe that to identify as a queer Asian American woman is to have successfully made it through to the other side.

It's tough work because there is so much working against us.

Our queer community continues to exotify us, preventing us from ever becoming a part of their norm or of being able to define the norm, or we become tokenized queers offered only partial acceptance into the greater community. Because our ethnicities are largely ignored by white people, they expect us to be like them and cannot understand when we are not. Our Asian and American heritages encourage us to be invisible, unspoken, non-identified. Our families demand us to conform to their expectations and fears. And, as well-raised Asian daughters and women, we are often both afraid and ashamed of the conflicts we experience from these contradictions and our sexualities; consequently we do not talk about the resulting trauma we suffer. We do not give voice to our responses to this all-encompassing negation of who we see ourselves to really be.

Therefore, I say to identify as a queer Asian American woman is a revolutionary act. Once acknowledged, we become changed forever.

The awe I felt by being with all these women was due mostly to the sense that we personally, and now publicly by attending the retreat, identified as queer API women. And in the relatively safe space of the retreat that we helped to create, we revealed the great inner strength, pride, and beauty in us, something we shared with each other and made manifest around us all weekend long. Somewhere, during the retreat, I realized I no longer wanted to deny or hide that I am a queer Asian American woman, too. Now, I no longer felt the need to.

As a result of the retreat, I gained a fuller sense of the term "sister." Before, being an only child, sister meant something I didn't have or was an alien term used by non-Asian feminists. There were no personal ties between myself and the term "sister," and I never included it in my vocabulary.

However, after the retreat I began to use the word. A sister became a woman who has shared with me her life and struggles to identify herself as she does. We have beaten great odds, often times alone, to be who we are today. We are kindred spirits who have somehow shared some similar experiences in our individual lives while offering support for our respective differences. Sister is also a way to communicate my love and respect for another woman. Perhaps sister is simply the result of two women who share themselves openly and honestly.

The retreat was a time for empowerment, a process I felt happen within and around me. For the first time, many of us were verbalizing our fears and pains, giving names and form for them. We were proving to ourselves that we existed. We spoke. We met and strategized. In essence, we created ourselves as queer API women in a culture that otherwise would ignore or erase our contributions, identities, and our very presence.

And we were angry. Women who felt excluded — bisexuals, those from Canada and Hawaii, foreign-born and immigrant, South Asian, those with a mixed heritage — said so. When they spoke, I immediately understood a part of their rejection and isolation because that, too, is my experience with its own particular nuances. Through my tears and shame, I recognized and respected the sheer boldness of the angry words these women spoke. As a Hawaiian woman said, "If this conference wasn't so powerful, I wouldn't have been so angry. For without this power, I would've just said 'Fuck it,' and walked away." We didn't walk away, though. Instead, we tried to work differences and difficulties to a point of mutual understanding.

The retreat gave us all a space and time to talk together, for us to find the specific common points linking our lives together and to educate each other on our differences, for us to be sisters. We decided to rename the network from Asian Lesbian Network to Asian Pacifica Lesbian Network so we could be more inclusive. At the next APLN retreat, I fully expect the name to change again, this time to recognize the presence and contributions of our bisexual sisters.

We decided to document the retreat using our own words, images, passion, and visions. Besides allowing us to remember the retreat, we would also be able to share the experience with our sisters who could not be with us.

We realized "I am a coalition within myself" (from an unknown speaker) and each one of us was our own queer API network for our area. I admitted my desire to accept the personal responsibility necessary to help bring about social change, and I came to see that I contain within me the drive, energy, and dedication to fulfill this desire.

I watched women like Mei Beck step forward to become leaders for the session discussing the future of the APLN. As the weekend progressed, women who had never been leaders before took their first steps to lead their communities. I listened as women spoke in public for the first time, the sound of their voices so surprising to them that they were at first tentative and cautious; by the end of the weekend, their voices became warm with newly found confidence in the worth of their words. I was one of the women who began to feel more comfortable about being an Asian American lesbian, eventually opening up and freely talking with the many women I met.

All weekend long, we exchanged addresses and phone numbers so we could remain in contact after the retreat was over. So many photos were taken. I think we were all trying to personally document the weekend, to take back home with us concrete reminders of the women we had met and the community we'd created this weekend. I know I'm afraid I will lose contact with this fledgling community and may one day forget how wonderful this retreat has been for me. This diligent narration has been my way to staunch any memory loss.

All these experiences added to my own empowerment. I've always been hesitant in my actions or in speaking my visions. I wanted role models to show me how things could be done, but, when I looked around me, all the possible role models I saw were white gay leaders who weren't always appropriate for me or my community. Suddenly, I found myself no longer alone or unusual. Now, I have 170 role models imprinted on my mind. I even have new goals for my life after meeting and hearing women who were more articulate, focused, committed, and passionate than I am. At the retreat, I began to create my own network of supportive, caring, and encouraging queer activist API women. As a presenter said to us, "I need every bit of your knowledge, love, support, and stamina." Yeah! The accrued stereotypes and myths of APIs disappeared from my mind like morning mists in the rising sun of our strength and visions as queer API women.

The retreat provided a point of self-reflection as well. My awe at seeing 170 queer API women came from the overwhelming and visible fact that, "Yes, Ann, there are other women like you in the world," who looked and dressed like me, had short hair, and were proudly outspoken. For the first time in my life, we were an endless sea of black hair, queer-identified sexualities, and Asian and Pacific Islander faces. As women, we were articulate, energetic, political, artistic, bold, dynamic, honest, open, supportive, encouraging, assertive, and confident (all traits I like in women, I must admit). And Asian and Pacific Islander. And queer. All at once. And all together.

Svati Shah

Lunch Vignettes

I eat my culture.
I snarf huge bites of puri
                    shak
                    bhatt
                    shrikhand,
and have visions of
the restaurant keepers
cursing in Gujarati
(words I've never heard)
and throwing me out
for my shaven head
torn jeans,
nose ring.

(For once) it's my prophesy left to starve
as the proprietor runs from
our table to the kitchen,
asks how long I'll be in town,
and graciously accepts
my accolades for his wife's cooking.

I eat my culture,
and remember my mother's table
feeling anglo vision
from two dearest
who never
bore a color standard before.

I eat my culture
till my stomach is distended.
Because I can,
I LOUDLY proclaim the event
"Better than sex."

I eat my culture,
making my mouth form phrases
that should be mothertongue
for brown strangers

who understand
despite
my
hesitant,
grammatical
constructs.

I eat my culture
Sometimes,
in lieu of
salty-creamy-sour-sticky-sweet
which began
as cumin
and turmeric flavored dishes
in her mouth
behind her mother's table
where, legs swinging,
she eats her culture, too.

Something We Both Know

i wanted to show Her another India
Where women publish for other women
and gay people live together
  talking about what to make for dinner
and beggars live blamelessly
and old men hug trees
  saying aloud that pollution is a sin.

Basically, i wanted Her to see a Mira Nair film.

She raged,
and repeated stories about frolicking freely,
(despite their poverty)
about praying nightly,
and burning lamp oil to study for finals.

Mostly, She recited stanzas —
of daughters who love their mothers with obedience and respect
    attend to their fathers despite their abuses
    smile indulgently at men and children
    cling to innocence
    and marry young.

i said that respect is not always obedience,
and that forced innocence is always denial.
i said that India-as-haven
only happened for the children who left.

She bowed her head and cried,
images of care-free
downed with swallowed anger.
Her scars gleam and bleed
when the frolicksome child
  vanishes into windy grey.

She asked again
for the girl who ran arms wide
to the Woman who grew with eyes full of sorrow
and stories full of days that never rain.

i said that the girl is mine,
and thought.
A true child of a Hindustani heart
would never have made her own Mother weep.

Vanessa Marzan Deza

distractions

oh excuse me i'm sorry
didn't mean to stare at your
honey-colored fingers
grasping the tip of a red pen
and think about how i want them
interlocked around my waist

oh yes we are in a meeting here
let me just button up my shirt and
cross my legs and try not to notice
how nicely yours curve into the chair

okay let me just focus my gaze
on the rim of this coffee cup
so i don't see your breasts brushing
up against the hardwood table as you
lean forward to make your point.

i speak to impress you
bring two fingers up to my lips
in mock seriousness
"hmm...yes, uhuh, is that so?"
i nod as you reply
and move your hands in eloquence
i am concentrating on the way
your mouth forms the words
pursing the o's
popping the p's
and i'm wishing i was a letter
caught between your teeth and
sliding between your lips
but all i can do is nod and go
hmm...yes, that's right
uhuh...yes
yes.
yes.
yes.

Rini Das

We Three: X, Y, and Z

This is bliss. The canon of vanity.
You cast contempt on the aseity
Of the grammatical fatigue.
She is liturgic with all the PC, MC
And jerks out the last drop of frustration.
I sit burnt out with promiscuity,
Fake, labels, diddle and charm.
Then you want to go to Vietnam,
And just labor, dabble
In the drowsiness of a joke.
She cringes for Africa, stares
Within and chokes over the tales.
Yet, lies restless and wants to go.
I have it bad and just wanna
Autograph and leave.
Begone! My Others.
For you: The variance of this
Inertia is too rustic.
For her: The blues are stirruped,
Temperance is blazed.
Vamoose!
Oh! Sistah! Scar not the reflection.
Leave me to the mundane.

Darlena Bird Jimenes

Solitary Bravo

> "One cannot become a part of
> where one is, unless one knows
> where one is from; then there is
> clarity to see where one is going."

THESE ARE THE WORDS THAT ENERGIZED ME AS I EMBARKED on a personal journey of discovery. As I awoke within myself, I found rainbow terrain, collage country. Always had I accepted my multiracial heritage, never had I celebrated my multiracial existence. Now, my horizons have broadened, and my consciousness has globalized.

As the various peoples of the world defy simplistic descriptions, so does my personal issue of self-identification as I become myself. Since heritage, race, ethnicity, cultures and the like can be categorized, segmented, boxed in every way imaginable, it continues to be important for me to emphasize the "oneness of my being"; I become the international fusion of all that I am and cease recognizing society's imposed "fraction-identification" of race/ethnicity.

Instead of "categorizing" myself by "placing an x next to the proper category," I decide to erase the boxes and encircle them all together, for they are all me. I am a proud multiracial polyethnic extraction; a unique blend consisting of (but not limited to): Native American (Cherokee/Apache), Latin-Caribbean (Puerto Rican/Cuban/Trinidadian), Asian (East Indian), African-Arab (Moroccan/Tunisian/Egyptian), and European (Spanish Creole/French-Italo-Portugese blend).

I am blessed with the distinction of belonging to two families of multigenerationally multiracial/blended peoples. With deep, strong roots with which to anchor, I can now grow and flourish and blossom. This allows me to continue on a journey of claiming, reclaiming and focusing on specific aspects of my racial makeup. I can remember going through stages in my life where I delved into a specific culture from my background, and I would get creative in order to avoid the tedium sometimes connected to "getting into your roots," especially for a child. So I would experiment with clothes, jewellery, cuisine, and my own ways of remembering my ancestors. Me as mixed Native American. Me as mixed African-Arab. Me as mixed Latina. I discovered myself as a dancer and later in my teens used music to express myself. This was now my cultural crossroads of "racial focus." Me as salsa-loving Cubarican. Me as flamenco dancing Creole Gypsy. Me as tabla tranced Indian. Into the college years (and all of the discovery that this time entails), I became even more focused on various aspects of my being because I tapped into the holistic energies of all of my heritages, and desired to exist in the most balanced, harmonious way that I could.

It has been a journey, maybe I should say many journeys. Now I discover me as an Asian woman. A woman of Asian descent. A multiracial Euroasian. A Trini Indian.

> "...latinos called me anglo,
> whites called me spic,
> blacks couldn't figure me out,
> they said "we'll just pick";
> Kid Everybody, Kid Nobody
> you have to check just one box,
> But I thought to myself
> with a chuckle and a grin,
> Fooled you all,
> Me — the sly Fox!"

For me, growing up as a cultural melange felt sometimes like being a cultural anomaly. Sure, I knew other biracial/multiracial kids outside of my family unit, but even at an early age I saw many of them begin to harbor the small, poisonous seeds of compromise, self-denial and ultimate rejection of parts or even all of who they were. Times began to get dangerous in my perfect fairyland where eyes saw no color yet marvelled at the rainbows.

When my little girlfriend Shang and I and her little brother would walk to school, the eyes of otherwise-friendly neighbors would start to glare, then leer at "too much difference happening too fast." We would be met by a posse of other kids who cornered, jabbed, and reminded us of a "yellow belly, chinky, jap, dotty-girl" existence that we never knew we had. I remember the experience as a child of attending a Protestant church in the community where my family lived. The congregation was mainly African-American. Given their behavior towards us and anyone else who was of mixed descent or of another race altogether, it seemed a credo of the church was "act Black, be one of us and you'll be accepted." Any other type of expression would be met with scorn. My parents didn't seem to mind, but I grew to despise what I termed "Black Face Sundays," because it meant pulling out and using a "cultural eraser" that I didn't want to own.

Riding the schoolbus one morning, Snapuhl and I were playing a hand-clapping game. She had been born in India and her parents immigrated here when she was a baby. With her colorful saris and a small bangle, she proved "too exotic." She and I had an instant link. We bonded immediately. We chattered and clapped and laughed and giggled; friendly and no longer friendless. We became girlfriends. At nine years old, your whole world becomes wrapped up in "girlfriends" — or so we thought. Our world was perfect until one day a little white girl saw us standing off to the side to ourselves talking and hollered, "Rotten, dirty yellow teeth, raggedy clothes 'cause you're so cheap!" The other kids rallied around her and continued to chant and holler at us until Snapuhl started to cry. I put my arms around her and comforted her as a schoolyard aide rushed over to disperse the taunting kids.

She warned them to leave others alone or there would be after-school detentions and calls to parents. The aide never did come over to us and ask if we were alright. We had to provide each other with our own comfort the best way we could. I told her that her teeth were just fine and that she was beautiful. We hugged each other and revelled in our own little bond of Asian sisterhood.

During the culturally repressive regimes that I called junior high and high school, I found myself in a quandry over my own strength to maintain who I'd grown to become — and was sorely tested. Seventh and eighth grades were the most challenging for me because I was ostracized by those who I had counted "among my own." Since the junior high that I attended was in a predominantly African-American community, everyone was expected to "play the game." There were two girls at school who were also melanges, Karen and Terry. Karen's mother was Sri Lankan and her father was African-American, and Terry was Puerto Rican and Native American. We three were never really close, but because of our various backgrounds, we found we shared a lot in common. There were a lot of petty jealousies and in-fighting (especially among the girls) over looks and hair and clothes; and at that time everyone wanted to "fit in." No one ever dared to be different, even on an unconscious level.

Given my personality, the war was on. I managed to remain the "Other" throughout those two grades. Nothing I said, wore or did fit in or was accepted. The war was lost. I retreated into my own shell. The ultimate letdown happened one day in the lunchroom. A group of girls were in line waiting to get served, and Karen and Terry were among them. They had long since "cleansed" their ethnic persuasions to become "total Black sisters," in order to fit in neatly. They all began to whisper about me as I sat alone at one of the tables eating the bagged lunch I had always brought with me. One of them asked audibly, "What is she anyway?" One said, "She talks funny, she got an accent or somethin'?" Karen laughed and said, "No, no she's Indian, that's why she brings all that funny lookin' food to lunch." Another said, "I think she's Puerto Rican, too. Terry piped up and said, "Yea, that's why she has hair like that." This went on for a time in between snickering and laughter. They ended this little performance with a unison rolling of the eyes towards me and "Humph, she is just so weird!" Imagine my surprise and disappointment to look up and see that Karen had uttered that last blow. They hooted and went on outside. I sat there alone, as usual, shook my head and thought about Terry and Karen befriending those other girls, as they scouted for someone else to taunt. All I could think was what a price to pay for "a perfect fit."

Fortunately, high school was in another district and took me far away from the killing fields of junior high. This school was much more integrated and it was refreshing to see all kinds of faces. After awhile though, I began to realize that there were two camps going on here; a white camp and a black camp, with very little room for anything else. I thought to myself, "Not again," and sighed. This time, I was going to make my own way. There were other "Others" (as they liked to refer to us) besides myself; a few Asians, a Native American and a few biracial kids. I did befriend two Chinese guys (whom everyone else shunned) and Michelle who was biracial and proved to be a "sometime" friend. Most of my high-school time was spent on me by me. I decided if no one wanted to be bothered with me, then I'd have to be my own friend first. There would be like-minded folks out there to connect with when high school was over. I convinced myself of that. It was a pretty lonely time though, with few close friends, and no "cliques" like everyone else belonged to. But they had nothing of substance to offer me, and wouldn't have accepted me in anyway, because I was different in too many ways.

One occasion in high school that does stand out in my mind was quite amusing. I was sixteen and in the eleventh grade. During an English class one day, the teacher was called to the front office for some business she had to take care of. Since we had been discussing a chapter in a book the class was studying, she made the rest of the period a study hall and forbid talking or discussion. The open space of our English "classroom" had long wooden desks, about four, around which eight to ten students would have chairs. I was at a table with the "quiet studious types" (read: the unpopular ones). For us it was a true study period. Two tables away were the "loud rowdy types" (read: The In-Clique). For them it was a true party period.

They were laughing and joking and talking about every subject under the sun. Suddenly, one of the guys glanced toward our table. They joked, "Look at that, they're really reading," and "Everyone over there has glasses on — you think that means something?!" There were roaring guffaws, even from some of the other tables around the room. Then somebody caught my eye. I looked away hastily and continued reading. There was an unusual silence for a minute or two. Then I overheard the strangest conversation in hushed tones. "... it's Indian and Spanish and maybe a quarter white..." "No, no, no she's American Indian and Italian..." "... Her grandmother is Cuban..." "... she's Black, Puerto Rican and Spanish, or is it French?..." My sometime friend Michelle (who alternated between the

Black Clique and the White Clique) was sitting at that table too, and said, "I'll clear it all up, I met her parents and they're very nice; she's a little bit of everything, White, Black, Hispanic, Asian, and Native American. She's not as weird and mysterious as everyone thinks, she's just quiet and shy." And so the forum on race relations of which I had been the sole subject was over. The bell rang. Class dismissed.

> "In rigid ideology, no trace of
>   gender diversity
> Part and parcel, all better no worse
> The spiritual order of my universe
> No one is wasted, everyone has their gift
> We encourage, inspire, empower, uplift
> I'm loved and valued, honored and cherished
> kissed and hugged and caressed
> It's just the natural way to be
> For the Ancients have said
>   I'm Twice Blessed"

Sexuality. All too complex. All too simple. There was never a problem within myself about my gayself. There was a myself and a gayself and they were one in the same. I have never known myself outside of a queer context. As basic as my breathing is my innate queer, homosexual, gay, lesbian, gender-liberated, gender-atypical, same-sex, appropriate-sex orientation, lifestyle, existence, energy. As early as I can remember there were my beautiful and quite natural thoughts and dreams of female friendship, love and bonding. As a child, I never talked to anyone about it, not out of fear or shame, but because I felt there was no need to treat any differently my feelings towards other girls than boys' feelings towards girls or girls' feelings towards boys; because in my mind it was all the same and all just as valid. An important aspect of my early years to me (looking back now) is that I never felt like "I'm the only one in the world who has these feelings; who's different." For some reason, even at six, seven, eight years old, I knew that I wasn't the only gay kid in the world, I just knew it! I didn't know the language to express it, but I felt that there were others like me, and it was just a matter of finding a way for all of us queer kids to connect.

I was always a "different kid" in every respect anyway, so the process of coming out (especially during the teen years) never seemed necessary for me personally. Coming out, I felt then, was an unfair "requirement" because straight kids had the luxury of naturally evolving into who they would become without fanfare or confrontation. As a matter of fact, their sexuality was encouraged from every corner — societally all the way down to the most personal relationships in their lives. During high school, my own personal and political coming out was not done verbally, but through my actions and the way I communicated movement-wise. My challenge to my peers was not to emphasize that I was gay, but to emphasize the fact that I was *not straight*. So, it wasn't that they would hear that I wasn't into their definition of dating, relationships, proms, dances, partying and the like, they would see it and feel it. So everyone knew, but no one said anything. That wasn't earth-shattering because no one really said much of anything to me anyway, so it worked out in my mind. I had made my point without so many words, just as they had always felt justified in doing.

In my family, the issue of sexuality was never directly addressed, nor was I ever formally confronted with a "Well, are you or aren't you?" It was what I termed an unspoken knowledge around the house. We weren't in the most social arena anyway, so the fact that there wasn't much dating or party-going really didn't surprise anyone. But somehow, deep down I knew that there were questions that weren't being asked about marriage, children, etc. It was almost like a wait-and-see game.

I sometimes felt closeted, but never in the closet. Everyone in my orbit was heterosexual at that time, and I felt deprived of the community that I knew was out there; partly because of growing up in a fairly sheltered, protective environment, the gay world, my world seemed so inaccessible to me. In my junior and senior years of high school, I had the displeasure of watching the only two lesbians who were verbally out (and a mixed couple at that, an Irish-American and an African-American) become part of a schoolwide scandal. (They had been "caught kissing" in the girls' room.) They allowed this to force them into isolation. Ultimately, they crawled *back*

(!?) into their respective closets never to be heard from again. They wouldn't even look in my direction when I was nearby; knowing glances and a shameful lowering of their heads was the only communication that we had.

This incident was so angering and appalling to me that it became the impetus inside of me that would eventually empower me to find my radical lesbian voice. This coupled with a very special friendship with John, the only openly gay guy in our senior class. He and I were shunned not only because of who we were, but because of the jealousy that the others harbored over our strong support system that we had built up. Nothing anyone said or did was allowed to intimidate us into a closet or anywhere else. John took so much harassment and bullying, but was such a fighter. Unfortunately, John was transferred before the end of the term and didn't get to graduate with us.

The inspiration that I got from his life and friendship and the anger from the seething homophobia that I had experienced during high school enabled me to graduate with a sense of strength I had never felt before. I gave myself the gift of the determination to live on the edge, to be personally responsible for my own well-being as a gay person and politically active, and to realize my voice and vision through personal celebration.

"I don't just listen, but hear
not just selective voices
but all of the voices;
For the dream of finding a place
that gives me a sense of home
becomes the art of connecting
as part of our extended family;
Through our collective queerness
We become who we might be"

In the process of discovering and connecting all of who I am on every level in my life, there had to be a recognition and awareness of all of the communities that I am part of (and that are a part of me). As I thought more about it and began to be more "in the life," I started realizing that identity plays a key part in the forming of a person's reality in any community; and that included the gay community. I suddenly realized that my "identity" started to give way to "identifications" — varied and diverse. I was finding out parts of my history — culturally gay — you might say, that I was eager to know more about; and claim as my own.

I have become Latina Lesbiana, Native American lesbian, radical sistah, Berdache, Asian/Pacific Islander lesbian, Caribbean queer, Khush. Many of my cultural communities are conflicted with my sexual minority communities. They simply do not want to acknowledge that a segment of their community or culture is gay, and that it is a natural part of the culture of existence; not a mistake, "negative influence," or aberration. This is one of the reasons that it became a central part of all of my activities and expressions to harmonize all of my cultures within their own gay contexts, and to find a place for that harmony within myself, for I am the point of fusion for it all.

It is one of my goals to try and integrate the networks within my various families and communities (both in gay and straight contexts). I try to show in my life by my existence and actions that gay is a way of being in the world and that we all share, as humans, a family of community, no matter what label we are either forced or choose to wear. It's not really about sexual preference or orientation or gender, but about human traits of love, respect, decency, and conscience. If the intolerant segments of my various communities can at least see these acted out and exemplified in my life, then the realization that we all share something basic as humans will have been made.

Having experienced life as a melange, a racial minority and a sexual minority, I continually emphasize to myself and those around me that having true knowledge of self keeps us free. Our challenge then becomes (especially as mixed race gay people), not to accept blindly what has been handed to us historically and societally. We must challenge conventions that sanction hate, fear and ignorance toward us and begin to portray our own cultural/political vision. We become, then, brothers and sisters in the name of love, hanging out with unconditional people and nurturing each other to be fulfilled.

"Take time to play, it is the secret of perpetual youth,
Take time to love, it is a precious jewel,
Take time to fight, challenge is in the air
Fearless warriors are tremendously cool;
Take time to create, it is essentially timeless,
Take time to dream, we never know what's in store
Take time to learn, let it go to your head
Fearless artists focus on what others ignore;
We are all creators, young and old
So take time to laugh, it is the song of the soul"

Bird is an artist. More specifically, a creative being, a cultural creator. Since we all create what we are, I found that art in my life and being an artist gives me tremendous voice and is a tremendous weapon. I could be called a "slash person" in every respect! Artistically, I describe Bird as an independent, multidimensional, interdisciplinary, multimedia, performance artist/dancemaker/soundscapecomposer/poet/animator/puppeteer/cultural arts activist. And it doesn't end here, for I continue to discover new roads to travel and new voices to speak with.

In all of my work there is a gay-affirmative energy; a space that is multi-sexual, ambigendered. A place to explore the pansexual, the intrasexual. I become the gender transcender. Within all of this, I have begun to actualize the marriage of my artistic voice and my awakening political voice. Where do I go from here?

The message that I was getting while creating was just as I do not want my voice or my life censored in society, I will not have my creative expression censored. One of the poisons of our community is internalized homophobia, which is self-oppression. If we're told who we have to be in order to fit in and belong to the dominant culture, and we comply without challenge, without question, then we are internalizing the homophobia around us. If we dare to be who we are in every aspect of our lives, then we are "living life in the outside tribe." This is where I knew I had to be.

The mainstream culture and viewpoint with all of its exclusions is just as clueless about who, what, where, and why we as gay people are, as we are about their senseless fear, hate, oppression and intolerance toward us. I decided the best way for me to confront these issues was through art as a medium, art as activism and activism within art. This new-found voice has allowed me to mine a treasure trove of ideas and projects that I am working on and hope to share with others.

One of my projects stemmed from developing a strong desire to work with and advocate for sexual minority youth, particularly those of color and within minority communities. After studying and reading about the grim statistics of gay teen/youth suicides, and realizing that they are so invisible and vulnerable to extreme oppression, I knew that more voices were needed from within the gay community to advocate for the youth segment — our future.

I desire to interact with gay youth from an artistic and creative perspective. If I (and others) could provide a forum and space for them to feel safe to be who they are, then they can concentrate on fully realizing their highest potential, especially as young artists. This is in the planning stages now, and I'm calling it GAiLY (Gay and Lesbian Youth). Its aim is to service the artistic needs, voices and expressions of gay, lesbian, bisexual and transgender (GLBT) youth, to empower through action, eliminate the "invisibility factor," and to educate and celebrate. An affinity group of GAiLY is called the Hormone Zone and serves as an art/theater group, floating club/party/activity source, and will provide a newsletter by, for and about GLBT youth in the arts/performance arenas.

Another project that I'm involved with is the Citizens For A Multiracial America (CMRA). I am a local representative for CMRA; and what we're about is fighting for and supporting the cause of a national voice for those of us who are Biracial/Multiracial, and those that are in our interracial communities (mixed couples, transracially adoptive or fostering families, and those consciously involved in positive, globally-inspired race relations). My specific area of interest is the GLBT communities within the interracial community. I am working diligently to protect our civil rights, educate the public about our interracial lives, secure a biracial/multiracial category for race and/or ethnicity on all school, state and government forms, find a place within to liberate and be multiracial and gay and/or interracially coupled and gay, and to build a national and international network in support of change and viable representation.

The Alternative Voice Network (AVN) is another activity of mine that I hope will serve as an ad hoc collective of people involved in various social, political, cultural, educational and global avenues; working together in the struggle to achieve human and civil rights, to affect positive social and political change, and to raise awareness and consciousness about issues affecting all of us on the planet. AVN's sister organization is the Alternative Artists' Kollective (AAK!) for short. AAK! is in its developmental stage and will be made up of gay and gay-positive artists, activists and advocates whose goal it is to give voice and engender community empowerment through alternative media and arts to those people and communities that are shut out of mainstream society, that are oppressed through marginalization, economic disenfranchisement, racism, sexism and homophobia. It will serve as a means to uplift spiritually, culturally, creatively and artistically through the evolving of a new gay community.

The political and cultural strands run through my work as a gay artist expressing myself personally and ethnically. The Word Shop is a cooperative of performing poets and wordsmiths. We create in an ethnically cultural, politically grassroots and indigenously social context. I perform movement poems with social poetry concerning the plights of oppressed women's and sexual minority communities worldwide. Two video projects of mine are *To Say Hello Again* and *Safe Shorts* Video/Poster Campaign. The theme of *To Say Hello Again* is the voices and visions of gay and lesbian artists empowered as a result of the AIDS epidemic to express themselves through dance, poetry, visual art, theater art and music; they share their stories of the pride, celebration, liberation and struggle in the quest to reclaim, rediscover, reaffirm and reacquaint with Life. The *Safe Shorts* theme is safe sex education outreach through open, out, graphic, erotic, sensual visual images used as a means to desensitize and demystify sex and sexual health issues, especially as they pertain to the sexual minority community.

In each artistic expression of mine, I find my own individual identity within it, and then become comfortable with it in its own genre. My performance piece "Running Towards Myself" explores through dance and sound an Indian woman's journey of discovery of herself as a lesbian. My dance work-in-progess "Cages" is a study of two interracial couples, one gay, the other lesbian. They are enclosed in their own cages that are symbolic of and explore society, intimate relationships, and the spatial interrelationships between the dancers as individuals, their environment and each other as couples.

My performance musicwork entitled "Yin Drums: In the Global Groove" celebrates the strength, beauty and timelessness of women, and the unique energy that is lesbian. It features drums and beats and movement and dance by women from diverse world cultures. An avant-garde video of the project is in the works.

In the experimental theater arena, I have written a performance play, a movement narration choreopoem and a playlet all dealing in vastly different ways around the issue of coming out. The play entitled "Purse" recounts the story of a gentle, triracial queen with red hair and his process of growing up, coming to terms, and coming out around his gay sexuality; all from the context of his childhood obsession with women's handbags. The choreopoem called "Tableaux — Recollections Today, Dreams Tomorrow" utilizes movement and poetic narration as we enter a combined male/female entity's dream through the frame of a surrealistic painting of a fantasy community that suddenly comes to life. The playlet "Captured Memories" (working title) is a sectioned piece concerning a gay couples' conversations, photographs, and personal diaries of each other, and their revelations to each other about their lives over a long languished three-day weekend. I am directing the video version of "Purse" and "Captured Memories."

My two latest pet projects are a direct result of my getting much more involved in the Asian and Pacific Islander community. What I have called the Gaysian Group will be an independent, informal organization specifically targeting our Asian and Pacific Islander gay, lesbian, bisexual and transexual community focusing on increased visibility and voice, education, political action, networking and empowerment. I am designing a newsletter that I hope will be distributed nationally and eventually grow and interface with other organizations and groups like SHaKTI and APLBN

(Asian and Pacific Lesbian Bisexual Network). The other is a unique endeavor that I hope finds its niche, Black Jade. This is a program providing networking and support services for the AfroAsian community (those within the African and Asian diaporas, African/Asian unions, adoptions and fostering, and people of AfroAsian and mixed Asian heritage); Black Jade will provide a place for our recognition, gay and straight, cultural and political; in the exploration of dual-heritage, bi-cultural empowerment and pride.

I am very proud of all I have accomplished and the myriad projects and activities that I find myself involved with these days. I have learned the importance of knowing, accepting and loving myself as I am, and the quality of valuing people for who they are. When we have learned to love ourselves enough to say, "It doesn't matter what the society thinks of us, but what we think of us," then we will have found the strength to know who we are. This is the process of overturning self-hate, starving negative stereotypes about us, redeeming negatives, empowering ourselves through suffering and celebrating the triumphs.

Brenda Joy Lem

Gold Gate (Gam Moen)

Linda Fong

Rice Dreams

There were times
when you, *ah ma,*
gathered us kids around.

In a hushed tone you began.
You spoke of a childhood
        of endless mountains
        swimming fields
and the tender beauty of the *ho fa.*

I would listen
        watching
the stories unfold in your face.
The tiny lines of
hardship and age would
soften
slowly,
your eyes would glaze over in
                distant memory
a slow journey back
to the ancient land of our foremothers.

In your memories
hid my dreams

144

Yet
there was more.
Bitterness
Seeping Bitterness
Your face hardened
in remembrance of the
nightmare of yellow fever.

How they left you to die.

After all,
You were only a girl
Useless in the fields
Useless
You proved them wrong
          by surviving
and toiling
Hard
Tasting the salty sweat of your upper lip.

But that was a long time ago you say,
quickly re-adjusting to the present.
You think I cannot see
your old wounds
but I can
Traces of faint scars
Traces of Us.

In a dream
I see you, *ah ma*
and you, *ah poh*
We are seated in the kitchen
making *tae*.
the room
filled with warm familiar cooking smells
      embraces us
We laugh
and speak
in our mothertongues.
Three generations of Chinese Women
      sharing and living
      our secret rice dreams.

---

ah ma: mother
ho fa: peach blossoms
ah poh: grandmother
tae: Chinese dumplings

Amy A. Zukeran

My Mother's Mother

I LOOK UP FROM MY COLORING BOOK, MY GRANDMA IS SAYING something to me in Japanese. Her eyes dance though they are misted blue by cataracts and her eyelids are heavy with years.

I can't understand her, but it is obvious that grandma is asking me a question.

"I'm coloring," I say. She laughs.

In an age-ravaged voice, she gently teases me about something. Her small mouth bows into a crooked smile. A webbing of deep wrinkles spread from the corners of her eyes to her hairline.

"She wants to know why the cows are purple?" My mom, sitting nearby, translates for grandma.

"Because they ate too many eggplants!" I exclaim, trying my best to keep a straight face. She laughs again and we enjoy our private joke.

Earlier in my visit, grandma caught me throwing her very ripe, purple eggplants at the cows. I just couldn't help myself — the eggplants were a perfect fit for my small hands. Now that I think about this, I'm sure the cows gathered by the fence, both out of curiosity and in anticipation of my pitching practice.

"And the pitch!" I muttered, mimicking a radio announcer's breathless style.

"AY," my grandma shouted, just as I let loose a knuckleball. She stood on the worn green porch of her house, flapping her arms and gesturing in my direction.

I didn't have to know the language to know that I was busted. And she knew I knew. I skulked away through the eggplants and string beans to find a place to hide from the punishment I knew would come.

But my grandma didn't tell my mom about the eggplant incident — not right away at least. Grandma waited a couple of days. In fact, she let so much time pass that the incident became a joke rather than the source of a sure spanking. My grandmother and I became co-conspirators.

Grandma met her husband as she stepped off a steamship that carried her across the Pacific Ocean to Hawai'i. Though barely in her teens, she was the picture bride Grandpa dreamt of.

Life was difficult for the young couple. The glittering streets of gold that drew thousands of hopeful immigrants to Hawai'i never materialized. Grandma worked the sugarcane fields just like grandpa — planting, cutting, and harvesting — save for those days when she was too pregnant with one of the eight children she gave birth to.

The sun freckled her fair skin and it grew leather-like and creviced. Backbreaking days followed, one after the other, but she never lost her pride to the monotonous tasks of field work. She retired after years of spine-twisting labor.

One look at Grandma's hands and you knew just how hard her life had been. Her fingers were large, flat, and slightly misshaped. Her nails were permanently stained. Sometimes the skin on her hands were so brittle and cracked that they snagged fibers from delicate fabrics.

These well-worked hands snatched up hens from the dusty backyard for our dinner. With one hen tucked under her arm, gracefully quick she would twist the neck of the other, assuring a swift and necessary death.

On many nights, these hands lifted me from the terrifying depths of a nightmare. Whispering the demons away, gently, gently, she would rock me back to sleep. In that chilled and darkened universe, only my grandma and I existed.

Years passed. I mourned her death alone in my parents' empty house — I couldn't bear to see Grandma still and lifeless. I didn't want to believe that she was gone.

On cool, damp nights, Grandma's memory — her milky bright eyes and calloused strong hands — fills me. And I thank the goddesses for the opportunity to know this woman. Grandma proved to me over and over again that when all is said and done, words have very little to do with love.

Kitty Tsui

Anita and Auntie
for Anita Taylor Oñang

THIS IS A STORY THAT BEGAN A LONG TIME AGO WHEN THE LAND was green, the air fragrant with the scent of jasmine, the water pure and the sun warm on my body. You ask, what is an old lady like me doing up here? I tell you, I am here to keep a promise I made to a girl who died before her time. A promise to tell her story and keep her spirit alive.

I was born many, many years ago, a Nanhai girl from Guangdong province in southern China. We were very poor, and I was lucky to be alive. In those days girls born to poor families were drowned in the village pond or sold to be prostitutes. My father had gone to the Gold Mountain to work as a tailor, so my mother was alone. She knew that only boys could live so she raised me as a son and even called me by a boy's name, *Siew Lung*, Little Dragon, because I was born in the year of the dragon! When I was ten years old my father sent for me to come to America as a paper son. My mother did not want me to leave her, she was afraid Father would kill me if he found out that I was not a boy. But I was young and daring and I was not afraid. I could work the land, carry buckets of water balanced on a pole. I could sew and mend. I wanted to go to Gold Mountain.

When we first sighted land I stayed on deck and strained to catch my first glimpse of gold on the mountains. But as we got closer and closer all I could see was land like any other land, no gold anywhere. I wanted to cry. I thought that people must have come before me and taken all the gold. But too much was going on. I hadn't seen my father for so long I was afraid I wouldn't know him. But when a man came up to me and said my name I knew it was him! My father took me to where he lived. Home was bunkbeds in a room with noisy machines that spit steam. I never heard so much noise! Do you sleep when the machine stops, I asked. He said the noise never stops. The machines are always working. Then I asked about the gold, and he laughed. And all the men in the room laughed too. I wanted to cry. I felt so stupid. But I held the tears in. Boys didn't cry and I was a boy. Physical work had made my back and my arms strong, my shoulders broad and my legs sturdy. Even in those cramped living quarters I never let on that I was a girl.

When I was fifteen my father got sick and died. It took all our savings to send his body home. There was no money for me. I left the laundry and travelled around doing whatever I could: picking produce on farms, working in the canneries. I kept to myself and never married. Having raised myself as a man I could not marry one!

When I got older I worked as a maid in a big hotel downtown. I became good friends with a young Filipino girl who had just lost her husband. Whenever we had the same day off, we would ride the streetcar to the end of the line and take her daughter, Anita, to the beach. We would wrap up good, even in the summertime. You know how cold and foggy it gets! She loved to be by the sea, reminded her of home. We would take a thermos of hot tea and food. I'd bring fried chicken and my favorite, cha siew bow, and she would make pansit or lumpia. Sometimes I think we got along so well because we both loved to eat. Not only that, we loved to talk about eating! On special occasions I'd take her and Anita for dim sum in Chinatown, and whenever she'd make chicken adoboe she'd always bring me some wrapped in aluminum foil.

But then she got married and moved away. I was glad for her, you know, she was young and pretty. But I was very sad. She was the only real friend I ever had. And I missed her little girl. She was like my own. Such a sweet little voice calling me Auntie. Auntie, give me a hug, she would always say. Give me a kiss, Auntie.

About a year ago there was a knock on my door. I'm retired now, home allaw time. But I don't like to answer the door. Too many bad men now. But they keep knocking and I say, I wonder who that could be? I go to the door and there is a girl standing there with a paper bag in her hand. I do not know her so I start to say, you got the wrong number, girl. But she is smiling at me and I think to myself, why does she look like I know her? Then she say just one word. She called me Auntie.

I was so happy to see her. Come in and let me take a look at you, I said. Oh, you are so pretty. You look just like your mother. How is she and what are you doing here, I asked. Tears came into her eyes. She said her mother had died from bad kidneys. But before she died she told Anita to come see me. I brought you something too, she said, giving me the bag. What you got there, I asked. The girl had brought me six cha siew bow. What a good heart you have, I said, just like your mother. But you stay and help me eat, okay? Me and your mother we eat a lot of food together but that was when I was young. Come on. I make tea and we eat together, just like the old days.

So that's how it began. Funny, huh? Young girl like her coming to see an old lady like me. She would come see me once or two times a week. We'd talk, eat. One day she said, have you ever wondered why I don't ask you to hug me anymore? I said, you young kid then, now you big girl, probably only want to hug boys, right? She told me she had a lump in her breast. It got bigger and bigger but she was afraid to go to a doctor.

Mama went to so many doctors and they let her die so I hated all of them.

When she finally did go they told her it was cancer.

So that's why, Auntie.

She started to cry. Silly, silly girl. Your Auntie's always here to give you a hug. Auntie always love you, no matter what.

They took her left breast and said she was okay. Then they said she had to have, what you call it, chemo...chemotherapy. Then radiation too. She was a good girl. Still came to see me when she felt okay. But she felt pretty sick most of the time — nausea, vomiting. And tired too, allaw time. Sometimes when she can't come she call me on the phone and ask how I am. I tell her I'm okay, but that's not the truth. I feel so sad. Her mama died so young and now... But we can't think about that. Anita is young still. Should be married with a family or at least out having fun. Not going in and out of a hospital.

Thanksgiving she came to spend the day with me. I cooked a big turkey stuffed with Chinese sweet rice, black mushrooms and sausage. Chinatown style, I call it. Gravy too. Sweet potatoes, cranberry and Chinese greens. She didn't eat too much but I packed some for her to take home. She says she's feeling better but she looks thin and is so pale. Christmas she couldn't come over. She said her back was hurting again.

New Year's Day was sunny and warm. Not usual for that time of year but must be an auspicious beginning, I thought. Perhaps this year Anita will be well. She called and said she had to tell me something. She wanted to go to the beach. You better wrap up good, I said. Not good if you catch a cold. We sat in the sun listening to the sound of waves. For a long time she was quiet. Then she said,

Auntie, I think I'm going to die.

What you mean die, I said. You young girl. Me old lady. I die first.

No, Auntie, I feel bad. When I lost my breast I cried and cried. I hurt terribly and I was frightened. I was afraid to look at myself in the mirror, I felt ugly, scarred. I was sure that no one would ever love me again. I had read somewhere that Amazon warriors of Dahomey had their right breasts cut off so they could be more effective archers. But I thought, I am not a woman warrior, just a scared woman in a lot of pain. I was angry at the doctors, at my friends, at everyone. Why me? I'm young, I feel fine, why me? Then I thought of all the injustices in the world: terrorism that kills the innocent, the earth raped by strip mining, Native American peoples relocated from their ancestral lands, the threat of nuclear war. History is filled with terrorism and injustice against women: African girls forced to undergo genital mutilation; Chinese girls limping on bound feet; young Indian widows burned on their husbands' funeral pyres; women killed at the stake for being witches. None of these women had a choice either. But it didn't make me feel any better. I'm very depressed, Auntie. The doctors are no longer talking remission. I'm going to die, Auntie. I'm very depressed and I don't know what to do.

What could I say to her? We cried and held each other, a young woman and an old woman.

A few days later she went back into the hospital. She couldn't sleep and the pain in her back was worse. The doctors found tumors on her spine and put her on morphine. I go to the hospital every day now. It's not that far by bus, only one transfer, and I walk half a block. Strange, I don't feel so old these days. One day when I was there she looked down at her chest and said,

Auntie, I feel like I'm a science experiment. All these tubes going into me...

And she gave me a letter.

Don't read it yet, not now. Later, you know when.

I stroked her hair, her face. I looked at the daughter I never had and I cried. She opened her eyes and said,

Don't cry, Auntie. I'm going home to my mommy. I feel like I'm going backwards. I'm a child, I'm a baby and you are my mother here to tuck me in for the night.

She closed her eyes and smiled at me.

I love you. 'Night, 'night.

Anita never woke up. On the day she died I opened her letter.

Dear Auntie. I send you all my hope and strength and love in your time of difficulty and sorrow. I send prayer and bright sun fire yellow, white, red flame of candle light to embrace you. Incense rises to the highest, the highest where we all come from and where we eventually will return. My heart opens to you more at this time than ever before. Don't cry for me, Auntie. I am with my Mama soaring on great wings across the sky. So many thanks to the Divine Force that continues to unite us as family, as friends for all time. A year is a year is a year... Falling asleep now. How I love you and hold you close. You will always be in my heart. 'Night, 'night, Auntie, till we meet again. I love you.

How I cried and cried and cried. How cruel is fate to take one so young while old ones like me live on and on and on.

I get sad a lot and cry too. When it gets bad I take myself down to the beach. I pack some food, fried chicken or maybe some lumpia and cha siew bow. I look out at the sky, listen to the sound of waves. I feel my friend and her daughter very close to me out there. When I get sad I remind myself that they are together in a place where the land is green, the air fragrant with jasmine, the water pure and the sun warm. There is no pain or injustice there.

One day I will join those I love and we will soar on great wings across the sky.

A Chinese Banquet
for the one who was not invited

it was not a very formal affair but
all the women over twelve
wore long gowns and a corsage,
except for me.

it was not a very formal affair, just
the family getting together,
poa poa, kuw fu without *kuw mow*
(her excuse this year is a headache).

aunts and uncles and cousins,
the grandson who is a dentist,
the one who drives a mercedes benz,
sitting down for shark's fin soup.

they talk about buying a house and
taking a two-week vacation in beijing.
i suck on shrimp and squab,
dreaming of the cloudscape in your eyes.

my mother, her voice beaded with sarcasm:
you're twenty-six and not getting younger.
it's about time you got a decent job.
she no longer asks when i'm getting married.

you're twenty-six and not getting younger.
what are you doing with your life?
you've got to make a living.
why don't you study computer programming?

she no longer asks when i'm getting married.
one day, wanting desperately to
bridge the boundaries that separate us,
wanting desperately to touch her,

tell her: mother, i'm gay,
mother i'm gay and so happy with her.
but she will not listen,
she shakes her head.

she sits across from me,
emotions invading her face.
her eyes are wet but
she will not let tears fall.

mother, i say,
you love a man.
i love a woman.
it is not what she wants to hear.

aunts and uncles and cousins,
very much a family affair.
but you are not invited,
being neither my husband nor my wife.

aunts and uncles and cousins
eating longevity noodles
fragrant with ham inquire:
sold that old car of yours yet?

i want to tell them: my back is healing,
i dream of dragons and water.
my home is in her arms,
our bedroom ceiling the wide open sky.

Peou Lakhana

Tha Phi Neah Yeung The... ?
(Only the two of us... ?)

I decided to do an interview/cross talk with Chamroeun because of the isolation and loneliness I often feel being alone and invisible. I met Chamroeun a few months earlier through my job. Before I met her I was the only Cambodian I knew of who is lesbian. I looked for a sense of family and community to the general Asian and Pacific Islander lesbian and bisexual community but felt invisible. I longed to meet someone with a similar historic and cultural background. Someone who felt and still feels the pain from the atrocities and crimes that were and are still being committed against and in Cambodia, my homeland. Someone who would understand the confusion, fragmentation, and fear of being bicultural. Someone with whom I can share an unspoken commonality, a commonality so common that I feel I belonged.

LAHKANA: I grew up most of my life in this country. I came to the United States in 1975 when I was nine. I'm twenty-seven now, so I've definitely been "Americanized." My soul is still *Khmer*, but I feel I've lost a lot being here. I dress differently, I speak differently, even my *Khmer* has an English accent. It's really hard... I'm in this country not by choice but because if I didn't leave I would have been murdered. On the other hand, I've also gained exposure to things that I don't think I would have been exposed to back home.

Coming out gradually probably works for a lot of people, but my style is different. Being a lesbian is part of who I am, being *Khmer* is part of who I am, being a woman is part of who I am and if my being a lesbian is going to turn you off to me immediately based on your biases, then you need to work on your biases. I don't think society's gotten there. I don't think we'll ever be there but that's how I operate.

CHAMROEUN: I was also raised in France for ten years. I was also in the army for five years. So, who the hell is... me? Who am I? I am all that has been in the past and I will be what the future will hold for me. But, all I am is a human being and I try to change with time and grace.

LAHKANA: So when were you in France?

CHAMROEUN: During my teenage years from age ten to about eighteen.

LAHKANA: And from France you came to the United States?

CHAMROEUN: Yeah, we make the best out of every situation, and I think you do more good by being flexible. That's a very good attribute of being a human being, I think from being Cambodian or from the suffering that we had, all the deaths, all the pain, all the suffering that we've gone through. I want to survive no matter where I have to be. You know, English is not my first language and I speak it very well; it's a matter of adaptation.

I like women. My sexual orientation has always been there.

LAHKANA: Did you feel like you were attracted to women even before you came to this country?

CHAMROEUN: Oh yeah! Of course! Since I was six or seven or so. I wished I was a boy. I knew I liked women back then.

LAHKANA: But there was no way of expressing what that was. Boys like girls, you like girls, so if you were a boy you could.

But I think the concept of being a lesbian, the way you label it, is more of a western thing, an "Americanization."

CHAMROEUN: When I was still learning the language, the culture, I learned the term for gay people.

LAHKANA: It's *Khtoey*.

CHAMROEUN: *Khtoey*, that's right.

LAHKANA: But it's so derogatory. It means limp-wristed or off.

CHAMROEUN: It is and it isn't. I mean I never had a bad experience saying that, okay, this is a gay guy. My experience with another gay person I knew when I was in Cambodia, actually the guy was more of a transvestite — he owns a house and has a reputation of being *Khtoey*.

LAHKANA: The community knew that he was *Khtoey*?

CHAMROEUN: Exactly, and he still is a rich man. Not ostracized at all.

LAHKANA: But *Khtoey* is used for gay men as you said earlier. Because of women's roles and the culture, it would be much more difficult for a woman to have an alternative lifestyle. Women need to be married, serve their families, and to birth sons.

CHAMROEUN: But I think it's a matter of who you are and how you handle it that will cause you to be ridiculed or accepted. You're a human being first before you've been labelled by anything else. Being a gay person is a small fraction of my life, so it's not that I don't want everybody to know that I'm gay. Yes, I understand there's a political agenda behind it as well for the visibility but it doesn't mean that you should just publicize and try to change perception so drastically. I think once people know who you are first, it doesn't matter whether you're gay or whatever, they accept you for who you are; they have a better understanding of who you are.

LAHKANA: How do you define community or family? When I came into this country in 1975 there weren't any Cambodians here, since the majority of Cambodians arrived after 1980. There were a lot of families here, scattered here and there with federal laws on sponsorship made to prevent ethnic enclaves. During this time, I was a part of a community, through weddings and lunar new year celebrations, through my parents.

Then I went to college and entered the predominantly white mainstream of a Seven Sister college. I thought I fit in but I didn't. I was tokenized and exoticized, although I didn't know it then. Slowly, after college I became more and more involved with the gay and lesbian Asian organizations. I'm very involved in the gay and lesbian Asian and Pacific Islander community at present.

You know, I still don't feel like it's my community because I feel it's East Asian-centric and I'm invisible. I have a different history. Only fifteen years ago, one third of my people and 80 percent of my family were murdered. I think that's part of the reason I'm radical and out. I don't waste time sitting on my ass. I could have been one of those dead people, but I survived and now I think about what I am going to do while I'm alive.

CHAMROEUN: The definition of community has a lot to do with family. Looking back, with all my family and relatives, the feeling of giving back has to do more closely with parents. Your parents gave you what they can and once you learn how to appreciate it you say, well, I have to do something, whatever I can too. I learned from my mother, she is very giving, very generous with her time.

Part of what I would like to do is to go back to Cambodia and adopt children or run an orphanage and give them some of the teaching I think is valuable for survival. I'd like to do this later on, like in my forties or fifties. I'm concerned for all those children. I feel compassion and empathy for all the people that lost their parents during that horrible genocide. But that's something for me in the future. It's an idea that I haven't abandoned, but I have to help me first and then I can help others.

LAHKANA: I want to go back to Cambodia too, in 1995 hopefully, or soon after that if I can do it financially. I want to work there. Probably in education/prevention and program development for HIV/AIDS in Southeast Asia. It's projected that by the year 2000 the continent of Asia will be leading the epidemic, concentrated in Thailand, India, Myanmar, and the Philippines. So I want to do something, I want to give back. I lived while most of my people died. I feel like I have a lot of advantages and privileges that other people don't. I'm going to do something to help the community.

What is a portrayal of a Cambodian lesbian identity? I mean, do you look more Cambodian lesbian or do I look more Cambodian lesbian? Because the way we dress and move in the world is different. Your energy is calming and deliberate. I want to call you *Mein* (aunty) instead of *Bong* (elder sister) and you're only one year older than me. I'm more of an *Onh* (younger sister). My mother always gets angry at me because I act so *A-Lim A-Leihm* (silly). You dress professionally in a more conservative way, and I dress street casual.

We're both Cambodian lesbians. But for me to walk into a Cambodian community setting in Stockton or the Tenderloin or in Oakland the way I am is scary. I am scared that my people won't accept me, that I will be judged because I don't have a Cambodian accent, that my Cambodian is not that great, or that I look the way I look. I want to be proud of who I am and say, well, this is who I am and I can do a lot and I love my people, but I'm not going to be what you want me to be in order for you to accept me. Or will I have to change?

CHAMROEUN: It doesn't matter how you label yourself or what you call yourself. You earn your respect. When you look at the lesbian community, the way they portray a lesbian is extreme, ring around the nose and ugly and all those things. Is this the definition of a lesbian? You don't see the invisible crowd. The extreme makes the media. As an individual growing up, you say is this what I'm supposed to be or identified with?

LAHKANA: You can't identify with it! It's not who you are. And the way the lesbian community is portrayed tends to be very white. There's a look, and yes, it's a stereotype. The "look" may be a choice, but I feel like it has a backlash. Lesbians of color are invisible and we are oftentimes forced to choose between our culture and our sexuality.

CHAMROEUN: Once you become more adult, you feel, so okay, it doesn't matter who they are — I'm going to start portraying a different type of lesbian. I don't expect for them to portray me. You need to go out there and portray yourself period.

LAHKANA: But it would have been easier for me if I had picked up a book about lesbians and there was a Cambodian lesbian writer in it. Or, if I had picked up an anthology of women of color or lesbians of color and I had seen that then. I think I would have come out sooner. I think that's part of the reason why I'm out and visible. Hopefully my experience can support another sister's process and make it a little bit easier.

CHAMROEUN: It's good that we do pave the way for people to say yes there's such a thing as Cambodian lesbians. When you came out four years ago, when anybody comes out basically, is when you feel pretty secure about who you are. And financially secure too, because if you're not financially independent I don't think you can easily say I'm out now. We are the first generation of Cambodian lesbians. I'm glad that you are out and loud.

LAHKANA: I've been out the past four years and I have looked and put the word out at conferences and all the Asian Pacific Islander lesbian bisexual things that if there are other Cambodian lesbians, out or not out, please let me know. It's really important for me to feel that I'm not alone. That I'm not a freak. Yeah, there are Korean lesbians, there are Chinese lesbians, etc. But there aren't any Cambodian lesbians. I met you just a couple of months ago and I felt so good. I was in tears almost, because it was like looking at myself in the mirror. I'm not alone. You know there's gotta be more Cambodian women who love women, who are lesbian/bisexual. There's got to be, and meeting you gave me a lot of hope. I came out here because there's a large Asian and Pacific Islander lesbian community, so I figured maybe I'll find a community for me. I guess a community for me means a lot more Cambodian lesbians.

CHAMROEUN: You know I have the same question. I think you have to look at the numbers. Yes, I know that 10 percent of the population is gay, lesbian, bisexual, out or in the closet, but again part of the Cambodian culture is that it's not something to say. It's such a taboo subject, though not everybody was raised the same way. My mother was more liberal, some of the people are very rigid and maybe most of them are very traditional. When you look at the population of Cambodia, there are only four or five million of us left, and most of us are in Cambodia. Right now, the ones here are more or less worried about their own survival — not being out or gay.

LAHKANA: Eating, sleeping, working — basic survival needs, because we're the most recent immigrants. Also, most of us are refugees dealing with a lot of traumas.

CHAMROEUN: That's right, so I think that's part of the reason that you don't see too many visible Cambodian lesbians. You're looking for a minority within a minority.

LAHKANA: Within a minority, so we got two people!

Patrice Leung

A Letter to Female Homosexuals

Yo Abby,

I need to get this out of my system so bear with me, babe.

My lover (or ex-lover — whatever she happens to be at press time) likes to shit on me for my "middle class" choices in life like my job, my house etc. In my opinion the lesbian community shits entirely too much.

Shove an anal plug in, womyn, or we'll never wrest ourselves from our own excrement.

S-M dykes get shit on (that's figurative, you shitheads).

Vanilla dykes get shit on.

Monogamous dykes get shit on.

Non-monogamous dykes get shit on.

Middle class dykes get shit on.

Fat dykes, Chinese dykes, Jewish dykes, Native dykes, Catholic dykes, New Age dykes, English-speaking dykes, French-speaking dykes, Anything-but-English-French-speaking dykes all get shit on.

The self-important "politically correct" dykes shit on apolitical dykes as well as on each other.

This list is of course incomplete unless it includes all of us who like to shit on ourselves.

We are so goddamned full of it!

As human beings we don't fit neatly into one category so the permutations that provoke shit are endless. Can you imagine the guts it takes to come out in our community as a middle-class, macrobiotic, S-M Lesbian of Colour?

It's time to cut the crap.

Unity comes not from uniformity but from accepting the fucking fact that individually we have been shaped by a unique combination of experiences and as a result we're bound to piss each other off.

Strength comes from realizing that in our fight against a homophobic world the least likely lesbian may be a fucking good ally. Shitting on her will cause alienation and weakness among us all.

We demand visibility, if not acceptance, in the narrow-minded societies in which we live, and yet it is interesting that even as our own views have been fuelled by passion arisen out of our own oppression so too do we seek to oppress each other using the tool with which we are most familiar: Bigotry.

The lesbian community has set itself up as a superior society. We are not. We are, each of us, imperfect. And we come from so many different places that living together is hard while hate is easy.

We'd be boring girls if we did not debate and disagree. Constructive criticism is necessary for our survival. But for fuck sake can't we be more tolerant of each other?

Save the shit for the real assholes.

Please.

Signed,
In A Shitty Mood
Vancouver, BC

WAKING FROM
A DREAM
OF LOVE

V.K. Aruna

AT&T
dedicated to all those women in long-distance relationships

Last night, as you flirted with me on the telephone,
I sat, wrapped in lavender mists. Naked under
a flickering candle. Mouthing sweet mischief in your
rapid Indian vowels, you whispered language magic
till I dissolved into silent wetness. Knees flung
wide in heated water, I listened to your homegrown
expressions of subtle seduction, drawing water between
my thighs, my skin settled back against the porcelain
of a recreated womb chamber. And when you paused
to gather a thought, the symphony of ripples from hand
cleaving water rose up to greet you across the wires,
leaving you speechless. And for one long moment,
we shared only silence and the quiet breathing
of two women desiring each other a one-hour
plane ride apart.

Susan Ito

Yoo Hoo

MARA WAS THE FIRST AND ONLY WOMAN I'VE EVER BEEN IN LOVE WITH. She was my ex-boyfriend Nathan's dental hygienist. Nathan was my dentist. We'd broken up during his first year in dental school, and six years later he was still the only person who could make me feel comfortable while I was getting my molars drilled. He whispered dirty stories to me, making me go all soft and limp while his rubbery fingers probed the inside of my mouth. Even though it was clear we would never be in a relationship again, Nathan and I still liked playing with each other. After he was finished working on my pathetic teeth, I would catch the tip of his latexed thumb and suck on it for a second before he took it out of my mouth. It made him crazy.

While Nathan tortured me with his stainless steel instruments, he kept me entertained with a running commentary on his social life. It was unbelievable; Nathan had seduced about ninety-five percent of his secretarial staff. After having their hearts broken, the gorgeous young women would quit, and sometimes I would see one of them working somewhere else on the same street, at Crown Books or Pizza Hut. They would walk by Nathan's office during their lunch hour, and leave little notes on the windshield of his car.

I could tell Mara was going to be different kind of employee, though. After she finished grinding every molecule of plaque off my teeth, she didn't totter out to the hallway to call him like the rest of them did, ridiculous in their fuschia heels. They would lean against the doorway like teenagers and giggle, "Doctor Naa-than?" I noticed the soft suede ankle boots and gray tights underneath Mara's white lab coat and thought, she's really beautiful. Not at all ridiculous.

She handed me a new toothbrush, patted me on the shoulder and told me not to forget to floss. Then she winked at me and called into the intercom, "Okay, Nathan, I think the old flame is ready for her laughing gas!"

I blushed, madly embarrassed, and started waving my hands around. I protested, "Oh, God, that was *years* ago!" She laughed.

I had to come back two weeks later to get a filling replaced. Nathan had me stop in for a quick polish with Mara first; he said he didn't like working on fuzzy teeth. While she whirred around the inside of my mouth with her vibrating toothbrush, she chattered away with an amusing monologue. She whispered to me that she had actually gone out with Nathan too, only a few times last summer, after he had come to lecture her dental hygiene class back in New York.

She stopped, held the instrument up like a telephone, and crooned one of Nathan's classic lines with perfect delivery, "Mara, you're so smart you're making me hard!"

I howled, and pink gel toothpaste dribbled down my neck.

Mara dabbed at it gently with a Kleenex and said to me, "I think you and I could be good friends, Leslie."

I liked her. I really liked her. I so much wanted a good friend. I had a couple of other women friends at the time, but none of them were intimate, true soulmates. I complained to my therapist, "I don't have one single friend that I could call up at 3 a.m. and wail to!" She nodded sympathetically and then firmly refused to have coffee with me. Obviously *she* wasn't going to fit the bill.

I showed up a few days later at Nathan's office, carrying a dog-eared copy of *Pilgrim at Tinker Creek*. Mara had told me she'd lost hers during the move out from New York, and felt bereft without it. It was one of my favorite books, too. We ate at Dakota Pete's, huge chicken-walnut salads, and a pile of lacy onion rings. Mara speared a cherry tomato on the end of her fork and waved it around in the air while she talked about her last relationship, a man named Patrick who had dumped her the day they were supposed to move in together. Her belongings were already stuffed into a U-Haul, so she had revised the rental contract and decided to drive it across the country to California, instead of across the Triboro Bridge to Queens. She had been in San Francisco one week when she took the job with Nathan.

I stared at her through the entire meal, feeling electrified by her energy, the way she laughed. Every word she spoke seemed to resonate in my head, like a song I had known a long time ago. Listening to Mara stirred up my blood, sent it bubbling to the surface of my face in hot, overwhelming flushes. It was a familiar but oddly placed sensation: I recognized it from crushes I had had on several men in my life.

I had a number of different boyfriends then, attracted to little pieces of each one, but unable to really imagine being serious with any of them. I wished that I could combine them all to form the perfect man: Phillip's intelligence, Jake's sexual passion, Charlie's sweetness. Each of them had tarnished sides, though. Phillip was smart as a whip, and we could talk all night, until my brain was happy and sizzled. But he was also moody, and compulsive, and his idea of a *really* romantic gift was a five-year subscription to *The Nation*. Jake was sexy and wild, but he also had a cocaine problem. And Charlie's doting attention ultimately made me feel irritable, like I was being followed by a drooly puppy.

Mara laughed at the stories about the three-ring circus that made up my love life. We sat in the fat green vinyl booth for a long time, drinking refills and more refills of coffee. Finally I was starting to twitch from all the caffeine, and looked at my watch.

"Uh... Mara..." I started. "I hate to tell you this."

"Oh my God, no." Her eyebrows jumped up. "What time is it?"

"Quarter to three."

"Nathan is going to KILL me!" We jumped out of the booth simultaneously, crashing into each other as we grabbed for our coats. Laughing like high school kids, we threw our money at the waitress and ran out the door. We rushed to her car and Mara leaned against the door, shaking her purse. "Oh God, tell me I left my keys on the table!"

"I'll run back there while you keep looking." I turned and hurried back to the caf_ and collided with the waitress. She gave me a dirty look as I squatted down to search under the legs of the customers sitting at the table where Mara and I had eaten. No keys.

"Are you sure you didn't pick them up?" I accused her. Just then, Mara appeared in the doorway, redfaced. She pointed down the street.

"What, did you find them?"

"Uh huh." She was shaking her head, snorting giggles through her nose. "They're locked inside, on the front seat of the car."

"Oh no."

"I'm going to call Nathan," she said. "I'll tell him I'll be in tomorrow. Today is completely shot."

"But don't you have afternoon patients?"

She shrugged. "Yeah, I do. They'll have to be rescheduled. I can fit them in next week... if I haven't been fired by then."

I stood next to her at the phone booth while she dialed the office. "Hi, Cindi, this is Mara. Yeah, I know. Listen, something terrible happened. I, um..." she looked at me and bit her lip. "I had an accident." She rolled her eyes to the sky, crossed her fingers under her chin. "Yeah, on the freeway, no, nobody hurt but it took *forever* to get everything cleared away, you know, police reports and everything."

I was staring at her with my mouth hanging open.

She continued, calmly, "I just can't deal with coming in for the rest of the day, but please, would you call everyone, apologize for me, reschedule? I'll be in tomorrow. Sure, I'm sure. Thanks a lot, Cindi." She hung up, grabbed my hand and cheered. "Free time! Leslie, let's go to the beach!"

We sat down on the sidewalk and waited for Triple A to come jimmy open Mara's car. I looked at my shoes. "Mara, don't you feel guilty? All those people who had appointments?"

She tilted her head. "Well, yeah, sort of, but Leslie, there were only five of them, and one of them cancelled anyway. It's not like they were scheduled for *brain* surgery. It won't kill them if their teeth aren't cleaned for another few days."

I protested, "But Mara, their schedules..."

She put her finger up to my lips. "Leslie, it was a mistake, but look, for us, it's a gift. Now we get to spend the whole afternoon together. To me, that's worth it." She winked at me. "It's even worth a temper tantrum of Nathan's."

I felt a tremor of something when she said that, "It's a gift." The skin around my entire body tightened and shivered, and I felt an extra gallon of blood push into my heart. I had been trying to be conscientious, but the truth was that I was ecstatic she wasn't going back to work.

We spent the rest of the afternoon at Ocean Beach with our shoes off, skipping along the edge of the freezing water. Mara ran ahead of me, singing "Runaway." Her hair was wild, whipped up in the salty wind, and I could hear voice, throaty and off-key, blending with the sound of the surf. I watched her, dancing like some sort of sea sprite, and my stomach did a little cartwheel. She was so beautiful. As she got further away, all I could hear was a little chorus, "Mah little run-run-run-ah runnawayyyy..."

She waited for me at the end of the beach and we shuffled our names into the sand. Then we climbed up the hill to Cliff House, and sat by the window, cradling mugs of hot cider. I looked out and saw our names on the beach, melting away under water. We didn't say anything for a long time as the fog rolled towards us, pressing up against the glass, pulling nighttime behind it.

Mara didn't drive her car to work for the next five weeks. She took the bus, got there on time every day, and made regular reports about the status of her car repairs. One day she showed up at the office jingling her keys, saying, "I finally got it back! And they did a great job — it looks just like new."

I got it in my head that I wanted a sports car. A little silver Fiat. I took Charlie with me to the used car lot and he looked it up and down, inside out, drove it around. He took me for a ride around the block, made a series of figure eights through the Toys-R-Us parking lot, then we flew onto the freeway.

I was screaming with excitement. I yelled, "I want this car!" I had the down payment ready, folded up as a cashiers' check in my pocket. The only minor detail was that I didn't know how to drive a stick shift. Charlie reassured me that it was easy, so I signed on the dotted line and he drove me home.

The next day we had our driving lesson. I stalled at five traffic lights and sweet Charlie was white-knuckled and cursing me after twenty minutes. The lesson ended with tears, mostly mine. He parked the car in front of my apartment and took the bus home.

I called Mara. "I've made a terrible mistake," I said.

"What?"

"I bought this beautiful car and I'm never going to be able to drive it." I pounded my fist on the kitchen table. "Damn, I'm going to have to take it back and trade it in for a stupid Dodge Dart or something. A dumb automatic."

I could feel her hesitation on the other end.

"What is it, Mara, you think I'm a real idiot for buying it?"

"No, Les, I'm just wondering..." she paused, "How come you never asked *me* to teach you to drive."

"No way, Mara. I've already driven a stake into my relationship with Charlie. I'm not about to do the same thing with you."

She persisted. She told me it would be easy, it would be fun. We went up north to the long rolling highway at the top of Marin county and I watched her hand as she drove, rocking the stick shift with just the heel of her palm. I leaned over and watched her left foot lift up in perfect synchrony, steady as a cable, the tension showing in the tendon on top of her ankle. The car hummed along gratefully. The road disappeared underneath us like a black, currentless river. Mara drove for an hour, maneuvering the Spider up and over hills, slowing for an occasional cow. I watched everything.

Then she pulled over to the side and opened her door. I got into the driver's seat and put my hand on the polished wood knob. It was warm. She leaned over and laced her fingers lightly over mine, and said, "It's like dancing. I'll lead." The car moved forward, slowly, and waltzed onto the pavement without stumbling.

Nathan started calling me more frequently, asking how "things were going" with my new friendship. I think he was getting nervous about the amount of time Mara and I were spending together. The days I came to meet her for lunch, I'd see him watching us through the window of the reception desk. The way we were always laughing hadn't escaped him.

"Leslie, you two don't, um, talk about me, um, do you?"

"Don't flatter yourself, Nathan, we've got a lot better things to discuss than your private parts!"

That shut him up. After that, he steered our conversations away from her name as smoothly and quickly as I'd learned to drive the Fiat around Mount Tamalpais.

One day Mara called me up and told me she was going away for the weekend. She asked if I knew any romantic places in Calistoga.

"Romantic? What is this?" I was startled, but intrigued.

Mara laughed. "I met this great guy, Les. Ramon. He's from Argentina."

"Really? Where did you meet him?"

"At the CopyMat. He was Xeroxing some brochures for his new business, I was waiting for the machine he was using, and we started talking. Les, I can't wait for you to meet him, he's really great!"

I bit my tongue to refrain from making a sarcastic comment about meeting prospective beaus in front of Xerox machines. "Well, have a good time, Mara," I said dully. "Listen, call me on Monday. I want to hear all about it." Suddenly I wasn't looking forward to my dinner date with Phillip. I called him up and cancelled, complaining about a stomach virus. I sat in my apartment and sulked for the rest of the weekend, eating frozen pizza and rereading *Pilgrim at Tinker Creek* for the seventh time.

I eventually got more or less used to Ramon. He was handsome, and very charming, and he attached himself to Mara's apartment like a fungus. Once, Mara and Ramon invited Phillip and me over for dinner at her apartment. Socially, it was a disaster. Phillip tried to engage Ramon in a political discussion about U.S. foreign policy in Latin America, and couldn't hide his disgust when he found out Ramon didn't know if the Contras were from El Salvador or Brazil.

The only redeeming part of the entire evening was the food. Ramon was a phenomenal chef. We all sat around the kitchen while he juggled little jars of chile and cinnamon. He made some kind of chicken dish, with onions and olives and spices in enchanting combinations. While he stirred and rattled the pans on the stove dramatically, Mara hovered around his shoulder like a surgical nurse, passing him utensils and bottles with devotion. I didn't like it at all. I sulked in a corner near the refrigerator and looked up at the little blackboard where Mara put her grocery list. In a dozen shades of colored chalk, she had drawn broccoli, and carrots, and a big orange cheese. Under the grocery items she had drawn a heart, and inside were the initials "R.E." I called over to Ramon, "Hey, Ramon, what's the name of your business again?"

He looked up from the stove, startled. He was probably shocked since it was the first time I had ever addressed him directly.

"Espinoza Electronics. Why, Leslie?"

"Oh, I was going to refer a friend of mine to you. Someone I know who has a broken radio." I looked back at the smudgy blue heart, and wasn't hungry anymore. The smell of the cooking chicken turned acrid, and I could swear I saw a green cloud hanging over the kitchen.

I was swimming in a thick, dark dream, when a sharp sound near my head jangled me, sat me up. The receiver was in my hand and I was already saying, "Hello," when I woke up. A tiny voice, hoarse and trembling, called my name. I couldn't tell who it was, and the dense weight of sleep almost compelled me to hang up and flop back down into my pillow. I said it again, "Hello? Who is this?"

"Mara. Leslie, it's Mara." Her voice was faint, almost a whisper, but with a high-pitched intensity I'd never heard before.

"Mara!" I turned the light on, rubbed my eyes. "What's wrong?"

She didn't answer, but asked in that creepy, tiny voice, "Can I come over?"

"Oh, God." I looked at my watch and saw that it was 1:45. "Of course you can, of course. What is it, are you all right? Do you want me to come get you?" There was a pit of fear and anxiety carving its round shape into my gut.

"No. I'll be there soon." She hung up, and I was left with the buzz of the phone in my hand. I put on my bathrobe and got up to boil water for tea.

She huddled into the corner of my couch, holding a round corduroy pillow up against her body. Mara looked half her usual size: the grey sweatsuit she was wearing was enormous. When she had come in the front door, the hood of the sweatshirt had been pulled over her head, making her look a little bit like an elf. Her eyes were puffy, her eyelashes stuck together in wet spikes. I wanted to gather her up in my arms and rock her back and forth, but instead I gave her a cup of peppermint tea.

"So what's going on?" I asked, as gently as I could.

Her eyes reddened a few degrees more, and she put her fist up to her mouth, pressed it there for a moment. Then she looked up at the ceiling and said, "I'm really scared, Leslie. I'm scared to death. It's Ramon."

I jumped off the couch. "Mara. Did he hurt you?" The room was getting really hot and I felt myself breathing in huge, noisy gulps.

"No. No, he hasn't touched me, but..." She looked up again, twisted the border of the pillow. "He kicked a hole in the wall of my kitchen. You can see all the way through. He broke some plates too."

"God, Mara. What happened? Did he threaten you?"

"Sort of."

"What did he say?" I wanted to kill him.

"He said I'd be sorry if I didn't start treating him the way he deserved."

I couldn't believe this. She already treated him like a prince. Baked him chocolate chip cookies, brought him cuttings of every plant she ever saw, called him in the middle of dinners with me to tell him she missed him. Frankly, I thought it was nauseating, but she had seemed happy with him so I'd never said anything.

She talked for a long time and I just sat there, feeling like I was drifting around in the middle of some horror movie. After a while her voice dropped down an octave or two, and she was sounding a little bit more like Mara. There started to be long pauses in between her thoughts, and I could see her eyelids making slow, heavy blinks. About the time that the sky started bleaching into morning, I took her and led her by the hand, like a sleepwalker, to my bed. She rolled up into a round gray ball and fell asleep. I watched her for about ten seconds, as she lay there like an armadillo, and then I passed out too.

"You know what I really want right now?"

"Ice cream."

"You're such a *genius*."

Mara and I walked around the corner to the place that had homemade vanilla bean ice cream. The night air was chilly, wet, fog hanging like a net of droplets on top of our hair. Still, we wanted that ice cream. We sat in the front window and watched people pass on the sidewalk, a silent movie.

I looked at Mara shaping the ice cream into a perfect peak, and a thought flashed in my mind, *her breast must look like that.* I grabbed that thought by the tail right before it escaped my consciousness, then dropped it like a live coal. I was shocked at the heat that had passed through me. I didn't want it to be true, but there it was. Not only was I falling in love with Mara, something in me wanted to make love with her too. The idea of it made me feel desperate, crazy. She looked up at me, smiled, blew a white vanilla bubble between her lips.

"Leslie, do you believe in reincarnation?"

"I'm not sure. Why, do you?" I was relieved to have a conversation to distract me from my thoughts.

"Well not really, but you know, I just had this weird feeling. Like I've known you before." Her eyes were serious, devastatingly beautiful, deep grey encircled by gold.

My heart stopped. "What do you mean?"

"Like, in another life, maybe we were..."

Don't say it, Mara. I will die if you do. Don't say lovers.

"Come on, Leslie, use your imagination. What do you think we might have been in another lifetime?" Her eyes glittered.

"Um, I don't know, let me think of something." I was stalling for time, felt trapped with my thoughts. *Don't make me say it.* I pulled the first silly thing I could think of out of the air...

"Goldfish." We both said it simultaneously. Her mouth dropped open. "What did you say?"

"Goldfish."

"That's what I said!"

"Oh my God, then it must be true!"

We started laughing, an uncontrollable, giddy shrieking that made everyone turn look at us. Mara pulled me to my feet and we staggered out to the sidewalk, wiping our eyes, gasping through high-pitched giggles. "Goldfish!" we screeched. "Swimming around one of those little treasure chests. In a round glass bowl in some third-grader's bedroom." I was hysterical, giddy, spinning around in circles on the sidewalk, when I looked at her. Mara was staring at me with dead-serious eyes, and then she caught my hand, kissed it full on the palm.

"Whatever we were," she whispered, "It feels like I've been you, or maybe you've been me. That's how it feels."

I swallowed, not taking my hand away from her face. "I know," I said. "I know."

Mara changed the locks on her apartment, and several times a week, she asked me to sleep over "for protection" although I told her I couldn't exactly vision myself duking it out against Ramon. He didn't bother her when someone else was around. But sometimes when I came into her apartment I could hear her talking to him on the phone. I knew it was Ramon because she would be speaking Spanish, and although I couldn't understand what she was saying, her words had a soothing, amorous tone. Ayy, m'ijo, no sea tan enojado, I'd hear her crooning, and I'd give her dirty looks through the kitchen wall. After she hung up the phone with a soft click, she'd pad into the kitchen in her fuzzy slippers, and shrug her shoulders.

"He's just a confused guy, Leslie," she'd say, and bright, defensive-looking spots would pop up on her cheeks.

"Confused!" It made me want to scream, and sometimes, I did. "Mara, that jerk put a hole in your wall, and almost beat you up! That's not confused, that's violent. That's sick. I can't believe you even still talk to him."

"I don't call him, Leslie, and what do you expect me to do, hang up in his face?"

"That's not a bad idea."

"He's all alone. His entire family is thousands of miles away, and I'm the only friend he has."

"You're too nice to him."

We slept together every night, curled up like shrimp, and told each other our dreams in the morning. It was like an ongoing slumber party. Sometimes we even used the same toothbrush. She left mushy notes in my lunch bag, and I kept a photo of her in my wallet. But still, Mara and I couldn't talk about what seemed to be happening between us. I wrote in my journal, "I'm in love," but I didn't say it out loud. She had erased Ramon's initials from the kitchen blackboard, and in its place had drawn a pair of pop-eyed goldfish.

One night we went out to Dakota Pete's. I fidgeted in the green booth and kept looking around like I was waiting for someone to come and rescue me.

Mara waved her hand in front of my face. "Hey, are you all right? You seem really nervous, Fish."

I swallowed. "Mara, there's something I want to talk about."

She looked at me straight in the eyes. "Go ahead."

"Well... you know we've been getting really close."

"Uh huh." She had a smile twitching at the edges of her mouth.

"What are you laughing about?" I was about to have a heart attack.

"I'm not laughing." She put her coffee down, and placed her hand over mine. "Say what you were going to say."

"Mara. I love you."

A shadow fell across the table, and I looked up to see the waitress hovering over us with a coffee pot. "Refill?" she asked. Mara was hiding her mouth behind a napkin, and I could see her eyes giggling.

I wanted to die. Here I was professing love for a woman, for the first time in my life, and the entire public was in on it. I stood up suddenly. "Let's go home."

She held my hand in the car, releasing it only to let me shift. "I'm sorry I was laughing, Leslie," she whispered. "I know you were serious."

I parked the car and turned the lights off. "I just feel really stupid, Mara, I don't know how to say this. I've never felt this way with a... girlfriend... before."

"Neither have I." She seemed unbelievably calm.

"I've never felt like this with anyone before." All of a sudden I felt something in my throat close up, and I knew I was going to cry. My mouth crumpled up and I couldn't talk anymore. I could feel the tears running into my mouth, down my neck.

Mara leaned in close to me and put her hands on either side of my head, underneath my hair. "What is it, Leslie?" she whispered. "Why are you so sad?"

"I'm just scared, Mara," I gulped. "I'm terrified. I don't know what's going to happen."

"Shh," she said. "We're going to love each other. That's what's going to happen." She touched the end of my nose lightly against hers, and rubbed it around in little circles, an Eskimo kiss. Then she turned her face to the side and our mouths met. It was soft, kind of salty from all my tears, and long; it went on for hours, days, weeks. I closed my eyes and drank up the taste, thinking the whole time, finally, finally. I followed Mara over to her side of the car, and unbuttoned her blouse with more coordination than I realized I had. The light from the street filtered through the foggy windshield and made a white canvas of her skin. White as vanilla bean ice cream.

For the next few months, life was sweet, but I felt schizophrenic. My co-workers kept asking me if I was in love. They saw the little daisies that fell out of my lunch, they saw the way I turned red and looked at the ceiling when I talked on the phone. The only way I could respond was to laugh and mumble something vague. I didn't know what to do with all their questions, or the questions that were rolling in my own head.

One day we spent several hours trekking all over the East Bay and into Contra Costa, on a search for Yoo Hoo. Mara was still feeling homesick for Brooklyn, and she was dying for a real Coney Island hotdog and a bottle of that fake-chocolate non-dairy beverage. She had a wicked craving, and couldn't talk about anything else. I was in love, and it gave me a mission.

We drove to this little hot dog stand in Berkeley that was alleged to carry Yoo Hoo. They had discontinued them the summer before, claiming no one ever bought them. From there we went to downtown Oakland, to a little mom'n'pop grocery, and then out to Concord. We struck out everywhere, but by then we were on a roll, driving East.

"Just a little further," I said. "I bet they'll have some at the next town."

Mara knew that I would've driven to Indiana if I had to, I was so bent on making her happy. We were on the highway then, laughing like maniacs. We kept going until the lanes narrowed and twisted, and we were in the mountains. Our legs pimpled up in the cold and I turned the heater on full blast. Then we both saw the blinking neon sign: Walden Pond Cabins.

"There it is, Fish," she said. "That's the pond where we came from." We checked into Number 17 and dropped our clothes on the ratty carpet. After making love a hundred times, we took a bath together, slipping against each other like seals. We didn't get out of the cold milky water until our fingers and toes were pruney and all the bubbles had fizzled into nothing.

It was a Saturday morning in August when I decided I had to ask. I stared at Mara while she slept, loving the way her mouth dropped into an open pucker, like she was about to whistle. My head raced with questions and I started hurling them at her the moment her eyes opened.

"Mara, what are we going to do?" I have to admit, I didn't even give her a chance to pee or brush her teeth.

"'Bout what? Aren't we going to Santa Cruz this weekend?" She had no clue what I was talking about.

I could feel my anxiety rising like bad coffee in my throat. I nudged her out of my arms so that I could sit up. "I meant, what are we going to do, about us. Are we ever going to tell anyone? What about having children? Are we going to live happily ever after, you and I?"

"Sounds good to me." She smiled and ruffled my hair.

"Mara, are you serious?"

"As serious as you are."

"What does that mean?" I felt cornered.

"Leslie, I love you. If you want to tell people all about it, that's great. If you think you can deal with it."

"Me!" I squeaked indignantly.

Mara sat up and put her bathrobe on. "I'll tell my friends if you tell yours. And we can tell Nathan together." Her eyebrow twitched wickedly.

"Mara, I have to ask you something. Have you totally given up the idea, of, you know, guys?" I held my breath, looking at her.

"Given up on them? Nooooo. I still think they're pretty cute." Then she bounced out of bed, and her words flew back at me from the bathroom. She said that she was going to find a man who wouldn't mind if we were lovers too. Not like a menage a trois, she wouldn't want us all mixed up together. I would be more like a pet rabbit that she could just take along with her. She didn't say it like that, of course, but that's what she meant. Then she turned on the water, and while she was singing off-key in the shower, I stuck my face into her pillow and cried. I knew then that we weren't going to have the courage to follow it through.

Just a few weeks later, Mara met a man at her gym. I don't even remember the guy's name, but she came home one day, all sweaty and giggly, and I knew we were in trouble. He was crazy about her, and left about a dozen messages a day on the answering machine. I kept my eye on the chalkboard in the kitchen, waiting for his initials to appear.

One night she went out to dinner with him and it took her forever to get ready. I watched miserably while she held up different earrings against her cheek.

"Mara, did you tell him about me? About us?"

She smoothed back her hair and said gently, "I did."

"And what did he say?"

She took a deep breath, and I saw her eyes blur a little in the mirror. "He said he didn't like the idea of me sleeping with anyone else, no matter what gender." She stood up suddenly, and grabbed me in a crooked hug. "But it'll be okay, Leslie, really. You and I have our friendship, and nobody can take that away."

I thought of Ramon, and the iron-shaped hole his foot had left next to Mara's refrigerator. I thought of the silky way her words had smoothed over him when she spoke to him on the phone. I knew that if I didn't walk out right then, that my rage would scare her half to death and she would end up trembling on the gym guy's doorstep.

I heard they got married a year after that. I think it was the same guy, but I'm not sure. Actually, Nathan told me. He showed me a Polaroid photograph that she had sent back to the office from their honeymoon.

They were standing at the edge of a blue-green lake, and the mountains in the background looked fake, they were so perfect. When I saw her eyes, crinkled together against the sun, and her hair, blowing crazy in all directions, my chest suddenly went all hollow, like the inside of a balloon. Then the balloon deflated and I didn't have any air to breathe. I had to go into the bathroom and make myself inhale, exhale in the mirror. I didn't come out for half an hour.

I went for lunch at the deli up the street, and was about to grab a Diet Coke from the refrigerator, when I saw a shelf lined up with those muddy brown bottles: Yoo Hoo. I took one to the cash register, holding onto the cold, cold glass with both hands, and I was shivering so much I was afraid I'd drop it. Then I brought that bottle home and wrapped it up like it was rare perfume. I put it in a wooden box that had once held oil paints, and surrounded it with a nest of yellow Kleenex. On top I put a little tiny gift envelope with a card inside, a card with a Chinese watercolor of a goldfish on the front. Inside I wrote, "Just wanted to say hi."

I took the whole thing to the "Handle With Care" packaging store, and they took the little wooden crate, and put that inside a cardboard carton full of plastic bubble-wrap. I had them send it by UPS Next Day Air, even though it was only going across the Bay to San Francisco. I didn't want to take any chances of it getting lost. They charged me $11.50. Mara never responded.

It's been over five years, and I haven't forgotten one detail of those months we had together. I haven't really been with anyone since Mara, nothing serious, anyway. Nathan still takes care of my teeth, but she quit working for him a long time ago.

Two weeks ago, there was a storm here, worse than any we'd had in decades. There was flooding, and mudslides, and my apartment building was washed right off its foundation into the supermarket on the street below. Hundreds of people lost their homes, including me, and several dozen died. The newspaper and television reporters swarmed through the shelter that had been set up for flood victims, and there were endless scenes of people running through the rain, their hair dripping with mud, their clothes all one brown color. I was one of them, the one trying to carry the screaming, drenched cat in my arms. Maybe she saw me there. Maybe she saw me being interviewed by the reporter from CBS, and knew that I had survived.

Maybe that's why Mara never called me, like the lady from the drycleaners did, like my computer programming teacher did, like my college roommate and second cousin did. They weren't watching the news, so they didn't know if I was dead or alive. They called my office, and they called my parents in Philadelphia, too, dozens of people, for the whole next week. Mara didn't call. But I bet she saw that clip on TV, where Nathan found me in the shelter and led me, wrapped up in a patchwork quilt, out to his car. Maybe she never called because she knew I had a place to go, and that I was all right.

Vanessa Marzan Deza

This Hunger in my Hips

sistah, sistah
this is for letting me drown
my sleepy, 4 am words of love
in the soft, sweat-scented
mass of your hair
caught between my teeth
spreading like dark seaweed
on the pillowcase
while we float in the currents of
the waves we made from
treading deeply/fully into
each other's secret oceans.

sweet, sweet sistah
poetry gets tangled in your curls
hanging softly over
chocolate brown eyes/framing invitation.

sistah, sistah
this is for letting me
come home in your arms
be reborn from your thighs
build my dreamhouse between your breasts
where pomegranate trees tremble wildly with fruit
and flowers sprout defiantly through
concrete streets and we water dandelion weeds
with the summer squash
and there's only one queen-sized bed
in this house where doors remain unlocked
and mothers don't ask what goes on behind them
and our early morning grins over
fresh brewed coffee
oven fresh biscuits and
garlic fried rice.

sweet, sweet sistah
many months have passed since
i've held your taste in my mouth
tongue is dry/unwhetted by sweat
from your forehead
body yearns with remembrance
hands remember the small of your back.

in dreams my fingers climb
the length of your spine
this love so fierce
fierce love pulling
you into me.

still i hold your memory
when i hold my hands to my hips
where the hunger of a thunder still
rumbles like the sea
trembles like pomegranate trees sprouting
through the concrete
calling calling
i found my first calling in the sway
of your strong, strong hips
sweet sweet sistah
this is for letting me come home in your arms
be reborn from your thighs
build my dreamhouse between your breasts.

Little Earthquake

Making Love to You

a thin veil of light blinds me to seeing
you lost among perfect auras i was dreaming
last night in a prayer i sent to moons
circling endlessly your tongue sensing my ripe flesh
caressing breasts softly tender lips in a gentle sea
washing my spine trembling a deep moan wailing to
waters pouring whispers shrouded in mystery
you i have found but where is myself darkened
in a scream of yearning lost to desire's body
torn in petals scenting your vulva rose arousing
my heart and spirit ribboned by skies of longing
kisses tasting skin in rapture your shimmering
thighs breathing deep the magic of our love.

Indigo Chih-Lien Som

the very inside

like the white fuzzy part of strawberries
or the slip on an avocado pit, you are
under the moons of my fingernails & deep
down in my lungs, i feel you like pollen
or blue veins. for you i will jump & stay
up there like a hollywood special effect
but here now in the stratosphere i am
frightened, your planets and milky ways
so alien violet & perfect. i will not come
down, but cry scratching at your starry
kitchen table until i have written a love
song for you, one unpublic & not like those
outside split-end top 40, a song that tastes
like your very inside.

Minal Hajratwala

Summer, Manhattan, 1991

Exiting the movie theater into the brightness
of mid-evening, signs and streetlights, you and I glow
with anticipation, not knowing
how to move from holding hands in a cold theater
to bed

We drop hands on the street
"Queer-bashing happens here," you whisper

In the bar your hand in mine quivering
cold from holding a drink with a twist
You smile so gently in this safe space
as if you are the virgin among women

"The old ways," you say, before AIDS, before politics,
"You could meet a woman and seduce her,
none of this talking talking talking"

And walking now to my apartment

On a doorstep a black man shouts at two white men
sitting close together: "I don't want no homos in my neighborhood,
go on over to the West Side"
A white man shouts back: "You calling me a homo, you
fucking nigger"

We pass
in silence

Then, high above the street,
your skilful tongue, your compact smooth body,
your strong fingers, large nipples, soft moans

Mina Kumar

Jeannie

NEELAM UNDRESSED AND GOT INTO BED AND DREAMT OF JEANNIE with the sweet pink pussy. Jeannie was as dark as espresso but her pussy was candy pink and pink champagne bitter. Neelam had always dreamt of Jeannie, even when the dream had a different name and even when she thought the dream had only dream logic.

Before she met Jeannie, it seemed such a strange, mysterious thing to like a woman. Neelam worried over what she was and why she was what she was and what women like her wanted and whether any woman would want her at all. She didn't think the latter was possible. There had been women who had liked her, liked the way she sucked their breasts, liked having her on their arm, liked dancing with her, but she wanted to be wanted. She wanted a woman to desire her body, as ludicrous and impossible as the idea often seemed. She told herself all lesbians really wanted to be wanted by a woman or wanted to possess a woman more than they wanted to make love with a woman, and she had a lump in her throat of the cries it seemed she would never utter. It wasn't so much that she wanted a 'butch' as that she wanted a woman who would desire the corporeal reality of her, her breasts, her stomach, her cunt, and this didn't seem altogether likely. Why would a woman want her pussy? She had never particularly been overcome with a desire to eat pussy. It didn't repulse her, and she was certainly willing to do it, but the idea didn't particularly excite her. She didn't know she just hadn't met the right pussy.

The night Neelam met Jeannie began with Neelam sitting alone in the park in Sheridan Square after yet another failed date. The only other people left in the park were sleeping homeless men. Neelam stretched her arms out on the back of the bench. Her blouse was short-sleeved, and the metal of the bench was cool against her skin. She sighed. It had been a long damn day.

The first thing that had gone wrong was that she got out of work late. There had been no time to change her clothes. She had rushed downtown to make her blind date with a pudgy, androgynous Chinese-American dyke who was not what she had been expecting. After the movie, they walked down Seventh Avenue and Neelam suggested they go to the Box for a drink. The Chinese-American dyke said she only went to Crazy Nanny's, the white bar, because she had heard that the women at Pandora's Box smoked crack in the bathroom. The date ended soon after.

Neelam continued sitting in the park after her date left. She didn't feel like moving. It seemed such a shame to be home on a ripe summer night. She took a sip of D&G's ginger beer and watched the women go by.

The furthest back Neelam could trace it was to when she was eight years old and living in Kluang with her mother and her stepfather. Her mother passed the long, empty days sitting in an enormous wicker chair in the garden, doing the crossword puzzle in every magazine or newspaper she could buy. When her mother went into the kitchen to get her lunch, Neelam would sneak up to where her mother had been sitting and carefully pull out from the pile the Australian tabloids with the halfnaked girls on page three. She would enter the house from the backyard and go into the room where she slept. There she sat hunched on the tile floor, poring over the pictures of bare-breasted girls, and listening for the sound of footsteps coming towards her, ready to shove the magazines under the mattress if anyone came to the door. "Why does that girl sneak the magazines away?" her mother once asked her stepfather. He had shrugged.

A cop came into the park to get the homeless men out and Neelam rose along with them. She tossed the empty bottle into the garbage bin and turned the corner.

The Box wasn't very busy. There were some women at the bar but the only people dancing were one couple and a vogueing transsexual. Neelam set her bag down on a chair on the edge of the dance floor. Jeannie was standing against the speaker with her arms crossed.

Jeannie was the one woman in the world who actually was the color of bittersweet chocolate. She was tall and Junoesque, if Juno wore a pair of tight jean shorts and a football jersey. She had big breasts and big legs and long, thin braids that flowed over her shoulders. Neelam walked by Jeannie and into a corner of her own. She wasn't in the mood for rejection. Jeannie was too femme for Neelam to think that she would have any success with her.

Although Neelam hadn't aligned herself yet, people presumed she was a femme because of the low-cut, high-hemmed way she usually dressed. She went along with it because she thought it would be slightly ludicrous to be aggressive when she was small and soft and unathletic.

It was different when she was a kid. Neelam still had her fourth grade class photograph of herself, tall and dark, standing in the back row with her arm wound around the waist of a small Chinese girl with big, moist eyes. She had towered over the petite Chinese girls in her class and she was always carrying them or tickling them. Neelam liked to regale her friend Billy with tales of herself as an elementary school butch, but there had also been a tall, older girl whom she had had a crush on. Neelam had anonymously sent her little gifts like a small hand mirror or a paper coronet of salted almonds.

Neelam had come to like only tall women. Tall, and strong, and curvy. Just like Jeannie, whom she purposefully ignored. Neelam tried not to want what she couldn't have and she was sure she couldn't have Jeannie just because she wanted her.

Another couple came on the dance floor but it was still more or less empty. Beams of colored light made swirling pools on the ground. Neelam turned and danced with her reflection in the mirrored wall. Jeannie was now standing against the mirror on the other side of the room, talking to a slim, dark girl in an orange Lycra bodysuit. Neelam watched them for a few minutes to see if they were together, but the girl in the bodysuit noticed her and Neelam had to turn away. Neelam went up to the DJ. booth to make some requests and then down to the bar.

The bartender, Jamie, was a puertorriqueña who looked like Nargis. "Mimosas are on special," Jamie said in her throaty voice.

"I'll have a screwdriver."

Jamie shrugged and smiled. Neelam could see the gap between Jamie's front teeth. "Are you having a good time?" Jamie asked, bringing her her drink.

Neelam didn't answer, and Jamie had another call at the other end of the bar. Out of the corner of her eye, she could see Jeannie dancing with the orange bodysuit girl. Neelam sipped her drink. The apex of existence in Indian philosophy was not to care about anything, to root out the "I," and Neelam was trying hard to reach this peak, but she couldn't help wanting Jeannie to come over and grab her.

It's the drink, she thought, setting it down. Alcohol made her want everything more loudly, and they always say you will never meet someone when you're looking. She sighed. She was sitting at an angle to the bar counter and the mirror behind her reflected her in profile, brooding over her drink like Amithab Bachchan in a gangster movie.

When she was a kid, she used to escape herself in masala movies. Nearly every weekend, her mother and her stepfather and herself went into the Indian section of Singapore, to eat at Komala Villas and to watch a film, preferably an Amithab film.

Neelam spent her Saturday afternoons mesmerized in dark, cool movie halls. The theaters had at least fifty narrow, steeply ascending rows and the screens were enormous. The movies were four hours long, plus the intermission when the crowds poured outside to buy salted or roasted nuts, candy, sundal, garam masala, kara boondhi, soda. Her mother insisted that they stay in their seats so they wouldn't lose them, and she handed Neelam film gossip magazines to read to keep Neelam quiet. And so in the middle of the movie, Neelam would read about the real-life exploits of the stars who towered over her on screen.

Neelam identified with Amithab completely. He was tall and angry and misunderstood, usually abandoned by his father, usually forced to rely on only himself. Amithab was the "angry young man." Amithab was a criminal, a man whom injustice forced outside the law, illegitimate, fatherless, a drinker, a clubgoer, a sophisticated lover of beautiful women, a wreaker of revenge, consumed by his past, lean and dark with a deep, rich voice, consummately urbane, strong and unafraid, melancholy, a man who won in the end or died. Neelam was all these things. But to her confusion, she also identified with the women in the movies. She wanted to wear makeup and lots of heavy gold jewellery and zari-bordered bright silk clothes and be beautiful and have designs in henna on her hands and brow and writhe and sing mujras like Rekha and Zeenat Aman and Parveen Babi and Helen and Bindu. She was torn between being Amithab and being the heroine, knowing that she was both. And if she was corrupted by being both, how would she have the only solace Amithab ever had — the love of a beautiful, sympathetic woman?

Amithab movies stirred her and consoled her and discomfited her. She watched Helen swivel her hips in the den of the dacoit Gabbar Singh and felt a strange wave of something between queasiness and joy. She watched the scene in "Muqaddar ka Sikandar" where the rich girl who will grow up to be Raakhee comes out of her house in the dead of night. The poor boy who will grow up to be Amithab is sleeping on her front steps. He has nowhere to go and no one to help him. The girl leans forward, and without waking him, covers him with the blanket. Which one did she want to be? The girl or the boy? She thought about it until her head hurt. The blanket, she thought finally, but it was an answer both witty and inadequate.

Neelam took her half-finished drink to the table next to the chair she had set her bag on, and returned to the dance floor. One of the songs she had requested had come on. She stood facing the empty center of the floor and waited for the music to enter her. Neelam danced with a slowly disintegrating edge of selfconsciousness. This was exactly what she needed after her lousy day. The DJ played all her house anthems one by one. "Coming on Strong." "Ride the Rhythm." "Let No Man Put Asunder." "Love Dancing." Neelam's moves became deeper and showier. She slid and glided on the waxed wooden floors. "But tonight is the night, that I'm gonna make you mine."

Dance was how she made up for not having any sex. The first black woman she had ever had a crush on had been Donna Summer. She was looking for some hot stuff herself. When she told her mother she was in love, her mother had said, barely glancing at her, "Well, as long as it's not Dionne Warwick. That would be going too far."

That was when she first came to the West. She was about ten years old. They lived in Scarborough, a bleak working class suburb of

Toronto. They were the only Indian family in their neighborhood. Lisa Erwin was a fawn-like girl in her new school who wore a burgundy cloak with a fur-lined hood. When they played tag on the snowy banks outside the school and Neelam was It, Lisa was always the first one she caught. The other kids noticed it and even remarked on it, but when someone finally called her a lesbian, it was because she kept her hands warm in the back pockets of her jeans. She accepted this. She had just read *Claudine at School*, and the relationship between Claudine and Aimee had felt so right that she knew she was one. It didn't seem odd that putting her hands in the back pockets of her jeans was what gave her away. When her stepfather picked her up to take her to the ophthamologist, she announced, "I'm a lesbian."

"Don't be silly," her stepfather said, and opened the car door.

From coming across his Hustler magazine in the closet when she was looking for a box of Kleenex, she learned more about lesbianism. She learned men thought it was really hot.

A few years later, as she did a Cosmo survey on sexuality with her best friend Robyn, she told Robyn about herself. Robyn said that she too would sleep with a woman. Robyn had checked off that she was willing to try nearly all the items on the questionnaire. It was impossible for Neelam to explain that what she felt was different.

Not that Neelam ever felt she was the only one. Neelam was from a post-Stonewall generation and there were books to tell her lesbians were everywhere. She also knew that they were with each other out of feminism and they would be with men except men were patriarchal bastards. Either that or they were lesbians because they were tomboys. She knew she was the only one who wanted the sex. She read all the lesbian-feminist-separatist books and *Surpassing the Love of Men* and two or three pages of *Rubyfruit Jungle*. She read *The Color Purple* and she loved Celie and Shug, but she couldn't identify fully. She had examined her own pussy years before. Besides, she didn't quite relish the idea of sleeping with a bisexual woman. Shug eventually left Celie for a man. That's the way it was. More importantly, Shug wasn't so much overwhelmed with desire for Celie as moved by her oppression. This was not quite Neelam's dream of love.

Neelam had stopped watching Jeannie, and barely noticed her when she brushed by. Neelam was dancing with her eyes closed the better to feel the beat. "You used to hold me, you used to touch me;" she moved her hands along her arms. She took advantage of the extra room, sauntering down the length of the floor before striking a pose. "You used to squeeze me, you used to please me."

Finally, the DJ played some lethargically slow Jodeci song and Neelam sat down. She gulped down the rest of her screwdriver. The no-name brand vodka hit her straight between her legs. Good music, booze, what else was there, she thought happily. A jug of wine, a house record and thou. Oh yeah, that. She crossed her legs and leaned back.

Other lesbians had close friendships that flowered into sexual love but Neelam couldn't imagine looking at her friends that way. It was not the way she wanted it, but she supposed that was the way it happened. Even after she got into the bar scene and saw women cruise each other, she didn't shake off this belief. She had gone out with one self-described "stud" who despised women and asked Neelam if she would have the baby if the "stud" made her pregnant. Then a femme who spent hours giving Neelam dewy looks turned out to have a boyfriend. Thus, Neelam concluded that the only women who would come to her were pathological or sleeping with men.

She wished she didn't want it. She wished she could be content with her work and her ambitions and her beautiful apartment and her hobbies. She wished she could be a repressed crone. But she couldn't. She wanted to be swept away.

As if on cue, the DJ played the Diana Ross song. There was no one left on the dance floor, but that didn't deter the DJ from her line-up. Neelam pushed the table away from herself so she could stretch out her legs and wait out the slow set. The transsexual who had been vogueing up a storm a little while back was sitting at the table across the aisle, next to Jeannie. Jeannie leaned over to whisper to the transsexual who turned around and looked at Neelam.

Neelam ignored it. The transsexual turned around again. What the hell was he... she... it looking at? What the fuck were they talking about? Neelam sucked her teeth. It was bad enough that she had to accept that a woman like Jeannie wouldn't want her, but did she have to also accept that Jeannie would make fun of her with some transsexual? Just as she was crushing the empty plastic cup, the transsexual loomed in front of her. "My friend is too shy to come over but she'd like to dance with you."

Neelam wondered if it was some kind of prank. She resigned herself to falling for it. Neelam looked down and nodded.

Jeannie strode to the dance floor and Neelam followed, her eyes lowered. They danced and Neelam felt too embarrassed to even look up. She was suddenly hyperconcious of her body and her movements were stiff and deliberate. A little liquor made Neelam feel dainty but a little more made her acutely aware of her heaviness. Jeannie asked her her name, and where she lived and where she was from. "I'm Indian," Neelam said, stopping to catch her breath. "As soon as I tell a woman that, she offers to teach me to dance."

"That's ridiculous," Jeannie said. She pulled Neelam to her as the first beats of "Housecall" started. "You know you have rhythm," she leaned down and whispered in the shell of Neelam's ear. Neelam blushed. Suddenly, everything was going right, and her anxiousness was eased. She felt like she was floating in a dream. She rested her face lightly on Jeannie's chest, the soft cotton jersey against her cheek so she could smell Jeannie's musk on it. Neelam put her arms around Jeannie's waist and gently scooped air with her hips. They were in a corner, near the speaker and through her half-closed eyes, Neelam could see the lights fading down until the dance floor was dark.

When they became tired, Jeannie bought her a drink and after Neelam had downed that, Jeannie took her outside for a breath of fresh air.

The outside air was in fact heavy and moist, hot summer night air that was waiting to break. Jeannie stood against the brick wall of the bar. "Do you want to see some pictures?" she asked. Neelam nodded. There wasn't anything else to do.

Jeannie fished her wallet out of her backpack and showed Neelam some faded snapshots of women in jaunty toques sitting around a table. "That's my grandmother when she was young." Jeannie flipped the page and showed her a heavily airbrushed studio picture of a woman with a big white bow in her hair and gleaming white teeth. "And that's my mother."

"Where's your girlfriend?" Neelam asked flirtatiously.

"I don't have a picture of her," Jeannie replied, putting her wallet back.
"You have a girlfriend?"

"Yes," Jeannie said. "Don't you?"

"No. What the fuck are you doing plying me with alcohol?"

"Being friendly." Jeannie pulled the strap of her backpack over her shoulder. "I wasn't making a move on you." Neelam pouted. "Come on, let's sit down." Jeannie led her across Seventh Avenue and through a few deserted side streets to a church with wide, white steps. They sat down on the top stair.

Neelam was silent. She has a girlfriend, Neelam thought. She has a girlfriend. There was always something wrong.

The first woman to make a move on her was a crazy closeted Bahamian bank teller. Neelam had been a little over fourteen and had noticed Rosemarie right away when she went to deposit the $40 she had earned compiling the listings at a real estate office. Rosemarie was tall and warm brown, with a big chest and expressive hands. The first time they actually spoke was weeks later, when they met by accident at the bus stop. Rosemarie told Neelam that Neelam cheered her so much that she wanted to know Neelam always, and she gave her her phone number. On their first date, Neelam brought Rosemarie a teddy bear with a pink bow around its neck, since Rosemarie had said she liked stuffed animals, and Rosemarie had bought her a brooch and a purse.

They rode the subway to a tiny Palestinian restaurant on Bathhurst, and Neelam shouted to Rosemarie above the train rattle that she was beautiful.

"I'm not beautiful," Rosemarie protested, smiling. "I am not beautiful at all. You should see me without my clothes on." She paused. Neelam began to wonder what she meant. "If you come to my apartment, I'll take my clothes off and show you."

The train pulled into Lawrence station. They walked through the fluorescent-lit corridor to the escalator to the street level and tentatively, Neelam took Rosemarie's hand in her own. Rosemarie squeezed her hand, her gold rings pressing into Neelam's palm. At the end of the dinner, which Neelam paid because Rosemarie didn't have much money, as they said goodbye in the subway station because they were going home in separate directions, they stood close and Rosemarie leaned down, her thick lips an inch away from Neelam, and Neelam reached up to kiss her lightly on the mouth. "You can't do that, that's a devil thing," Rosemarie said. Neelam drew away in surprise.

Rosemarie, it turned out, was a Pentecostal. They talked a few more times, and she accused Neelam of trying to seduce her. Neelam wondered if she had misread the situation? How could one misread "let me take you home and show you my naked body"? Did women generally buy presents for other women they barely knew the first time they went out together? Did women generally make friends in the subway station? Neelam stopped calling Rosemarie. It was all too complicated.

The next woman she went out with was years later and in a different country, but the situation was just as ridiculous. This woman was a Texan "stud" who told Neelam, "You are attracted to black women because you want a 'big, black buck,'" and Neelam wondered if this was true why she was with a woman who was decidedly wimpy in bed. Later, the Texan told her that they should be just friends and then told Neelam she wanted to fist her. And then she said they should be just friends, and then she told Neelam she wanted to eat her pussy. After a few rounds of this, getting neither friendship nor sex, Neelam gave up and the Texan ran off with a Dominican girl who it later turned out was pregnant by her live-in boyfriend who knew all about the Texan, so there was a modicum of karma. Then the Texan became the mistress of a rich butch chiropractor who took the Texan on all-expenses paid holidays to Puerto Rico, so maybe there wasn't any justice after all.

And Jeannie had a girlfriend. Neelam sighed. Her butt hurt from the rough concrete stair. And the air was like a layer on her skin. She watched the flies buzz around the streetlight in front of the church and screwed up her eyes until it was all a blur. She could hear crickets and cars and some people having a conversation around the corner. Why were there crickets in the city? *"And, girlfriend, I told that boy he was out of his mind. He can take his fine self and jump in the river. This is no ordinary woman. I do not need to be taking this,"* a husky voice said. The other person laughed. Neelam was suddenly hungry. She realized she hadn't eaten dinner. She had bought a bag of sour cream and onion bagel chips right after she got off work, but she had had to stand and hold the bar on the train so she hadn't had a chance to eat it and then she forgot about it. Neelam took it out of her bag and ripped it open.

"Do you want one?" she asked, as chips tumbled from the packet. She held one out.

Jeannie shook her head.

Neelam ate it and held out her salty fingers.

Jeannie looked down at Neelam's outstretched arm, her fingers tipped with a paste of onion flecks and salt, and then back at Neelam's face. The streetlamp's yellowy light made Neelam's light skin and her white blouse glisten. The street suddenly fell silent. And Jeannie said, "You know how bad I want to suck them."

Neelam felt her pussy clench. She barely perceptibly leaned towards Jeannie and then they kissed, Jeannie's tongue sliding into her mouth. Jeannie said, "Are you trying to make me unfaithful to my girlfriend?" and kissed her harder. Just then, a man came out of the church and Jeannie pulled Neelam towards her to let him pass by. Neelam sat, triumphant, between Jeannie's thighs, Jeannie's arms around her waist. The alcohol was beginning to wear off and everything seemed in sharper focus. Jeannie's arms felt heavier around her, Jeannie's bare legs warmer beneath her hands.

Soon a white straight couple came to sit at the bottom of the stairs, and they rose. "Do you want to go the Pier?" Jeannie asked. Neelam nodded. That *was* after all what gay people did. Jeannie led her through the dark maze of the West Village. They passed a group of fags and the flaming bald queen at the forefront cackled, "Now that girl has got some beautiful big breasts." Neelam laughed, embarrassed.

"Even fags notice," Jeannie teased her.

"Please, I can't even get a girlfriend."

"I can't believe you don't have a lover."

"Neither can I," Neelam replied.

This was not strictly true. Sometimes she could and sometimes she couldn't. For one thing, she was short. She somehow felt she hadn't fulfilled her potential by being short. When she was a kid, everyone thought she would take after her uncle who was six feet tall, but around sixth grade, just as all the other kids started growing, she stopped. Now, she was short. And plump and unathletic. It seemed incongruous. Lesbians were supposed to be tall and lean and androgynous, weren't they? Either that or shapeless feminist blobs. Renee said that was a white lesbian thing. But that was who wrote the books. Except for "Tar Beach." Maybe Jeannie would take her home and plunge vegetables in her. Not that this was her particular fantasy.

The Pier was fairly desolate, even though it was a warm, sultry night, maybe because it was Wednesday. There were some banjees at the other end, but that was it. Before they crossed the highway, Neelam said she needed to use the ladies' room, so they stopped in at Kellers.

When they entered, Neelam saw that they were the only women among the dozen people in the place. The rest were what Neelam thought of in decade-old slang as "rough trade." Jeannie checked the bathroom for toilet paper, and gave Neelam some cocktail napkins before standing guard over the lockless door. The toilet was filthy, but Neelam couldn't afford to discriminate after two drinks. She washed her hands.

When she came out, Jeannie was sitting at the bar. "Will you buy me a drink?" Neelam gently pushed her luck, emboldened by Jeannie having kissed her. Jeannie nodded. Neelam climbed onto a torn leather barstool and ordered a gingerale. It was something cheap at least. Jeannie didn't order anything for herself. They sat for a few minutes watching two skinny men in jogging suits play pool. Neelam sipped the cloyingly sweet ginger ale. She felt giddy like a little girl, a spoilt little girl. She didn't often have a chance to feel this way and it did feel good. She put her drink down. They went across to the Pier.

"Why don't you have a girlfriend? Are you really picky?" Jeannie asked, heaving herself onto the low wall. Jeannie had just been laid off of her job as a secretary in some city government office.

"I just want a good-looking, tall woman of color who is goal-oriented and doesn't have any diseases, addictions, or severe neuroses," Neelam replied. It was her rehearsed spiel. She, who had once said she would never sleep with someone who hadn't read Flaubert, had gone out with a sorter at UPS who was thinking of getting her GED, a greeneyed 28year-old prison guard, various fillers of the unemployment rolls, and a drug dealer or two. And Marita, which was not worth mentioning. "I don't know what it takes. Tell me about your girlfriend."

But Jeannie wouldn't say anything beyond the woman's name and that she was from Barbados. She wouldn't tell Neelam what she did. "She's not a prostitute, is she?" Neelam was suddenly afraid.

Jeannie sucked her teeth. "I wish she was. Then maybe she'd be making some real money." She looked down at Neelam, who was standing in front of her. "What do you do?"

"I work at a museum up in Harlem," she said. "And I write book reviews for a magazine and tutor high-school kids." She said it with an edge of spite.

"I guess you're very productive." Jeannie looked over at a group of Latino homeboys carrying a stereo who were coming toward them.

"Freud said civilization was built on sexual frustration," Neelam replied, carelessly, looking at the lights on the river.

"You're sexually frustrated?" Jeannie asked, with a slight smile. Neelam nodded. "So what is it you want in bed?"

Neelam looked up at Jeannie. And Neelam told her.

"You got a light?" a mustachioed Latino asked. Jeannie produced a fake gold lighter from her bag. Each of the men lit their blunts. "You want one?" another one asked in a heavy accent. Jeannie and Neelam shook their heads, and the men left, a refrain of merengue trailing after them.

Neelam and Jeannie were the only ones left on the Pier. The sky was gray and troubled, and behind them the river was like a slick, black sheet smudged with Jersey lights, and it seemed as if the river and the sky had exchanged places. The street lamps were dim. Neelam could make out the edges of a big neon pink sign for a triple X place of some kind a little up the highway. A police car screeched past. Jeannie was looking down at her hands. Neither of them said anything. A hesitant breeze rustled the edges of Neelam's palazzo pants. "My nails are kind of long," Jeannie said at last. She paused. Neelam looked up at her, wondering what was coming next. "Do you have a nail clipper at your house?" Jeannie asked, drawing Neelam into her arms.

Neelam pressed herself against Jeannie. "Yes," she said, putting her arms around Jeannie's waist. "Yes."

She drew back. Jeannie was beautiful. She looked a little bit like Monie Love. Her lips were thick and wide and juicy and she was wearing red-red lipstick. Jeannie seized her by the shoulders and Neelam felt Jeannie's fingers pressing into her flesh and Jeannie's braids grazing her ears and neck as Jeannie kissed her. Neelam felt as if she was melting between her legs. "Let's go," she said. "Let's take a cab."

Jeannie hopped down from the wall. Neelam was walking to the island in the middle of the highway to catch an uptown taxi.

Jeannie grabbed her elbow.

Some guy rolled down his car window and some other guy in the back seat shouted, "Are you lesbians?" "Yes," Neelam said over her shoulder. She was laughing.

"Baby, I can eat pussy," the man said, craning his head out of the window.

"Yeah, but you don't have a pussy for me to eat," Neelam shouted back.

Jeannie squeezed her hand. "Listen," she said. "You know I'm not working, right, so we have to split the cab." Neelam pouted. This was not exactly romantic. Nothing ever happened to her the way it should. "Alright?" Neelam shook her head with a toss. Jeannie began to walk away towards the mouth of Christopher Street.

"Jeannie!" Neelam called out. A taxi had stopped and Neelam was holding the door open. They got in and Neelam leaned her head on Jeannie's shoulder and watched the lights swim by and Jeannie slipped her hand between Neelam's thighs.

It had been a couple of months since a woman had touched Neelam. Since Marita. Neelam inwardly winced. Marita was in her late thirties and not quite pretty, with a voice corrupted by years of smoking. When they met, Marita had had her hair natural and this had excited Neelam. Neelam enjoyed courting Marita, she had never done it and it had its pleasures. She had refused to let Marita touch her the first few times they were together, holding Marita's arms behind Marita's back when they kissed and moving away if Marita resisted.

From the beginning, she had known Marita was living with someone but Marita had said they were breaking up and Diane was in the process of looking for another place. Weeks later and with no progress on that score, and since she found Marita's kisses slobbery and repulsive, and after the rather annoying discovery that Diane had courted Marita similarly when they first met, Neelam let go. She had liked the idea of being courtly with an older plain woman who had never been cherished before, but she was hardly going to follow in some squat, uneducated former lover's footsteps. It was somewhat humiliating to think that she couldn't draw Marita away from Diane. She had a whole lot more going for her than both of them put together. She had declined when Marita suggested they stay friends. She didn't find her interesting on that level. As she joked to Billy, "You date someone because you wouldn't want to know them as a friend." Besides, Marita had gotten braids. Perhaps it was Halle's remark that Marita resembled a girl they had gone to school with, a girl whom Neelam found quite unappetizing, that finally soured her attraction to Marita. That and the uncomfortable sensation of sleeping against someone with narrow shoulders.

After Rosemarie, Jeannie was the first woman that Neelam had been with who wasn't skinny. Neelam cuddled up to Jeannie. It was so nice. Broad shoulders, a big chest. Jeannie pressed her hand down.

Finally, they got to her apartment. "It's a little messy," Neelam said, opening the door.

"Do you live alone?" Jeannie asked as she entered the small studio apartment littered with books and papers. After a quick glance at the time, Neelam went into the bathroom to run the bath water. To her surprise, it was nearly one in the morning. How had it gotten so terribly late?

Neelam felt soiled by her long day. Besides, she had taken a leak at Kellers, and she didn't want Jeannie to touch her without washing herself.

She had a beautiful bathroom. The building had been a house once, and the rooms had been redivided, so the bathroom was quite large. She had an old tub with claw feet. The walls and the shower curtains were blue and the cloth mat was nubby pink and blue, and a pastel fish of 3D jigsaw pieces stood on the window ledge. The enormous counter around the sink was full of tubes of lipstick and bottles of perfume and her pink soap pig and other pretty things. Her toothbrush was in an small jar full of cowry shells. Neelam picked up the cherry-scented bubble bath.

Jeannie had locked the door and was sitting on the edge of her bed. "Can I use the phone?" she asked.

"Yes," Neelam said, over the sound of the gushing water. "Who are you calling?"

"My girlfriend," Jeannie replied. "I told her I'd be there when she got home from work, so I have to call and make up something."

Neelam said nothing. Jeannie was not being particularly tactful, but after her own behavior right before they caught the cab, she had not much right to complain. Besides which, Neelam knew from Jeannie's gaucheries that she wasn't used to this kind of thing. But she couldn't help herself with me, Neelam thought happily.

She unbuttoned her blouse and took off her pants. She was wearing a lace white one-piece with satin cups. Nice underclothes gave her an extra bit of confidence on a date, but she didn't think of why she was wearing it. It suited the moment, that was all.

Jeannie came in and fingered its satin spaghetti straps. "I guess you were planning on bringing someone home with you," she said.

"I've never done this before," Neelam said truthfully, but the idea of her as a deliberate, lingeried seductress was not displeasing. She reached over and turned the water off. She put a finger in the tub. The water was nice and hot. The mirror was covered with steam. Jeannie pulled off her jersey and hooked it on the doorknob.

Neelam undid her ponytail. "You are beautiful," Jeannie said.

"I know," Neelam replied. And at that moment, she did.

"I know you know."

"But no one loves me," said Neelam, sadly.

"You know if I didn't have a girlfriend, I would scoop you up," said Jeannie. Neelam raised her eyes. And then Jeannie scooped her up.

They sat in the bathtub with Neelam's back against Jeannie's chest. Neelam could feel Jeannie's thick, stiff nipples poking against her. Neelam splashed the hot, soapy water over Jeannie's strong legs. There should have been music in the background, but Neelam knew it would spoil the mood to go turn some on. Without a great deal of gentleness, Jeannie entered her. "Didn't you ask about the nailcipper," Neelam reminded her, wriggling away.

Jeannie rose. Neelam washed herself quickly.

Jeannie upset the contents of the jar that held the nail clipper and clipped her nails, letting the cuttings fall on the floor. "There is a wastepaper basket right over there," Neelam remarked, getting out of the tub.

"Now you'll have to clean before you invite the next person up," said Jeannie.

Neelam wrapped herself in her blue towel. "There doesn't have to be a next person, you know," she said, tentatively, going into the other room.

But Jeannie had a girlfriend, she thought. She felt cold in the bed and got under the covers. She threw the towel on the floor. "Turn off the light," she said, and Jeannie did.

And then Jeannie crawled into her bed, shoving the blanket aside.

Neelam knew what the inside of her pussy felt like. She had felt it. And though it was fine, she couldn't imagine a woman wanting to be there. What for? It wasn't that she thought it was icky, just unexciting, and yet she wanted a woman to want it. Her fantasies always abruptly veered into trying to imagine why exactly a woman *would* want it. She knew that she wasn't overcome by the desire to be inside another woman, so why would another woman want to be inside her? Women probably did it out of politeness. Billy said he sucked dick because he liked his dick sucked. This was simply not good enough for Neelam. But fags have anal sex, which they can both feel. What a ridiculous thing a lesbian was. Two polite women doing boring things. Didn't any woman want it? She was forced to admit that she never looked at a woman and wanted to suck her pussy or get inside her. The thought just never occurred to her. She never thought at all about the act of sleeping with a woman she knew. Neelam somehow felt that it was impinging on the woman because the woman might not want to sleep with her. Neelam rarely appeared in the fantasies she used to get off on and the other kind rarely managed to overpower this kind of discussion. When she did succeed in suspending her disbelief, she felt like she had cheated. The only way she believed a woman could want another woman was out of pathology, like the Texan. The Texan wanted to be a man. In fact, the Texan liked to pretend her lovers were men. The Texan wanted to be a fag. This was too much for Neelam. She never had much luck when she tried to explain her quandary to other people. They would describe scenarios where two women could come at the same time, but that wasn't the point. She wanted a woman to be stimulated by what was stimulating her, not by the idea of stimulating her.

"You think too much," Marcia said.

"What choice do I have? I never have any sex," Neelam replied.

As Jeannie got inside her, she wondered what was going on in Jeannie's mind, but knew better than to ask. Why were women so ridiculous, she wondered. Why couldn't she just believe?

"Do you have any lubricant?" Jeannie asked.

Neelam reached for her breast. "We have to do this the natural way,' she said. "Besides, I'm so wet."

"You're so tight." Jeannie looked down at Neelam's pussy. "And your clitoris is overgrown."

"Overgrown?" said Neelam. Not again. She pulled her thighs a little closer.

"It's enormous," Jeannie said. "It looks like a little dick."

"Oh, stop!" Neelam was half-laughing and half-insulted. It was no doubt the reason she was a lesbian, at least according to medieval Europeans. That and the porno magazines of her stepfather's that she came across as a child, and her domineering mother, and some inner perversity that disposed her towards the impossible.

She leaned over to suck Jeannie's breasts. There was not a whole lot else she could do in the position they were in. Jeannie's pussy was beyond the reach of her hand. She wondered if Jeannie was having a good time. Neelam wondered if Jeannie was bored with probing the guck of her pussy. Straight women had it so easy. All they had to do was lie there and a man would be satisfied. Besides, everyone always said that the only thing a straight man wanted was pussy. Straight women didn't have to ask themselves how and why and if this was true. Why did a woman want pussy, and did any women really ever want it at all?

Jeannie made her lie back, and plunged deeper inside her. Neelam arched up to accommodate Jeannie more easily. Jeannie tried to put it all inside her. Neelam clenched her teeth. She didn't want Jeannie to stop but it was beginning to hurt. Jeannie's powerful movements made Neelam's whole pussy shake. Finally she couldn't take anymore. "You're hurting my clit," she cried out, squirming, her body involuntarily lifting off the bed.

Jeannie said breathlessly, "Can't you move it?"

Neelam was dumbstruck. Jeannie was staring at her as if she expected a response. She doesn't want to stop, Neelam thought with astonishment, she wants to be inside my guck. If she is unwilling to stop, then it means she wants to. And suddenly she realized that it was possible and Jeannie wanted her and everything tumbled into place. As ridiculous as the comment really was, it thrilled Neelam. She felt as if her lungs were full of clear mountain air, and she was almost crying. She moved Jeannie's hand out of her and pulled Jeannie on top of her. "You didn't even come yet," Jeannie said, reproachfully.

"It doesn't matter," Neelam replied, ridiculously happy. She wants it, she wants me. She really does. It's not just to make me happy. She wants to.

They lay in silence for a while. Then Jeannie shifted to lie beside her. "I have to go soon," said Jeannie. "My girlfriend is expecting me." Neelam rose and put on her ruby-colored satin nightshirt.

Neelam turned on the light and looked at Jeannie, her dark, beautiful naked body. Jeannie was about to draw the covers over her, but Neelam stopped her. "Don't," she said. She parted Jeannie's legs. "I've never really seen a pussy." This was not strictly true, but it was close enough.

Jeannie laughed and unclenched her thighs. "I'll let you see mine," she said in her rich voice. And she did.

Neelam remembered Jeannie fondly, even though she never saw her again. As a sleepy Neelam stood by the door to lock it after Jeannie left, Jeannie paused awkwardly and said, "I guess I'll see you at the club." Even while lying in bed, she had said she would keep an eye on Neelam in the club to see who else Neelam was picking up. The next few times Neelam went into the Box, she expected to see Jeannie, but she never did.

Right afterwards, Neelam felt cold and sluttish and guilty, but not for long. She was full of Jeannie, and when a friend from high school whom she hadn't talked to in years called up, she helplessly started telling Kathy about what had happened.

Kathy was initially discomfited by the turn the conversation was taking, but then her curiosity overcame her other emotions. "So when did you know you were...," Kathy asked.

"What is there to know?" Neelam responded. "It has nothing to do with knowing. It has do with your pussy getting hot. Ask me when I knew a woman could feel the same way about me. That's what you have to realize. That's what you have to learn. Your pussy getting hot is an involuntary physical reaction. It's the other thing you have to figure out or find out or have shown to you, because the world does not want you to know." Kathy was silent. "Alright, when I was in fifth grade, after reading Colette," said Neelam, to keep the conversation rolling.

Neelam didn't always have the faith, but thinking of Jeannie always improved how she was feeling. Once, after eyeing a dark, hard dread all night, just as she was getting her coat from the coat check because it was obvious that this eye contact thing was not working and she was ready to go home, the dread touched her elbow. The woman made mildly flirtatious conversation and asked for her number, and just as Neelam was settling in to enjoy the moment, the woman said, "Let me ask you something. I see a lot of Indian girls with acne on their faces, is that a really common thing?"

Neelam reeled from the shock and rushed out the door. It had been almost a year since that time with Jeannie and that was the last time she had been with a woman. She felt ugly and empty and she felt like it would never happen. The drinks she had downed and the year of celibacy made her feel weak and insecure. She would never find anyone, she thought, crying, but then she stopped, because she thought maybe she was overdoing it and besides she would find her woman. At least the women were getting better and better, so one day, she would actually have a girlfriend.

She undressed and got into bed, remembering Jeannie's pussy. It had such pink petals. She had wanted to suck it, but it would be her first time, and she knew she would be terribly depressed later if her first time was in a one-night stand. She had contented herself with a swipe of her finger to taste Jeannie, and Jeannie tasted slightly bitter, like appleseed or pink champagne. Jeannie's pussy was so pretty and rimmed with dark, tightly napped hair like a pink rose surrounded by baby's breath. She had leaned closer to the pink jewel at its heart, and she had seen, Neelam remembered with a smile, Possibility.

Lê Thi Diem Thúy

Foresee

you said
why does it take so long to be

night time?

i never thought it would take so long
to get dark

and you were waiting for
the kiss
the confession
the surprise
the aching
denial
the aching
desire

say
a fire comes
and
takes us
say
we just didn't know
it would be
like
this

we didn't know it could be

let it be
let it go

you grasp hands full of
sand
let it fall between your toes

if i win the lottery
i will have a house
on skinny legs which
always threatens
to fall
into the ocean
and
it has
a winding staircase
which
falls down
into the ocean
and
every morning
every time
i wake up with you
climbing
with me
down
into the ocean

then

it's night time
coming
dark

like i always knew
it could
be

Ana Bantigue Fajardo

Island Dream

Long ago before the whites came
you watched me
from afar
as I paddled my *banca*
up on to the shore
returning from a fishing trip.
You noticed the way
my muscles
tightened
as I drove my paddle
gently through
the ocean waters.
My brown skin
perfectly baked from
the tropical sun,
my rich black hair
dripping with sea water
and sweat —
You noticed the
intensity of my Pinay —
Pilipina eyes —
the way I was one with
my canoe
> with my paddle
> with our mother sea

You waited for me
to ride the wave in,
and you watched as
I slipped my *sarong* off
and lay on the sand
to rest.
You noticed the way
my breasts were
flawlessly molded —
Parang Mayon Volcano,
ang inisip mo. Kay ganda.
How beautiful — you thought.
It was then you could wait no longer
so you approached me.
Malacas na babae, kailangan ko kita.
Strong woman, I need you.

Vanessa Marzan Deza

Warm Weather Thoughts

mid-july waiting
on the one freak day
that bay area summer
was actually hot
HOT... huffpphh
at the bus stop
smelling the thick and sweet
overripe melon scent from
oakland chinatown
inhaling the overpowering perfume
of a powder-haired granny
seated by me in a thick woollen jacket
i suffocate for her/filling my lungs
with tea rose scent so strong
i can taste it bitter in my throat
i can't stand this heat
that makes noses bleed
and dogs drag their bellies
on the lawn.

been waiting for 30 minutes or so
warm air blows up my skirt
from the #40 bus exhaust
here under the sun
with my bareback warmed
by the wooden bench smoldering
in 103 degrees weather
sandaled feet soaking in heat waves
rising from the sidewalk
summer dress pressed
wet against my thighs

i think of your cool tongue
lifting up the hem
my hands thrusting deep into
your sweat-drenched hair
bringing you so close
your breasts graze my hips
as you plant a kiss on my navel
your cool tongue burns my heated flesh

travelling
down
down
down
you brush against mute lips
licking, coaxing them to speak in
moans — wet and drawn — come from
between my legs
travelling up to escape
long and drawn from my throat
silence comes only when
you hold my hips steady
steady
steady
and
beep beep beep
here comes my bus
and i need to unstick myself off this bench.

Minal Hajratwala

Brewing Secrets

You ask me for a secret and I
have nothing to say
My secrets are too dark
to be told over
this pale beer
golden as champagne
sticky on the table where you spilled it
with one wild sweep of

That hand on the door of my car
"Don't think I've forgotten," you say,
"You owe me a secret"
I shake my head, mumble
The secret is

this smile is a mask
as fragile
and opaque as what I peel
from my body each night
The secret is

I want to weep
when we embrace

Between our bodies
are layers,
each as thick
as this wooden ale-stained table,
as my skin
       not pale amber but
       the color of Guinness,
as the secrets
I do not tell

Ami R. Mattison

Misplacing Alissa

MY LOVER HAS A LOVER WHOSE LOVER IS ALISSA. I KNOW ALISSA from my lover's conversations with her lover, which she repeats to me. Alissa is a chemist. She works for DuPont. In her spare time, she photographs urban architecture and sells prints to local corporate offices in Dallas. Also, Alissa avoids travelling by airplanes. She refuses to eat eggplant and to own cats.

While on her second business trip during the month of April, my lover calls me on the telephone from Texas, four states away from me along the southern coast. Over the phone, my lover tells me the story about how she met her lover: My lover and her would-be lover drove for drinks to a small bar, just the other side of the border. As they drove back, they stopped at an overlook. They walked to the edge of the cliff and looked across the canyon. They kissed.

"I don't understand," I say. "You were standing atop a mesa? Looking down at the canyon? And she kissed you? Just like that? Kissed you?"

"Well, it went something like that," my lover says. "I mean, she says she likes me. She says she wants to know me better."

"She wants to know you better? What does that mean? She wants to fuck your brains out?" I laugh to let my lover know I'm hurt, but my lover says nothing.

Then, she says: "April is a *nice* woman. I like her."

My lover's voice is sincere; her sentences are precise. I wonder what she isn't telling me. I ask, "You met a woman? Named April? During the month of April? What if it's bad luck?"

"It might be good luck," my lover says.

"It might," I say, "be."

When my lover returns home from her business trip, we discuss non-monogamy over a pasta dinner and a bottle of cabernet. Afterwards, we drink cups of coffee and smoke pot. Also, we have sex on our new futon, the one that we've wanted for the past four years. Then, we sit cross-legged, facing one another, and smoke cigarettes.

My lover says she loves me. She says everything will be okay. I try to ignore the compressed pain in my belly. I want to believe her. I tell her she should do what she wants to do.

I think, maybe, I can find another friend, too. Already, I have a woman in mind, but I'm not sure if she does women. I think nothing of not knowing this information. All I can think is to find someone else to fill up my time when my lover is involved with her lover.

"Do what you want," I say, again. "Maybe, it'll be fun."

After a few weeks at home, my lover takes another business trip for three weeks. She schedules the weekends before and after for pleasure, for time with her new lover. She calls me on the telephone to tell me she's having a great vacation in Texas.

I want to tell my lover these things: Our flannel bed sheets still smell of her; our collection of house plants are wilting, except the potted palm; and the light bulbs are burning out, room by room.

Instead, I tell my lover that our dog misses her. "During your absence, the dog has taken to strange behavior," I say. "She won't eat. She's tired when I get up in the morning. I think she's having a hard time sleeping at night."

My lover breathes into the telephone. "There's nothing wrong with the dog." She tells me: "Exercise her more, and she'll be tired at night."

I say nothing.

"Look, if you don't want to do this, then you need to tell me," my lover says. "You need to tell me now, before things get deeper and more involved."

I say nothing.

"Don't just sit there and say nothing," my lover says.

"I'm standing," I say.

"Stop it." I hear my lover smoking a cigarette. I hear her inhale deep and then blow smoke in one hurried rush. "Don't do this to me," she says.

"I'm not *doing* anything," I say. "Rachel. I'm not doing anything to you. I'm trying to keep things going here while you're gone. There are bills to pay, you know. The house has to be cleaned. The dog and cats have to be fed. And the dog, the dog is acting very strange."

My lover breathes deep. "I told you: walk the dog."

I don't like this telephone conversation. I don't like the tone in my lover's voice, careful and controlled, as if she's talking to a child or to someone very dull and thick-headed. I tell my lover not to worry. I tell her: "I'll take care of the goddamn dog."

I take another lover. I know her from my classes at the university. She's intelligent and a performance artist. She wears wire-rimmed glasses, which make her very attractive. She reminds me of every nice woman I've ever known. Her name is Clover.

"Clover?" My lover asks, "What kind of name is Clover?"

"She's vegetarian," I answer.

"It figures."

"Perhaps," I say. "But April during the month of April is trite, almost obscenely trite."

My lover says: "April is a *nice* name."

"Yeah, if you like rainy months."

My lover is silent on the other end of the telephone line.

"April, Clover," I continue. "Maybe I should find a woman named May. It might make things easier to remember."

"Nothing," my lover says, "could make things easier."

I want to tell my lover more important things. I want to tell her about the disturbing dreams that wake me and keep me up at night, about my increasing inability to eat, about the recurring burn in my belly. Instead, I ask, "Whatever happened to simple names? Whatever happened to Alissa?"

My lover says, "Alissa is not simple. She's giving April a very hard time. Alissa is difficult. Alissa is impossible."

My lover tells me that Alissa has avoided April for two weeks. Alissa says she's busy. She goes to dance bars every night. She attends concerts to listen to live progressive rock music. Alissa told April that she took a new lover. Alissa says she's having a great time.

"She doesn't seem unhappy," I say.

"Well, she's been very difficult with April."

"Maybe I should be so difficult," I say.

"This phone call is expensive," my lover replies.

I say to my lover: "I miss you, Rachel."

"I know."

"I wish you were here with me."

"I know," my lover repeats. "You tell me, *everyday*."

My lover repeats to me stories about Alissa's childhood. Once, Alissa's spiteful cousin threw the family kitten into a black wood-burning stove. Alissa has nightmares about it. She dreams that a cat is burning alive, hears it screaming to death, as she searches for the source of an awful stench throughout a house with many rooms. When she finds the black wood-burning stove in her dreams, it's cold and empty.

I'm impressed by Alissa's dream. I find it difficult not to reduce Alissa's pain to overwrought Freudian symbolism. I decide Alissa is reasonable in her refusal to love cats. I try to imagine Alissa, looking like every nice woman I've ever known. I can only think of her as forever a horrified child.

I remember photographs of myself when I was a young girl. I imagine Alissa with dark hair, dark eyes, dark skin, like me, standing on our front porch on the first day of grade school and wearing a green and yellow plaid dress, her long hair pulled back with a bright yellow ribbon. Her hands are by her side. Her face is serious, unsmiling. My older brother stands beside her. He holds two fingers, a peace sign, over her head and laughs. My mother takes the picture.

Clover invites me to dinner.

"I have something I need to talk about," Clover tells me.

I swirl wine in a glass. I hold its stem between my fingers. These days, I'm reluctant to engage in conversations that even approach double meanings. I think, I've had my fill of underlying agendas. However, I decide Clover is honest and trustworthy. Clover is direct.

"I don't think we should continue this relationship," says Clover. "I'm not in a place where I can have any demands on me. I really need some space right now to sort through my mixed emotions."

"I understand," I say, though I don't because this is the first time Clover has mentioned her mixed emotions.

Clover takes a breath, holds it, and looks me direct in the eyes: "I'm trying to work things out between me and my boyfriend."

I spill cabernet on the white table cloth. I look down at my plate of lettuce. I set my glass precisely over the wine stain.

While Clover talks in a hurried, rehearsed way about some guy named "Scott" or "Bill" or something, I think: *Boy. Friend.* I let the two words swirl around in my imagination until they crash together and dissolve to a red stain.

Clover tells me that I'm an intelligent and attractive woman. Clover says she cares about me. She says she's my friend. She says, "I'll call you soon."

During the days, I try to write. Instead, I stare at the purple computer screen and blink at my reflection on its glass surface. Sometimes, I glance through my address book for names of friends to call. All my friends have answering machines. They're never home. Also, I spend hours creating schedules. I schedule time to eat, time to walk the dog, time to write, time to read, time to do research at the library, time to take the car (the one in Rachel's name) to the shop for repairs. I never keep the schedules. I forget to eat. I put off having the car serviced.

One day, I throw the dog's food bowl at the computer screen. The bowl doesn't break. The computer screen remains unscratched. I think: I'm the only thing that breaks around here. I'm the thing falling to pieces.

At night, I try to sleep. Instead, I have long conversations with myself, aloud. I never know who else I'm talking to. Sometimes, I talk to my lover who ends the conversation by saying the phone call costs too much.

Sometimes, I talk to an imaginary therapist.

I tell my imaginary therapist that I'm suffering from an inferiority complex. I tell her I'm masochistic as hell, neurotic and compulsive and manic. I tell her I'm sadistic as hell and suffering from megalomania. I tell her I have a great relationship with my lover.

One night, while talking to myself, I allow myself to cry. I lie face down in my pillow. I cry until I choke on tears and snot. I tell myself to stop crying. I tell myself I'm weak. I tell myself everything will be okay.

I tell myself I need too much. My lover tells me this, as well. I tell myself that I miss my lover less and less. Unreasonably, I tell my lover I miss her more. I fear I can do nothing now without my lover. I tell her: "Our life has gotten out of control."

"I don't understand," she says. "The cats shouldn't be any trouble. All you have to do is feed them. Throw the dog in the backyard if you don't want to walk her. I paid the bills for the entire month and mailed them already. Don't drive the car if you don't want to have it repaired, and you can fix the screen door yourself for cheap."

She breathes into the phone. "Why do you tell me these things? I can't do anything about them. I'm in Texas."

I want to tell my lover I hate our pets, our two cars, our house and the things in it. Instead, I remain silent. My lover is silent, as well.

"This phone call," I say, "is expensive."

Still, Alissa refuses to speak with April. Alissa sees no reason to discuss their relationship while April is involved with my lover. Alissa believes relationships shouldn't require work. If relationships need to be talked about, Alissa thinks, then they shouldn't exist. Alissa hates to process.

I disagree with Alissa. At night, I argue with her. "Communication is vital," I say. "How do we know what each of us wants, if we don't tell one another?"

Alissa remains unpersuaded. She's a stubborn child who dances escape to hard punk music. I drink my beer. I talk and talk, and Alissa remains mute, shaking her dark fist to a silent beat. I reach for her. Then, Alissa tells me that I'm a cat.

My lover tells me I should go to therapy. "Something is wrong with you," she says. "Something is very wrong. You aren't yourself, at all. Talking to someone may help."

"I'm talking to you," I say.

"I don't understand you anymore," my lover says. "You've changed. I don't know you anymore."

"You know me," I say. "You're just not listening."

My lover gets angry. She tells me that she calls me every day. She tells me that she can't do *everything*. She tells me that she's working hard to make money, and I don't understand the kind of pressure she's under to support both of us, since I bring in hardly any income at all because I'm a student and a writer, and I'm not even going to classes anymore, and I'm throwing away an education, and I'm not writing either, am I?

My lover asks, "What the hell is going on? Talk to me."

These are the things I don't tell my lover: I write words, lists of words for hours and hours during the day. I cry for hours and hours during the night. I don't go out of the house anymore. I don't even try to call my friends anymore. I only pick up the phone at seven o'clock when I know it's her calling me. I don't like her anymore.

I don't tell my lover these things because I've already told her. She told me to stop telling her; it hurts her to hear such things. She said she didn't understand; she couldn't do anything to help. She said she was in Texas.

"What the hell is going on?" My lover repeats. "Why the fuck won't you talk to me?"

"This phone call is expensive," I say.

"Don't hang up."

I push the telephone button with my thumb. I hold it down for a long time and then release it. I listen for a dial tone. I lay the receiver off to the side of the phone. I decide to go to therapy.

My therapist's name is Valerie. At first, I think she looks like a tightass. Then, I decide she's just precise and tidy. The first thing Valerie tells me is that I'm normal. I suspect she says this to everyone.

"Seems like a normal problem to me. You're having trouble with your schoolwork, and you've never really had trouble before. When did this trouble begin?"

"Oh, around April or May or maybe March," I say.

"And did anything traumatic happen at about that time?"

I bite my bottom lip with my upper teeth and raise my eyebrows.

"No, not that I remember."

Valerie smiles at me. "Well, we'll figure it out."

Of course, Valerie reminds me of every nice woman I've ever known.

She asks, "What do you think the problem is?"

I laugh, and she asks me why I'm laughing.

I answer "I don't know" to both questions.

Valerie asks me to tell her about my childhood and my family and my relationship with Rachel. I try to be honest with Valerie. I try to be honest with myself. Except, everything I say sounds melodramatic. I sound like a bad paperback version of lesbians, I think.

Valerie is patient. Valerie is kind. She says, "I can see that you're in pain." She says, "You're making perfect sense to me." She says: "I understand how that hurts you." And, "Do you feel jealous?" And, "Perhaps, that's why you feel out of control."

While my lover is away, I go alone to laid-back dyke bars, punk-fag disco dance clubs and mixed leather bars. I ask women back to my house. They have names like "Jody" and "Steve" and "Joan." They all look like every nice woman I've ever known.

When my lover returns, she says she doesn't want to have sex with me anymore if I'm going to have sex with so many other women. "You'll do anything that moves," she says.

I tell her to fuck off.

My lover and I stop having sex. I move my things into the extra bedroom. After a few days, my lover asks me to sleep with her at night. She says I misunderstood about the "anything that moves" comment.

My lover leaves for Texas again. I stop cruising bars at night. I start crying again. I try to remember the days when my lover and I fell in love.

I remember rainy spring afternoons and hours of sex to Billie Holiday's voice, when work at my lover's construction job was cancelled. I remember sitting for hours in uncomfortable chairs, our cold dinner plates on the table in front of us as we talked and talked. I remember her blue eyes, her blue sweat shirt, and her paint-covered jeans. Now, I imagine her, standing in the sun with one hand raised: hello or goodbye.

Dana takes classes at the university. Also, I've seen her at the poetry readings and women-only events that I stopped attending sometime around the month of April. This is the story of how I met Dana:

I was in the grocery store, and I saw Dana, pushing her cart along the opposite side of the baking goods aisle. I pretended that I didn't recognize her, but she stopped and smiled at me.

"Hi," she said.

I nodded my head at her.

"Did you have a nice summer?" she asked.

Dana didn't notice that I wasn't in the mood for a polite chat. Before I could stop her, she launched into a story about her summer vacation. She said she worked in a record store and at a coffee shop, too. She told me about going home to visit her family. She told a funny story about her parents and how they try to ignore that she's lesbian.

I'm in the grocery store. I'm standing in the baking goods aisle. Dana is talking to me. I'm laughing.

I asked Dana if she wanted to go for coffee sometime.

"How about right now?" She asked.

We walked to a coffee shop in the same mall with the grocery store. Dana sat across from me and sipped decaffeinated coffee from a thick white mug. She told me more funny stories. I laughed, and I kept on laughing.

While I command the dog to perform tricks for a biscuit, my lover sits on the futon, writing out checks to pay the house bills. I give the biscuit to the dog, sit on the futon, and look over my lover's shoulder. Then, I tell my lover the story of meeting Dana, but I leave out the laughing part.

We sit in silence for a few minutes.

Finally, my lover asks: "Are you going to finish your schoolwork from last semester?"

I light one of my lover's cigarettes. I tell her I don't want to talk about school.

"You don't want to talk about anything," my lover says. "You haven't wanted to talk about anything important for weeks, for months."

We begin to argue. We accuse each other and talk in loud voices. Finally, I cry. My lover sits in a rocking chair, silent, her body rigid and her eyes looking down. She stabs the ashtray with a half-smoked cigarette.

"I'm done talking to you," my lover says. "I don't want to process anymore. I'm tired." She walks out of the room.

Now, I'm numb from crying. I look at the bills scattered on the futon. The check my lover was writing is made payable to "Southern Bell."

"Change happens." Alissa tells me, during one of my imaginary conversations with her. "We don't choose these things, you know."

I tell Alissa that I hate her now. I imagine my fist square in her face. Then, I imagine busting a hole through my bedroom's puny plaster walls. I call Alissa every obscenity I can think of and even make up a few. I turn my name-calling into a game. I string curse words together into one unbroken, meaningless obscenity: "Jesusfuckjesusfuckjesusfuck." Then, I want to die.

"Change happens," Alissa repeats.

"I know this feeling," I say. "I *know* this feeling."

"Because its old," Alissa says. "Because you've been here before."

When I enter the room, I find my lover sifting through papers on her desk.

"What are you doing?" I ask.

My lover's hands slide in two directions across the desktop. Sheets of paper fall like toy airplanes to the floor. "I've misplaced her."

"Who?" I ask.

My lover presses her lips together, gathers patience.

"Alissa," she says and blinks innocent.

"She's here? Where is she? What have you done to her?"

My lover laughs. She kneels and gathers her papers. "I've misplaced April's photograph of Alissa. It got mixed up with my things. April wants it."

I help my lover look for the photograph of Alissa. I find it, first guess, in a paperback my lover is reading, between pages 38 and 39. I question my lover's judgment about using April's photograph of Alissa to mark her place.

I blink at the photo. Alissa looks nothing like I've imagined her. She has short brown hair, and her eyes are red from the camera's flash. She stands in front of a Christmas tree. To her right is a fireplace with two stockings pinned to the mantle. She's smiling. She holds two fingers in the air — a peace sign.

I turn the photo over. On the back, someone has written in blue ink: Alissa, Xmas 1989. I look at Alissa's picture again. She looks like every nice woman I've ever known. Then, she looks like a stranger.

My lover walks up behind me and glances over my shoulder. Together, we stare for a moment at the photograph. "Thanks," she says, and she takes the photo from my hands.

"Rachel."

My lover turns and looks at me. She smiles and waits.

I pause, and my lover turns her head to one side. She stops smiling for a moment and then smiles again, as if I'm an amusing mystery. Creases line her forehead. She blinks, and her face is newborn again. She says, "Claire."

At night, I awake to the sounds of a new neighborhood. Next door, the rooster crows, and down the street, a dog barks, seemingly out of some persistent misery, perhaps from the cold night. I sit up and light a cigarette.

For a few minutes, the dog stops barking, but the rooster crows again. Now, I hear only the sound of myself, sucking smoke and then blowing it away from me. I press the remaining cigarette to the ashtray's glass bottom. Then, I think of Rachel.

I remember when Rachel lay next to me, every night for several years before the month of April. I remember her body's curve against my back. I try to remember if I ever woke during those nights to check her breathing, to touch her, to make sure she was still there, if I kissed her then, if I smoothed her hair with my palm. I never did. During those years, I always rested easy and slept hard in my lover's arms. At that time, I remember, there was no need for comfort.

Now, I think of Alissa, several thousand miles away from me along the southern coast. I wonder if she's awake, unable to sleep, haunted by a dead kitten's screams. I wish for her peaceful dreams. I want to give her something. Instead, I bend my knees up near my chest, wrap my arms around them, rest my head on my arms. Then, I try to imagine this moment as an ending, as some renewed sense of self. Instead, I think of my past, piece together my private devotion, my thoughts of Alissa, for Alissa, during the month of April.

Ka Yin Fong

Amita and Vinita

Neesha Dosanjh

Dusk to Dawn

the wind
whispers
    petals
        through
           my
                window
    tonight
pain
is my lover
she
strokes my limbs
encircles
my waist
snuggles
against my breast...

the wind
whispers
    petals
        through
           my
                window

    tonight
pain
is my lover
velvet of night
my desire

red moon
laments
in my doorway
fear
creeps
into my bed
covers my skin
like a fine sea mist...

wandering
through
corridors of
unsettled sleep
i
      struggle
          to
               rise
                   into
                       the
                           sun...

i
grasp
the hands
of anger
for it is she
who shelters
my eyes
leads me
through harsh
white of day
    into
        cool
            calm
      evening
shade

the wind
whispers
     petals
        through
          my
             window

       tonight
    again
pain
is my lover
resting
faithfully
aginst my body...

Indigo Chih-Lien Som

in my sleep

my girlfriend becomes
a godzilla
tiptoeing up the
stairs/& i
am a round
grey mushroom

she sees me
there casting my
small gray shadow
on the white sheets
& blue pillowcase

w/ her green awkward
claw she gently
lifts me high to
look & wonder if
i am poisonous

i feel myself softly set
on a protected edge
of shelf/& the reptile
mass roars away to
her task
the destruction of western civilization

she returns
beautiful warrior monster
& finds me/gorgeous
fungus by the tapedeck

in her joy she breaks
me carefully in 2
one half offered
to my beloved family
who eat me in breakfast
omelets & experience
subsequent psychedelic journeys

my girlfriend inserts
my other half
into her scaly dinosaur vagina
like a magic tampon

becomes her soft
self again/& i am
her fierce flannel bed

Brenda Joy Lem

Enchanting Forest

May I become your enchanting forest?
A place of refuge
from tempest storms, perhaps,
you could come to me
enter my body
like a familiar lover.
In a calming embrace
I will become your private garden.
Like the tongue that traces
my rib cage, my breast
you meander.
The night, heavy
in quiet repose
overwhelms.
Human vulnerability revealed
the unclothed, uncivilized
nature of the body;
soft, sensuous, innocent.

Little Earthquake

Love Poem

i was thinking tonight of clouds,
how dark they are in form,
hiding skies with their bodies,
blocking the red eyes of sun, blinding moon.

as they disappear each layer of night appears
in a miracle, unfolding slowly and filling the air with calm
i was touching the clouds, gazing at their fullness
celestial and voluptuous, they dance alone
embracing stars, fragile dark wonders float above earth

i thought of you undulating
moving beautiful in grace,
bursting as a cloud may joyously burst into rain
desire rages inside me as i feel you
in the ocean of my dream
shadow of your beauty surrounding my soul.

Naomi Guilbert

Letter from Bali

i never expected happiness
but i never expected this either
this slow slow pulling apart
of the heart
this constant and meaningless grief

what else do i have to do?
i've stopped showing you my poems
stopped seeing with your eyes   behind my eyes
all the small things that would delight you —
the colour of a certain flower in summer
the changing shape of the moon

i wish i could leave
all regrets behind
i wish i could take back
what was never wanted
send   instead   my indifference
unrequited   sincere

Linda C. Parece

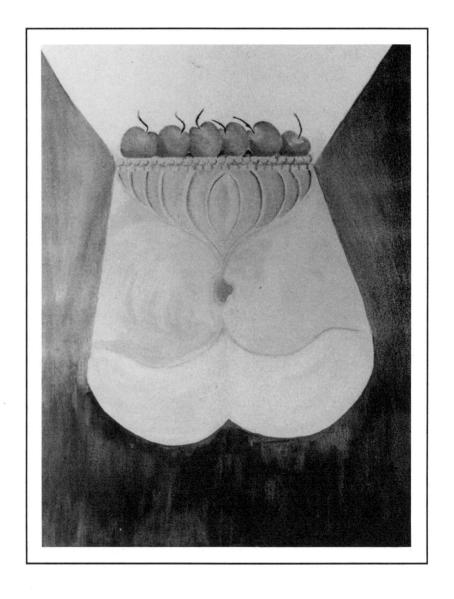

Suniti Namjoshi

When My Love Lay Sleeping...

When my love lay sleeping,
                                    it was not I,
it was the sun who splashed her
with sticky honey.
                                    The sun
put it there. I merely watched,
patiently
                    And it was the air,
mistaking her breasts
                              for gentle hills,
or, not mistaking at all,
                              but finding
a landscape so pleasing and rare,
                              who caressed her,
sleeping.
                    And it was the grass.
Its flickering tongues licked
                              at her feet,
crept up her thighs
                              and played
with her hair.
                    Oh it was the lascivious grass
that made my love sigh
                              and show herself
to me.

Lisa Asagi

Swirling Tales, and the Concept of Tea

Once, there was this woman. Once, she was the world and I slept with my face in her nape. Sometimes she'd reach over, rest her hand near the hollow of my neck and count for the room how often my heart moved. Maybe one day this will all find her in the middle of a story, sheets of words laid around her. A way in which to keep her warm, having to stand so long in my memory. Perhaps a well-thought out tale about love, passion, the human condition, etc. But this isn't possible at the moment. I can't stop thinking about her. Can't stop interfering with the nature of motion, have it grow out of me enough to encircle, gradually expand into one big picture. Paintings, photographs — are not excused from the concept of time, but they can sometimes get away from gravity. Unlike a story.

> The earliest remembering she ever shared with me was to tell of her first airplane ride. When she was seven. To Maui. Said that she has never been able to fly in her dreams since, but she can pilot airplanes in them. So far about sixteen, only three of which have crashed. No one ever dies. There was one three years ago that actually stopped in mid-air. "What did you do?," I asked. She stood up and walked to the back, climbed out and realized the plane was floating in water. Then she woke up.

> > In August I walked through a Paul Klee exhibit and hated everything, until I reached one notebook paper sized sketch. It was pencil, watercolour and everything barren, insect-like except for one thing. It was supposed to be the moon, but it wasn't. It was a musical note. It's called a fermata. It looks like an upside-down bird's eye. In musician's terms it means an extended pause.

This is not about how I keep seeing things about her. Even if it were, no one would know. My body used my mind, it believes it is still falling and so it stutters. It says nothing at all and then it says too much. At this moment, I am working for a documentary filmmaker. For lunch we talk about rendering. Rendering is an honest word. It feels responsible for considering all seemingly unrelated ideas so much so that sometimes it prolongs, searches for connections in contradictions in order to show exactly how feeling can actually exist in the middle of a street at 11:57 p.m. and as always, Tuesday night.

Look. Looking is standing at a bus stop or the desire to fall in a wide open space for an indeterminate length of time. It really is. And this is based on the fact that it has become impossible to adhere to visible landmarks to establish a sense of placement in the current of general time. It has nothing at all to do with maps, but it involves a lot of research into the understanding of why we love to understand.

Once implies a decision of a singular beginning. This is true. Once, a story really did have the privilege of feeling alone. But at first or in the end, it has to grow into something much larger than it can admit.

On the way to work one day
she got into a three-car accident
and came out of it with a half
inch cut inside of her mouth
and a bruise to hide it. She
couldn't eat for two days.
That was when I painted her
kitchen. She said that the
smell didn't bother her as
much as she thought it
would, but the curious
thing was that the scent
of the paint almost
in her mouth. She couldn't
describe it really. But I
think I know what she
meant because whenever
she got really hungry we'd
end up on her bed and
her mouth was of a firming
taste, slightly chemical
tinged with a baseness
of blood.

One morning while
I was taking a shower,
she came in with a bucket
of warm earl grey and
poured it over me. I got
her back the next day
with a warm stew pot
of country peach spice.
Then it was black
cherry and I almost
got fired. The next
day it was almond
sunset and this was
how I spent three days
of suspension.

One night she played for me.
It was the first time she ever
played her piano when we
were alone. It was a nocturne
she said she'd been working
on when we first met. I was
standing near her left cheek
and remember how much
I wanted to touch her but
was afraid it would make her
stop, in some way it would
interfere with the motion,
risk the chance of this
moment even taking place.
Every Tuesday night after
that, I would ask her to
play it for me again. I
would lie very near with
my face on the side of her
piano watching her make
all the sound come out
and into my body. Watch
her. Sometimes the edges
of her eyes, her mouth
would almost slip into a
smile and she'd catch her
glance before it could see
me watching her tell me
too many things.

This past Wednesday night, I drove back from L.A. and had to stop in Grapevine to water the car. Almost nine. Maybe it was because the air was so warm and the sky was trying so hard to turn dark, that I felt far enough to slide into a strange sense of how even the smallest of details — the windshield, a street sign, the color of the air just above the road in the headlights, the chin of the woman in the passing car — are easily enslaved by hope or filed as greatly forgotten.

This past Thursday I almost got fired. Well, somebody had to say this.

Mona Oikawa

Stork Cools Wings

I MET LISA IN MY TAI CHI CLASS. WE WERE THE ONLY TWO ASIAN WOMEN in a room full of tall white men. Our one consolation about this setting was that from the moment we saw each other we knotted a bond of sisterhood, tight as the clasps formed by our hands in the mirrored movements we practise in our strengthening exercises. We quickly discovered we are both third-generation Canadians: she is of Chinese origin, I am of Japanese descent.

A few days ago, I went to Lisa's house for tea. The conversation turned, as it always does between us, to being Asian women in a racist society. By the light of candles and burning incense, we talked about our own racism. We compared the stereotypes fed to us by our parents about each other's cultures — she in bowls filled with long and separate grains of rice, me in short-grained sticky servings. We both cried when we talked about how we had internalized racism toward other Asian peoples and now knew it was a reflection of our anger turned inward, the scars of self-hate and self-denial. Before I finally left at 1 a.m., we hugged long and hard. I had not wanted to leave.

Week after week I watched Lisa grow stronger, thighs spreading through *tor yus* and *don yus*. My favourite moment is seeing her hands flutter earth and skyward through stork cools wings, beautiful hands poised in mid-flight. When she carries tiger to the mountain, I, too, leave the earth transported by a secret vision of her firm brown body flying and alighting on me, lifting me to sheltered summits rising in mist above my bed. This image has burned deep into my source of yearning, and keeps me restless, night upon sleepless night.

"The class is starting," Lisa whispers, gently pulling my hand. "Are you okay?"

"I'm fine," I answer with an embarrassed grin. "I really have to watch your movements closely. I'm having trouble with my brush knees."

Lisa hurries to take her special sunlit spot. "Let's practice them then. Meet me at the Sun Yat-Sen statue tomorrow at 2 p.m."

The next day, the sky glowed fresh from a morning rain. We completed one set, hands and legs in perfect harmony, two Asian women, stroking and striding together.

"Your brush knees look better." Lisa states, weaving her long black rivers of hair into soft entwining coils. "I think it's a good idea for us to practise together... Not to change the subject, but I just read your story on Asian lesbians and safer sex. Do you really use Saran Wrap?"

Nearly choking on the tea I am sipping from my thermos, I wonder why she is asking me this question. I knew she had ended her relationship with a man over a year ago, but despite my daily fantasizing, I assumed she was still very straight.

"I'm not really an expert on safer sex. I actually have never used Saran Wrap. In fact, the latest research indicates that plastic wrap may not be an effective barrier against the HIV virus, so I wouldn't recommend it." I'm trying to hide my insecurity, I think to myself, as I hear the familiar academic-trained voice come from somewhere inside me.

"It's all pretty scary to me." Lisa says, her dark brown eyes piercing my veil of confidence. "What do you use then?"

The truth is I hadn't been able to make love to a woman since I met her six months ago. "We can talk about it over dinner, if you wish. Want to come back to my place?"

"How long have you been into macrobiotics?" Lisa asks, tasting the azuki beans I'd cooked in garlic and ginger.

"I took a course over a year ago. But actually, these foods are a part of my history. I guess I'm just trying to reclaim them."

"That's how I feel about Tai Chi." Lisa's hands are beating the air to illustrate her point. "But I get angry when I feel I'm depending on white people, like our teacher, to help us learn our histories."

As we pass the teapot between us, Lisa reminds me about continuing our safer sex discussion. "Can I see a dental dam?" She smiles with the warm openness I have come to cherish. "I assume you have a ready supply of them?"

"I do have a few somewhere." I am shaking with nervousness and excitement. I go into the bedroom and open the creaking drawer of the dresser my grandmother gave me. I reach for the box of bubble-gum flavoured dams and carry it to this beautiful woman with hand outstretched.

"How do you use them?" she asks very seriously. Now, I am confused. Does she really want a demonstration?

I tell her matter-of-factly, how the lube can be applied to the side covering the skin, and how either partner can hold it in place. I don't elaborate with descriptions of the leather straps I've seen for allowing hands their wandering freedom, or the garter belts like the black lace one that sits unused in the same creaky drawer.

"I really think I should be tested for HIV," Lisa says quietly. "My ex and I were non-monogamous and I never asked him to wear a condom with me. I haven't been with anyone else since we broke up, but I know I have to practise safer sex. I don't want to put myself or anyone else at risk. But I'm scared of being tested. And scared of not knowing what to do when I want to sleep with someone."

My eyes do not leave her face as I admit, "I'm afraid too. I've thought of being tested. Even though I was monogamous in my last relationship, I did have unprotected sex with my lover, and a lot of women before her. I've decided it's best for me to practice safer sex. I feel it's an issue of respect and not differentiating between certain types of lovers — making categories of safe and unsafe people. It's some of our practices and not protecting ourselves that may be unsafe... But I do miss being able to do some things without barriers."

"Maybe we could go to the clinic and get tested together," Lisa says, taking my hand in hers. I feel her pulse with the tips of my fingers. Is it racing as fast as mine?

"I have to think more about it. But I'd be happy to go with you if you decide to take the test."

"It's late. The subway has stopped running," Lisa yawns. "Can I stay here tonight?"

"We'll both have to sleep on the pull-out couch. I still haven't finished my loft." I am trying to calm my voice by clearing the tea-cups and picking up crumbs from the table.

"That's fine." She is rummaging through the cabinet in the bathroom. "Do you have an extra toothbrush?"

I put the dental dams back in their hiding place. I try to stop thinking of how I would like to use every one of the thirty-six dams in the box with the woman who will share my bed tonight. I am flushed from the sight of her holding the six-by-six inch piece of latex between her incredibly beautiful hands.

I really must stop fantasizing, I tell myself, crawling into bed beside her. I must not turn or my face will be a breath away from her back.

She, however, is not as careful in this bed made for one-and-a-half women. Her hand is on my hip now, and I try to move away. She must be asleep, I chant silently, my heart beating up through my throat into my mouth.

But her hand is moving toward my breast and I am wanting her, hoping her fingers will rise to fondle my nipples, erupting at the feel of her.

"Where are the dental dams?" Lisa whispers softly in my ear.

"In the bottom drawer of my dresser," my voice is barely audible.

She scrambles away from me and I know she has found the other box in my latex stash.

"What do we do with the gloves?" she shouts.

"They are used for penetration," I reply.

"We will need them then," she says, lighting a candle and placing it by the bed.

I reach for her. Our mouths join, our tongues search first tentatively, then lustfully. She is on top of me now. Rubbing the inside of my thigh with her knee, she moans, "This is how I do brush knee." I grasp her knee hard between my legs, while she lifts my T-shirt and begins to lick in circles around my breasts. I take her beautiful hands in mine, raise them to my lips, and pull each finger deep into my mouth, one by one.

I move her beneath me and begin to travel the paths of our foremothers, through crevice and moss, uncovering treasures with mouth and hand. When I reach the hollow of her navel, she pleads, "I want to go down on you first."

"You're very butch for a woman who's just coming out," I tease.

"I know you haven't thought of me as a lesbian, but I have wanted you ever since I saw you do your first Tai Chi set." She is hovering above me and I am captive of the sight. "And that night you came to my house, I didn't want you to leave."

Lisa is going down my body with her tongue. In leaps and bounds, she is stirring within me feelings of joy and hope and love. She slides a lilac-coloured dam over my wetness and says, "You are dark like me, so dark, so beautiful." She begins to lick me slowly, then with urgency. I am entering that other plane of consciousness, panting in rhythm with each of her mouthfuls of me.

She stops suddenly. "What's wrong?" I ask. She sits upright.

"I don't care for the taste of bubble-gum and rubber. I want to taste you."

"We can rinse the dam, it helps... And there's a little bottle in my fridge door with a drawing of a Japanese woman on it. Get it," I urge frantically. It seems she is gone forever. Unscrewing the bottle cap, she returns.

"What is this stuff?"

The tension is subsiding between my legs. "It's *ume** paste. Smear it on your side of the dental dam."

"It looks like dried blood," she says.

"That's why I like it." I answer, adding, "It's actually dried plums, very macrobiotic." She laughs and I feel a cold sensation as she spoons out the thick red paste while the dam is still on me. I will not need any lube tonight.

Lisa's tongue is licking upward and around. She eats the *ume* noisily. "It is salty. Your blood is delicious." I rise and come quickly beneath her.

We wait long moments, hands clasped tightly, brown skin breathing on brown skin.

"I really think it's time for you to practice your brush knees." Lisa smiles, her lips showing spots of *ume* red. "But please use this for my dental dam." She pulls my black lace garter belt from the green and white dental dam box, over her legs, and up her powerful thighs. "There are lots of things we could use, you know," she says, passing me the bottle of *ume*

"Like what?" I ask, pulling her face into mine.

"Come to my house tomorrow and I'll show you."

I climb Lisa's soft brown body, my wings circling her head. Her delicate hands flutter through my hair and around me joyfully. Incense wisps of jasmine and cherry blossom rise in clouds above our bed. 'Til the light of dawn, we carry each other to the peaks of Tian Shan and Fuji-san, arms and legs in perfect harmony, two Asian women stroking and striding and flying together.

---

*Note: Technically it is *umeboshi* paste. *ume* means plum. *umeboshi* is pickled plum.

Little Earthquake

Rati[1]

i am swallowed by the tongue of night her
fist buried deep beneath bruises these quiet
purples and blues screaming red gently rocking
her moan on my lips i travel to the country of
breasts with boundaries of flesh covering
a remote heart of bone disintegrating dark
pauses her fragrance drowning my body in
fluid melodies of grace of earth of shells
breaking sound silence streaming wetness
bathing dawn's face all tremors locked in her limbs
shining gold smooth mouth biting soft pleasures

open your eyes from blackness as you swim
into surrender of crimson touched raw
tasting love this love my love yes love
we love and love

---

1 *Rati* is the sanskrit word for sexual love.

Lani Ka'ahumanu

Ode to a Fierce Butch

I am
a woman
who fancies
a butch
with
smoldering fires
and
simmering desires
evident in her gaze

I am
a woman
who willfully
stays
who skillfully
plays
with her own satisfaction
in mind

I am
a woman
who takes
a butch
on her back
on her belly
on her side
yes, I will sweep her
right off her feet
yes her feet
spread wide

And
in my own way
and
on my own say
make that butch
come to her core
shudder and beg
oh yes
beg for more

Tomiye Ishida

Akairo
(The Color Red)

A snap of your watch
and my pussy aches...
Involuntary pangs of desire
ignite my body.
Single fluid motion
slides watch and rings off
your fingers reaching
down to open me and plunge
into the hot, wet embrace of my cunt.
Thrusting fist of love
and lust
deep inside
fiercely satisfying.

A moan escapes the back of
my throat
as my body arches
bowlike into your rhythmic
movements and closer to the
tender curves of your mouth.

A lingering kiss
soothes the fire between
my parted legs
and yet it draws me upward...
Spiralling intensity
The sky turns red
as thunderous waves crash mightily
over our sweat-soaked bodies,
breaking down all restraints.

We collapse together
this woman and I
in the warm, salty ocean
her breasts close to mine
Hearing only her breath
and the soft sound
of waves lapping gently
over our tangled limbs.

Indigo Chih-Lien Som

Just once
before I die
I want someone
to make love to me
in Cantonese

> *my mother*
>
> *tongue not*
>
> *in my mouth*
>
> *no longer mine*
>
> *my second tongue*
>
> *now my only*
>
> *one/mother*
>
> *tongue some*
>
> *where in me*
>
> *deep/not*
>
> *my own*

> Just once
>
> I want to remember
>
> language I've never
>
> known/Give me words
>
> I never heard
>
> at my grandmother's
>
> kitchen table

Make the tones
fall from my
throat/like
fairytale flowers
& toads/until new
sentences snake
across your skin

let me moan
mothertongue
in your mouth

Nila Gupta

Your Love Has Undone Me
for love

what have you done to me
prying my arthritic fists open
all these years clenched tight
around the poles of my banners

sweeping aside my pickets and barriers
my red rage and chants and slogans
simply, as if cobwebs and dust

what have you done to me

gathering me into your arms
as i stand shocked and defenceless
in my greatest moment of nakedness
i want to fight you off

but the touch of your hands on my body
the feel of your kiss on my body
had undone me

why have you done this to me
i hear women screaming
from somewhere deep inside me imprisoned
and i cannot be free, until they are free

i see the white bullyboys
cornering my family again and again
their spit on my face
and there is no rest for me

i cannot sleep
i hear little girls crying
every night before I go to bed
and my eyes have run dry

what have you done to me

this woman needs a rock
this girl who shouted into the wind
for help
cannot rest
until help
comes

you have undone me
with your talk of love
and forever
with your kisses
and caresses

you have undone me
and your love has made me soft

now, when another woman is killed
another black youth shot
i march hand in soft hand
with a million women
and you

your love has undone me
and i am no longer afraid

LIFE
STRUGGLE

Vanessa Marzan Deza

A Litany for Our Survival

"so it is better to speak
remembering
we were never meant to survive
— audre lorde"

> for a mother who has raised four children
> fatherless in a foreign land
> a ph.d. from u.p. gone to waste
> working as shift manager at taco bell
> run for the border
> immigrant/exiles from a different shore

> a ph.d. from u.p. means
> precision when chopping tomatoes
> (or teaching seventeen-year-olds how)
> at 2 a.m. she closes the store
> walk by the hoodies hanging
> on the corner eating taco bell
> run for the border

> late nights i put my brother
> and sister to sleep
> stay up with kuya, the eldest one
> watching cheers and taxi re-runs
> and tom vu telling us to join
> his make-money-quick seminars

we hear her pull up the driveway
hurriedly turn off the tv as the
car door slams/under the blankets
in a room shared with my eleven year
old brother baby sister / i lie still staring
at the ceiling listening to my steady breathing
a thank you sigh she had come home
safe this time

this is a litany for our survival

six years ago when we waited for
her safe return home
driving through gardena streets
inner-city in suburbia
driving her work crew home
to inglewood and wilmington

a story she told me as
i massaged her calloused feet
with vicks vapour rub one day
was how a white man with his wife
sneered at her through their car
rolled down the window at the drive-thru
and said, "we'd like some WHITE milk, please"
my mother replied, "i'm sorry sir, but
all our white milk is rotten. would you care for
some fresh, brown chocolate"

in those days she'd stay up
unable to sleep
sometimes i shared in her insomnia
she almost always held a wine glass
that she handed to me for refills
in the kitchen i'd pull out the gallon
jug of pinkish julio and gallo
hesitating to pour even more
knowing i'd be sent back if i didn't.

this is a litany for our survival

she almost always sat engulfed in
cigarette smoke
feet tucked under her thighs
on the faded flowers of a
hand me down couch from
a rich relative's garage
            (run for the border/exiled immigrants
            from a different shore)
at fifteen i hated wearing the clothes
discarded by my cousins
hated even more when they came
to my room and recognized their
old sheets on my bed.

            "when we first got to the states we
            had nothing/your no-good father
            be thankful we help your family"
            rich auntie says handing me
            a cracked plate to take to my mother
            "here's the vacuum cleaner"
            she says later and i drown in the thick
            carpeted halls of her $600,000
            real-estate prime home.

i remember doing the laundry with
my brothers and sister
by the boys market and thrifty's
buying presents for each other
        (run for the border/exiled immigrants
        from a different shore)
during half-priced sales
styling in our blue bandannas
white sneakers and thin cotton shirts
head held high in pride
buying with our own money.

        for her birthday we got her
        delicate porcelain swans
        and ice-frosted fake crystal glasses
        my mother was beautiful then
        as always even in an
        off-pink nightgown and
        smeared mascara
        asleep with hands gone limp
        to her sides/head on a throw cushion
        i put the wine glass away
        crush the cigarette till
        the red ember went black

this is a litany for our survival

Nila Gupta

Identification Card

everywhere i go
i'm asked to pull out my identification card
along with the appropriate rhetoric
the appropriate posture
to pass
if i pull out the wrong one
at the wrong time
they tell me to choose

at the Coalition of Visible Minority Women's meeting
i'm a woman of colour
at the South Asian Women's Group
i'm South Asian
at a hearing at the 519 on gay bashing
i'm a lesbian
at the Michigan Women's Festival
i am a lesbian of mixed race

at my work at the Human Rights Commission
they won't study
discrimination
in their own house
against lesbians and gays
or women etcetera
but they've formed
an anti-racism committee

i tried to tell them all
that they have to have an integrated analysis
but that won't wash in 1992
there's always a reason
to leave a part of me behind
so they can have a bigger part
for themselves

very rarely
am i just who i am
to them
except to myself

and sometimes
with my lover
in the wide expanse
of her smile
i catch a glimpse
of myself
whole
in her eyes

Alice Y. Hom

In the Mind of An/Other

I OFTEN WONDER WHAT WHITE LESBIANS THINK WHEN I WALK INTO A lesbian nightclub. Am I the first Asian Pacific lesbian they have seen? Do I exist in their minds? Do they see me as an exotic sex kitten or as a submissive/passive plaything as perpetuated and manipulated by the media? Do the stereotypes of Suzy Wong, of prostitutes, and of geisha girls in the mainstream heterosexual world become transposed and translated into the dyke world? Do the images of an obedient domestic or meek, unassertive girl come to mind? Am I a tasty treat — dim sum to be sampled and an hour later they are hungry again? Do they see me as butch, femme, or androgynous? As a woman of color does that mean I am a better lover than my white counterpart? Will my exoticism make her come better? Maybe they are surprised to see me because Asian Pacific women stereotypes are so ingrained in the heterosexual context that Asian Pacific lesbians do not even come to mind. Considering the power of social conditioning it would not surprise me if the stereotypes about Asian Pacific women are internalized and believed by lesbians.

What do they think?

Once my Korean dyke friend and I were accosted by a white lesbian at Crystal Images, a Connecticut lesbian bar. We are minding our own business, watching the women dance and my vision is temporarily blocked by a woman with her hands in a prayer position, bowing and murmuring, "An-yo." We stare blankly at her and she asks if we understand Korean. "All Asians look alike," was the thought that raced through my mind. "No, I've been colonized and led to believe that English is the only acceptable language. So much so that I cannot hold a decent conversation with my parents in Chinese." She went on to say that she had some Asian friends and that they were "just the cutest things; small and dainty like China Dolls." "Fuck you!" flashed through my mind. I went to this bar to be empowered with other lesbians and I was disappointed. I did not have that validating experience I sought. I was not in the mood to educate (I'm tired of educating white women). I did not want to waste my breath on unhearing ears.

What did she think?

When I am in a lesbian club or bar I am always scoping. If I am not dancing, I like to watch. I take it all in with a sweeping glance, the sweaty, undulating clothed and black lace bra clad bodies on the stage and dance floor swaying to the backbeat of house music. It is another world, far away from the dry, sterile, mainly heterosexual academic environment that I live and breathe during the day. I feel good to be in this atmosphere of women prancing, pressing and thrusting at each other, arms and legs touching everywhere. My face is flushed with energy and streaked with sweat as two women sandwich me; laughing and losing balance as they freak with me. We fall to the floor like dominoes, my back leaning against one and the other on top. A new position. My eyes wander to a short-haired woman, skimming over the torn jeans cuffed above big black shoes and white T-shirt neatly tucked in by the big black belt and covered by the ubiquitous black leather jacket. She looks like me. I notice all the short-haired women — black, brown, red, grey, and blonde and dyed. My fetish for short hair is well-known amongst my friends. They tease me about it because they say that I want to go out with myself. An element of narcissism always pops up in same sex couplings.

What do I think?

I ventured into Girl Bar, a Los Angeles lesbian club, for the first time and saw around twelve lesbians of color out of 100, which made me sort of happy. At least there was a representation of color. Creamy-white clubs make me feel uncomfortable and different. I saw another Asian Pacific lesbian and we looked at each other but that was it. Did she see me as competition? Did she turn away for fear of being identified with another Asian Pacific lesbian? Did she think she was the only Asian Pacific lesbian, as I sometimes have felt when I go to new places? Was she happy to see me, as another sister in the sometimes white, alienating dykedom? I am always excited when I see another Asian Pacific lesbian because it makes me feel less lonely. I realize that there are others like me who face similar experiences. Yet, I was afraid to approach her because of my own insecurity. Many of us are caught in the process of de-colonizing our minds that have been fucked up by dominant society and culture. Internalized self-hate causes some Asian Pacific lesbians to turn away or run when they encounter other Asian Pacific lesbians.

What does she think?

The majority of lesbian literature and culture portrays only white lesbians. Sappho is nice but she does not represent me. Images of lesbians of colour are minimal. Even when we are represented (see the November/December 1990 issue of *On Our Backs* with Kitty Tsui) there is a distinct reification of her exotica in that erotica. The caption highlighted her great popularity with the readers. I read it as proof that Kitty is seen as an exotic "other." A double invisibility shrouds the Asian Pacific lesbian. Although snow queens and rice queens are more visible in gay clubs, I would argue that there are snow dykes and rice dykes out there in lesbianland. My Asian dyke friend does not go out with other Asians. She does not find them attractive because she grew up in a white neighborhood believing that she was not attractive. Self-contempt is "natural" for the lesbian of color given the dominant culture's overpowering influence in all aspects of our lives. Media, books, magazines, schools, and people interact to create a system where dominant culture (read white) remains in power. It is a common sight to see Asian Pacific lesbians at clubs and rallies, where we notice each other but we actively and consciously remain distant. We mirror each other, but we are afraid to look in. We are magnets that should be attracted to each other, but we are polarized.

What do we think?

I go home and my mom comments on my short hair. She says in Chinese that I look like a boy. In the same breath, she presses the same old line that I should only go out with Chinese boys. My oldest sister echoes her sentiments. "I bet you have a lot of white boyfriends," says she. "No way!" I answer honestly, smirking and throwing a knowing glance to my other sisters that know. Will they accept a nice Chinese girl? My family knows that I am different, especially from my appearance. I get insinuating remarks about my genderfuck look but my sexuality is never questioned. I walk in greeting my mother's friends and they exclaim in unison Chinese, "Oh, so this is the daughter that has been away to college. She is so pretty and smart." But I catch their eyes scrutinizing my butch/androgynous attire and I see their surprise as I am introduced as a daughter and not a son.

What do they think?

An Asian Pacific lesbian faces an alienating lesbian community and a hostile Asian Pacific community. The Asian Pacific community denies her existence and the lesbian community does not validate her existence. I am homeless. I want acceptance from both communities. I want both communities to understand my experience. I cannot separate the various identities that I possess in order for approval. Both communities must realize and acknowledge that Asian Pacific lesbians have played an active role in shaping and implementing their agendas. And tokenism will not be accepted. While I am waiting for both communities to get their respective acts together, I am finding empowerment and validation in Asian Pacific lesbian groups and with other lesbians of color. We look to each other for support and guidance.

What do you think?

Indigo Chih-Lien Som

internalization

the other day
(cdve been today)
i was at work
& looking out the window
i saw
a white guy
zipping by on his very
cool motorcycle
with blond hair flying behind
all fine & free
he looked like the American
Dream or something

& i
in spite of everything
i the hip radical
woman of color writer
so proud of my culture
& like having my period & all that
& really
having struggled for so long
to become who i am

yes
for one second
one third of a heartbeat
i wished again/still
that i cd be him & free
instead of
me

sister
i know it's
happened to you
too

Lisa Kahaleole Chang Hall

Ashes
for Auntie Dickie

My aunty locks the doors
against my cousin Patrick
Last week the vacuum disappeared
went up his nose
Years ago, I watched him throwing flame
We stood outside as he flipped
matches all around   like little fireflies
they helicoptered down
sputtered out
against the sand

He comes and goes, my golden cousin
Flames flare up or flicker
Last year they bent the bars and
let him out for the
last days' watch of
my great-uncle's life   he did not run
When that long week
was over   the canoes sailed out into
the ocean bearing ashes   his sister
accidentally left   wrong boat
bereft of all the rest
Calmly she sat alone   hair whipping
out in the dancing breeze   her friends'
voices rose in anxious chorus —   What
do you want us to do?   What shall we do?

She told them — Nothing
Patrick will take care
And when the right time came he
lept into the sea
sleek seal swimming   dolphin   shark
sunlight flashing off his hair
he swam against the current
ashes held up   to be received
his sister reached out
to meet him   standing firmly
in the prow   mu'umu'u flaring
like a sail her hair a dancing corona
These spirits flew up   along with
those ashes and fell into the sea

Wherever you are now, my missing cousin
Our hearts are burning for you
Mixed up creatures that we are
I'll pray to Pele
that like phoenix
you'll return
transcendent in your ashes

Margaret Mihee Choe

Suddenly, You Realize...

I. Mick or Chink?

OUT OF DESPERATION AND A CHRONIC LACK OF BUTCHNESS, Maggie occasionally hired herself out as a temp. She wasn't overly organized — one look at her apartment would tell you that — and her office skills were less than exemplary, but it was easy work for her to get. Maggie dimly felt that the invariable ease with which she was hired had less to do with her skills than with her temp persona: a dutiful, quiet Oriental housegirl, perhaps akin to those Japanese "office ladies" she had read about. Her employers (she imagined) felt she could be counted on not to stumble into work at eleven in the morning after tying one on the night before, not to pop her gum in visitors' faces, not to be a troublemaker.

It was ironic that the one true asset that Maggie could use to advantage in offices was not her appearance but her excellent telephone voice. She so relished working the phones that in more energetic moments she considered getting into the voice-over business. On the phone she could be charming, discreet, diplomatic, flirtatious, or commanding as necessary. On the phone she wasn't her drab self, but someone else entirely. Discovery of a telephone alter ego had come as a surprise. On the phone, when she left a message, she would say in her exceptionally clear, regional-accentless voice, "This is Maggie Choe." The person at the other end of the line would repeat back to her, "Maggie Shea?"

"Shea?" Maggie wondered. There she would be, having a mundane conversation with some other office drudge like herself, when that one little syllable would throw her off balance. It was, perhaps, like being a drag queen, except there hadn't been any intentional identity transformation on her part. Had there? Maybe it was all those times in her formative years when she had opted for Burger King instead of her mother's homecooking. But what was she to do now? Develop an accent? At first, she corrected the error by spelling out her name, but gave that up after too many people mispronounced her name when returning her calls. A couple of times, recalling the Spanish custom of people going by both their mother's and father's surnames, she had given her name as "Maggie Oh Choe," and, sure enough, it had come back to her as "O'Shea."

Maggie came to think of her alter ego with fondness, even admiration. She pictured her as a rather formidable, can-do gal, wearing lipstick of a threateningly lurid hue; stockings with flawlessly aligned seams; and Tallulah Bankhead heels that clacked viciously down the street, in a beat that said, `These shoes have been registered as deadly weapons.' Maggie could see her stopping at a certain office building to pick up her lunch date: her best girlfriend, a woman who wore too much perfume, who smoked cigarillos, who liked her drinks stiff and her women supple, the wise-cracking Emi Ohara.

II. The Gyopo Blues

I was camped in front of the international travel section of one of my oh-so literate city's big bookstores. In anticipation of my first trip to the Far *West* (North America, not Europe, being my point of reference and departure), I was browsing through the few inches of shelf space afforded to guidebooks on Korea. Sooner or later all the guidebooks, under the heading (euphemism?) "Entertainment" or "Night Life," directed me (*Me? Are you talking to me?*) to bars employing *kisaeng* and other types of hostesses. Now, I had wanted to meet Korean women, but this is not quite what I had had in mind. One book recommends that readers (me?) draft a Korean (*Who? My mother? Her brother? His in-laws?*) to take them to such establishments. Another book makes references to the "mamasan" with whom one must negotiate. I tried to imagine the bargaining scene between her and me. Would she give me a discount or just try to recruit me? Yet another book states that "(Koreans) go elsewhere for the pleasures of the flesh and it's a mind-boggling experience to take a look at where they go." (*Zoos?* I speculated. *Hardware stores? National monuments?*) Just before the frustration completely shattered my will to buy a book, I recalled Korean women "comforting" Japanese soldiers in World War II; Korean men going on sex tours to the

Philippines, to Thailand. I didn't feel any better for having thought these things, just less *weissefeindlich*. I thought to myself: a *gyopo* ("overseas Korean") who speaks Korean with the proficiency of a slow toddler — and that's on good days; an American looking for her roots. Maybe I'd go and write the damned book myself, "The Gyopo's Guide to Hanguk."

III. California Girls

So I'm in California visiting my Orange County cousins, and I'm with my favorite cousin Kevin in — where else would we be in California — his car. We're parked out in front of his old high school, waiting for his younger brother Harvey. (When Kevin's parents came to the U.S., they offered my mother and me the American naming of their baby. Though we were restricted to something his parents could more or less pronounce, "Ke-Bin," still I regretted not coming up with something more meaningful than "Kevin," at least until they named their second child Harvey, "Ha-Bi." I mean, why not call the kid "Egghead" and get it over with?) Harvey is going through a jock phase, trying out for all the teams: basketball, baseball, football, volleyball. Football? Basketball? I was amazed when I heard. These are big American sports, meaning sports for big Americans. Harvey did get decent height from his mother's (and my) family, but that merely makes him average on an American height scale. Average-height Asians named Harvey don't go in for baseball, Lenn Sakata notwithstanding. Average-sized Asians go into martial arts, table tennis, badminton, sports red-blooded Americans don't bother with, I insist. But as the high-school doors open and release the students, I begin to see how Harvey would get it into his head to try out for sports. Everyone is Asian. Or so it seems to me, whose graduating high class of almost six hundred had exactly one Asian.

I find myself observing the girls. Goddess preserve me, the girls. They look like they're in a (soy) milk commercial. Looking at them feels like driving a stretch of smooth, traffic-free road with the radio blasting the one song I've been dying to hear (but didn't realize it) and having the roof of my sensible car peel back beneath a sky, clear blue and securely lined with ozone. The easy confidence of the girls, their natural hipness relaxes me, seduces me into another realm, into which Kevin, I now notice, has also made his way. He sees that I have caught him following the girls with his lustful, nineteen-year-old's gaze (but he doesn't read the heat of my own gaze), and he blushes.

I blurt out, "D'you think Asian girls are pretty?"

He looks puzzled. He looks at me like I'm Chief White Man and I've just asked him how much he wants for his prime beachfront property: *what a weird question.* "Some of them, sure, I guess," he says. Somewhere I have retained enough sense to realize that this is the correct response.

I am embarrassed. Call yourself a feminist? Don't I know by now that all women can be beautiful? That Miss America is a patriarchal conspiracy? Yeah, but I still need the double eyelids, a more prominent bridge of the nose, leaner cheeks (moon faces need not apply!), a perm, and heels to be beautiful. That I have chosen to acquire none of these means I have forsaken beauty for something else, something more meaningful, I've told myself.

The engine of Kevin's car roars into my consciousness, and the "Frankie Goes to Hollywood" tape Kevin had been playing picks up where it left off:

...Don't do it

When you wanna go to it.

Relax! Don't do it

When you wanna come,

When you wanna come...

I wonder if Kevin's parents' English is good enough to understand what their number-one son is listening to. Harvey, whom Kevin has already spotted, is sauntering toward us, talking with a girl. Her eyes are bright and her teeth are perfect. She is loose-limbed and sunny California to the core. She is beautiful.

Once Harvey is in the car, Kevin begins the obligatory teasing. "Hey, wasn't that Michelle Yi?"

"Yeah, so?" Harvey is always on the defensive, always trying to prove himself. Even so, his eyes crinkle with good humor.

"I thought you weren't going out with her anymore."

"I'm not. We're just talking. She's too much of a jock."

Jock? My ears perk up. "What do you mean, 'jock?'" I knew there was something about her.

"She's, like, captain of girls' volleyball."

I roll my eyes at the windshield. "But you play volleyball. It's something you have in common."

He mutters a vague assent, but the discussion is over. Maybe he just doesn't want to lay open his love life in front of his cousin who, in Korean terms, is more of an aunt, someone of his mother's generation, even though I'm closer in age to him than to his mother. I'm content to sit, watching the fast food restaurants and mini-malls flash by. I've been here before; as a child I was taken to Disneyland, hardly twenty minutes away from where we are. But suddenly, I realize, I've never been here before: Asian America.

Heidi Li

Often It Is a Stilted Eye
Which Contains One Woman's
Love for Another...

Innocent cadaver, your bleached clean
blood along with the look in your eye
tell me that I am still your ultimate

sin.

But do you remember how we once touched,
woman to woman, with the softest
parts of ourselves exposed?

Together we mixed the colors upon colors
of our emotions in the separateness
and wholeness of who we are/were.

Yet like rocks tossed upon hard ice,
we finally fell, shattered by your fears,
and your hatred of what you could not be.

Lesbian,

    Dyke,

        Witch,

            and Castrating Bitch.

How you could not embrace your own
self-empowerment.

Instead like a burnt offering,
you sacrificed yourself to the few
startled gasps of privilege

your heterosexuality
offers you now.

Oh woman, with your built-in desire
to self-destruct, if you only knew
that my woman love for you
is still yours

to someday claim.

A Visit Home

MY WALK UP THIS HILL NEVER SEEMS TO CHANGE. YEAR AFTER YEAR I climb the return journey home thinking, "What will I say?" Before our shared silences slip in to a mandatory sort of ease, before we begin to doubt what little there is to say, I always wonder, "What will I say to you today?"

Sometimes the walk is short, at other times it seems to continue on, but you are always the same — changing and shifting beneath surface I can only begin to see. We are, Mother and Daughter / daughter and mother, two distinct beings linked by our experiences — our separateness.

With each step I somehow climb closer to you. With each step I ask myself, "What is it that makes us women, mothers, daughters, Our Selves?"

Perhaps, it begins with our knowledge of each other as women who breathe, cry, shout and laugh — as women. Continues with how we see each other through different eyes, still knowing how we will never be, can never be, completely different from the Other that yearns and moves in each of us. Coming home, I am my mother's daughter. Yet I may by choice not be my daughter's mother. I want to say these words to you today in order to begin a dialogue of truth.

Mother, your unspoken, broken marriage is not just a lie. As my key settles into the front door, as I walk the stairs and my eyes finally see you, I hope there will come to be more than just the birth of a new silence between us.

PART II

You are sitting at the kitchen table reading the mail pretending that I am not here. I am watching you. We are alone. Separate, together, always pausing as we watch the pattern of our mothered-daughtered lies settle between us.

"So, you finally came home."

How are you? It's been a long time, months since you've been back. I've missed you.

"Hi Mom..."

Mother... do you wonder how much you and I speak alike in our silences.

"Did you have a good ride home?"

I walked the hill again. Wondering this time how I was going to tell you that I was a woman of color conscious of, proud of being — an Asian lesbian, a feminist, an artist claiming my own creativity, your daughter — the many parts of myself all at once sharing one single heartbeat.

"It was a pretty good ride... not too crowded on the train. How are you doing?"

Mother, did you know I was thinking of you? While riding on the bus from Trenton, I saw so many women. Women of all colors — yellow, brown, red, and white — all turning away from one another. Still I saw the scattered parts of all our lives... sensed the possible wholeness of each of our experiences shifting together. Yes... I saw.

"I'm okay."

How could you see me in those women when all we share are our separate breaths of silence?

"Well... how's work going?"

Because I saw the nooses and the veils, all our color-filled bindings twisted among our fears... and realized how much we women continue to lie to each other and our denied Selves.

"Okay... it's been pretty busy these last few months at the processing lab, not enough people on our floor, so I've been working a little harder these days."

Why do you say such things? Are you just trying to hurt me, spite me for who I am?

"Your job sounds like it's been pretty demanding lately."

No, I just want to bring you the freedom I'm finding in choosing not to lie, not to hate, and be hated for all the things I am.

"Yeah, I suppose... are you hungry?"

You think you are bringing yourself so much happiness, but what you speak of carries its own emptiness and lies.

"Actually I am."

Mother, when we speak to each other in silences we see our own emptiness, we feel each other's lies. Yet with fearlessness, spoken words we would — could — begin to see each Other in our Selves.

PART III

It is dusk. We raise our hands slowly. We look at the bowls, the bits of food, and the long walk up this hill that divides us inside.

I want to speak open words that will reach you, but you look intently at your bowl of rice. You are chewing phrases and thoughts I don't know how to speak. Is it only the idiosyncracies of language which separate us? When will the cord of motherhood be acknowledged? When will its presence be joined with the female power within us?

"Mom, did you choose freely to have — adopt — Steve and me?" I ask nervously, not quite sure where to begin with such an awkward, uncomfortable question.

"Of course," you say.

"Didn't Dad just want a boy?"

"Yes, but he wanted you too," you reply quickly, not once looking up from your bowl as you speak.

"What did you want, Mom?" I ask, probing further, not once looking away from your downward turning face.

"It didn't really matter to me... both of you were fine."

"But, do you think it made any difference that you adopted us, instead of giving birth yourself?" I looked imploringly at you, at your still downward turned face, as I wait for your response.

Finally, you look up. You look directly at me. You do not glance away as you begin speaking.

"No. I loved you both as if you were my own. At first, I wasn't... you're not used to a kid not being yours from birth... maybe, at first, you don't love it, because it's a stranger to you... but soon, you love it... like there was never a difference."

How hard these words must be for you to speak. And still, I must ask this next question of you.

"Mom, would you recommend adopting, I mean... regardless of whether or not a woman is capable of giving birth herself?"

"What do you mean?" Your voice tightens as you ask.

"You know, what if I was thinking about adopting a child at some point, instead of giving birth to one?"

You look at me as if I'm making no sense. You respond, nonetheless.

"Dana, if you can give birth to your own children then do that first. That's my advice to you."

Mother, you cannot tell me why. Looking at me — your adopted daughter — you say to me in words you do not speak that there are lies that you can neither contradict nor believe in yourself.

PART IV

It is now late evening. Nothing more is said between us except our "Good nights." Waiting for you in the kitchen, hearing you in the den, I follow you now as we go to our separate rooms. I cannot speak to you yet. Not until Sleep joins us in a dream.

Mother... I see you staring at me, looking surprised. You are becoming angry, because you don't like what you see — me staring back at you with my womb exposed. As it drips blood, it is an unfilled, uncertain cavity of skin, muscle, and movement.

"Why," you scream, "are you killing me, killing yourself!"

Mother what other words can I say to you except these words that follow me now wherever I go? "Is this really our death you see, or life as it always is for us? Take my arm with you if it is."

You reach for me, holding my hand as you begin, knife in hand, to cut away at the skin. With your other hand, fingers shred away the muscles of my forearm. You repeatedly say to me, "I must cut it off too."

Mother, in my dream can you actually feel my pain or was the lie of Self denial your only truth? Pretty soon you will cut away at the bone itself. I will be without an arm, but with a womb. One day both of our mothered emptinesses will be seen as Being whole not just lacking.

"How many arms have you lost yourself?" I ask as you continue to cut away.

You don't reply. But you let go of my arm and it swings. As you look closely at your hands you begin to scream at me. Who are you seeing when you cry, "Where is my womb? What has happened to it, to me!"

Oh, what was once thought to be dead is now living, and what was believed to be living is now dead. In my dream, we say this to our Selves — as sweat not blood — drips from both our bodies...

Tonight our rooms are not as silent as I had once thought.

PART V

It is now early morning. We are on our way to the train station. I am already beginning to think about what I will say to you the next time. These same words are always spoken in a broken Mother tongue. With your face turned forward, I can see:

How —

the red smear across your heart

was the pinprick you could not contain

the red drops of blood flowing

from between your legs

the anger you could never show

Mother and Daughter / daughter and mother. Yes you are my mother and no lie can erase this truth for me. With your face turned forward, I can see:

How —

in the stillbirth of my emotions

this is what I've come to know.

This red/brown earth breeding

in our bodies, wrapping us in ourselves

calms us now... releases us

from the gouged spirits, patches

of flesh which drip

from us all

like a dying flood.

Mother as we reach the station, all that is left between us now are the remains — the ends to see settled as last.

"Bye, Mom, I'll call you sometime this week... okay?"

"Fine, have a good ride back and call me soon."

"I will Mom... take care of yourself, okay?"

"I will... you too."

"Mom..."

When we say goodbye, we never hug, never touch.

"When you talk to Steve next time, tell him I said hello."

It's just always been a part of our being strong, Dana... as women... we had to become tough inside in order to survive.

"I will. You should call him yourself and see each other more often."

But Mother, we also needed to be strong for our Selves, for each other, not just for the rest for the world.

"I'll try, Mom."

But we had each other, didn't we? No matter what happened, how much we did or didn't express our Selves, I was still your mother... and you were always my daughter.

"No, don't forget to call me soon."

Yes, you've never denied that.

"Don't worry, I'll give you a call sometime this week... Thursday probably."

No matter how you came into this world, into my life... I never denied you were my daughter. Not inside, never inside my heart.

"Will I see you again in a couple of weeks?"

But did you choose to?

"Probably in about three weeks, Mom."

Does it matter if — how I made the choice?

"Okay, Dana, I'll see you then."

Maybe not. As long as we can see who we've been and who we hope to become. We are our own possibilities, our own choices.

"See you, Mom."

Yes Dana, you will always have your own choices to make.

"Bye, Dana."

I love you.

"Bye Mom."

I love you too.

EPILOGUE: I still walk the hill every time I go home wondering how will I reveal myself to you as your daughter, a potential mother, an Asian lesbian, a woman by myself — someone who is both known and unknown to you.

J. Kehaulani Kauanui

olelo kupuna o hapa
kanaka maoli wahine

I am the memory of my family   for my father who won't talk   his
        father and father's father   I am the memory of my family
I have to be   the genealogy has been given to me   but the names are
not enough   I want to remember the time   of my great great grandfather
who grew up at the time of the overthrow   who survived the mass deaths
    who converted out of fear   for the teachings my grandfather left on
    Moloka'i   the knowledge of the *kahuna*   the teachings of a "heathen"
for my great great grandfather who tried to kill his own son   but instead
    killed the woman he married   and his son who survived his father
    only to try and kill his own son   for my father who survived him
                        but is now silent

    I am the memory of my family   bypassing my father   going to my
Aunties   sidestepping Grandma   asking my Uncles   I am the memory
    of my family   to remember what mormon amnesia won't   the ways
they loved   the ways they battled   the ways in which they ascended our
    lineage   I am the memory of my family   for my Dad   who doesn't
    think I need to know   for myself   trying to tell him my own memories

---

Kahuna is healer.

Neesha Dosanjh

Little Girl Blue

hands drawing water
from an endless well
of love
massaging oil into
a budding mind
painfully sewing sequins
onto a skirt
cut
from her favourite sari

rolling dough for rotis
crushing cardamom for tea
mixing...

THIS IS WHERE POETRY RUNS DRY

shrill voice rings
in my brain
fists and feet *pound*
into my back

grab a stick
grab a shoe
beat that little girl blue

beat laughter
    out of her eyes
        joy
out of her belly
    power out of her soul

THIS is what i saw
MY mother do

grab a stick
grab a shoe
beat that little girl blue

who does
she think she is?
LAUGHING like that
doesn't she realize
what i sacrificed
giving birth
to a GIRL

stop laughing
shut up
SHUT UP

don't you know
i hate you
source of my misery...
reminder of all
that i lost...

dirtydirty
slutwhorebitch
shouldvekilledyouafteryouwereborn

grab a stick
grab a shoe
beat that little girl blue

who does
she think she is?
LAUGHING like that
don't you know
they'll put their
hands
all over you
cut out your tongue
scrape out your insides
tie up your tubes

grab a stick...grab a shoe...beat that...little   girl   blue

Canyon Sam

Invitation

THIS WEEK I GOT THE INVITATION IN THE MAIL FROM CATE IN SAN JOSE.
It was on Starbright Astroglow Pink Coral paper and I could see
she'd made it with her Mac. A graphic of a cake lit with candles was
on the cover, festooned with, *You Are Invited to a Birthday Dinner*, and inside
the particulars in a lovely Medieval but easily readable typeface: *Saturday
October 3, 6 PM. Yet Wah restaurant, 23rd and Clement. For Lou's 50th. Birthday Cake
will be served at Elaine's.* That was my mom's house, one block from the
restaurant.

The decade birthdays in one's later years are important in Chinese
society — cause for celebration — probably left over from the days of
rampant starvation when only Taoists on mountaintops lived to see the age
of 50 or 60 or older. I was third generation Chinese, "ABC" or American
Born Chinese. When I walked into Chinese restaurants, the first-generation
proprietors openly sneered at my lumbering L.L. Bean boots, or my black
leather fanny pack which looked, I suppose when I wore it in front, vaguely
obscene to them. But I did retain a feeling for certain Chinese traditions
with which I'd been raised.

My cousin Lou turning 50 was a momentous occasion. She was the
eldest of my generation and would inherit the role of elder and tradition-
bearer when my parents and Aunt Camille, all now in their mid-70s and
early-80s passed on. Growing up, I was raised close to my first cousin Lou,
my elder by fourteen years, her sister Cate, and brother Jeff; they were
something like older siblings to my two brothers and I. All of us spent a
good part of our childhood and youth living together in my grandparents'
house in Fresno, California, because Lou, Cate, and Jeff's mom had died
when they were children and they were raised by their maternal
grandmother, my mom's mom.

Lou is one of the prides of our family. She gets along with everyone. My brothers are each close to her, admiring her for different reasons. My older brother Mark admires her for her success. He's kept every scrap of history of her professional career and civic contributions of the last 32 years in a series of albums: a color photo of her standing beside the new, cherry red Ford MG she won along with her four-year Ford scholarship to Cal Berkeley; the program from her law school graduation in 1969 where she graduated Summa Cum Laude; her first front page byline in the *San Francisco Examiner* newspaper; the letterhead stationery of her Montgomery Street law firm where she, Louise H. Yuen, is the eleventh senior partner listed after ten Jewish males, followed by dozens and dozens of other partners and associates that joined after her in the 70s and 80s; the videotape clip of her auctioning prizes during the KQED Auction when she was a member of their Board of Directors; the embossed invitations to On Lok's annual fundraising banquets at the Hilton — she was a long-time donor to the Chinatown organization that served the elderly.

My younger brother Winston respects her for her money. He likes to go antique shopping with her in classy boutiques on Sacramento Street and then needle her for days to buy items he's selected, like the $7,000 chandelier he's convinced is perfect for the living room of her Pacific Heights Victorian. He likes to drive around Atherton and Woodside with her on Sunday afternoons scouting estates and California-style mansions for sale. She told me once that when she asked him where he might get the money to buy a house he wanted — at 33 he has never supported himself, my parents support him and his wife both — he answered that my dad would give him the money. He likes to help her choose imported Italian wallpaper, gold-leafed picture frames for tapestries she brings home from overseas travel, and marble floor tiles and countertops for her remodelled bathroom, without concern for cost. He spends weekends leaning over, licking wealth, status, and luxury from her bowl.

I'm the different one. The only girl, in between two brothers. My cousins studied business, pharmacology, computer technology; I studied poetry, theater, socialism. I spent years working for grass roots political causes for no money and hitchhiking through underdeveloped Third World countries with a backpack. In the late 70s I threw myself into a human chain of 7,000 protestors protecting low income housing at Chinatown's International Hotel while Lou's Financial District law firm represented Four Seas, the corporation who owned the square-block property and had ordered the demolition. But we never discussed politics in my family, along with a lot of other subjects. In my early 20s, when I couldn't afford a car, Lou let me drive her Ford Maverick when she bought her new Porsche; she gave me her old living room sofa when I finally moved to a place with more than a bedroom. I'd come around on family occasions, and leave the table when my relatives started talking about annuities, Nintendo, the Jaguar they will buy their six-year-old only son when he finishes medical school.

Last New Year's afternoon we were at Lou's house having juk, rice porridge made from the leftover Christmas turkey. It was a cold, grey, wintry day and the trees along the street of her house were sinewy and bare. Her house was painted burnt orange, the living room decorated in sunburst orange: it was her favorite color. But the dining room we sat in was in Old Americana style, with blue and white paisley wallpaper and cherrywood Victorian wainscoting.

"I just noticed something about your brothers," Lou exclaimed.

"What's that?" I said.

"Well, I invited Winston over to decorate the tree Sunday night, and I had been talking to your mom on the phone saying the beautiful gold ornament I used to put at the top of the tree — the one with the tall curly spire and the Nativity scene inside — had somehow got crushed in storage, and that I didn't have anything for the top of the tree."

"So Winston and I are decorating that night and the doorbell rings: it's your older brother bringing over this ornament from your mom for the top of the tree. That's so nice of your mom. So we're all three there decorating the tree for a while — I got Perry Como on singing carols, we're hanging the ornaments and stringing the lights, your younger brother was on this side of me, and your older brother was on this side... and pretty soon I notice that each of your brothers speaks to me," her eyes open wide, "but they never speak to each other! Jeez, jeez, jeez!" She chortled in disbelief.

"You just noticed that, Lou?" I asked.

"Yeah! They never talk to one another!" She was making little gasping noises as she laughed.

"They have never talked," I said. I put my hands underneath me, between my thighs and the seat of the Queen Anne chair.

"What?!"

"They have never talked to each other. Ever."

She blinked. Her mouth opened.

"At least in my memory," I said rocking on my hands. I looked at my juk — the green parsley sprigs floated beneath the surface, the red ginger shreds marbled the broth. It was getting cold. "If they did, it was when we were real little, little kids. I don't remember them ever talking. And my memory goes back to about four or five." I dipped my ceramic soup spoon into my juk.

"Gee whiz," Lou whistled. "I guess I never noticed it, because whenever we get together there's so many people around. You know there's twenty people. Gee Willikers."

I happened to be in the neighborhood, so I dropped in at my parents' house one evening years ago. They live on a wide, quiet residential block near Golden Gate Park in a two-storeyed, stucco-fronted house.

My mother answered the door. She looked shrunken and bent. Her face was drained of color, her cheeks hollow, her eyes darkly anxious. She cowered behind the door.

"What's wrong?" I asked.

"Your brother," she quaked with fear, "is upset."

My elder brother was in one of his rages.

"He's mad at your father," she muttered, climbing up the carpeted staircase near the front door. "You stay down here, he won't like it," she said, taking two stairs to a stride, her white knees popping up through the front of her raspberry pile robe.

"It's Deb, it's Deb," I heard my mom plead in a high voice upstairs towards the back of the house. Then I heard muffled low voices. I could tell my brother was trying to keep his voice down. Witnesses irritated him.

"Nah... nah," I heard my dad baying in his keeping-the-peace voice. You're overreacting Elaine. Whatever you want, son, it said.

More low threatening murmurs from my brother.

"I will not let you... I'm going in with 'im, I'm going in with 'im," my mother clipped in a rushing, panicked voice. A door slammed. The voices trailed off. I ran up the avocado green carpeted stairs to the sunporch adjacent to Mark's room. Both my parents were inside with him. I knew he had the doorknob lock pushed in.

"Sit down! You're going to listen!" Mark thundered. I heard everything through the cheap balsam wood door.

My brother resumed a tirade, raging at the top of his lungs. "But you *told* me to apply! You *said*. When I asked you! How could you say that when you didn't know? How could you *say* that when it was the complete opposite?"

Unintelligible mutterings from my father answered in the same tempered honey tone. I could smell fear through the door like an animal scent.

"What are you doing saying things you don't know anything about? I put six weeks of training in..." Mark's voice was whining and raging in the same sentence.

My mother in a tight anguished voice was pleading, "That's not true, that's not true. No, he did not mean that." I could hear my brother stomping and circling around, imagine my parents huddled together in the center of the room, my father squeezed onto some old toy chest amidst stacks of papers. My mother would be clinging to him, leaning her body against his side protectively, her eyes on her son as he paced in front of them, clicking the heels of his shiny black leather boots on the hardwood floor. He was punishing my father for lending bad advice. In my brother's twisted logic my father was responsible for his losing his new job as a parking control officer, a meter man.

My father said, "They have a predetermined drop-out rate that wasn't met, so they had to cut someone... Perhaps they're under budgetary restrictions... City government sometimes..." His voice was patient and eerily calm as if he was reading from a procedures manual at work, explaining some technicality to some disgruntled client.

"You're just speculating!" Mark cut in. "There you go again, talking off the top of your head. Why would they advertise that they had nine positions and go through all those candidates and hire nine people, if they were gonna cut back to eight?" He stopped on a question to set another trap for my dad; if my dad spoke up, he'd slash into him again. My dad said nothing; Mark seized the momentum: "I lost this job because you don't know what the hell you're talking about!"

My brother was indecisive to the point of paralysis, to the point where he's never moved out of my parents' house in 39 years, and didn't work till he was 30, despite a college degree in urban studies and a high IQ. Two or three months ago my brother was agonizing over two job offers: a temporary six-month position at the DMV as a test monitor that paid well, but held only the possibility, not the guarantee of a permanent position; or a job as a Parking Control Officer at a lower salary — a permanent job, contingent on three months' probation. So afraid was he of making the wrong decision that he was unable to make a decision at all. He hounded my father morning, noon, and night every day for two weeks angling to squeeze an opinion out of him. Mark took the meter man job, then a week and a half before his six-week training period ended, before his three-month probation was anywhere in sight, he was dismissed.

"Don't give me these excuses! You're just trying to get out of it! Don't interrupt me *again*..." he shouted. I imagined his jowly face twisted in rage, his thick neck purple with straining veins, his little yellow teeth clenched tight. I wanted to put a gun to his head then and there like a rancher puts a rabid dog to sleep. To put him and the whole family out of its misery once and for all.

"AND I SUFFER FOR IT! YOUR LAMENESS! YOUR STUPIDITY!" he shouted. A loud crash hit the floor. The floor shook under my feet, indeed the whole room quivered, the feather-light door, the molded door frame, the sheetrock walls.

"Don't you touch him..." my mother begged, the pitch of her voice rising in fear.

I ran downstairs and punched the buttons on the ivory phone in the hall: 9-1-1. Focus, focus. I didn't want to see what I saw in my mind's eye: his face trembling in front of my father's, his fragile impulse control losing the battle against his outrage, his thirst for vengeance, his meaty, steak-fed hand rising in the air, my father flying off the toy chest like a swatted fly, my mother's helpless horror.

I called the cops and then I called Lou who lived about three miles away. Lou was home and said she'd be right over. The patrol car bounced over the curb pulling up at an angle across the sidewalk, its high-powered blue beam flashing in circles in front of the house, streaking the stucco. Lou parked her sleek silver Mercedes in front, but out three feet from the curb like in the action movies where the detectives screech to a halt and leap out.

"Eddie!" I said, seeing the police officer come towards the front door in the night shadows.

To my surprise and relief, the officer was Eddie Chow, an old acquaintance from high school, a basketball star who'd become a cop. He had filled out a good deal, stood tall and imposing in his dark blue uniform and black leather gunbelt, but I remembered him as sweet-natured. He and Lou and I dashed upstairs and huddled in the sunporch — it was full of discards from Mark's room: a broken Smith-Corona typewriter, a torn lampshade, dusty stacks of five-year-old *Time* and *Business Week* magazines. We could hear everything as if we were in the same room.

"Now this goes on my *record!*" Mark thundered. "I've lost *income*, I've lost the other *job!* Because of YOU!" He spit the last word of each phrase in fevered rhythm. We stood back several feet from the door, wincing with every scream. A crash from a heavy, weighted object smashed to the floor.

"I'm gonna break down the door," Eddie breathed hoarsely, shoulder-ing past me, gripping the top of the black nightstick hanging from his belt.

"No, no, wait," I cautioned. It would only escalate things.

"Gollee, what is he doing? What's he so mad about?" Lou asked. I could tell she was shocked to hear him in his out-of-control state: no one outside the immediate family had ever witnessed him before. "My God!" she shuddered, as another crash shook, this one a duller, more diffused thud against the opposite wall. My heart was beating hard and quick in my chest.

I couldn't tell if he was actually hitting them, but he was lathering up, getting awfully close.

"I'm gonna go for it," Eddie said, pressing by me.

"No, Eddie, please... just wait." I had already asked my mental health friends about it before: 72-hour lock up was the only option. A 72-hour detention was all we could get, then he'd be back home and even madder. He'd make them pay for his humiliation. After a three-day psychiatric detention in some city ward or jail cell, my brother'd probably come home and burn their house down. One time he was mad at my father for some slight, and for two years slammed doors whenever my dad was in the house until my father left the premises. My brother blamed a member of the family for any misfortune that befell him. My father was being set up again. Once Mark could get an admission of guilt, he could extract a prize, but that would come later. In his early twenties, using leverage from a 23-page written indictment against my father, he got a summer trip to Europe.

My dad was talking: "... Civil service procedures will allow you to apply again in... " He was swimming, talking to himself as if trapped down a well in his own world, repeating how everything was fine no matter how high the water surged around him.

"Tsk! Tsk! Tsk!" My brother snorted and clicked his tongue in exaggerated disgust with each heavy breath. His breathing was labored, agitated like he was catching his breath from one round, but keeping his adrenalin in high drive for the next.

"NO! DAMN IT!" Crash!

"Son, son...," my mother was crying.

"Don't protect him! Stay out of the way!" Mark yelled.

My eyes and Eddie's locked. He was chafing to break the door down, but I knew the repercussions on my parents in the long-term for this action would be unimaginably awful. I checked Eddie with my stare.

Lou slumped against the wall taking big gulps of air. She was pale. She could spin streams of elegant prose off the tip of her tongue with the barest of effort — I heard her dictate a letter once at my grandparents' house when she was still a young, new attorney — but her 25 years' experience as a high-powered corporate lawyer never prepared her for this kind of battle. My brother had been the prized first-born of my mom, their favourite aunt. The entire family doted on him when she was growing up. She could tease him, she could reason with him. She could reason with anybody, it was her profession. But not now.

I wish I had a stun gun and a straitjacket and the means to ship him into outer space, out of our lives. Forever. I could only hope he wouldn't touch them.

After twenty more minutes, I detected my brother's flailings beginning ever so slightly to lose their force. He repeated things for the tenth time in a pouting, almost droning chant.

"And what are you gonna do? Eeehhhh? EEEEEEHHHHHHH?!... You're going to make this up to me... Two thousand dollars a month guaranteed income I lose because of you!... Because you can't make proper decisions... You..." Sometimes he trailed off. On his inhalations he gasped in soft, spiteful spasms. He had peaked, and now was circling to a descent. I knew from experience that he could light up again at any moment, but I sensed he was doing perfunctory final laps, milking every last minute in a show of force and control. They just had to wait now till he tired enough to let them go. But at least he wasn't going to physically harm them.

I could breathe again. The world started to right itself, the satiny oak floors in neat, tightly laid strips, the starched linen and lace curtains, the hard square corners of the aluminum window, the door frame, came into focus. I shooed off Eddie and Lou, knowing he'd be so furious at outside intervention and so humiliated to know anyone had heard him that it'd likely set him off again.

After another twenty minutes, my mother emerged. I say the fuzzy gold letters, "MARK," on the bedroom door open back and close forward again. When I was thirteen, my parents built the back addition on the house so we three kids each got our own room. They had to, my brothers were going to murder each other. Mom put our names on our new doors in contact paper: MARK. DEB. WINSTON.

She was swaying unsteadily as she walked, as if she might faint if you touched her. Her face was ashen, her eyes swollen and red, her cheeks damp.

"You should leave," she half-whispered. "He thinks we called you." I knew my brother: he liked his prey completely helpless. There was no "Thanks for being here," no "I'm glad you were here."

"Go, go," she said, brushing my elbow with trembling hands, her raspberry robe sleeve drooping from her bony wrist.

Three weeks later at Mother's Day lunch at my folks' house, the extended family was at the dining table for dessert — Lou, Cate, Jeff, my mom, younger brother, our Aunt Camille, and her son Ray and his family. Mark was upstairs in his room watching TV, which is where he spent family get-togethers. Somehow the conversation turned to him.

"Jeff suggested you just give Mark one of the apartment buildings and say: "You're on your own, fella..." Lou said, chuckling nervously over her mandarin orange pie. I got the sense that Lou had told Cate and Jeff about Mark's tantrum. The TV was on loud and there were couple other conversations going on at the same time, so not everyone heard. My younger brother looked at Lou with first a puzzled, then a hard stare. Lou had a tiny kiss of whipped cream on the side of her mouth. Winston rolled his eyes and curled his lip derisively at the thought of our brother. Cate heard, but just blinked and kept her mouth shut; she wasn't going to take it on. I think my mom heard, but pretended not to: "Ice cream with your orange pie, Nicole?" she sung, silver spatula in hand, addressing the fourteen-year-old, sloe-eyed daughter of my cousin Ray.

My parents made Lou executor of their estate when they drew up their wills after my dad's 70th birthday. She was the oldest cousin, carried the most moral authority in the family, and had legal clout to boot. Hadn't she been chosen to dress down my younger brother when he almost flunked junior high school? Wasn't it her shadow I couldn't escape when I dropped out of the University at Berkeley, knowing my hard-won A-s and B+s could never approach her remarkable, effortless scholastic achievements there? It was a brilliant stroke for my folks to designate her to handle legal matters between my brothers and me upon their death — much more effective than my mom's trembly warnings: "If anyone contests the will, everything goes to St. Anthony's Dining Room."

But I realized, after this scene at the house and after the Christmas tree night, how much Lou *didn't* know — even in the midst of hearing and seeing some of it herself. No one knew. I realized that even Louise H. Yuen, ascending to the mantle of elder in our family at the age of 50 — with all her prestige and power — even she could not help us.

Patrice Leung

December 1989

IT WAS ALWAYS THE HARDEST MONTH FOR HER.

The day had dawned (if you could call rain dawn) hours earlier and yet she remained wrapped securely in her quilt as she had for the past two and a half weeks. It was the month of her birthday, of course, and as her twenty-ninth year drew nigh she had retreated to her bed.

There were forays to the kitchen and toilet but for the most part she lay on her futon listening to the banal offerings of AM radio. The hype was endless, the superficiality infinite, and together they prevented her thoughts from becoming concepts. Noise as a condom.

In the odd moments when she wished for quiet her mind wandered, but not aimlessly. The day was fast approaching when she had to acknowledge her knowledge. And she became frightened and felt alone. Quickly, she turned on the radio.

She wasn't socially inept. Oh, she had friends and family and a potential lover. She was usually employed. She wasn't ugly and she wasn't too attractive. She wasn't stupid and thankfully she wasn't a genius. She just was. And whatever she was she needed to control at the moment.

The noise from the radio was becoming identifiably repetitive so she switched stations. Through the cracks in her closed blinds she noticed the dull grey had turned into a dark void and she was thankful that she had survived another day without incident.

To sleep is to escape. From even the most real nightmare you can awaken. And so she yawned and willed herself to sleep.

She awoke at 7:20 a.m. to a voice on her phone machine. One of her ex-lovers was wishing her a happy birthday all the way from Montreal. There it was 10:20 a.m. How typical of Lynn to be so thoughtful and thoughtless at the same time.

She did not answer even though there was a tone in the voice that begged for human response. Instead she flipped on the radio and tried to drown the memories of her night's dreams.

At 11 o'clock she wrested herself from her quilt and sat up. She shut off the radio. Leaning forward she slowly opened the blinds and stared silently into the rain. Then she smiled. It was her birthday.

She proceeded to the bathroom, had a pee, took a shit, brushed her teeth, and languished under the shower.

She got dressed and sat at her desk. She chose her black mechanical pencil and some white lined paper. The time had come.

Dear Patrice (she wrote),

Today I must face what I have learned. My innocence is irreparably tarnished. And I grieve. And am scared.

I used to trust the world in spite of what I thought I knew. The world was violent, unfair; repercussions both of what was natural and man-made. But the atrocities were always distant, geographically and emotionally.

And then it became personal.

You know how I like to say that I'm from peasant stock. From the southeastern part of China. That hardworking, intelligent, honest, and cultured blood courses through my veins. That my arrogance is based on genetic superiority.

However, on June 4th I fell off my pedestal. My pride turned to shame as I realized that we as Chinese are not above barbarism.

Tiananmen Square.

A massacre.

The crushing of human lives by tanks and guns and sick, old men. No act of repression has ever touched me so deeply. It was so painful to see my own blood that even now I cannot write without tears.

I used to be invincible. And then they killed fourteen women. In Montreal. But it really doesn't matter where, does it? One man pulled the trigger but I see other men behind him, smiling from the shadows.

Because they were women.

It could have been someone I love.

My lover.

My sister.
My mother.
My niece.
My friend.
Myself.

I knew intellectually that there are those who hate me for who I am, for exactly those things of which I am most proud: Chinese, Woman, Lesbian. But this is the first time in my life that I have actually *felt* this hate. This intensity sears my gut. And for the first time I am scared of the world.

Remember the few times when friends dared to jump out at me from behind corners? I would jump but never scream. Instead I said, "Fuck You!" and then laughed. It's just my way. I've always met fear with anger, because fear is used so often to control and I refuse to be manipulated.

Anger has always been my power. My motivation to act. To regain control of the situation and myself. But how do you control a semi-automatic rifle when it is pointed at your soul?

My anger is powerless this time. I cannot bring back the murdered women. I cannot kill their killer because the bastard beat me to it. I cannot stop the sickening anonymous phone calls to rape crisis centres and womens' organizations which threaten even more Montreals.

How does one find and kill the men who hide their hatred behind anonymity? Maybe I should just choose one at random and hope for the best.

I could choose one easily. Lots of men pass by my window. Or I could spot one in traffic. Or in church on Christmas Eve. No, it won't be hard at all. Some man at work is bound to piss me off.

Then I would haunt him day and night. Stake out his home. Observe his patterns. Call him. If his lover answers, speak, and apologize for the wrong number. If he answers, be silent, and then hang up. Anonymous, of course. But not out of cowardice.

I will merely appropriate their use of intimidation on us and twist it slowly and meticulously into my own vision of torture.

If he moves I will follow. And one night I will catch him alone and slice off his penis with a serrated knife. And he will bleed for me and for all the women he has hated and killed. And I will not take his penis, Dr. Freud. He can have it. Stuffed in his mouth to stifle his screams.

Then I will choose another man. And after that another. And so on and so on. But I won't tell two friends. Not even one. This is private. And I have a lot of catching up to do.

Fourteen women.

The three-year-old accused of being sexually aggressive.

Bill Van Der Zalm.

The lesbians abducted and gang-raped near Commercial Drive.

The prostitutes abducted, raped, and murdered in Vancouver.

Martin R. De Haan II.

My ex-lover who was sexually abused by her father.

Don Getty.

The man who threatened over the phone to kill me, you stupid Chinese woman, because ICBC settled in my favour against his drunken driving.

Brian Mulroney, Ronald Reagan, George Bush.

The anonymous male caller who wants me to suck his dick.

And so on.

In the course of writing to you I have changed. I am no longer scared of the world. I am scared for the world.

I always thought adulthood meant finding a comfortable space for myself in the world, but no one told me that to get there I first had to learn to hate, and to fear, and to mistrust.

I have been forced to acknowledge that pain exists and that I must challenge it continually. Anger and Words. These are presently my most powerful allies in my struggle with pain. It would be easier to wrap myself in ignorance but that would not be living.

Take care.

Love,

Patrice

She read what she had written and then re-read it aloud. As she placed the letter beside her typewriter she looked out the window and saw the wind and rain gently orchestrating the branches of her neighbour's willow tree. She walked to the closet, grabbed her jacket and pulled it over her head. Then she opened the front door and went outside.

Elsa E'der

Who Will Remember Me
When I Return To America?

I Jazz

Jeeeez us! in Oakland too! it's 9:30 on a
thursday night the 33rd street church voices walk
right through locked windows, doors
even the blinds shutup/my silence understood
I am waiting for music to find me/waiting
half-assedly balancing the checkbook
expense theory against cost/who's counting/Jeeeez us!
they implore such wicked history

    sing the songs that collapse the borders
       the songs that collapse the borders
          songs collapse the borders
            collapse the borders
              the borders

of empty pages bleached white
clean pages
flat and neat and all alike/unlike the violent cost
unlike the j a z z
Hawaii Filipinos made sure I knew
the j a z z

II Blues

my tribe breathes fire
and laughs pulling
notes out of the sky/thorns out their eyes
to place them/when they remember
on five thin lines
scratch paths between cultures
So They Can FIND US In America
five thin lines when they remember
the net weaving song
over the ocean
to the Philippines:
this is the FIRST BASE of all Bases
this is the pitcher's mound
these are the blues baptizing us
in America.

> after the priests stole their land
> my people drew plans on the shoreline, lines
> when dogs devoured... /lines
> from ports of Cebu to lines and lines of planting/lines
> in the hopeful empty hands of farmers/we will remember
> our roots are the rumours in a line

because some-peoples'-time-is-worth-more-than-others
now it is clear/if my people had stayed
we would be squatting on somebody's rich
rich somebody's soil
starving

III Rock-and-Roll

I am an American Filipino
I am not pure
I do not dance tinikling
I cannot speak Tagalog

    I understand that
    understanding is as deep as
    the lines in my grandmother's hands
    I am waiting for the music to find me
    I listen for the sound of
    silent screams en la noche
    I speak the language of broken angels

I am the children's children of
blood in the land
the Philippines
do not belong do not belong do not belong
to the Filipinos

    yet they tell me
    my kind of people are
    stupid enough to work the land/they
    tell me they are disgusted because I do not speak their words/they
    tell me we should hire someone to scrub our floors because we don't have
    time to do it ourselves/they
    tell me Filipinos are hispanic/oriental/malaysian
    therefore we are the latest fashion/they tell me
    they are Filipino American/they
    tell me I should be proud
    of these people
    they tell me they have so much to do
    but they hire people cheap
    they can't do it alone/they
    tell me I am not who I am

the exile told me:
the first thing he thought when I came to
the states was: "who's going to do my laundry?"

IV Prayer

tonight in Oakland, it is Jesus again
not rage in an apartment near
34th and Neldams-on-Telegraph

it is some night in the nineteenth month
of inconsistency/I
suspect have 33 years
     of migration my self
     laborers, mirror of saints
     woman, lover of women
     warriors and blues
     Cebu, Ilocos, LaPuente, San Francisco
     Honolulu, Los Angeles, San Francisco
     blood in the land
     the Philippines
     do not belong do not belong do not belong
     to the Filipinos

I put my hand inside the wound
the borders/inside I have betrayed
the friends who love
my fear/lovers
hating my love/enemies who
fear my hate/I too
have prayed before
the earth
dead warriors
and women
in the cities

I am the children's
children of discontent
blood in the land
flame and smoke and flame
a solid ghost
weary of the earth vestments of
warriors   Indios
born in the city of angels/Los Angeles
woman born in the city of angels
I speak a broken language

we can burn this place
this wasted time in exile from
exiles in a place called *home*(?)
in a place I call home.
I have prayed
before we can burn this place
this place
we can harvest.

Lynne Yamaguchi Fletcher

Custody

You've won. Your sun-browned son, twelve-tall,
Nephew I helped deliver, stays yours — *ours* —

For as long as you can hold him.

Grief cleaves victory from your voice.
Song sparrows flock the backyard feeder.

There was ugliness. Your boy's father
Tried to make you out a buffoon, your husband

An old man, stepfather out of step.

Your voice quits.
A mourning dove searches the ground for millet.

Among the sparrows, chickadees, brazen, black-capped,
Snatch seed, their greed not theft but

Wanting: his Dad. Unhappiness

Roots in him like thistle.
Sister. You will not be comforted.

Beside the trunk of the puffball tree
A young cardinal, black-billed, orange-breasted,

Not yet in his red.

All morning, it has mimicked the male's
Brilliance, the bright peck and step and plumage . . .

He chose his father's. The judge chose you.
All family hurts, you say, and hang up.

A pulse of wings and it's gone.

Recurring Dreams

In the first, crocodiles
wait below as one by one my family
slips from a single-log bridge
into a chasm. I cross last.

I cross.

In the second, I am sorting zippers
in my family's notions shop when
the radio barks a news flash:
An unidentified

monster on a rampage
is killing people all over
the city. I am cleaning
the bathroom when I hear

sounds in the shop. I know
who is here. I hide in the
waste can, come out when hush . . .

Pieces of my family are all
over the shop. (This is before
Vietnam stains TV.)
A hand

rests on the counter.
I am alone.

In the latest, which comes
when I am awake but
desperate for real sleep,
exhausted from the daily
in, out
remembering to breathe,

I take a scalpel, begin
at my chin, slice
downward, a smooth
unzipping: choir robe.
What I feel is longing,
the slip of the heavy satin

from my shoulders. What does this
have to do with the others?

What is rage but
pain turning
inside
out?

Donna Tsuyuko Tanigawa

Junks Inside Me

I.   da scar on my arm
stay open   again.
look like one mouth/all red inside
lips thick brown scab.

dreamt i at da beach
was morning time
took one razor and shave my legs
ran da blade over chicken skin
cut/cut hair follicles

den growths start fo' grow
some look j'like potato spuds
or cauliflowers on my cunt/stay warts
others look like accordion files
folded j'like one Japanee fan

da cuts stay pink and moist/mucus
hanging from my calves
me, I jus' accept 'um.

II.   wen tink dat i one daisy
da kine at Tani's Store
stay in da can of water/bunched
together in cellophane.

but i one daisy
i told dem' all.
j'like one daisy
fragile/plain/wild
and short lived.

wen da sun come out
in da afternoon   i live
but only fo' couple days
sun stay strong here.

den i saw dat i wasn't one daisy
i wanted fo' be one, but
dey only live short.

III.   strange how my husband
is one head banger
thrash/sistah/thrash she tell me
i no like heavy metal
    (mom used to say heavy metal fo' dinner
    only she mean dat we goin eat from da pot)

for her birthday i bought
one CD of Metallica
thrash/sistah/thrash
i told her no play wen i home

eh, i read one book
on psychosis.
babies that bang their heads
are bent on suicide, da man said
psychic pain inside.

as one small kid/i wen move
around plenty
had bed rails two sides
j'like one jail
i wen like fo' have da bed
against da hollow tile wall/wood panels junk
stay more cool, i told um.

but i used to wake up wit
big red bruises
blood on da white paint too/tan-ko-bo
on my head.

i nevah tell nobody but
i used to bang my forehead
on da cold cement wall/was up
i nevah was sleeping/no tell

IV.   guess what my bank code
number is   da one fo' da $ machine?
O-D-I-E. smart, eh?
i figgah dat since i goin die soon
good fo' have one reminder.

i try fo' hurt myself
i get five bumps inside my lip
j'like tiny okole-holes
or braddah's face/stay erupt

remember da girl   used fo'
bit her fingertips
until could see da meat hang

i came already   you know.
8:36 pm on May 27
stay wit da devil already
you wit me, he said
undress/take off your clothes
eh, da Polaroid picture of my cunt.

cut your gums/slice 'um like cabbage

write dis' down: Look at your naked body.
Feel it.   Touch yourself.
Meet Jack again. four sips, Mr. Daniels.

prepare fo' suck your arm/clotted blood

i feel it coming one more time
kinda like one slow twitch
or extra cup of coffee

i can hear it again
no be mad/at me
i thought pills would kill da noise
lithium   something blue   brown

sorry, no can let da burn heal/curling
iron work good
bile come out/secretions
poisons/yellow stay now/lymph
thick crust on my shirt sleeve.

V.   dream at da ocean again
a group of girls by da water
we find a box/stay floating
inside get someone's ear lobe
and nipple   I put the
items inside j'like jewellery
no care what da other girls tink.

Lihbin Shiao

Butterflies

A GE 24, ERICA CAN'T REMEMBER YEARS OUT OF HER CHILDHOOD. Her friends seem to remember minute details. Erica can't even remember the color of her room when she was five. She tells people: "If it were important, I would remember." It's only in the morning that this memory loss haunts her. Propelling herself out of dreams resembling slide presentations in dark rooms, Erica misses the warmth of nubby bed covers with crocheted nipples and the long strings her mother used to sew on blankets to keep her from kicking them off. "Mom," as Erica refers to her, tells her that she used to have nightmares almost every night. And Erica's younger sister, Masha, would have to sit in the bathroom while she took her showers. But Erica can't remember dreams or the past anymore.

She imagines she's rewriting her history in this way, a blank slate. When Erica walks down the street to work every morning, she stares at men in windows. Her eyes bounce off the eyeballs of men in the glass. She notes the slope of their necks, the curve of shoulders and the backs of their heads. She likes to play games. Some men stare hard, others turn away embarrassed, mumbling something about wives, strange looks, and the devil. But Erica never bats an eyelash; they are no more real to her than the slide presentations of colors, shapes, and smells in the hour before awakening. She doesn't feel threatened by them.

The aroma of toasting bagels comes out onto the sidewalk at 7:15 every morning. The Bagel Place's narrow space of grey counter, its polished tile floors and small stools are illuminated by the bright morning sun from the store window wall. Clocking in and greeting a few co-workers, Erica pulls her apron strap over her head and behind her neck and ties the back strings around her waist securely. Her friend, Laurah isn't scheduled to work today; so, Erica settles into her morning routine uninterrupted by Laurah's game of pulling her apron strings loose and asking her to try a new type of hot coffee or chocolate drink she'd concocted in stolen time.

Erica spends only the mornings at work. The afternoons she whites canvasses with gesso to sell to artists too busy to do it themselves; she'll lay back reading a book, or she'll work out. These afternoon hours she takes for herself; they keep her sane after the tiring demands of customers, polite or most often, otherwise. Her home is not always a haven though.

The crash of a cup in slow motion. The accompaniment of words that she can't quite comprehend. Someone is screaming. Erica awakens: 4:18 am; the couple upstairs with two kids, Narhee and Ja, are fighting again. Her slide presentation is interrupted. Erica is disassociated for a minute until she realizes that somehow her dream coincides with this concrete incident. Erica flips on her lamp; she and the other neighbours wait for someone else to call the police; 911 traces the caller, and nobody wants to be the somebody responsible. When the police do come, they come late: some with eyes full of sorrow; others with a hard look, thinking of what they've done to their own wives. Their arms hang at their sides, useless.

"I hate you," Haiwon shrieks.

"You are useless," the man's voice rages.

Setting cold milk to heat, Erica sneaks upstairs a half floor: "Pssst." Narhee and Ja usually sit in the stairwell playing cards and wait for the fight to boil over. But this time, without a response from the two girls, Erica climbs the stairs to find them huddled in the stairwell corner. Ja, the older sister, eyes angry, crying, is kissing Narhee's cheeks, eyes and chin, not wanting to miss a spot. Narhee is seven and Ja, twelve.

Ja picks up her little sister, more than half her own weight, and without a word, descends the stairs with Erica. The hot chocolate doesn't put them to sleep tonight; Narhee's arms have bruises the size and shape of poking fingers. Erica does not ask. A pressure cooker contains Erica's tired frustration over this frequently occurring scene, the top clanks loudly.

Narhee and Ja spend the next two days in her apartment before their mother can walk downstairs to claim them. As usual, she has no marks on her face; her long sleeves and high neckline are dark enough markers. Ja's eyes search the tightened muscles of her mother's neck, and angrily she stares her mother in the eye. Haiwon cannot keep her gaze. Her inability to protect herself and now her daughter makes her humour forced. She leaves with her two children quickly.

The next day, Narhee comes downstairs with a small knock and a brand new doll to meet Auntie Erica. The bruises on her arm yellowing already.

"This is Sasha, isn't she pretty?" Narhee's voice lilts.

"She's very beautiful, Narhee," Erica answers solemnly.

"Daddy thinks so too. He says she's my little girl, just like I'm his little girl now. He let me name her. And he told me I'm old enough to be responsible for dressing her, combing her hair, and making sure she's a good girl."

Packing boxes, Erica calls the child abuse center that night. She's been putting off this confrontation, her adult self with her child self for as long as possible. In the early morning, she says goodbye to Narhee and Ja. Narhee tells her to visit them soon; Ja's eyes stare fixedly at Erica and into herself. Erica tucks her address into Ja's front pocket. This is not the time for pictures, goodbye or no.

It takes Erica hours to lug her fourteen small boxes, her easel, blankets, canvasses, and rugs up the stairs of her new apartment. Finally done, instead of unpacking, she locks the door and calls her closest female friend, Laurah from a pay phone.

Coffee, eggs, bacon, toast, home fries, and blackberry pancakes relaxed their limbs, soothed Erica's emptiness. Holding hands over the plastic top of the small breakfast table in Cypress' Home cooking, Erica told Laurah she'd moved.

"Why, I thought you liked your apartment." Laurah's voice always has a musical quality.

"Yeah, well, I'm having problems. Remember, the two kids you met last time you were at my place?"

"Yeah, Ja and the shy little girl."

"Narhee. Her father and mother fight all the time, and they live right above me you know. He beat her really badly this time. It was two days, Laurah. Two days before she came and got them. Narhee had bruises all over her arms the first day and the day after her mom took her back, she came back telling me she was daddy's little girl. I can't do it anymore,

Laurah; nothing's getting better. I called the abuse center..." Erica stares at her hands making a steeple.

"Yeah. At least she'll join the statistics," Laurah says sarcastically.

"I'm scared."

"Why?" Laura asks softly. "It's their problem, not yours."

Erica tangles her hands through her long hair, cupping her forehead. "But I'm scared. I had a nightmare last night and the thing is, I remembered having had it over and over as a kid. The room is dark, the door's closed, and I'm covering my ears. A lot of colors and sounds, but I couldn't remember the rest after I got up."

Laurah's arm stretches across the table, recapturing Erica's smaller hand within her own larger one. "Do you need someone to spend the night?"

"No, I'll be okay; maybe things will be better now that I've moved. It's a nice looking neighbourhood."

"That always helps," Laurah says doubtfully.

"Sorry to dwell on such depressing topics. Let's talk about something else. What's going on in your life?"

"Oh, same old shit. Dealing with Oma. The same old cycle breakup, makeup, etc. She's impossible. But it's unimportant compared to what you're going through. I care a lot about you, Erica."

Short stubby fingers, brief cuticles, short straight hairs on the digits closest to the hand, bulging veins grip a slender neck, the other hand poking into somebody's waist. Another person replaces the trapped one, her long hair is being pulled as she tries to escape. She escapes; his hands full of long strands of ripped out hair. The phone rings.

"Hello?" Erica answers sleepily. It's taken a little more than a week for her to get the place to look lived in.

"A-rica," her mother's peculiar accent comes across the line like she lives next door though she really lives 600 miles away, "are you sleeping?"

Erica rolls her eyes and sighs, "Yes, Mom. I went to bed early; I had a long day. What's up? Can I call you tomorrow?"

"Oh, you're sick. I just wanted to remind you to pick up the package I sent you federal express. It will spoil if you forget."

Erica doesn't speak with much if any of a Chinese accent, but it's taken her years living away from home to be able to detect even slightly the accent her friends told her her mother has.

"Yes, Mom, I'll remember," Erica interrupts impatiently, too tired to argue with her mom about not being sick, just tired. She knows she should be thanking her mom, but she's just too tired to say anything requiring much thought. Their relationship has been made of a long history of miscommunications. Talking to her mother, Erica finds herself fragmented: Chinese/Asian/Asian-American/womyn/bisexual.

Getting off the phone, Erica vaguely remembers the last two slides in her dream. Lately, she isn't as quick to dismiss their possible significance; lately, her dreams seem to be seeping into her daytime self. Erica sees slide-like images coming from she doesn't know where when she's wide awake at work.

She sees the face of a customer twist into pictures of people she's sure she's seen before, but Erica can't quite make the connection. In the slope of a man's neck in the mornings Erica sees the slope of another man's neck, but his body is in the dark; she can't see him, but she knows his eyes are staring at her.

"Laurah, I think I must have had a lobotomy earlier on in life. Some part of my brain was disconnected from the rest of it or maybe it was just lopped off. What do you think?" Erica makes light of her inability to remember.

"Seriously, Erica, maybe you should take my suggestion and go to counseling."

"Yeah, and here the same things I was taught to say to people to who called the crisis center? I already know what they're going to say to me."

"But these are professionals..."

"Right. So, I have to pay a shitload of money I don't have to hear some professional tell me that I'm hiding something from myself? Probably some traumatic incident in my childhood that I need to acknowledge, accept, and deal with," Erica essays half jokingly, half fearfully.

"You should confront this problem."

"You sound like the psychological services commercials on TV."

"Humph, can't I say anything helpful?" Laurah asks.

"I'm sorry; I'm just making light of it to deal with it. Let's talk about something else," Erica says more gently.

"As much as you know I hate it when people say this to me, I'm going to say it: really, it'll take time. Look, I'm always around, just call me if you need anything or feel like talking."

But Erica doesn't feel as if Laurah was getting any of this.

Two weeks. Ja buzzes Erica's doorbell, and Erica buzzes her up.

It's late afternoon and it's just starting to get dark.

"He broke her legs a week ago," Ja says right off the bat.

Erica sighs heavily, "Are you okay?" At twelve, Jaiun is too grown up.

"I called the police. I told them he was beating her in the bedroom. They didn't believe me after I told them how old I am. Mom caught him in Narhee's bedroom again; he had the top half of her pajamas off."

"Has he ever touched you, Ja?"

"Humh, no, I used to bite him whenever he came near me even at Narhee's age. I would scream real loud too. He knows I hate him," Ja recounts.

The hot water whistles, and Erica pours it over honey and a tea ball of dried jasmine flowers and green tea. The two of them sip solemnly. Ja watches Erica and imitates how she holds her cup and sips when Erica sips.

"I want to be like you one day, Erica," Ja says seriously.

"Why?" Erica asks awkwardly.

"You live by yourself. Nobody makes you do anything you don't want to. And it's always peaceful in your apartment."

"Not always. Do you want to spend the night?"

"Yeah, but..."

"I'll call your mom."

"She can't come to the phone; it'll be him."

"I'll take care of it; unless you think you should go home and take care of Narhee?"

"No, he always waits a week or so, so Mom can put up a good fight," Ja says sarcastically.

Erica calls, but even beforehand, the matter is settled.

That night, Ja curls on Erica's futon with her. Ja can't remember feeling this safe; she sleeps soundly. The two face each other, holding hands.

The next morning Erica remembers all her dreams. Slide presentations in the dark. The light pours into the room through the bedroom curtain. Ja is in the kitchen cooking Erica a breakfast of thin flour pancakes with sliced green onions. Erica showed her how to make them many a morning at her old apartment.

After Ja finally leaves around lunchtime, Erica allows herself to think. She wanders through her two rooms. The color of her room when she was five was blue. *His piercing eyes would stare down at her; he threatened her without words; he had to control everything in the house; he strolled into her bedroom without knocking; "I'm your daddy," he would answer her protest. He would choke her with her own hair to weaken her.* Picking up the phone, she dials Mama; her fingers finding the numbers without looking; the ringing sounds too loud to Erica's frightened mind. Her breathing shallow. Suihua, her mother, answers, "Hello," as if she were next door as always. Erica hangs up. She doesn't know the words, couldn't say them to her mother even if she could find them. Erica grasps scissors from her top righthand desk drawer, and twisting her long black hair behind her neck, she cuts it. She lets the severed mass fall into the wastebasket. The hopelessness of this gesture comes up from her stomach like nervous butterflies that flutter out of her mouth in a noiseless downward jerk of her jaw.

In Korean:
Haiwon: silent one
Narhee: butterfly
In Chinese:
Suihua: water flower

C. Allyson Lee

Recipe

Separate carefully the following ingredients
(with the help of family, friends, co-workers and the general public):

Why do they always hang around in groups or gangs?

Why don't you stick to your own kind?

So how come they let them into this country if they
caint speak English?

No, I don't speak Chinese.

They *all* look alike.

No, we aren't sisters.

They *all* do that.

They give the rest of us a bad name.

They talk so loud and get so pushy.

Why are they always so wimpy and reserved?

If I could be born all over again, I'd be born white.

If you marry a white boy, we'll cut you out of our will.

You'll have to try three times harder in order to be half as
good as white person.

Those Chinese work such long hours without complaining.
They do what they're told and they never ask questions.

They're driving up all the housing prices and they're
taking away all our jobs.

Why can't you get a decent respectable job like everyone else?
Something like business, accounting or pharmacy?

They're everywhere, taking over the world.

We didn't get the vote until 1949.

See how dorky they look, with those thick glasses and flat noses?

> Attractive Straight White Male,
> middle-aged business executive
> looking for that special little
> China Doll, preferably short,
> petite and obedient. Object:
> to fulfill typical fantasies of
> the stereotype of Oriental ladies
> anxious to marry a Canadian in
> order to get out of Hong Kong or
> the Philippines and willing to
> do anything to pamper and please
> her man. Photo required.

Do *you people* celebrate Christmas?

That Lo Faan looks ridiculous in that Chinese silk dress.

Tch, tch... another Chinese driver.
Those people are such lousy drivers.

Oh no! Not another Chinese Volvo fender bender.
How embarrassing!

You know, I just read a really interesting book on *China*
the other day...

What's the use of studying drama if there is never going
to be a Chinese actor allowed to play Lady Macbeth?
(Take *my* milk for gall!)

You know, I went to really good *Chinese* restaurant the other day.

Look at all these Lo Faan in this restaurant.
They're ordering exactly what *we're* having! Bunch of "Wanna Be's."

More crime! Violence! Must be *Asian gangs* again.

Look at all those whites wanting to do martial arts,
trying to be like Bruce Lee.

Do you cook Chinese food at home?

Do *you?*

Do you speak Chinese?

Do *you?*

I didn't know *you people* could sing jazz!

We all have vocal cords, too.

Where do you come from, *originally?*

My mother's womb — how about you?

Have you ever been back to Hong Kong?

How can you go back to some place you've never been?
I'm not Shirley MacLaine.

Wow — lookit that beautiful Chinese girl.
Such nice, almond-shaped eyes and lovely black hair!

Just because the person who passes me on the street is Chinese
doesn't mean that I have to look him/her in the eye and
acknowledge him/her.

Hey, some of my *best friends* are Chinese.

You should be playing with more Chinese kids!

Why don't they go back to where they come from?

Why don't *they* go back to where *they* come from?

Exclusion Act.

A dollar a day on the C.P.R.

Mix in a blender the following ingredients (in any home, school, workplace or public place):

Chink

Chinaman

Gook

V.C.

Slant-eye

Rice Gobbler

Gwai Lo

Lo Faan

Throw in a dash of guilt, shame and embarrassment, and a pinch of intimidation, resentment, jealousy and fear. Reinforce solidly with threats, condescension and a patronizing tone.

Subtly fold all ingredients together in a large, liberal multicultural bowl.

*Place in a large pressure-cooker and seethe at the following temperatures
(NOTE: the temperatures may be altered depending on attitude):*

        1950 Colourblind, Invisible

        1960 Don't Wanna Be

        1970 Third Generation Canadian-born Chinese

        1980 Woman of Colour, Visible Minority

        1990 Asian Canadian
                  Asian Pacific Lesbian
                  Asian Lesbian of Vancouver

Cook patiently for one generation and release pressure briefly no more than once a year.

Stir up frequently, to taste.

Do not clean out the pot after any explosions.

Season with Japanese soy sauce; no one will know the difference.

Guaranteed to stay in the stomach a lifetime; you won't be hungry again, even after a couple of hours.

Serves millions.

OUT OF FIRE, GRACE

Merle Woo

Yellow Woman Speaks

Shadow become real; follower become leader;
        mouse turned sorcerer —

In a red sky, a darker beast lies waiting,
        her teeth, once hidden, now unsheathed swords.

Yellow woman, a revolutionary speaks:

"They have mutilated our genitals, but I will restore them;
I will render our shames and praise them,
Our beauties, our mothers:
Those young Chinese whores on display in barracoons;
the domestics in soiled aprons;
the miners, loggers, railroad workers
holed up in Truckee in winters.
                I will create armies of their descendants.

And I will expose the lies and ridicule
the impotence of those who have called us
        chink
        yellow-livered
        slanted cunts
        exotic
in order to abuse and exploit us.
                And I will destroy them."

Abrasive teacher, incisive comedian,
Painted Lady, dark domestic —
Sweep minds' attics; burnish our senses;
keep house, make love, wreak vengeance.

Nila Gupta

Oh Canada

Oh Canada
I stand on guard for thee
where women are murdered
and white men go free
where the press is free
to support white supremacy
and police still shoot
black youth
and we still get called paki

Oh canada
nightmares are my legacy
thrown on the tracks of the TTC

oh canada
your imperial history
has shackled our countries
and brought us to our knees

oh canada
we toil and toil for thee
and immigrant women on Spadina
still don't get pay equity

oh canada
are we really free
when gays and lesbians get pelted
with beer bottles on Church & Wellesley
and my lover and i
are not considered family

oh canada
we are the brave
and white men are the free

oh canada
let us stand on guard
against thee

Linda Wong

Mini Liu, Long-time Activist

IN MANY WAYS, MINI LIU — A CHINESE-AMERICAN DOCTOR, LESBIAN, activist, and cofounder of the Committee Against Anti-Asian Violence (CAAAV) in New York – is both a "typical" and an atypical Chinese woman. The confluence of both her familial and personal experiences – most particularly during the Vietnam war era – seemed to have informed several of Liu's political choices, choices that either fit well with the consciousness inherited from her family, or were at direct odds with it.

Liu came from an academically privileged family whose visit to the United States was abruptly made permanent following the outbreak of the Cultural Revolution in 1966. Emigration officials, fearing perhaps that the Lius' university education in chemistry would only abet Mao Zedong's communist takeover, barred them from returning to China. Such prohibition kept the large influx of Chinese academics arriving after the 1965 lift of the national origins quota, "permanently" situated in the States. While the experiences of Chinese academics afforded the luxury of studying abroad were far from ordinary – the majority of China's citizenry were composed of poor peasant farmers – they apparently informed Liu, as well as the regular family occurrences that made her *so Chinese* in more common ways.

Liu remembers the atmosphere at home in Baltimore, Maryland, as being "mellow," where public conflict was rare and ideas were exchanged through example and innuendo: "(The) messages we got from our parents about what they wanted us to do and how they wanted us to behave, was somehow trickled down without their imposing it on us," Liu said.

This method of communication easily partnered the Chinese notion of *li*, – the idea of a harmony or code of behavior between "superiors" and "inferiors" and the notion that an individual is nothing except in relation to other people. In the context of *li*, communication through innuendo merely put conflict away into the private realm of individual thoughts so that the public realm of the group and outward interactions would not be disrupted.

Coming from a family with such a typically strong and unspoken ties, Liu, not surprisingly, majored in chemistry, the major of her parents and one that Liu readily attributes to their influence.

After graduating from Harvard University in 1971, and remembering but not really participating in the organizing efforts against the Vietnam war, Liu began her graduate studies in chemistry at MIT. After one year, she realized that she "really wasn't committed to studying some tiny little subject to death" and so decided to become a doctor instead. Liu readily admits that she "had no idea what it meant to become a doctor" and considers herself lucky that she likes the health care field.

Her move to graduate school in chemistry at UC/Berkeley was the start of her formative political education. While in school, she started working at a free clinic and later ended up at the women's health clinic. Liu said that by "working at the free clinic, I began to develop a little different idea about what it meant to become a doctor. And, in fact, at that point, I wasn't so focused on being a doctor, but just on being in the health care profession, providing health care to people who couldn't normally get decent care."

Working at the women's clinic also affected Liu's awareness of her own sexuality. Identifying herself as straight at the time, Liu said, "I think that was when I was first exposed to lesbians per say... I was sort of attracted to a few (women), but I never really thought about it, and I was still with men at that point."

Later, Liu went on to medical school at George Washington University in D.C. and became more aware of her changing politics after the first Christmas break. Her boyfriend at the time was reading communist and socialist literature, including works by Mao. "I read some of [these works]," Liu said. "I was just really taken by the idea, the vision of a different kind of society. And that's when, I think, I became more consciously political based on heading for a certain point, not just a general liberal notion of trying to serve other people. (I had) this feeling that there could be a society where there was a sense of equality, a sense of respect for everybody, and a sense where society worked for everybody rather than just for a few people." Liu made this realization in 1974.

This realization, while away from the context of her family, in many ways fit both the notion of *li* and the iconoclastic feelings of the Vietnam war era. The sense of "family" or belonging appeared, For Liu, to transfer from her own blood relatives to the whole of society. Yet the anti-authority, antigovernment feelings of that era also influenced Liu as she began questioning how parts of American society was structured. Liu, a Chinese American, seemed to be a mixture of the simple dichotomy postulated by Francis Hsu in *Americans and Chinese: Two Ways of Life* in which he says that the Chinese are more situation-oriented than Americans are while the Americans are more individual-oriented than the Chinese.[1] Hence, according to Hsu, the Chinese are "inclined to be (more) socially or psychologically dependent on others" than Americans while the "American moves toward social or psychological isolation."[2] The Chinese, thus, try to conform to reality, while the American tries to make reality conform to himself or herself.[3] Liu appeared to be pulled in both directions as she began to seek political change but was also seeking a community who wanted these changes as well. It also is not without a little irony that the Chinese in China were also undergoing such societal upheaval under Mao.

After medical school, Liu went for a family medicine residency program at Montefiore Hospital in the Bronx. This New York program in social medicine "had a lot of radicals" in it, said Liu. "They had a different vision of not just family medicine, but also of the notion of you're part of the community. The doctor is part of the community and community's health. You deal with the bigger problems.. You deal with public health issues like just access to care, the quality of water, or lead poisoning, or occupational diseases."

Liu's awareness of workers' issues was also heightened when the doctors of the health maintenance organization in which she worked had a strike. Liu didn't cross the picket line, a decision that may have been partly made from the consciousness-raising of the J.P. Stevens campaign in which she had participated in D.C. Liu had participated in that campaign to support the unionization efforts of textile workers.

Liu eventually established herself at the Gouverneur Hospital in the Lower East Side, where she has been working for the past five or six years, although she has been in the neighborhood twelve years in total. At the clinic, which is close to Chinatown, Liu sees Chinese as well as Latino patients, many of whom are working class and/or are immigrants. Liu attests that the best part of her job is her relationship with patients where she often shares "everything they go through in life." "I'm really like their family doctor," Liu said. "I see the husband and the wife. I see the kids. They were adolescents or kids when I saw them and now they're adults. It's sort of an old-fashioned idea."

Once settled with her practice, Liu helped found the Committee Against Anti-Asian Violence (CAAAV) in 1986. At the time, the group to which she belonged, the Organization of Asian Women (OAW), wanted to do an educational forum about anti-Asian violence. "At that point in New York City, there were no groups actually doing work on anti-Asian violence – working with victims or anything like that. And when we started to call around to other Asian-American groups, we found out that the Organization of Chinese Americans and the Japanese American Citizens League were also thinking of addressing the same topic. So, we formed a coalition of about seven groups, and did this forum, which turned out to be a huge success – 250 people came, maybe two thirds of whom were Asian."

Many of the organizing seeds were sown for a national consciousness of anti-Asian violence in 1982. Vincent Chin, a Chinese American, was killed by two unemployed auto workers in Detroit who mistook Chin to be Japanese. The auto workers blamed the Japanese for the their unemployment, and thereby, clubbed Chin to death by shattering his skull. Neither of the murderers got any jail time for their crime.

Putting consciousness into action, Monona Yin of OAW, who currently is CAAAV's fundraiser and policymaker, helped co-chair the forum in New York. She was also one of several people, along with Liu, to be a part of the original coordinating committee for CAAAV. The group was formed in the fall, and already by the winter an event occurred which galvanized the organizing efforts of CAAAV. Michael Griffths, an African-American man, was beaten and killed in a white neighborhood in Howard Beach. He and two friends were driving late at night when their car broke down. After getting out of the car to walk and find help, they were attacked by a carload of white teenagers with baseball bats. Griffths, in an attempt to get away, crossed the highway and was killed by an oncoming car.

"So, this was a really huge rallying case in New York," Liu said. The

African Americans took the lead [in organizing]. The Latinos also. Since CAAAV was already there, we added our voice to protest the death of Michael Griffths and also the way the police dragged their feet and treated the other two Black men as criminals at the beginning of the case. There was a lot of activism in the city. There were forums all over. There were a lot of multiracial panels and CAAAV was always the Asian voice."

At that point, Liu said, CAAAV "really took off. If we hadn't been there, [racial violence] would have been a hidden problem for Asians. It wouldn't have occurred to people that Asians had similar problems."

Another event galvanized CAAAV. Soon after the Griffths case, a Chinatown family was beaten by the police in the family's own home. "I think OAW in particular felt like it was important not to just speak out about anti-Asian violence and just sort of talk about ourselves as victims of violence," Liu said, "but also as the worst sort of illustration of how racism affects Asian Americans. We feel like we are always fighting against this myth of the model minority and that Asians don't have this kind of problem with racism. So, we felt it was very important to deal with that issue very directly and forcefully to make it clear to people that this institution of racism is all-pervasive and affects us also."

In the beginning, Liu said that CAAAV was mostly "reactive": someone would have a problem, and CAAAV would organize a campaign around that problem. But once the goals were achieved in these campaigns, "that was it," and there wasn't further work to be done. The problem with reactive campaigns, Liu said, was that "we really weren't building a base in the community."

Refocusing their vision toward community-building rather than victim-advocacy, and adjusting to the reality that 85 percent of Asians in New York were foreign born, CAAAV went into different Asian communities to find out what the issues of concern really were.

One of CAAAV's first projects under this readjusted vision was addressing the problem of crime in a housing project in Queens. The building was composed of both Chinese and African-American tenants, and CAAAV effected the long-range plan of helping the Chinese better their language skills so that they could work with their English-speaking counterparts on the issue of crime. This, said Liu, was a better plan than the more passive approach of simply assigning a police officer who spoke Chinese to the beat.

Besides community building, CAAAV is also incorporating economic justice issues. "It's all linked," Liu said, "The racism issues. The economic justice issues. The reason we're organizing (Indian) cab drivers is that first of all, there are a lot of South Asian cab drivers in New York – something like 43 percent of the new drivers are South Asian... Because of the racist way society is set up, that's the kind of job that Asian immigrants and I think most immigrants and immigrants of color have been forced into... (Cabdriving is) a really dangerous job. You work long hours and make little money. So, we're trying to respond to where the needs of the community are by expanding the definition of anti-Asian violence."

Liu's political work took her into realms other than anti-Asian violence as well. At a December 1990 protest of the play *Miss Saigon*, organized by Asian Lesbians of the East Coast and the Gay Asian and Pacific Islander Men of New York, Liu came out as a lesbian. Her journalist friend, Ying Chan, a writer for the *Daily News*, profiled Liu in an article in which Liu said she "felt relieved. I wanted to come out for a long time but just didn't know how to do it."

Liu had her first woman lover at the age of thirty and said that her residency program was half people of color and half gay people. "It was very easy to be out in that program."

Yet the the reticence and innuendo learned from her family affected her coming out process. "The way I usually deal with being a lesbian," Liu said, "is that I usually don't tell people. So that's my dilemma... I never found an easy way of telling people."

Liu first became aware of infatuations with women in junior high school but was not really interested in dating at the time. Later, in medical school, a book on the coming out process "opened possibilities" for Liu even though she had not consciously identified herself as lesbian. In New York, Liu thought that the next person that she'd date would be a woman but said that she "had no idea what that meant. But once I got together with my first (woman) lover, I realized this was a total transformation of my life – I'm never going back... When I got together with my first lover, (I realized) that this is what people talk about when they talk about love. I had learned all these love songs when I was growing up (but thought it was) baloney. I thought it was some kind of social construct because I had never felt anything like that until I started getting attracted to women."

Coming out to her family was not easy. Liu wanted to avoid doing it, but her lover pushed her to face her family. Unbeknownst to Liu, one of her brothers also came out as a gay man. And contrary to what she anticipated, her mother became extremely upset while her father was supportive. After her mother began crying and saying that Liu could get back together with her old boyfriend, Liu's father said, "She doesn't want to," and abruptly left the room. When he came back into the room, everyone "suddenly just changed the subject and we didn't talk about it again."

Putting painful or problematic events away into private thoughts or out of consciousness altogether, away from the public realm, is a common coping mechanism of Chinese families. Liu said that her family "basically knows" about her lesbianism and her current lover Debi. As long as there isn't any explicit public display of Liu's lesbianism, Liu's mother seems to be able to cope with her daughter's sexuality. Liu partly attributes her father's supportiveness to his talks with her gay brother. Liu's father also "sort of acknowledges that [homosexuality] existed in China, but he also feels this is somewhat a phenomenon of this country," Liu said. "But, bottom line, he feels that we're adults and he respects our choices."

Regarding her coming out process via the *Daily News*, Liu said that while her coming out was "backwards" in that she came out after working years in a community rather than before, there were no major bad effects to the announcement. "A lot of people feel that being a lesbian is a disadvantage to doing good organizing work in the community, and I really haven't found that to be true," Liu said. "Ultimately, people will really respect you for what you do."

---

1 Hsu, p.347
2 Hsu, p.347
3 Hsu, p.347

BIBLIOGRAPHY

Francis Hsu, *Americans & Chinese: Two Ways of Life*, (New York: Henry Schuman, Inc., 1953).
Ronald Takaki, *Strangers From a Different Shore*, (Boston: Little, Brown & Co, 1987).

Ann Yuri Uyeda

Love Letters from the Movement
(Excerpt from a work in progress)

5 May

DEAR HAEJUNG,
How are you doing? I hope this letter finds you in good health and spirits. How's the weather in Washington, DC? Since getting back to San Francisco, I've been busy re-immersing myself in the Asian American community here.

This past Saturday was the 8th annual Empowering Women of Color conference at the University of California, Berkeley, located across the San Francisco Bay. A writer friend and Asian lesbian sister who lives in San Diego came up along with eight of her women friends. They all attend the same college in San Diego and belong to an Asian American women's feminist political collective they helped start on that college campus. They started out as a discussion/social group for Asian American women before deciding to become the collective.

The women are pretty awesome! It was nice for me to just hang back and listen/watch them in action. They are all very aware, articulate, political, and analytical about their lives as Asian women living in America. My friend is openly lesbian with them, and they accept that well (since sometimes I find Asian women have this weird thing about sex and sexuality). Whatever may be the sexualities of the women, they are all comfortable about their own sexual identities and don't seem to have hang ups about other women's sexualities. Although this was my first time meeting them, they all made me feel very welcomed, and, by the end of their stay the next day, I claimed myself as being a sister in their group.

These women are also a lot of fun. Watching them, I remember how natural it is for Asian women to touch each other as a form of communicating intimacy and love (i.e., nothing overtly sexual). The women would hug, hold, and kiss each other frequently. They'd lean up against someone else or stroke her hair. It wasn't a big deal. And I realized that, as an Asian dyke, Asian American lesbians don't do touch each other very much. As queer women, I think we've become too fixated on the sexual content of our verbal and non-verbal communication — sometimes, everything could mean or be construed to indicate our sexual interest in another. But as queer women of Asian heritage, we deny ourselves the joy of touching another in fun, sisterhood, or friendship. After all, so many of our Asian sisters continue to do so without fear of conveying loaded messages or double meanings.

After the conference on Saturday, all eight women came to my place to caffeine up before beginning their nine-hour drive back to San Diego. As we stood around the kitchen, drinking our coffee, the conversation turned to an evening when my friend and two of the women were hanging out at someone's home. They decided to take all their clothes off except for their underwear, I think because it was hot and also because they were all a little curious to know what their bodies looked like. This event sparked a great deal of interest in some of the women who were not there that night, and we finally decided to sit down and do the same thing with all of us.

I began to feel a little alarmed at this point. After all, I am attracted to women (and as you know, especially Asian women), and these women are very attractive. My own homophobia surfaced, too, as I thought, "What if they get the wrong impression if I look at them?"

But we undressed, shirts first, and sat for a while just looking at the different ways our breasts were shaped, how they sagged and pointed. We varied greatly in size, color, and balance. We compared the amount of hair on our bodies, the size of arms and wrists and hands. We looked at everyone's back and neck. We checked out the amount of hair we had under our arms. My friend talked about the wonders of making love to women and how it feels to have another woman's breasts rub against her back or her own breasts. I talked (with some embarrassment, feeling like I was revealing top-secret stuff about lesbians) about the wonders of seeing and feeling a woman's breasts for the first time, and the incredible sensation of being fucked by one as we make love. We discussed how sensitive our breasts are, which seemed to vary by size.

With some sadness, we put our shirts back on and then proceeded to take our jeans off. Our underwear stayed on (although that would have been educational, too) as we looked at our legs, flexed muscles. Someone told me my body looked "like a white woman's!" because my legs are much longer than those of most Asian women. Without discussing the comment, we realized how terrible it sounded, but it was the only way this one Asian woman had to explain how my body differed from hers.

I was pretty proud we all felt comfortable enough to do this. I was especially proud my new-found sisters weren't homophobic. Internally, I mourned that when I am with my women lovers, we do not spend time like this looking, comparing, and appreciating our bodies.

When I explained this scene to my gay Chinese friend, Jeffery, I thought he would scream out like gay men typically do when they find out what lesbians and women really do when we're away from men. Instead, there was thoughtful silence on his end of the phone. "There's no way," he replied, "that my gay Asian American men friends would ever sit around and do the same thing." Or Asian American men in general, too. We speculated about what this meant for him.

Outside of men's muscle mass and penis size, this curiosity to know what our entire bodies look like seems to be something more common in women than in men. The feminist movement has been clear that for us to reclaim the power of our bodies, we need to first understand and appreciate them. Then we can assume responsibility for our bodies and begin to slowly reshape the mainstream, patriarchal constructions of women's bodies and sexualities. But there is something more special about reclaiming this power with other Asian American women; after all, it is really the body of an Asian woman I am most familiar with, through myself and my mother. My invisibility in the mainstream culture (except for those damn exotified/fetish-ized/passive images), along with persistent racism, encourage me to forget the simple pleasure and normalness of my body as an Asian woman's body. By appreciating my body, I like to think I also appreciate the beauty of all Asian women. When I "scam" on Asian women, I am really seeing and responding to my own beauty and strength. (That's how I try to rationalize that I'm not objectifying my sisters.)

Our home is becoming the new lesbian vortex for the Asian American community here. We're housing several women from the Sacramento/Davis area who'll be in town next weekend for an APS (Asian Pacific Sisters) party. Several other women will be staying with us for Gay Pride during the last weekend of June. (God, after the quiet March on Washington, I'm looking forward to just cutting loose at our parade — SF has the reputation for being the most outrageous, and our parade begins with a two-mile long contingent of Dykes on Bikes! Truly a hot scene!) I've become more radicalized (unfortunately for my poor parents...) since returning from DC so who knows what I'll do this year as I march. I'm also a bit scared to see what my roommate will do this year. Last year, she just about had safe sex in the middle of the street... are you sure you still want to move here? We're just a bunch of wild wahinis (Hawaiian for women)....

Since returning home, I've begun to slowly process the March on Washington, where we first met. Six years of marching in gay pride parades all over California, yet somehow this march still managed to be very significant for me.

I'll always remember when the Asian and Pacific Islander (API) contingency stopped (I think this was before you joined us) at one group of *%#$! fundamentalists who had clumped together at several points along the parade route. As usual, the fundamentalists were armed with their judgmental signs, shouting simplistic sermons on homosexuality amplified by bullhorns. Whenever I pass these groups, I get a little scared — never can tell exactly what they might do. Well, at one point, we stopped and pointed our index fingers at them, shouting, "Shame, shame, shame!" the standard response from queers. However, this time was different: when I looked around me, there were all these queer Asians and Pacific Islanders making a deafening roar which drowned out the fundies!

As we continued marching down the street, I became angry, thinking these fundamentalist Christians had a lot of nerve to show up at my parade and then try to interrupt the festivities! So at the last group of fundies near the Mall, I was so pissed off that I just lifted my shirt up and flashed my breasts at the protesters. Logic just doesn't work with them, so I went for pure shock value. And I got it — I watched the expression on one white man's face turn (in all of about ten seconds) from shock to interest to guilt at his interest and back to shock again. I think I'll add that tactic to my repertoire (and thanks to my roommate who was bad and bold enough to march the whole damn parade shirtless — I think that empowered me to try and be as bad and bold, if only for a few seconds).

And after walking around DC and talking with some of the queer Asian Americans I met, I remembered how isolated so many of us are. As queer Asians, I think we fight the isolation by constantly looking for our homes, that place suffused with so much significance and family history. We yearn for the patterns of kinship which have sustained us across centuries and generations, which have helped us to survive the shock of arriving and adapting to this country. Yet, identifying as queer often means the loss of these things. Whoever (another dead white man) said, "You can't go back home again" certainly wasn't a queer Asian American. For us, we were never truly home in the first place. Perhaps that is one of the many truths tying our various lives together — we search for home and for family who will accept and love us for who we are.

I met many brothers and sisters out there who are doing courageous work because they are alone as self-identified queer APIs. Or there are only a handful of them. Or they are trying to create API-only space in hostile places. Or the queer Asians or Pacific Islanders they do know are not proud and are instead "white-washed." Or there are no positive, appropriate role models...

... and I sit here in San Francisco, often trashing my own queer Asian American community here because I don't think it's doing "enough" (political work by APS, co-gender programming, spearheading regional/national/international organizing efforts...). Or deciding not to help out with the Asian Pacifica Lesbian Network retreat for this year because "I'm too busy with other stuff." Or opting not to go to something queer, queer API, or simply API because "I'm too tired tonight," or "Geez, I went to something in the community last week." Or wanting to leave the Asian American lesbian and bisexual women writers' group I helped start because I had a confrontation with one of the women in the group.

That's freedom. That's luxury. That's (to use a phrase we seemed to use a lot when we talked this weekend) privilege. And I've "paid" for it in that I've moved here, and I scrimp my money to afford to live in the City. And I seem to think part of "paying" for it means I can opt not to support or do something in my various communities.

But not when I remember my other brothers and sisters who don't live here. In some ways, I think they're doing the real shitwork. After all, I have community here. I have loud, rowdy, and proud brothers and sisters doing equally good and important work here. I have many role models around me. There are images of us here. I can see and celebrate our presence in the flesh.

So I've been reminded of the difficulties of being queer API and simply Asian and Pacific Islander outside of SF. And I'm realizing that it's for my own good to support and sustain my various communities. I'm trying hard not to take for granted the tremendous wealth I have here as a queer Asian American activist and writer.

I guess the March has allowed me to re-evaluate and recommit myself to the queer education and civil rights movement.

And I got to see that there is movement within the movement. There were many more people of color and APIs this year than in 1987, the year of the first MOW. The favorable/neutral media coverage of queers and queer issues is making it easier for people to "come out of the closet." I'm proud we were part of the largest march for civil rights in the United States.

Most importantly, I tasted freedom. I experienced, on a small scale for a short while, what it would be like to have my civil rights as a queer Asian American woman guaranteed and protected by the laws of this land. I became part of the queer norm that weekend in DC. And I realized I would never put myself back in the closet again, not for any degree of tokenized acceptance/privilege given by straight/homophobic society, or for the convenience or comfort of someone else who can't deal with my sexuality.

I marched as a whole woman. And that wholeness was my freedom. For the first time, I felt pride for the work I do as an Asian American lesbian. The excitement, the crowd, the march, my Asian and Pacific Islander brothers and sisters: all combined together to form an incredible sense of pride, collective commitment, and bold energy. When I felt all this at once,

I wanted to cry in the middle of Pennsylvania Avenue, holding the "Asian/Pacific Queer and Proud!" banner. I was finally home. But instead of crying tears, I felt my soul burst into flames, the fire burning away all the internalized shame, racism, and fear I've collected over all these years.

So I returned to San Francisco a more radicalized queer Asian American woman, in a city where it is somewhat safe to be all that openly. And with a smile I wonder how much social anarchy I can be a part of.

Jeepers. Sorry for the length of this letter, but this is the first time I've been able to write about how I felt about the MOW and meeting those Asian American women of San Diego. Lots of thoughts, coupled with unemployment, make for long letters. Write back as you can. I look forward to continuing our dialogue...

Ann

20 May

Dear Haejung,

Another letter to you, Haejung, in bits and pieces, as it comes to me and then vanishes, sometimes to reappear later or simply disappear forever... I'm sorry it's not as coherent as your last letter to me. The last time I wrote to you, I talked about some of the activities I'd been involved with and my community work. This time, I'm going to write about different things, the more mundane and quiet things happening in my life...

Today has been one of those days I tried to describe to you when we last talked by phone, a day filled with moments of meaning, so that as I write this at the day's end the entire day has been important and fully lived. The moments are, thankfully, not tied to man/machine demarcations of hours and minutes, but instead occur as whole pieces, with each piece having its own inherent beginning and ending.

Today has been a woman's day.

I wanted to begin the day with a visit to the museums in Golden Gate Park, which are open for free on the first Wednesday of the month. But by the time I had finished a letter, it was one o'clock already and I had an appointment later at 3:30 pm. Looked like my second month of unemployment would pass without my getting to the museums on the first Wednesday.

After lunch (something with rice to ease that intense need I always seem to have to eat rice), I read a little and then got ready for my appointment to discuss some business matters with a modern dance group in the City which performs works from and about the Asian American experience. This meeting turned into a three-hour discussion. I spoke with the Administrative Director, a beautiful and talented Asian American woman. She believes strongly in the group and is doing as much as she can to keep them going. I enjoyed our time together. We get along well and talked some about ourselves.

Then, on to Golden Gate Park for a quick run. With all this time during the day, I want to begin exercising regularly again. The weather here is turning to spring: warm, sunny days followed by cool, breezy evenings with layers of delicious fog sweeping in low from the ocean a mile or so away. It's great running weather, but I'm so out of shape I can run just over a mile before I can't breathe any more and have to stop. Sixteen minutes! Geez, I'm out of shape, but I've got a goal to drop my time for a mile and gradually add on the mileage. By the end of today's run, I'm sweating some and feeling my muscles already aching slightly.

As I run this evening, my mind settles, and I feel my core center. Each step shakes free those things not a priority to me, each breath brings me closer to the "really real." I recognize my focus on the running track to be the same focus I bring to my writing and community work and inter-actions with those I love. No thinking this time, just feeling. I like to run simply because I don't think, a rare condition to be in when I'm conscious.

Gotta stop by the market on the way home — there's a potluck tomorrow evening for the volunteers who helped with the NAATA (National Asian American Telecommunications Association) annual film festival this past April. I've been told to bring a green salad, and I pick over the ingredients: red and green leaf lettuce, two carrots, tomatoes, radishes, mushrooms. I contemplate a purple bell pepper the same hue as the eggplants I see for sale in the Chinese markets in Chinatown and on Clement Street, but at $3.99 a pound I pass. I want to buy something special for my own dinner tonight; I make a selection, then head on over to pay for my basket of food before returning home.

Home. When I was in Washington, DC for the march last month, I yearned for this — the familiar, the safe, a place to write and eat and read and sleep.

I drag everything into the kitchen, and find my roommate Kim home and up after a long afternoon nap. She's in a baking mood, and tonight we're treated to banana muffins and chocolate chip cookies, courtesy of various ingredients contributed by us! I clean my salad stuff and begin making enough for my potluck. As we cook, we swipe samples from each dish being made. I make a pot of coffee for us both, using vanilla flavored beans I'd bought earlier at the market. We find the coffee soothes us in ways wine just wouldn't do tonight.

"And artichokes?" I ask, digging through my stuff in the refrigerator. Two small ones go into a pot of boiling water, and 30 minutes later we eat them with eggless mayo spiced with mustard in one dish and ginger tamari sauce in another. Kim holds up the inside half of her artichoke and comments, "Looks like a woman, doesn't it? Artichokes are such a lesbian food!" I hold up one of my halves under my nose and smell it, letting my mind wander. Kim continues, somewhat blissfully, "Such a great food to feed to your lover..." We both agree that, tonight, in our home in San Francisco, it's a fine time to be a couple of Asian American dyke friends sharing a rare evening together.

We talk of our respective days. Then, as we invariably do, we rip into the socio-political stuff. We are involved with very different areas of activism, Kim with the Women's Action Coalition and Roots Against War, an anti-war protest group made up of a broad coalition of people of color. I'm involved with some arts advocacy work and queer, co-gender coalition building with Asians and Pacific Islanders. In spite of these differences, however, our community work stems from our shared perspectives as Asian American queer women.

Tonight, we name the anger we feel for our Asian sisters who continue to be eroticized as exotic sex objects by white men, sisters who fall victim to comparing themselves with hopelessly unreal standards of perfection constructed for white women. I explain the sadness I have for my sisters who look like the "norm" established by white men for their erotic/exotic fetishes (long, black hair; delicate and fine facial features; smaller statures) and the methods my sisters use to cover up their incredible beauty and strength so they will not attract the unwanted sexual attentions of men.

We rail against a society that continues to tell us that the high number of out marriages occurring in the Asian American community to white people (who I prefer to call "The Other" as my way of making the majority standard be Asian American instead of white-European-American-Caucasian-male). All the stories and personal accounts say how normal and expected these out marriages are, part of the process of becoming "Americanized." But Kim and I know the pain and internalized self-hatred that would once have prompted us to exclusively look for relationships with The Other to further deny the deep-rooted self-hatred we harbor for being Asian and because we look different. To be seen with The Other often allows a certain degree of acceptance into the white mainstream, a type of "racial privilege."

We describe our anger at people of color who offer slack responses to critical issues when they should know better simply by the reality of their own life experiences. We define past episodes when people of color have turned against us, against our brothers and sisters, in essence "sell out" to win some margin of acceptance by the mainstream society. We name the slackness to be the adherence of stereotypes, easy and blanket concepts of people and their cultures constructed to avoid unpleasant and discomforting realities of diversity.

Kim reads me part of a paper written by another Asian American woman detailing a broad organizing effort to protest the play, *Miss Saigon*, in New York City. The coalition formed in the protest efforts is amazing, and we contemplate the type of work we could do here in the Bay Area with a similar type of coalition. Our politics are such that there is no need to explain why anyone would want to protest the popular Broadway play.

Most importantly, Kim and I take the time to celebrate our lives here in San Francisco. We remind each other of how much we have here and how far we have come to call this city our home. We have moved here from elsewhere to open our options, to fully live lives defined as queer women of color, Asian American lesbians, activists of the feminist/anarchist/anti-patriarchal kind. For a moment, we recharge, putting aside our issues, activism, and organizing. For a moment there is only this kitchen with two women talking, eating, reading, and drinking. We do our dishes, then part our separate ways for the evening. Half-jokingly we say, "See you in two weeks!" Unfortunately, the ebb and flow of our lives is such that this type of time is hard for us to find. The reality is that it will be at least another two weeks before we have the time to spend as we have tonight.

In my bedroom, there is silence and the faint odors of food cooked earlier this evening. Outside my one window, the wind picks up strength. Sounds from the street dwindle into night silence. I sit at my desk in front of the window, writing to you and waiting for an almost-full moon to cross the sky before me, filling my room with its brilliance. The moon, the lunar presence: often a symbol for women and women's power. I sit waiting for her, a perfect end to this day, a woman's day.

It is the subtle, slow things which fill my heart with satisfaction and gratitude. For today, there has been no urgency, crisis, or other need clamoring for my attention. Today has simply been, and I've been relaxed enough to allow myself to be, too. The process has been so easy, with each moment unfolding to reveal its own inherent beauty and perfection. I momentarily look around me to take inventory: a purple mug with the last swallows of coffee; the taste of artichoke on my tongue; stray breezes caught against the walls of our home; sounds of Kim cleaning the bathroom and singing to a song on the radio. And outside, a clear night sky allows me to once again see the joyous moon travel the heavens in her nocturnal wanderings.

I'll end my letter to you here. Please write back as you can and as you have time to. I wish you were here — I'd love to show you my city (even if we don't have trees like you do in Washington, DC). Again, I'm glad we met and talked. I'm especially you glad you decided to march with us, otherwise we'd never have met! Funny how these things happen. Please take care of yourself. I'm sending you my best wishes with this letter.

Love, Ann

Joyoti Grech

Debi Ray-Chaudhuri:
Working towards a new language

DEBI RAY-CHAUDHURI IS A ZEN SAINT OF LIFE, ART AND EVERYTHING. *She also just graduated with a Masters degree from the School of Visual Arts in New York. I went to see her final year show and came away full up to the top of my head on her living, kicking, magic work. She uses colours like words and music, in a way that inspires and reveals the "great histories" of people of colour, which she understands to be both a strong base and a way to the future. Her thesis is entitled "Liberation? Art? Theory? Possibilities for a new language," and these themes run throughout her visual art work. She talked with me about this and about her campaigning work as an artist with the Committee against Anti-Asian Violence.*

JOYOTI: In talking about your work you speak about creating a new language with which to articulate some of the things you just described. How do you use your work in that way?

DEBI: I guess over a period of time, any artist develops a set of symbols or a way of working that seems to gravitate towards certain problems. I guess in my work particularly there's a problem of abstraction and figuration which I think is present in a lot of South Asian symbol systems. There's questions of colour that are used that sort of deal with identity. I guess that as somebody who's grown up in the United States I have a lot of exposure to different kinds of colour sensibility, but in my work I find that the colour sensibility that I'm drawn to is really very Indian, if you want. What else? Oh, a certain use of animals, body parts or a kind of space which is certainly not representational space in the sense of being within any kind of Western system of representation.

JOYOTI: Do you want to talk about that in reference to a certain piece of your work?

DEBI: Okay, for example, in this painting called "Chamula" which basically has a dismembered figure and a boat and various abstract shapes as part of it, you're not supposed to necessarily draw any conclusions about where things are in relation to each other (except for maybe the head and the leg seem to be very specifically disconnected) and I guess that's — just to have a sense of, inside of a picture, how can you represent space? I wouldn't say I never use a Western system because there's are paintings where I do that — and I also use for example the idea of a figure as being a unit, or as a space in which certain things can happen. Like in that particular painting there's a figure that you can see through, to things that are happening underneath which are essentially abstract. But the way that they work is sort of like paint on the body or even like some bone structure or some kind of structure underneath that's part of the body, which in fact is part of the whole painting.

JOYOTI: Especially with your colours: I remember when I first saw this painting the colours seemed to me very Bengali and the figure in the painting appeared to me as a Bengali woman. Which seems to me something to do with what you were saying about the language of imagery and colour. But you were using it to describe an anti-colonial experience in a completely different part of the world. Do you think there's a conscious connection between the two experiences?

DEBI: Well, I think the connection here is, I'm looking at it. And obviously there's elements of the visual language that I learned growing up that are Bengali and I think my sensibility about colours is probably from Bengal — it's definitely not from Ohio! But I think that if I tell any story I'm going to be telling it through my lens, I guess. And I guess that's the way that there might be this connection — what parts of the story I choose to emphasize are obviously going to be affected by my way of seeing. The Indians in this picture are Native Mexican!

JOYOTI: Do you want to briefly describe the history behind the painting?

DEBI: Well, I don't want to reduce the painting to the simple story, but the starting seed, the unifying idea, is that we went to Mexico, to a town called Chamula, where the indigenous people threw out the missionaries from the Church. In fact, it was a violent overthrow. Now the church is maintained as a place of worship for the indigenous people who have their rituals as they've known them for thousands of years. And it's a very interesting combination of saints and also different kinds of worship — which reminded me a lot of a temple in India that I've been to. This happened in the 1950s, which is a very recent example of response to colonialism that doesn't put the colonial on top — so that's kind of inspiring!

JOYOTI: That lines up with the work you've been doing with the Committee against Anti-Asian violence.

DEBI: Well, first of all, I've done four different kinds of artistic work with the Committee. First of all, I did the art for the brochure. Then we had a chance to use the window at Art in General, which is a street-level set-up. It was in June of last year (1992) and it was the 10th anniversary of the murder of Vincent Chin so we decided to do a memorial in which we gathered up various debris that was relevant to the case, like a baseball bat and McDonalds garbage. We wrote out a text on very American-style plastic material, explaining what had happened to him, and included a photograph of Vincent Chin and the text in Chinese, because the window's actually very close to Chinatown. That caused a little bit of an uproar at first because we were using garbage and the gallery owner was like, oh, you know, why are you putting garbage in the window, there's enough garbage anyway. But we wanted to make a point which was how his life was treated as garbage, thrown away.

Also, just recently there was this case where a Japanese exchange student was murdered. He was asking for directions to a Halloween party at a house. I guess the husband there just felt like he had the right to shoot him — and a jury has just recently supported him in this position. This is just an example of the general devaluing of Asian life in the U.S. And also there's the perception of the Asian person as an outsider, a threat or foreign. What happened in this case is very tragic: the husband didn't understand what the guy was saying. It's hard to imagine he would have shot a white kid or that there would have been that kind of reaction. So obviously this kind of violence just goes on. A lot of people say, oh Vincent Chin, that happened ten years ago, can't you find something new to talk about? But really, that kind of attitude still persists and when you look at the immigration laws and at the history of the way Asians have been treated in the U.S.A. that kind of attitude is still very prevalent.

And that's something that the Committee against Anti-Asian Violence tries to educate people about. I mean, not just educating Asians about their own history and the history of violence against Asians but also, you know, going to colleges and talking to white people and other people. Just sort of raising consciousness about what the effects of violence are — and how people can respond to that.

Another piece I did for the Committee was this. We had started a campaign around Marky Mark. Marky Mark is a rap singer. He's white: Irish and German-American. He's from Dorchester, Massachusetts, and he uses a lot of Black influences in his music, and ideas about racial harmony when he talks to crowds. He emphasizes the relationship between Black and white, but in 1986 he was convicted of physically and verbally harassing Black elementary schoolchildren. And then in 1988 he was convicted of physically assaulting a Vietnamese man with a five-foot pole. Actually, he assaulted two men, and when the police came he said yeah, I'm the one who attacked the fucking gooks. And he was very open about the fact that it was a racist attack. Now Marky Mark is big rap star of sorts — and very popular in the gay community. He's some kind of pin-up, goes around with his Calvin Kleins, he's really pushed Calvin Klein underwear to the forefront, so to speak. Anyway, there's these highly visible ads with Marky Mark wearing his underwear. So we designed a campaign where we made up these stickers that say: Marky Mark — Convicted Racist, and describe the different counts against him. We plastered all different parts of the city with these bright neon orange stickers. We also made a life-size cut-out of Marky Mark and pasted that. It made Marky Mark's people very nervous because obviously the guy doesn't really have a lot of talent so he's basing his fame on his image. They were worried that this was tarnishing his image. So we managed to force them to make a statement describing the incidents and recanting them. That he did these things and they're wrong and other people shouldn't do them and blah blah blah.

He's supposed to be making these public service announcements on

MTV that will speak directly about anti-Asian violence — which is very unusual.

JOYOTI: So that's a big victory!

DEBI: Yes! It was actually pretty exciting because they had all these big-ass media people, we were in the *New York Times* and *People* magazine and this and that. Everybody picked up on the story. It was a grassroots thing and it really took over. It was intense.

JOYOTI: What do you think of the issue of identity, how do you identify yourself or having to identify yourself?

DEBI: Well, identity is obviously a political necessity and it's something that we use in different contexts. But for artists, who are generally in the habit of articulating themselves [through their art], it's sort of the lot of so-called "minority" artists who have to identify themselves as a this or a that and then speak from that position. And in fact that position kind of limits who we're allowed to speak to and what interpretations can be brought to our work. Therefore, I generally try to resist those kinds of definitions — as an artist. I think maybe it's also good practice not to cling to these identities — or what we define as identities — because they give you a shortcut in thinking but they don't always reveal as much as they appear to reveal. There's a tendency also to make assumptions about what you can know about a person from a given set of identities. I think it's also important to see it in the plural: identities. Because most people don't live in categories anyway!

JOYOTI: Just to finish, you've talked about how your racial identity has informed your work. Would you like to talk about how your sexual identity has influenced your work?

DEBI: Well, I'm a lesbian, and I do a lot of work that is very specifically referring to me and my lover or indirectly about women's sexuality. I think also there's a way of talking about sex that is particular to lesbians — a kind of humour and also frankness. I have piece that actually combined that Marky Mark figure and a rather large painting of two dogs fucking. It's kind of a very frank, simple painting — in some ways. It's a complex painting in other ways.

I guess it jars a little to hear people ask me, you've talked about how your race identity affects your work, because I could identify certain things as Indian. But I would generally say it permeates all my work — Indian-ness and lesbian-ness and all of those things!

I think there's a certain kind of direct vision about sexual matters. But does that have more to do with being a lesbian or more to do with being Indian? I don't know.

I guess I do very specific paintings, which are women and most often me and very specifically my lover. I also had a piece that was a commemoration of our commitment to each other which is you know — a lesbian wedding.

I find it difficult to split the two things apart.

JOYOTI: Yes, you're right, it's all part of the whole...
Anything you'd like to say to finish up? Your hopes for the future?

DEBI: Well, I'm always excited at the different kinds of people producing art. I really think that this is an important time; we are seeing the breakdown of these major schools in the United States. I guess I would say that post-modernism kind of opened the door in a way, but really there's traditions of visual story-telling and visual... events, I guess that's the only way I can describe them, that in general people of colour have great histories. Not just histories but also really vital to the future. And I especially enjoy seeing work by lesbians of colour and especially the development of that language. I feel that over time I hope not to have to be a singular example. I don't like that position at all!

Joyoti Grech

Leolani M., Native Hawaiian Islander

O NE SPRING DAY WITH THE WIND BLOWING AT THE NEW PALM TREES
*on Dolores Street, Leolani M. took time out to talk with me about her work as a
founding member of San Francisco's Asian Pacifica Sisters. Along the way I
also learned her views on the Hawaiian homestead campaign, the first APLN retreat in
Santa Cruz, and some of the challenges involved in networking and organizing an
international women's event. She started off by telling me a little about her native Hawaii.*

JOYOTI: Leolani, how do you identify yourself?

LEOLOANI: Pacific Islander. I'm 63 percent Hawaiian, and
German, Chinese, English.

JOYOTI: What is happening in Hawaii right now, with the
sovereignty movement?

LEOLOANI: The Hawaiian movement — about Hawaiian
homestead land? There's a movement of our people concerned about our
land. The U.S. government is still holding on to it. I feel that most
Hawaiians come from poverty — unless they get a better education and a
good job. Most people who qualify for Hawaiian homestead used to be half
Hawaiian but now I think the percentage is going to be 25 percent.

JOYOTI: Who decides how much percentage a person is
Hawaiian? Is it the government, or you the person?

LEOLOANI: I think it's probably going to be changed by
legislation because you could hardly find an individual of full Hawaiian
blood — unless they come from the island of Niihau. That's pure Hawaiians.
For instance my family, my mother, my mother's mother, was half Hawaiian
and half German. And my grandfather is half Chinese and half Hawaiian. Of
course they never knew how much the percentage was. And I never knew my
father's side — his mother was Hawaiian and his father was English. So
there's the percentage mix — and I came out to be 63 percent!

But after 63 percent, the percentage of Hawaiian blood goes down and down, so now the qualifying percentage [for the state] is 25 percent. But there's also a long list for homestead land. People on the list who've been on the list for many, many years — over twenty years. Just waiting for openings for homes to be built — and space, and money also. It's funded by the government. There is money, but it hasn't been released.

JOYOTI: How do you feel about the whole idea of the U.S. government giving land to Hawaiian people?

LEOLOANI: That's strange because the land is ours to begin with — but they have control over it. It's kind of strange that it belongs to us but it really doesn't belong to us. When you say Hawaiian homestead land you still got to lease it at $5 a year. It's really not ours. It goes back to Hawaiian homestead after you die or if there is no one in the will, you forfeit the land. And yet you have to pay taxes on it every year. The house is ours — but the land isn't.

JOYOTI: The term API is used as a kind of umbrella. Do you think that's a strong umbrella? Do you think there's common ground to work on between Asian people and Pacific Islander people?

LEOLOANI: I guess it started with the APLN. People got confused — they didn't know who was what but it's only because we became an organization, and we filed as APS — Asian Pacifica Sisters — which should cover all Asian women and all women from the Pacific Islands and the Pacific to wherever how far back. I think India — there was a woman from there who came to the retreat and protested that we too were recognized as Asian women. So we had to swallow that one because we didn't know how far in the Pacific to reach out to. So I would think it has to do with APS, APLN, trying to reach out, actually, to all women of minority groups — not to women of the "other side:" white, Black [laughs]. I guess we always tried to concentrate on women from the Polynesia area and beyond in the Pacific, but I don't know how far.

JOYOTI: Tell us more about APLN and APS.

LEOLOANI: APLN is the network. They were the people who organized the retreat in Santa Cruz which was our first APS retreat that we've had so far. Oh, it was beautiful — women came from all over: China, women wrote from behind the Iron Curtain, in the Soviet Union. They couldn't come across the line to be with us. It was such a sad letter one of the girls read to us at the retreat. It was kind of like a sad feeling because this person was held back from coming to this retreat. Hopefully there will be a stronger organization that can help her come the next time. Their laws held her back — there was no freedom for her to come and be with us at this special gathering. Oh, it was so neat — you met individuals from all over. Across the nation — from the Philippines, from China, from Oregon, from Washington State! You name it! It kind of gave you chills just to meet how many women we have out there that wanted to be a part of this gathering for the first time.

JOYOTI: Tell us how you were involved in the organizing of that retreat.

LEOLOANI: Well, it was from L. She's a founder and she had the newsletter *Phoenix Rising*. As I understand there was over 600 women on this list — but not all of them members. Then L. had a meeting over at her house to organize, to bring us together as APS. So we, as individuals, came to another meeting and created a name and created the board. And this board went on for at least three years. I stayed on for another two years organizing social events. I thought it went really well. A lot of political [stuff] got in the way — a lot of headaches! People did get confused as they came to our group — what is our purpose, our reason of organizing? We wanted to do so many things — to reach out to newcomers to San Francisco, educational, culture, the social side of our activities — the fun side, go camping, see the nature of California. That was my interest, not so much the political part.

But the political part was important too. That helped us grow and reach out and help others who came to us for fundraising. APLN came to us to help with the retreat too — and *Phoenix Rising*, who wanted to reach out to individuals wherever they were. That was important. I hated the political part — because it always seems to hold us back from going ahead; there were many meetings that we've had that went in circles many times and it always had to do with new individuals that would come to the meeting not sure of what we're up to or where we're going or all of that.

There was a heck of a lot of things going on! We had the deadlines too for *Phoenix Rising*. We had to get all of our information to them so they could send it out. And of course we had the picnics and the social part of things; we had to come together and make that process work. It wasn't easy.

JOYOTI: To finish up, would you like to tell us about something you've seen as a victory that you've been involved with helping to bring about?

LEOLOANI: Well, the very first parade I remember I thought was very visible — the women of Hawaii. We had K. come from Hawaii. She too was in the political movement. And of course she corrected us in a lot of Hawaiian statements — because we had this T-shirt made of different languages, saying "For the Love of Women." And of course we didn't know Hawaiian, right, so we just stated the line "Ke Aloha o Wahini." "Wahini" is "women," "Ke Aloha" was "the love," and "o" was "of," which we thought. But it was wrong! But I don't care — being that it was from our heart. There was a deadline to make this T-shirt and we did the best we could. So she came and she said, that's not how it's supposed to be. And to me, it was from our hearts, and not because it was an error. Maybe if I have time I'll show you the T-shirt — it's a T-shape of all the different languages: Filipino, Chinese, and others. The fulfilling part was making the haku for the heads — which is flowers for your head, and then the flower leis that we wore. And it was just neat — more so because we were right behind Sister Boom. Sister Boom is an instrumental band that gave us more vision and the flowers, I think, and the banners. I feel like we were such an ultimate part of us that we came together to express that yeah, we're from Hawaii and we're gay.

Because Hawaiian women, a lot of them are in the closet — but now I hear that they're having a Gay Parade back in Hawai'i too. About the same time we have ours!

V.K. Aruna

The Myth of One Closet

I.

"IMPROPERLY FILED. REJECTED."

Three words that translate eviction. Ghost moving in fog, she wonders, pack first but store where? Leave for but go where? Goodbye but for how long? Lover is here, conference next month, film in progress, manuscript incomplete... should this all go in boxes?

"NO APPEAL NECESSARY. WORK AUTHORIZATION REVOKED."

Like she is not even here: the woman whose plants need watering, ceiling needs repair. The woman with ivy creeping over her kitchen window so the sun has stopped breaking in.

She asks for voluntary departure.

Dictionary definition: Voluntary — "proceeding from the will or from one's own free choice; intentional, volitional. Done without compulsion. Performed without legal obligation."

Eviction by some standards can also mean voluntary departure. Tonight, her sobs do not come, trapped inside tunnels of fear that lead her back to the same place... same place every time. Because her mind will not see beyond deportation. Yet.[1]

II.

I wonder how many lesbians realize that closets are not identical, that different realities define our closets, and that the difference in our closets defines the ways in which we choose to Come Out. Nonimmigrant lesbians do not only contend with the risk of anti-lesbian violence, housing or job discrimination, we also contend with immigration — a reality that citizens do not face by virtue of their "legal" status in this country.

As a nonimmigrant, I am not free to cross borders openly as a Lesbian. Laws that allow visitors into the U.S. for conferences on AIDS do not apply to me. Hence, the question becomes: Does the politics of coming out invalidate the politics of a double identity? Particularly, when it is a myth that there is only one closet and one way to come out? When what is safe for some/many lesbians is not necessarily safe for all?

It is true that many nonimmigrants tell ourselves that the INS has better things to do than go after some Lesbian from Bombay/Hong Kong/Chile living in Trenton/DC/LA but we also know the risk. We understand why some of us never march on the outside of Gay Pride contingents in case of cameras. Why many of us fear going to bars in case of a raid. Why we only do radio interviews, never have our photographs taken, or, get married. Why I: hardline, separatist, feminist, lesbian, seek the protection of my closet without apology while standing in a public forum, talking about fighting homophobia while using another name.

For even with a pseudonym, there is risk. As there is resistance. As there is humor — when I am able to laugh at the fact that I can be in a room and be two persons at once talking about "each other" as if we are old friends. But I am also constantly aware of the identity games I play — Who am I supposed to be today when I go to this conference? Who did I say would speak on that panel? Was that call for so-and-so or so-and-so? For someone who is an incest survivor, the secrecy feels horribly familiar as does the threat of exposure. Still, I go through the obliteration of being in closets while finding ways of being out without being caught by the INS.

And the question remains: Does the politics of coming out invalidate the politics of a double identity? Even as I am suspended between borders, between definitions of legal and illegal, resident and non-resident... alien... I survive by remembering that Going in and out of closets is a strategy for working to remove the conditions that make my closets necessary in the first place.[2]

1   I sometimes call the first part of this piece, "Eviction." It was written in 1989 and first appeared in the lesbian of color issue of *Sinister Wisdom* #47, "Tellin' It Like It Tis'," Fall 1992. In a heterosexist culture, lesbians will always be undocumented/evicted women. In a country like the U.S., where immigration rules impose special (unofficial?) restrictions on gays and lesbians who wish to obtain permanent residence here, the terms, "undocumented" and "illegal alien," are a double irony for the lesbian who refuses to marry in order to become "legitimate" in the eyes of the INS — because on one hand, her legitimacy is possible only because the lesbian agrees to pass (even if only for two years) as a heterosexual by marrying. On the other hand, she may have left her home country to avoid marriage, only to end up marrying to remain in the U.S.

As an alternative to a greencard marriage, a lesbian can "place herself" in the hands of an employer who chooses to sponsor her greencard. Although many lesbians are fortunate enough to be sponsored by universities and corporations that see sponsorship as merely a formality, many more lesbians suffer the indignities and exploitation that result from the inherent power imbalance in a work-related greencard sponsorship. Such an arrangement can and, often, does replicate the abuse of power that sponsored wives go through with their real or paper husbands. And such an experience is not limited to women working in sweatshops or tomato farms. Neither is it limited to women receiving wages "under the table." On the contrary, women working legally for progressive, social-change and even feminist organizations are vulnerable to their employers precisely because they depend on these employers for continued sponsorship, are at risk of being "laid off" because of budget cuts, and can be viewed as a liability rather than an asset to the organization. In other words, such employees are more expendable than other employees who are citizens. If such a lesbian happens to be undocumented, i.e. without legal immigration status in the country, she recognizes the risk to herself if she loses her job with the greencard sponsor. She is not eligible for welfare benefits. Her application for a greencard is jeopardized, and she can be deported.

It is no wonder then that many lesbians "choose" to risk marrying for a greencard because, at least, while they are married they can live and work as temporary residents; have access to emergency welfare benefits; leave jobs that treat them badly; and travel a little more freely in and out of the U.S. In this scheme of survival strategies where is there space for a feminist lesbian who finds marriage oppressive under any circumstances? What kinds of support does she get from other feminists who are U.S. citizens or immigrants? What kinds of networks have been set up for women like her who do not have the required paperwork to obtain housing, medical care, unemployment benefits, workers' compensation, foodstamps, and if she has children, AFDC? Currently, in Congress there is much debate on granting waivers to undocumented battered women married to greencard sponsors who are abusing them. When will there be a debate about making immigration possible without marriage, whether that marriage is heterosexual or gay? There is also an informal underground that helps undocumented women negotiate a system as greencard wives. How does such an underground benefit lesbians who don't wish to be wives? When will U.S. feminists who reject marriage as an option for themselves stop treating this as an acceptable option for lesbians who are not citizens or immigrants? In and of themselves, immigration policies and quotas are exclusionary and, as in many countries like the U.S., they are also blatantly classist and racist. Recognizing "legitimate" marriage as a means of granting citizenship or permanent residence adds to the injustice because it reinforces the system's heterosexism. Unless immigration laws change, all women, whether lesbian or heterosexual, will be forced to choose between institutionalized heterosexuality (marriage) and non-negotiable immigration regulations. They will be bartering one oppression for another to buy their "freedom."

Perhaps it is time to create sanctuary for lesbians who wish to live and work in the U.S. without taking the marriage route. Such formalized sanctuary might include the following: establishing "corporations" to specifically sponsor lesbians via job opportunities; providing pro bono legal services to lesbians who want to file for immigration but cannot afford the services; serving as a systems advocate for lesbians who are facing deportation proceedings; ensuring that lesbians detained by the INS do not have their civil rights violated; establishing safe spaces for lesbians who are "temporarily" undocumented until they find a way to become documented; fighting to keep politically active undocumented lesbians from immigration penalties that could include deportation. The sanctuary I describe needs to be accessible to all undocumented lesbians so its usefulness is not based on the goodwill of a few U.S. lesbians. At the same time, its success will rely on the discretion and creative imagining of those involved in it.

There are many lesbians who are "illegal aliens." There are many undocumented lesbians who are "illegally married." Unless feminist lesbians in the U.S. work on immigration issues, we will always be suspended between closets.

2   An earlier version of "The Myth Of One Closet," Parts I and II, was first published in *Sinister Wisdom*, "Tellin' It Like It Tis'," issue #47, Fall 1992.

J. Kehaulani Kauanui & Ju Hui "Judy" Han

"Asian Pacific Islander":
Issues of Representation and Responsibility

THE RELATIVELY NEW TERM, "ASIAN PACIFIC ISLANDER (API)," is an interesting development in racial formation in the United States. Presumably constructed in order to include Filipino Americans, the term is currently used interchangeably with "Asian American." Examples include Asian Pacifica Sisters (San Francisco-based group for lesbians and bisexual women), Asian Pacific Islanders for Choice (one of its kind, dealing specifically with reproductive health issues and rights), and Asian Pacifica Lesbian Network (a nationwide coalition), and countless others.

Certainly, we find comfort and safety among those who we consider similar to us. Collective identities like "Asian Pacific Islander" help us resist, survive, and maintain our sanity in racist and xenophobic cultures. However, we must constantly engage in rigorous critical introspection, no matter how difficult or high-risk such processes may be.

Many Asian Americans superficially claim the term "Asian Pacific Islander" for its "inclusiveness," but this results in little more than lip service. Expanding boundaries and including *more* does not equal being inclusive. Rather, being inclusive is about *responsibly recognizing all those who already belong*. This common misperception of "inclusiveness" results not in Pacific Islanders being included, but being *engulfed*, swallowed whole and remaining ever invisible among (East) Asian Americans.

"Asian Pacific," a United States Census term, is not only limiting but also misleading. Since when have there been any mutual political or cultural identifications among such disparate groups as Vietnamese, Sri Lankan, Korean and Hawaiians? What, for example, are the issues that link Japanese Americans to the Marshall Islands? Which, raises an important point: how many Japanese Americans would acknowledge the imperialist projects and the impact of multi-national Japanese corporations on the "development" of Hawai'i or the dumping of nuclear waste in the Pacific? In the Marshall Islands, 97 percent of the people are ethnically Marshallese. Languages spoken there are Marshallese, English, and *Japanese*. Do we know why? Shouldn't *this* be an "Asian Pacific" issue?

Of course, both "Asian American" and "Asian Pacific" as well as "people of color" and "women of color" are politically constructed categories. We use them strategically, and for the most part, they have been necessary and useful for many of us. They have served many of us well. Nevertheless, the "API" identity has not served *all* of us well, and we need to talk about these differences.

If we intend to address heterogeneity and diversity within "API" communities, we need to start by talking about our own practices of hierarchy and exclusion. For instance, issues around the model minority myth and stereotypes of subservient Asian Americans often get presented as "API" issues, ignoring the fact that they affect Pacific Islanders in *significantly different* ways. Stereotypical passivity of Native Hawaiians/*Kanaka Maoli* is linked more to supposed laziness and stupidity than submissiveness. It is uncommon for Samoan and Hawaiian women, for example, to be stereotyped as mysterious, meek or demure, as East Asian and Southeast Asian women often are. The eroticized images of Native Pacific Islanders are not geishas, not possessing East Asian women's perceived coyness. They are imagined to be simpler, without elaborate schemes to please men, or so goes the white male fantasy. Their appeal is in their carefree and easygoing "primitiveness." Their imagined exotic beauty, perhaps, is closer to the stereotypes of African American women than Asian American women. In the end, however, Asian American and Pacific Islander women as well as American Indian women are thought to be very good hostesses, or as Dan Quayle once so succinctly articulated, "happy campers."

Issues of interracial (sexual) relationships also raise a unique set of implications for Pacific Islanders, which are closer in nature to Native American/indigenous peoples' concerns than to Asian Americans' anxieties of "outdating." For Native Hawaiians, for instance, blood quantum determines whether you are Hawaiian (and how much) in the eyes of the government. Asian American questions of *preserving* tradition contrast with indigenous peoples' struggles to *recover and reclaim* what has been systematically devastated by such imperialist nations as the United States.

Difference is not otherness. And minority is not expendable. Instead of weakening us as a group, our acknowledgment of differences and active diversifying of political interests and practices can be only empowering. By recognizing the fundamental differences in the experiences of those outmigrating indigenous Pacific Islanders who can no longer *afford* to live in their homeland, and the experiences of those Southeast Asian refugees fleeing their war-torn homelands, we broaden our understanding of U.S. (and other) imperialism and learn to make connections across similar and various struggles. As Lisa Lowe writes in "Heterogeneity, Hybridity, Multiplicity: Marking Asian American Differences," such critical introspection makes way for "greater political opportunity to affiliate with other groups whose cohesions may be based on other valences of oppression."

By stopping short of truly acknowledging the heterogeneity and diversity of the groups of people "API" claims to represent and include, we replicate the relationship between the "dominant" and the "minority." By maintaining the same politics of marginalization and exclusion, many "API" groups can only remain dishonest and irresponsible in their claim to be anything different than the oppressive institutions they oppose. Answers like "there aren't many Pacific Islanders on campus" should be alarming for those of us who are familiar with claims that "everyone should have equal representation according to their number, that's what democracy is all about." As the logic goes, number counts and the minority is expendable, and "API" can only be hypocritical.

Finally, "API" must be based on coalition politics, not identity politics. A coalition is a group of people with recognizable and *recognized* differences taking a particular direction for the time being; an alliance is an arrangement for the mutual benefit for people who are in fundamental agreement. We must reopen, redefine and continuously question the boundaries of "Asian Pacific Islander" because a coalition is a temporary unity. And "API" can work only as a coalition.

Eveline Shen

In Search of a
More Complete Definition of Activism.

B ODY WORK IS ESSENTIAL TO SOCIAL CHANGE. I FIRMLY BELIEVE THIS. I've noticed that usually when we think about activism, we refer to actions such as organizing communities, participating in rallies or marches, and coordinating volunteers for the hotline. These types of activism are directly linked to social justice; obviously, we can't reform society merely by talking or thinking about how we want things to be. However, because we are so familiar with these external forms of activism I would like to focus on the more internal forms of activism: the acts of combatting internalized oppression through self-acceptance, the acts of gaining self- knowledge, and the acts of self-nurturance. The work we do internally is just as important as the work we do to try to change the rest of the world; they complement each other. We cannot do one successfully without doing the other.

My body is the site where the results of oppression manifest themselves.

IN THIRD GRADE: *I run off the soccer field during half time dying of thirst and open a can of soda. Diane comes up from behind, playfully grabs it from my hand and takes a gulp. My first thought is one of relief that a white person would feel comfortable drinking out of the same cup as me.*

In High School: My best friend Susan and I are walking towards class, laughing and talking about how much fun we had the day before, ditching class and going shopping. All of a sudden she turns to me and says,

"You are so cool! You know Eveline, sometimes I forget that you aren't White". I smile to myself, taking her remark as a compliment, hoping that I can continue to fool her.

During College at a Peer Counseling Center: I pace around the room, extremely nervous in preparation for my first lesbian panel in which I will come out to a

group of 80 of my peers who previously assumed I was straight. The director comes over and gives me a hug saying, "Why are you so nervous? We are all friends here.
This isn't going to change how anyone looks at you.
Your worries are so silly."
At the Women's Center: The day after we showed Elena Feathersone's video on Alice Walker, I inquire to the director about the lack of diversity (read 90 percent white) in the audience. She replies, "You know, there is only so much we can do. We try our best to be inclusive but we can't force them (women of Color) to come. Maybe they just aren't interested in feminism." I quietly excuse myself and seethe in silence. At night I lay awake for hours berating myself for not saying anything.

Living in this society takes a huge toll on our emotional, spiritual, and physical well-being. These pressures will wear us down to the bone if we are not aware of how deeply penetrating they can be. If we don't face our internalized oppression, we will not have a grounded place from which to do our external acts of activism. I am not implying that this internal work is more important than external forms of activism and that focusing solely on ourselves will make everything better. Nor am I stating that the only way to deal with internalized oppression is through personal introspection — often times, external acts of activism will positively affect us internally. If we ignore these ugly and painful messages that we have ingested into our bodies, our minds, our spirits and our soul, we will end up turning against ourselves, becoming our own worst enemy.

For me, it is essential to examine how oppression continuously affects my psyche and self-concept. It is essential to take stock of the tremendous amount of energy I use in this struggle to be Me. I fight to continue to find ways to center my experience, feelings and beliefs in a world which is doing its best to marginalize me; I undermine my sense of truth and reality by asking myself if I am being "too sensitive" about events or interactions that I initially deem as racist, sexist, classist, or homophobic; I attempt to reclaim and accept parts of my body and my sexuality on a daily basis; I am forced to keep anger and rage about being oppressed in check, whatever that means; I try to filter out societal messages about what I should be like, act like, and talk like; I work to unlearn the oppression that I have internalized; I struggle to carve out a space for myself in a world which doesn't want to have room for my image; I work to counter the invalidation and the hatred of my sex, my race, my sexual orientation.

DURING A THERAPY SESSION: *I'm in a place where I have felt validated and supported in looking at the emotional scars of my body. In beginning to deal with my internalized racism, I am trying to explain to my white therapist that there may be several factors which cause me to feel unsafe in talking to her about issues relating to race. I suggest that we explore how race affects our therapeutic relationship. I go on to say that therapy is a very white, middle-class way of dealing with life and express my excitement over finding out that there are different ways of doing therapy which might be more culturally appropriate in working with clients of Color. She gives me a blank look (you know — the look which makes you feel like you are totally crazy) and tells me that I am dealing with this in my head and that this is merely a strategy of "resistance." I leave the session weeping uncontrollably with the overwhelming feeling there really is no safe space for me. Anywhere.*

Along with analyzing how pressures of oppression affect us, we must also take time to learn about ourselves; how we cope with certain situations; what and who push our buttons; what style of communication we use; how we deal with emotions; how we handle ourselves in intimate relationships; what things we run away from; how we deal with power. This knowledge will not only help us internally but also be tools in working and interacting with other activists.

DURING AN INITIAL MEETING: *I am talking with two other community organizers who happen to be straight white men, about ways in which we can best reach our communities. For the first ten minutes, the men do all the talking, giving me no eye contact. I immediately retreat, the way I tend to do when I feel invisible. I sit back with my hands crossed in front of my chest angry and hurt that they aren't including me in the conver-sation. I then catch myself and realize that if I don't participate soon, I will completely disengage myself as I have done before. This disengagement protects me. But I refuse to allow a history of feeling invisible prevent me from participating in what could be a potential source of support and knowledge. I have to give this group a chance, take a risk, and see if their actions remain exclusive. I take a deep breath and try to enter the conversation.*

Finally, we need to find ways to validate and nurture ourselves. We need to gather around us people who are truly supportive: who will encourage and celebrate our growth, who will comfort us when life sucks, and who will validate us for being the wonderful human beings we are. It is imperative that we reach out to those who have forged a path before us and those who can serve as guides along the way. I realize that this may be difficult because as APL&B's, we don't exactly have role models jumping out at us. We also need to take time off from activism so that we don't burn out. We need to do so with the knowledge that the world won't stop spinning and that somebody else will step in to do the job. I've been surprised at the times when I left a leadership role that others filled the gap. We activists can have very big egos at times.

In writing this, I realize that this self-exploration is a necessity for me. But it is a luxury or priority that many of us don't have. Many of us have to devote our energy and time towards day to day survival: food, shelter, clothing, a decent job, or deportation. My parents, for instance, who immigrated from mainland China were forced to exit the country during war, to adapt to a society which is fundamentally different from that which they grew up in, to leave their family behind, and to exist on relatively little money while trying to finish their education. I understand that I have certain privileges that my parents didn't have. But I feel that I have a responsibility to use my privileges in a way that will be productive to myself and to those around me. I am a true believer that the work I have done on myself has made me stronger, more confident and empowered as a human being and thus, as an activist. In order to change the world around me, I must start with myself.

Trinity A. Ordona

The Challenges Facing Asian and Pacific Islander Lesbian and Bisexual Women in the U.S.: Coming Out, Coming Together, Moving Forward

This essay was adapted from a speech and slideshow presentation given by Trinity during Women's History Month in March 1992 at California State University-Long Beach. Trinity, an out lesbian for over twenty years, has presented her slideshow, "Asian/Pacific Lesbians: Coming Out, Coming Together," in over twenty public and private venues to Asian and Pacific Islander lesbians in the U.S., Canada, and Japan.

VOICE AND VISIBILITY ARE KEY CONCEPTS TODAY IN THE VOCABULARY of Asian and Pacific Islander lesbian and bisexual women (A/PLBs) in America. Until very recently, the homophobia and bi-phobia in the Asian and Pacific Islander communities was such that many thought gay and bisexual people were "nonexistent" or that these practices were cultural aberrations due to Western influence.[1] Today, a more visible and vocal A/PI gay and bisexual movement are challenging these erroneous ideas.

Another reason for our invisibility is the racism in the gay and lesbian mainstream community. The most blatant expression of racism in the gay community is the lack of presence, visibility, participation, and leadership of gay people of color. There are no signs designating "white only," yet white lesbians and gay men almost exclusively hold the reins of leadership and dominate the membership of most all gay organizations — political clubs, churches, publications, athletics, professional associations, and businesses. In other words, the gay and lesbian community mirrors, with little exception, the racial marginalizations that permeate American society. Gay organizations loudly decry the "lack" of people of color in their groups, yet so few have programs that address our specific needs. Too often when gay POC are involved, there is inadequate effort to sustain participation, develop leadership and consolidate commitment. The gay community's strides against exclusivity have generally been lip service.

So we struck out on our own to address our needs and develop our leadership, communication skills, organizational abilities, business acumen, and artistic talents. Like the African-American, Native American, Middle Eastern and Latino gay people, we A/PLBs have started to network, link up and form our own groups. Unfortunately, it is not the kind of community organizing that gets publicity from either the gay or Asian press. We are a growing community and new movement. But where have we come from? Where are we today? What are our future challenges?

Decades of Change

To contextualize our process and progress, we must go back several decades. In the 1960s, there were 1.4 million Asian people in the U.S. — less than 1 percent of the total population. The island peoples of the Pacific Basin under U.S. control also numbered about 200,000. Yet our communities were undergoing irreversible political and social changes during those tumultuous years. Decolonization movements were rapidly transforming the oppressed peoples and countries of Asia, Africa, Latin America and the Pacific.[2] Within the U.S, the civil rights, women's and anti-war movements drew thousands of young people into political protest and social change. Linked by common histories of land and labor exploitation, young Asian and Pacific Islander activists also began to organize their communities in Los Angeles, San Francisco, Seattle, Honolulu and New York. Immigration, law and labor reform, ethnic studies[3] programs, bilingual/bicultural education projects and social service agencies for newcomers, elderly, women and children were initiated. In the meantime, the 1969 Stonewall Rebellion[4] gave birth to yet another movement as thousands of lesbians and gay men "came out" in droves under the banner of the Gay Liberation Movement. Though few gay people of color were active in the early years of the Gay Liberation Movement,[5] small groups of gay people of color, including Asian lesbians, formed social and political groups in San Francisco, Los Angeles and New York City by the late 1970s.

Beginning in 1965 and through the next two decades, however, demographic changes were rebuilding the Asian and Pacific Islander communities from within. The 1965 Immigration and Naturalization Reform Act ushered in a new era of massive immigration, with the majority entering from Asia and Latin America. In less than fifteen years, the Asian community *doubled* in size to over 3.5 million, or 1.5 percent of the U.S. population. Another decade later in 1990, the population doubled again, reaching 7.2 million, or 3 percent of the U.S. population.[6] Today, 60 percent of the Asian community in the U.S. is foreign-born, with newcomers from a wider range of Asian countries. Among the Chinese, Japanese, Filipino, East Indian and Korean people who had immigrated between 1870-1950, the Asian community now includes immigrants and refugees from India, Pakistan, Goa, Sri Lanka, Bangladesh, Vietnam, Cambodia, Laos, Burma, Tibet, Thailand, Malaysia, Indonesia, Taiwan, Hong Kong, and Singapore.

In addition, large numbers of people from the Pacific Basin emigrated to the U.S. mainland, further complicating the changing population demographics. The people of American Samoa and Guam were granted U.S. national status in 1950, and Hawai'i became America's 50th state nine years later. For decades, these islands had served as key strategic military bases. As U.S. nationals, they were not subject to immigration regulations and entitled to take up residence and employment in the U.S. Soon, thousands of Samoan and Chamorro[7] families emigrated freely to Honolulu for military-related jobs, and then to the major ports along the West Coast. By 1990, there were 50,000 Guamanians and 63,000 Samoans in the U.S. For Hawai'i, statehood brought tourism on a grand scale and soon, millions of visitors came yearly to the "island paradise." High-rise hotels, condominiums and shopping centers escalated property values sky-high and well beyond the reach of most. Soon, Hawai'i had the highest cost of living in the country! The lopsided economy forced many Native Hawaiians to leave home for job and education opportunities on the continent. Today, over 100,000 Pacific Island peoples live in California alone, including half of the total Samoan and Chamorro[8] population.

A Mirror Reflection

The A/PLB community of 1993 reflects the generational, nationality, linguistic, ethnic, religious, and citizenship demographics of the Asian and Pacific communities in the U.S. For example, Asian Lesbians of the East Coast (ALOEC) was founded in New York City in the early 1980's and is still active today. Asian Women United, a nonpolitical support group of mostly second and third generation Asian-American lesbians, was formed in the San Francisco Bay Area in 1978. Their newsletter, *Phoenix Rising*, is still published today under the auspices of a successor organization, Asian Pacifica Sisters (APS). APS was founded in 1988 to coordinate activities and address the concerns of A/PI lesbians and bisexual women in the San Francisco Bay area. The current membership includes a large segment of foreign-born Asian women or whose parents immigrated to the U.S. since 1965. Along with San Francisco and New York, A/PLB communities can now be found in Washington DC, Boston, Pittsburgh, Chicago, Minneapolis, Seattle, Sacramento, Los Angeles, San Diego and Honolulu.

Reflecting the broader ethnic diversity of the community has been the emergence of South Asian lesbians and bisexual women whose network extends to Canada, England and their home countries in the sub-continent. As early as 1986, a group of South Asian lesbians and bisexual women produced a newsletter, *Anamika*. In 1990, a network of South Asian lesbians and bisexual women began producing a national newsletter, *Shamakami* with local groups mainly in Toronto, New York, and San Francisco. In addition, Pacific Islander lesbian and bisexual women have begun to network, including some *Kānaka Maoli*[9] activists in community and land rights struggles.

In addition, age and generational differences among women are now more pronounced. In San Francisco, a support group of older Asian lesbians (35 years and above) called OASIS - Older Asian Sisters in Solidarity was formed in 1991. In 1993, the first co-gendered youth organization of Asian lesbian, bisexual and gay men (17-25 years old) called FABRIC (Fresh Asians Becoming Real in our Communities) was formed in San Francisco. Across the country, networks and friendship circles have formed among Filipino, Vietnamese, Korean, Japanese, Malaysian,

Thai, Chinese, and mixed heritage Asian lesbians and bisexual women. Many individuals, organizations, social networks and support groups socialize together at dances, benefits, film showings, house parties, writers groups, rap groups, and softball, basketball, and volleyball games.

Significant regional, national and international conferences have also been pivotal in creating overlapping and interconnecting networks of individuals and organizations. The first Asian/Pacific Lesbian West Coast Regional Retreat was organized in 1987. A year later, the Asian/Pacific Lesbian Network (A/PLN) was formed as a project-oriented national coalition of individuals from the East Coast, Midwest, West Coast, and Hawai'i. In 1989, the A/PLN organized the first National Retreat which brought together over 140 women from the U.S., Canada, and England. A second West Coast Regional A/PLN retreat was held in October 1993, with future national A/PLBN[10] tentative activities set for the "Stonewall 25 Celebration" (New York, 1994) and the Second National Retreat (East Coast, 1995). Other milestones have been the A/PLB contingents at the 1987 and 1993 National Lesbian, Gay and Bisexual People's March on Washington, the National Lesbian Conference (Atlanta 1991) and the 1991 anti-*Miss Saigon* campaign in New York City and San Francisco when a nationally prominent gay rights organization used the racist and sexist *Miss Saigon* Broadway musical as a fundraising benefit. Outside the U.S., recent international gatherings include the 1988 North American Conference of Asian Lesbians and Gay Men in Toronto and the Asian Lesbian Network conferences in Thailand (1990), Japan (1992) and Taiwan (slated for 1995). Also reflecting the changing international demographics of a large overseas Asian population, Asian lesbian groups have formed in Peru, Canada, England, the Netherlands, and Australia.

The dynamics underlying these activities to identify, create and connect with each other are rooted in our similar and different experiences as Asian and Pacific Islander people, women, and gays. Indeed, the emergence and beginning unification process of Asian and Pacific Islander lesbian and bisexual women has been an emotional, moving experience. As a community of women and a movement for social change, we stand at the crossroads of three dynamic trends of change with far-reaching domestic and international dimensions. Asian and Pacific Islander peoples have already been noted as the "fastest growing population in the U.S." The 1990s has been hailed as the "Decade of the Woman" and the "Year of the Queer." Sāmoa, Guam, Hawaiʻi, Belau (Palau), Aotearoa (New Zealand), Tahiti and Kanaky (New Caledonia) all have Native Rights movements for various forms of political and economic autonomy. The centuries-old unequal social status of women continue to be vigorously challenged in all corners of the world. And the international Gay Liberation Movement and the AIDS pandemic have forced a spotlight on homosexuals worldwide.

In this broader context, we are emerging at the threshold of history-making social changes, both here and in Asia and the Pacific Basin. The future of viable communities of Asian and Pacific Islander lesbian and bisexual women will be largely determined in the decade of the 90s by the social and political foundations of our organizations, networks and institutions. The national and international bonds of common identities and shared oppressions, which undergird the radical growth of our community, now challenge us to consciously shape our future.

---

1 While not within the scope of this essay, there is documented evidence that homosexuality was an accepted practice in China (Hinsch, 1990, p. 2-4), Japan (Benedict, 1946, p. 188-89) and India (Ratti, 1993, p. 13) prior to Western influence. In particular to the peoples of the Pacific Basin, modern anthropology has distorted much of the record on homosexuality and bisexuality. The theoretical models used in the recent past to analyze homo/bisexual data came from Western psychological concepts of sexuality. Most anthropologists based their evaluation of homo/bisexual practices in other cultures on the deviance model of psychology and sociology, contrary to the values in the culture studied — most of whom accepted these practices within their social system. For further discussion of this, see Evelyn Blackwood, The Many Faces of Homosexuality, 1986.
2 In the Pacific Basin, U.S. possessions acquired between 1893-1899 included the Hawaiian Islands, Guam, and American Samoa. Additionally after WWII, the U.S. administered, under the auspices of the United Nations, the Trust Territories of the Pacific composed of the Northern Marianas, Carolines, and Marshall island groups.
3 In all but Hawaii, community efforts to build Ethnic Studies programs focused on

Asian-American Studies. In Honolulu, both Hawaiian Studies and Asian-American Studies programs were started.

4 Notably, white lesbians and Puerto Rican and Black transvestites and drag queens were among those that fought the police at the Stonewall Bar.

5 One exception was Jose Sarria, a popular Latino drag queen and the first openly-gay candidate for Supervisor in San Francisco in 1961, sixteen years before Harvey Milk.

6 Statistics taken from "Asian-Americans: Growth, Change and Diversity," Robert W. Gardner, Bryant Robey, and Peter C. Smith, Population Reference Bureau, Washington, DC, 40:4, 1989, p 8. For comparison, with other racial/ethnic groups (1992): white, 75%; African-American, 12%, Latino, 10%, Native Americans, 0.7%; see "America's Minorities: The Demographics of Diversity," William P. O'Hare, Population Reference Bureau, Washington, DC., 47:4, 1992, p. 10.

7 Chamorro, the indigenous people of Guam.

8 In the 1990 Census, listed as Guamanian.

9 *Kānaka Maoli* (pronounced kaa-na-ka mau-li) is Hawaiian for Hawaiian people or Native Hawaiian.

10 The Asian/Pacific Lesbian Network (A/PLN) recently changed its name to include bisexual women. The new name is Asian/Pacific Lesbian and Bisexual Network (A/PLBN).

Cross-Racial Hostility
and Inter-Racial Conflict:
Stories to Tell,
Lessons to Learn

In 1990, Virginia R. Harris and I published an article[1] on developing unity among women of color. It was a beginning articulation of an often-overlooked and underestimated problem: conflict and disunity among people of color. Since then, I have experienced many situations where inter-racial conflicts have arisen. Practice is always harder than theory. All of them were difficult and many ended poorly. Here are two stories[2] that did not.

COMMONLY-SHARED IDENTITIES AND OPPRESSIONS do not automatically bequeath lasting unity. In fact, it has generally eluded heterosexual women of color and lesbians of color. In 1983, one of the first Lesbians of Color conferences was held in Malibu, California. Attended by some 250 women, the conference began with euphoria but ended with confusion, frustration and accusations breaking down along color lines between and within groups of women of color.

When women of color first meet, it often feels wonderful. But later after the "honeymoon" is over, we find ourselves pained by insensitivity towards each other, in-fighting, and unaddressed conflicts. This is true of group dynamics across class, gender and sexual orientation lines within the same racial and ethnic groups and between different communities of color. People of color have not acknowledged the unique racial dynamics of cross-racial hostility between and among us, problems which have no ready answer. Short of slogans, "united we stand, divided we fall," there is little to draw upon when conflict emerges. For decades, we have devoted time and energy to the "race question between whites and blacks." Yet Pacific Islander, Asian, Latino, Middle Eastern and Native American peoples are usually left out of the discussion and the "race problem among people of color" is never broached. Too often, coalitions of people of color have been organized with the assumption of unity and inadequate time to build trust and lasting relationships beyond the event. Women of color are no exception. Yet, I had my hopes up when I went to Boston.

In Our Own Way

Boston, MA — In October 1991 I attended the "I Am Your Sister" Celeconference to honor the work and contributions of Black lesbian poet and leader, Audre Lorde. It was an inspiring event attended by a thousand people, mostly women from all over the U.S. and the world. To the organizers' credit, a good part of the conference's success was their politically astute policy that half the participants were women of color and impoverished women.

Given the widespread popularity of Audre Lorde's work and who can usually afford to attend national meetings, the race and class ratios would have easily gone askew if participation were determined on the traditional "first-come-first-serve" paid registration process. All participants alike were therefore subject to an application process in which one's anti-racist and pro-feminist work was the primary selection criterion for applicants. Then, equal numbers of white people and people of color who met the criterion were registered. Scholarships were also available to those qualified applicants also in need. In my estimation, establishing a political criterion to the conference composition and the more equitable race and class balance it provided undercut tendencies towards tokenism and alienation which oftentime accompany national gatherings.

Tensions were there, though it did not break out in ugly floor fights. From the beginning, there was very little Asian and Pacific Islander visibility[3] in the conference program. Throughout the three-day weekend, there were only three Asian and no Pacific Islander women presenters out of at least 50 stage presenters. There was no featured Pacific Islander or Asian woman speaker. African-American women's voice and perspective overwhelmed the program from beginning to end. I tried not to notice, but it was too obvious after a while. At first I thought to myself, "Well, Audre

Lorde is an African-American woman and I guess it's only right..." [*that we get left out like this, as my feelings completed the sentence*]. By the second day, however, I walked out of the auditorium when continued disappointment and confusion brought hot tears to my eyes.

Within the Asian and Pacific Islander women's caucus, we also had our own problems. When the first caucus meeting ended, we could not agree on what to call ourselves: Asian, Asian/Pacific, Asian and Pacific Islander, Asian-American, Asian Pacific American, etc. However, the discussion was open and democratic, and it felt good to be together as the fifty of us crowded into the little room. In our discussion, these questions arose: "Is the quiet, submissive Asian woman 'fact' or 'fiction'? Why can't we express our feelings, especially angry feelings, which Black women do so easily? Is there something 'wrong' with us?" Clearly, comparing stereotypes of Asian women to stereotypes of African-American women was at work among us.

It was also at work in the conference, too. The next day in the auditorium as caucus reports were being given, our two representatives waited their turn patiently. Somehow, other speakers from the floor were called on out of order and recognized instead. The precious time ticked away and for a while, it looked as if we might not get to speak. Then one young Filipino woman fearlessly jumped to her feet and got the chair's attention. Once she got the microphone, our caucus report soon followed and all the Asian and Pacific Islander women in the audience were asked to stand for acknowledgment. A sense of pride and relief rippled across our rows. Seconds before, I could tangibly feel tensions mount among our caucus members as we waited "so" patiently to be called upon. Did anyone else share our fear that we might be left out again?

The caucus met throughout the weekend over these issues of self-assertion, expression and invisibility. Ultimately, we decided not to directly confront the organizers or upset the planned program. Instead, we created a space to speak for ourselves. On the last day of the conference in front of the whole auditorium, a representative group of twelve caucus women[4] presented a performance piece. We wrote it the night before. Several women had never written poetry or performed before. We were the first to speak during the open-mike session.

We entered the stage single file from both sides, formed a single line and opened our presentation with this collective choral refrain:

I have to write, in order to say.

I have to speak, in order to be heard.

I have to be heard, in order to be seen.

See me now, see all of me.

I am part of you, just as you are part of me.

Then stepping forward, one after the other, each woman told a part of her story.[5] In 20 minutes, the audience collectively experienced a unique, creative combination of individuality and diversity. We were no longer a group that "looked the same," blended into some kind of hodge-podge of racialized stereotypical sameness. The audience saw that we did not look alike; they heard our names and other words spoken properly in our native Korean, Mandarin, Vietnamese, Hindi and Hawaiian languages. They learned that we were immigrant, refugee, American-born, adopted and mixed heritage women; they met lesbian and straight women. They felt our anger and saw our hurt. After the last woman spoke, we ended with this closing choral refrain:

I have written, I have spoken.

I am here, we are here.

Now can you hear us? Now can you see us?

Just as you are part of us, we now, are part of you.

Of the 12 women, seven of us were lesbians. A mere coincidence? I think not. Being a lesbian or bisexual woman in a bi/homophobic society is being a lifelong contrarian. So we have learned to struggle against homophobia, bi-phobia, heterosexism, racism and intra-racial/cross-racial hostilities wherever we are, whenever we can and however we must. We brought that experience with us and shared it that weekend in Boston.

Getting Called Out

Santa Cruz, CA — The Santa Cruz redwoods was the site of the most recent gathering of Asian and Pacific Islander lesbian and bisexual women in the U.S. Held on the weekend of October 22-24, 1993, it was primarily a regional mobilization that brought together over 150 women from San Diego, Los Angeles, San Francisco Bay Area, Seattle, and Vancouver, with some participants from as far away as Honolulu, Chicago, Minneapolis, and New York. The Second West Coast Retreat was organized by a Bay Area group of the Asian/Pacifica Lesbian and Bisexual Network (APLBN) who had spent over a year planning and fundraising for the effort.

On Saturday, two *Kanaka Maoli*[6] women helped to open the Retreat with an Hawaiian ceremonial chant and an invocation to the Native American people upon whose land we now stood. One of them joined the morning plenary to address the question, "Moving Beyond Visibility." Later that afternoon, they rejoined to lead the workshop, "Specific Islanders: Inclusion vs. Appropriation, Coalition and Hawaiian Sovereignty." As usual, we were already running behind schedule, so I came to the workshop a little late. They had not started, hoping that more people would show up. We started anyway, but with less people. Lisa and Kehaulani, the workshop leaders, came prepared with a lot of informational material including a powerful 10-minute video, "Spirit of Fire."[7] After an hour-long presentation on Hawaiian sovereignty and the land rights issue, we saw the video. The Hawaiian people's history of land grab and genocide by the U.S. government and big business, was juxtaposed against today's Native Hawaiians whose "life in paradise" is one of homelessness, joblessness, incarceration, and poor health and education. When the lights came back on ten minutes later, the room was hushed and everyone silent, except for the sniffles from a few tears. We were all touched so deeply, so emotionally, that none of us could speak. Soon everyone was misty-eyed.

Then the hurts, disappointments and anger began to surface. Among the questions asked were: In 1993, the United Nations Year of the Indigenous Peoples and the 100th Anniversary of the Illegal Overthrow of the Hawaiian Kingdom, why are so few people in this workshop? Where is everybody else? Why wasn't this a plenary presentation? How did this happen? Why are there so few Pacific Islander women here at this retreat? Is the "P" in APLBN real or token?[8]

Lisa and Kehaulani talked about repeated blatant instances of insensivity by other Asian lesbians and bisexual women. In fact, Lisa, when invited as a plenary speaker, made the condition of her participation the inclusion of this very workshop. Otherwise, she said, "this workshop would not be here and neither would I." Kehaulani, reflecting on their opening prayer, asked: "Why do people want Hawaiians for song and prayer, but then are not here to learn about our problems and take some responsibility?" Upset and self-critical, two workshop members and part of the Retreat Planning Committee also revealed they had suggested several ways the Retreat could acknowledge the 100th Anniversary, "but nothing came of them."

Immersed in guilt, anger, confusion, and compassion, we wrestled with these issues. The discussion revealed the many and deep problems of an Asian-dominated discourse that has repeatedly tokenized Pacific Islander peoples and their distinct identities, communities and struggles. The general practice of Asians, Asian lesbians and bisexual women not excepted, has been to marginalize Pacific Islander peoples within a monolithic (supposedly more "unifying") identity as "Asian Pacific." Therefore, sameness and power over, instead of difference and coalition with, have mistakenly become the operational framework for our politics.

While noting this is a pervasive problem in the broader Asian community, however, the Asian women in the workshop decided to take responsibility to change this practice among ourselves. We spent the rest of the workshop time on how to address the problems in a straight-forward, non-blaming way. The next day following the morning plenary panel, we took over the Retreat. With the cooperation of the Retreat organizers, we told the assembled group of nearly a hundred women the events of the preceding day. Then educational materials were distributed and the video was shown again. Soon, a powerful, emotional silence gripped the audience as the truth of the historic and continued oppression of Native Hawaiian people, and our own collusion by ignorance, came crashing home. Doreena, one of the main organizers of the Retreat, took the microphone only to be choked up in tears and unable to speak. We all cried with her.

That afternoon's "guerrilla workshop" was the first open struggle within the APLBN against this kind of tokenism by Asian lesbians and bisexual women and the beginning process of reconciliation with our Pacific Islander sisters. This story is but one contribution.

1 "Developing Unity Among Women of Color: Crossing the Barriers of Internalized Racism and Cross-Racial Hostility," Virginia R. Harris and Trinity A. Ordona, *Making Face, Making Soul = Haciendo Caras: Creative and Political Perspectives by Women of Color*, 1990, pp.304-316.

2 It is not my intention to provide a comprehensive report on the two events discussed here, but rather to focus on some of the underlying problems and tell how they were handled by the women involved.

3 Other groups also felt seriously underrepresented and the stage was not wheelchair accessible. During the open-mike session before the end of the conference, the Latina, Native American, and disabled women's groups voiced these same criticisms.

4 Sensitive to our own tendencies to be divisive, we were conscious to be broadly representative in the performing group. The group was composed of: a Filipino-American from California; a Chinese-Canadian woman from Vancouver; a Vietnamese "boat" refugee and now student at an East Coast College; a Korean-American woman from Massachusetts; a part Japanese-white American woman from the East Coast; a Japanese-Canadian nisei, working class dyke; a part Hawaiian-Okinawan-white American from Hawaii; a Korean woman adopted as a child and raised in New England by white parents; a 4th-generation Indian woman from Trinidad; a Chinese foreign student from Taiwan; and an Indian woman who immigrated to the U.S. as a young girl.

5 See "Who Am I" by Peou Lakhana, pg.40 and "Who Am I" by Anu, pg.19 for some of the poems that were read that afternoon.

6 *Kānaka Maoli* (pronounced kaa-na-ka mau-li), Hawaiian for Hawaiian people or Native Hawaiian.

7 "Spirit of Fire," produced by Jeffrey Hirota and distributed by Nā Maka O Ka 'Aina, 3020 Kahaloa Dr., Honolulu, HI 96822.

8 While seven *Kānaka Maoli* women attended the 1993 APLBN Retreat, the overall participation and leadership of Pacific Islander women had declined since the APLN was formed. Ku'umea'aloha Gomes, a leading Hawaiian Sovereignty activist from Honolulu, was one of the founding members of the APLN in 1988. Reflecting her leadership and influence, the first National APLN Retreat in 1989 had broader and more active participation in the workshops, caucuses, plenaries and cultural programs by Native Hawaiian and Guamanian women as well as Asian women from Hawaii. Ku'umea'aloha has since returned to Honolulu where she devotes her energies to Hawaiian peoples' struggles. In light of the popular resurgence of the Native Hawaiian sovereignty movement and the controversy surrounding the same-sex marriage lawsuit in the state of Hawaii, Ku'umea'aloha helped form a new organization of *Kānaka Maoli* gay men and lesbians, Na Mamo Manoa, and is active in both movements.

Anu

Response to "Room of One's Own"

Virginia, you said I needed a
room of my own to write
I have my room
Two rooms, in fact
Carpeted, furnished
Nine months temporary "refuge" until graduation
I have pens, pencils, borrowed computer
        Reams of recyclable paper even.
Then why do I struggle with pen and word,
                with sound and shape
trying to squeeze a flood of thoughts
                        on one page?
Why sometimes am I deluged with
        random words, inappropriate cliches
                no organization, no coherence
        just a war in me battling to gain expression?
Why at other times am I a blank desert, no horizon,
                nothing to say, immobilized
envying cigarette smoke for its freedom to form creative shapes
                before it disappears into nothingness?

No, Virginia, a room is not enough
        to write about the struggle of identity
                the colonizer and the colonized
        to make expression of my life as a convenient construct
                of centuries of brutality and exploitation

Tell me how to write *honestly*, in my room, about
      home, my home ravaged by colonialism for 300 years
      and now burning with fires of hate and exploitation
      where privilege is the narrow line
            between education and starvation.
Can I write about it, in my room, in this "land of the free"
      without being tokenized
      without speaking for every Indian voice
      or
without hearing "This is what they do if left to themselves"?
I no longer know what is Me and what is Indian.
Can I make that separation?
You say I need to, in order to write.
A room of my own does not remove me
      does not give me the necessary "objective" voice
Writing forces me to see faces I can otherwise choose to forget
Destroys attempts of erasing
      "Your aunt died yesterday"
      "Your brother can get no job"
      "The land is on fire"
      "20 people died of heatstroke"
      "30 more because of the cold"
      "And millions are starving to death."
Writing threatens my stability
      my ability to cope with the horrors of violence
In speech I modify, distort the truth, tell "white" lies
To prevent myself from screaming out loud
      At friends, American friends, products of
            hamburgers, Coke and TV
     who have no conception of my reality
Writing is my voice of true expression
Poetic license forces me to be honest
Because, Virginia, what I write is not easy,
It has no language, no place in the order of things
It is an illegal alien

No, Virginia, a room is not enough
        to write "objectively," "critically"
        about the contradictions of my
            Indian/Lesbian-Lesbian/Indian identity
I've forgotten my language
Hindi is now unfamiliar to my tongue
I know not any word for myself
        but Khush
        and even that is a mocking translation
Do I have the strength to put on paper
        my lack of a dream life there,
I cannot envision
        living in India
        preserving my "American" individualism
        loving a woman
        building a home with her
        defying family, friends
        ignoring disapproval, silence
        and still speaking, still fighting
        to prevent erasure
Life there, as life here, would be a compromise
        between complete silence
        and complete battle with the system
Both will destroy me
        faster than the cigarette burns into my lungs
No, Virginia, a room of my own is the illusion of safe space
        just the distance of 10,000 miles
        shattered every time I hear my mother
            over the phone, $2 per minute
        "Your brother hasn't mentioned you for two months now."
and it is not enough for me to build a revolution in.

Virginia, you said I need a room of my own to write, to create in
No, I say to you
I NEED MORE
I need the Words
Words in languages I have been forbidden to know
I need a language which does not carry the historical baggage
                                        of my erasure
A language with expression for love-hate contradictions
                                    which plague my life.
I need a voice, confident to speak
A voice to counter charges
        of "emotional," "hypersensitive,"
        of "biased," "reverse-racist"
I know I do not yet have those words, the language or that voice.

Virginia, I thank you,
I thank all brave and courageous women
who lived in a hovel with 15 others
or had 15 rooms all to themselves
The colonized women
The colonizer women
The lesbian women
The straight women
All the women who fought and struggled
whose work allows me to have a room of my own
But I still need more
We all need more

Remember, You, women like you, like us
        with (y)our multiplicities of privilege
        have rooms of (y)our own, a voice, a word
        because of others like you, like us,
        who cook our food,
        who clean our clothes
        who labor in fields and in our homes
        are silenced
We cannot be satisfied with just a room, four walls,
                        our enclosures
        while others have not even a voice which is heard
lest our rooms, our enclosures, give us the illusion of safety
        and close in like walls of a prison
            suffocate the very breath
                we have struggled to take.

Sharon Fernandez

Mina Kumar

Representations of Indian Lesbianism

LESBIANISM APPEARS IN SOME OF THE EARLIEST INDIAN TEXTS: the Arthashastra, the Laws of Manu, the Mahabharata, the Ramayana. In the epics and in the legal codes, it is portrayed as a negative, or punishable, practice. The next type of representation of lesbian sexuality is as a part of the range of human sexuality. This is the view of the Kama Sutra, and this is perhaps the reason for the appearance of lesbian sex in the friezes of various temple complexes, including Khajuraho, and in Mughal or Rajput miniatures. In the colonial and contemporary post-colonial period, discussion of lesbianism has been influenced both by Western modernity and Western prudery. While there has not been much work out of post-colonial India by self-consciously gay people, the South Asian diaspora has produced many images of South Asian lesbianism in popular media.

The materials discussed in this essay have all been read in English translations, and that is one reason for their remarkable heterogeneity of form. The range of the materials is also shaped by the uses to which Indian lesbianism has been put by Indians and by Westerners. Ultimately, the politics that disseminates certain kinds of representations is as important as the representations themselves.

The earliest text found to mention lesbianism is the Arthashastra, Chanakya's treatise on government written in the third century B.C. It prescribes the punishment of a fine of twelve to 24 panas for this activity. The fine was "much less than participants in certain heterosexual activities", and less than that for male homosexuality, which was fined "between 48 and 94 panas."[1] In Pratab Chandra Chunder's interpretation of key lines, "A woman having sexual connection (*prakartri*) with another woman who desires such connection and belong to the same status has to pay 24 panas and the latter only twelve panas... The text connotes mutual sexual passion between women. But for her own pleasure a woman ravishing an unwilling woman is liable to pay 100 panas in addition to the payment of the bride price."[2]

The Manava Dharmashastra was written within the first two centuries A.D., and in the Laws of Manu (VIII), "lesbian love between girls is punished with a heavy fine and strokes of the whip; and the married woman who thus stains a maid is at once shaved bald, and with two fingers cut off is led on an ass through the city."[2]

The Mahabharata and the Ramayana both describe events that supposedly take place at least a millennium before, but the first extant written texts are from the first half of the first millennium AD. In the Mahabharata, Nilakantha states that when two women have sex, "one of them holds an artificial male organ," and this usage is censured.[4] In the Ramayana, Hanuman witnesses women in Lanka embracing "as if they were making love to their male lovers."[5]

The Kama Sutra, written in the sixth century A.D., describes oral sex as both a homosexual and a heterosexual practice, and the same term (kakila) is used to denote simultaneous oral sex. The Kama Sutra describes lesbianism within the context of the languishing maidens of the harem. A "phallusshaped plant"[6] is mentioned as a sexual aid.

In the period after the Kama Sutra, written representations of lesbianism seem to be missing. Instead, the era from the second half of the first millennium AD to the late medieval period offers visual images. Temple sculpture of this period often depicted sexual acts, often in celebration of the marriage of Shiva and Parvati, and some of these acts are among women. Giti Thadani has photographed one such sculpture of a lesbian orgy at Khajuraho.[7] While lesbian depictions are not the rule, they are not exceptional. As Banerjee notes, "passionate people did not rest content with natural modes of sex-enjoyment... (There are) a few cases of aberrations in connection with sculpture."[8] It is likely that the various Mughal and Rajput miniatures that depict lesbian sexuality were part of illustrated manuscripts dealing with sexual matters, but at this point, individual miniatures are in the hands of different owners, and their context has not been ascertained.

Contact with Western civilization stimulated new genres of representations. The analysis of lesbianism as a product of single-sex schools that is prevalent in manuals about women's sexuality owes much to

Freud, Havelock Ellis and the cult of romantic friendship. Anthropological studies such as Kapur's study of the Kumaoni provide examples of lesbian sexuality well integrated within the range of village sexual experience. "Modern" writers began to pursue previously taboo subjects. Ismat Chugtai's short story "Lihaaf," which depicts a woman who turned to her maidservant when her husband ignored her in favor of various boys, became a *cause célèbre* when it was prosecuted for obscenity. Another of her stories, "Apna Khun," involves a woman who poisons the maid she loves when her husband decides to marry her.

In the West, the Indian lesbian played a bit part in the literature of the Sexual Revolution and the Lesbian-Feminist movement. *The Jewel in the Lotus*, for example, refers to "the aromatic gardens of the Red Fort at Delhi, the Fort of Akbar in Lahore and the Kaiserbagh Palace at Lucknow (were full of) zenana women with highly developed organs...[who] practiced sapphic venery in hammocks." Susan Calvin's *Lesbian Origins* places lesbian amazons in India, and Judy Grahn's *Another Mother Tongue* discusses an American woman's affair with a Tamil Dalit in contemporary "matriarchal" Kanyakumari.

The last decade has seen the emergence of materials by lesbians of South Asian descent about lesbians of South Asian descent within the context of a nascent "gay rights" movement, in India and most especially without. The Indo-British film maker Pratibha Parmar's documentary *Flesh and Paper* examined the lesbian Indo-Canadian poet Suniti Namjoshi. Parmar's *Khush* and Shakila Maan's short *Ferdaus* both depict lesbianism within the context of South Asia. Hanif Kureishi's film *Sammy and Rosie Get Laid* features a minor South Asian lesbian character within the context of London. Small periodicals for South Asian lesbians began to appear in New York, London, San Francisco, and Toronto.

The shape of the materials gathered for this essay is first determined by the fact that they are all in English. If there is other relevant source materials in regional languages, they have not been discussed in English texts.

The focus on ancient Sanskrit texts has been determined a great deal by the colonial encounter. Westerners tended to privilege ancient Sanskrit texts because they were considered closer to the "shared Aryan roots" of both European and Indic civilization. Indians, on the other hand, returned to these texts in the effort to shape an "Indian" identity in counterpoint to Western civilization. Thus, the validity of particular translations is not entirely certain given the unsubtle politics of cultural reclamation. Just as religious reform movements such as the Arya Samaj sought to make Hinduism relevant to a new world order, colonial and postcolonial writers are often at pains to prove the wisdom and pertinence of their significant texts to the modern world. Chunder, for example, goes to extraordinary and ridiculous lengths to decode the Arthashastra as having a (negative) opinion on sado-masochistic sex. His interpretation of certain passages as referring to lesbian rape where others have read it as heterosexual rape is therefore something worth questioning. On the other hand, A. L. Basham's remark that the lack of homosexuality in ancient India proved that it was "far healthier than most other ancient cultures"[9] indicates that there was also a parallel impetus to ignore a lesbian presence in ancient texts to shore up opposition to the depraved West.

If lesbian sex is explicitly outlawed in the two legal texts (even if it is not a comparatively serious offense relative to certain variant heterosexual practices), lesbianism is implicitly degenerate in the epics. In the Ramayana, for example, Hanuman sees the lesbian sex in Lanka, the land of rakshasas, and its presence may serve to indicate Lankan debauchery more than any lesbian presence. On the other hand, there is the intriguing fact that Surpanaka, the demoness who sparks the major battle of the Ramayana, is described as trying to devour Sita, and has her nose cut off in response. The reason given for this attempt to devour is Surpanaka's unreciprocated lust for Sita's husband, Rama, and his brother, Lakshmana, but the association of phallic castration with the nose-cutting is certainly tempting, given Hanuman's later remark about seeing lesbians in Lanka. In the Mahabharata, the two women Nilakantha refers to are condemned "for using an artificial penis."[10] It is interesting that the weight of the disapproval seems to fall on the dildo, considering that Lillian Faderman has shown that in Western European history, its use severely exacerbated the criminality of lesbian sex because of its implication of the assumption of male prerogatives.

The discussion of lesbianism in the ancient texts, especially the specificity of Manu's description, implies its existence as a social concern. It was explicitly differentiated from the rest of society, whether as a crime or as a practice of demons. In the Kama Sutra, however, lesbianism is simply another, if lesser, part of human sexuality. In this same era, the rise of Tantric ritual elevated sexuality and non-conformity (and the role of women, in its emphasis on female gods). In this context, the sculptures of women in amorous embraces at Khajuraho and other temples is part of the expansion of eroticism in religious and cultural life. Later Mughal and Rajput miniatures also depicted lesbian sex, perhaps as part of erotic manuscripts. Thus, in visual art, lesbianism was implicitly part of the social fabric.

Nayan Shah raises the concern that visual images that translate as "lesbian" to the contemporary eye may in fact not be construed as such within their cultural context.[11] This is certainly an important point, and care has been taken to control for this. The images refered to in this essay are explicitly sexual, and involve either stimulation of the breasts or genitals. While different cultures have differing levels of socially permissible physical contact, a woman's breasts and vulva are universally recognized as sexual zones. In one painting, the two women have their salwars down, and their shaven vulvas face each other in an imitation of the missionary position.[12] The aggressor is much darker, and is wearing a turban, in a kind of desi butch-femme. As in the American pulp novels of the 50s, the darker one is the butch. Other, more diffusely homoerotic, depictions in the books cited seem to indicate that the paintings were created for the "male gaze," and the male erotic gaze at that, which is not so explicitly true for the temple sculpture. The sculptures in connecting sexuality to religion connect more closely to society (though primarily upper-class society in the case of Khajuraho) and therefore cannot be said to cater solely to male fantasy in the same way as the paintings, which had a more explicitly male audience.

Another aspect of the colonial encounter with the West is that social reform for women became an important expression of modernization. Both Mayah Balse's *The Indian Female: Attitudes Towards Sex* and S. N. Rampal's

Indian Women and Sex examine the changing mores of the Indian middle classes and in their way advocate better roles for women. Their modernization involves wholesale and self-conscious acceptance of many Western psychological concepts (Oedipus, for example), while emphasizing the extent to which Indians still accept their religious traditions. Rampal, for example, vocally opposes male chauvinism, but begins his book with, "Our women are by far the most beautiful in the world. The women in overdeveloped countries are losing their femininity so fast that one can hardly call them beautiful... Beauty is a certain sensitivity in a woman which touches the man's heart in a particular way."[13] Both Balse and Rampal relegate lesbianism to the languishing maidens of urban single-sex hostels, though Rampal admits cases in village society. Rampal tends to conflate homosexuality and masturbation, giving one combined figure for the premarital practices of city girls, apparently because their causes are the same: "just the sensation of affectionate touch of each others' (sic) apart from lack of chances to indulge in sex with males freely all lead to homosexuality and masturbation."[14] While masturbation with a foreign object is noted without comment, a dildo is described as a "substitute phallus being used by some female acting as a male."[15] Rampal relates "a very interesting case study" where a woman became pregnant from the unwashed genitals of her married lover (who had presumably just slept with her husband), thus legitimizing a folktale used to warn women that even lesbian sex is not free from the dangers of pregnancy.[16] He also describes a woman who turned to a female friend after rejection from a boy, and after her marriage discovered that she didn't enjoy intercourse as much as "that peculiar relationship which she had had in the past."[17] Despite showing a greater amount of tolerance towards lesbian relationships than the contemptuous Balse, Rampal's main stress is increasing the liberality and sexual skill of Indian men, and repeatedly connecting educated urban women with variant sexuality, from prostitution to nymphomania to bestiality to lesbianism to a preference for white men. Lesbianism in these texts is a passing girlhood fancy or a product of education. Many of the books by Indians in this essay cite Kinsey, Ellis and Freud, revealing the Western base for these analyses of Indian lesbian sexuality.

In contrast, anthropological studies such as Kapur's *The Sexual Life of the Kumaonis* and the anecdotal evidence in *Lotus of Another Color* suggest that there are parts of India where lesbian sexuality is well-integrated into the village erotic landscape. The small town or urban bourgeoisie are invariably more concerned with issues of sexual repression; in village life, in contrast, sexuality may not be as differentiated. Kapur reports in his case histories several incidents of lesbian sex, but does not comment directly on them. It must also be noted that this information came indirectly through informants. A middle-aged Thakur woman thought that since the onset of her menses prevented her from socializing with boys, "there would be no more (sexual activity) for me till I married but an elderly woman took an interest in me."[18] Another Thakur woman said that "sometimes another woman helps me to relax and a woman knows that it is a slow process of enjoyment for another woman."[19] Kapur notes that "Dom women also said they sometimes slept with each other. Evidences of homosexuality were however very meager in all castes though not completely absent."[20] This is somewhat at odds with the fact that he refers to the two Thakur women as "representative cases."[21] Kapur's main focus is on the inability of the men to satisfy their wives, and he does not analyze the lesbian relationships in any way. Like Rampal, Kapur stresses that men should be more considerate. Lesbian sexuality is effectively marginalized even as it is noted.

Even when a modern or "progressive" Indian writer such as Ismat Chugtai discusses sexual relationships between women, the framework is not consciously "lesbian." The female characters do not differentiate themselves because of their sexual practices; even if their sexual expression is in opposition to their circumstances, their lesbian practices are their solace, not their method of contestation. They are not involved in the politics of their sexual choices. In this, the undifferentiated homoeroticism is similar to that of other Middle Eastern writers, such as Alifa Rifaat in the short stories "The Long Night of Winter" or "My World of the Unknown." This lack of radicalization is not only true to its milieu in some sense, it also provided a defense from charges of obscenity or immorality. Ismat Chugtai's lawyer argued successfully in her 1944 trial for obscenity that "Lihaaf" "could only be understood by those who already had some knowledge of" lesbianism.[22]

In the West, there has been considerable pornographic interest in the sexually variant Other. The reproductions of Mughal and Rajput paintings discussed in this essay are found as illustrations of Burton's translations, uniting material from vastly different eras for the Western gaze.

A similar ahistorical interest developed when both India and the Sexual Revolution came into fashion in the 60s. Examining the sexualities of other cultures was perforce a way of legitimizing variant sexuality through its universality even as other cultures were sometimes inaccurately and racistly depicted as depraved, as is the case in Edwardes and Davies. Bullough, for example, uses Tantric disfavor for female virginity to generalize that "what was undesirable in the West was desirable, or at least tolerated, in India,"[23] a notion that Rampal directly contradicts. Edwardes depicts harems full of women with over-sized clitori where "lesbian passion in women [sic] was... acquired to supplant heterosexual needs," and opines that Tamil boys are addicted to fellatio.[24] Obviously, these representations are completely at odds with the attitudes of Indians themselves. Indian accounts, such as Basham's comment cited earlier, tend to locate homosexuality within other traditions.

Western Lesbian-Feminists also discussed matriarchal and lesbian culture in India to legitimize their movement. Susan Calvin posits amazons in ancient India, but Judy Grahn goes further. Her naive perspective about Kanyakumari and the misinformation of the woman, Linda, whom Grahn refers to as having had an affair with a Tamil woman, make her account suspicious.[25] The word for male homosexuality is given as "two turbans together,"[26] but few Tamil men wear turbans, and this usage has not been substantiated. The ensuing extrapolation that "homosexual relations are taken as everyday occurrences and a major basis of social relationships,"[27] seems unlikely unless "homosexual relationships" is given the attenuated meaning of non-sexual romantic friendships, and even then they are not generally the "major basis of social relationships." The Indian lesbian in Western texts, therefore, is a construct related less to Indian history than to Western political movements.

Suniti Namjoshi articulated the problems of the diaspora lesbian, estranged from India by her lesbianism, but still conscious of her Indian heritage. The diaspora communities have become the major source of Indian lesbian representation. In the last decade, self-consciously gay texts have come into being as part of a Western "gay rights" movement. In 1985, the collective *Anamika* began its two years of producing an eponymous newsletter out of New York. In 1990, another collective began producing *Shamakami* out of San Francisco. In 1993, *Sami Yoni*, a journal for South Asian lesbians and bisexual women, started publication in Toronto. *Shakti Khabbar* out of London is another forum for lesbian and bisexual women of South Asian descent. (Many other periodicals such as *Trikone* and *Diva* often represent lesbian issues.) The films and shorts with South Asian lesbian characters have all come out of London, still attenuated from the realities of the Indian lesbian. Pratibha Parmar's *Khush* has come under severe criticism for reproducing the colonialist gaze. "*Khush* reminds us," writes Daleep, "that the equations of power, the mechanics of exploitation and abuse are still the same, but rendered by whites of a different hue. In fact in *Khush*, we see how deeply internalized, how insidious, is the programming to objectify, and reduce us."[28]

The few examples of representation of the Indian lesbian gathered together in this essay do not paint a coherent picture. The attitudes towards lesbianism expressed by Indian writers may more clearly be reflections of attitudes towards the rights of women, and the role of sexuality. The legal texts very stridently oppose any kind of sexual variance, and Manu, as Ranjana Kumari points out as part of her argument on the inherent sexism of Hinduism, is certainly a patriarch. The record of the Arthashastra is more mixed: its anti-lesbian fines may not be so much an opposition to self-determined female sexuality as an effort to keep sexuality under the domain of the ruler. The good women of the religious epics, even active women like Savitri, are committed to their husbands — as Arjuna's duty is to be a good warrior, a woman's duty is clearly to be a good wife — so the opposition to lesbianism is perhaps opposition to female agency outside the family (which Surpanaka, the demoness, represents). Later, with the rise of Tantrism, and Shakti, female power, and eroticism gained importance, in opposition to the previous Brahmanical puritanism. Further analysis of connections between the expanded role Tantrism gave women and lesbian depictions is definitely necessary. In the erotic paintings of the Mughal period, lesbianism is robbed of its seriousness, it is reduced to the merely titillating. This lack of seriousness was exacerbated much later by the theories of Freud and Ellis and other Westerners. Victorian prudery consumed by the elites at the feet of colonialism compounded the lack of consideration given to lesbianism. Contemporary Indian analyses of lesbianism reflect both homophobia and Western psychological theories about lesbianism's adolescent transience and unimportance, both amply demonstrated in the reactions to the marriage of two Bhopal policewomen.[29]

Most importantly, the representations of the Indian lesbian in this essay have all been created by others. The vagaries of translation may account for the missing Indian lesbian writer, but is jarring to see that in a tradition so rich in women's writing, there is no obvious counterpart to the significant lesbian poets of other traditions, from Wu Tsao to Bieris de Roman. The female homoerotic poets of Moorish Spain (e.g. Walladah, Muhjah) do not seem to have established parallels in the Moghul courts. Even today, the lead has been taken by women in the diaspora. The Indian lesbian has been represented as criminal or degenerate or a figure of erotica, at best she is seen as a minor part of the range of humanity. We have yet to hear her own voice.

---

1   Bullough, p. 263
2   Chunder, p. 128
3   Kumari, p. 17
4   Banerjee, p. 139
5   Ibid, p. 31
6   Banerjee, p. 139
7   In Ratti, p. 165
8   Bannerjee, p. 142
9   Cit. Chunder, p. 129
10 "ABVA" in Ratti, p. 30
11 In Ratti, p. 122
12 In Fowkes, p. 63

13 Rampal, p. 1

14 Rampal, p. 62

15 Rampal, p. 63

16 Rampal, p. 145

17 Rampal, p. 178

18 Kapur, p. 34

19 Kapur, p. 65

20 Kapur, p. 75

21 Kapur, p. 32

22 Kishwar and Vanita, p. 5

23 Bullough, p. 376

24 Edwardes, The Jewel in the Lotus, p. 107

25 "Rape is unknown in this region, and the men are very shy around women," p. 108

26 Grahn, p. 109

27 Grahn, p. 110

28 Daleep, p. 11

29 Thadani, in Ratti

ABBREVIATED BIBLIOGRAPHY

AIDS Bhedvav Virodhi Andolan. "Homosexuality in India: Culture and Heritage." *Lotus of Another Color: An Unfolding of the South Asian Gay and Lesbian Experience.* ed. Rakesh Ratti. Boston: Alyson Books, 1993.

Balse, Mayah. *The Indian Female: Attitudes Towards Sex.* New Delhi: Chetana Publications, 1976.

Banerjee, Sures Chandra. *Crime & Sex in Ancient India.* Calcutta: Naya Prokash, 1980.

Bullough, Vern L. *Sex Variance in Society & History.* New York: John Wiley & Sons, 1967.

Cavin, Susan. *Lesbian Origins.* San Francisco: Ism Press, 1989.

Chunder, Pratap Chandra. *Kautilya on Love & Morals.* Calcutta: Jayanti, 1970.

Chugtai, Ismat. "The Quilt" in *The Quilt & Other Stories.* London: The Women's Press, 1991.

Daleep. "Oriental Mystique" in *Trikone,* San Francisco, Vol. 8, no. 2.

Davies, Nigel. *The Rampant God: Eros Throughout the World.* New York: William Morrow, 1984.

Edwardes, Allen. *The Jewel in the Lotus: A Historical Survey of the Sexual Culture of the East.* New York: The Julian Press, 1960.
— *The Cradle of Erotica.* New York: The Julian Press, 1962.

Frieze at Khajuraho. Photographed by Giti Thadani. *Lotus of Another Color.* Ed. Rakesh Ratti. Boston: Alyson Books, 1993.

Grahn, Judy. *Another Mother Tongue.* Boston: Beacon Press, 1984.

Kapur, Thribhuwan. *Sexual Life of the Kumaonis.* New Delhi: Vikas Publishing House, 1987.

Kumari, Ranjana. *Female Sexuality in Hinduism.* Delhi: Joint Women's Programme & the Indian Society for the Promotion of Christian Knowledge, 1988.

Kishwar, Madhy and Vanita, Ruth. "An Irrepressible Spirit: An Interview with Ismat Chugtai" in *Manushi*, New Delhi: No. 19.

Miniature. *The Perfumed Garden.* ed. Charles Fowkes. London: Octopus Illustrated Publishing, 1989.

Miniature. *The Illustrated Kama Sutra.* Trans. Richard Burton and F.F. Arbuthnot. London: Octupus Illustrated Publishing, 1987.

Namjoshi, Suniti and Hanscombe, Gillian. *Flesh and Paper.* Charlottetown: Ragweed Press, 1986.

Rampal, S.N. *Indian Women and Sex.* New Delhi: Printox, 1978.

Thadani, Giti. "Inverting Tradition" in *Lotus of Another Color.* ed. Rakesh Ratti. Boston: Alyson Books, 1993.

Merle Woo

The Politics of Breast Cancer

This article was originally published as a discussion bulletin for the Freedom Socialist Party Convention, held July 3-5, 1993, near Seattle, Washington.

I HEARD SOMETHING HARD SLAM AGAINST THE WALL DOWNSTAIRS. THE THUD came from Karen's room.[1] She was now pretty much confined to her bed. Her breast cancer had metastasized to her liver, and she was growing weaker and was in pain every day.

I went downstairs to check. She had been reading one of a multitude of books on surviving cancer, and it was this book she had thrown against the wall. She was furious. When I asked her why she was so angry, she told me that this author, in talking about why women get breast cancer, pointed the finger back at the woman: there is a cancer personality. Women who get breast cancer allow cancer cells to flourish because they have a negative attitude about getting well; they don't do anything about rebuilding their immune system. They don't show any significant signs of changing lifestyles, for example, they continue to eat fatty foods, smoke and/or drink alcohol. They don't think positively!

Karen and I were furious that this kind of message should get such wide publicity. This was the same, old, blame-the-victim excuse for an epidemic that is killing women at astonishing proportions; it excuses the National Cancer Institute (NCI), the National Institute of Health (NIH), and the American Cancer Society (ACS), for not making breast cancer research a top priority.

We are going to have to take to the streets and demand funding that will save millions of women's lives — take to the streets just as we did for abortion rights in the early 70s. We're going to have to educate and be visible like AIDS activists. The AIDS movement, the breast cancer movement, the disabled movement need to coalesce! The federal government, the NCI and the NIH aren't going to give more funding without public pressure.

We're going to have to use breast cancer and the way it is so coldly deprioritized as a major indictment against capitalism and the primarily all white male medical establishment, exposing their misogyny, racism, and class bias.

Breasts are symbolic of the sexism in American culture. Women's breasts, like the buttocks, have been objectified and separated from the whole body and intellect — this dehumanization is indicative of rampant and pervasive misogyny.

It is a shock to note that most of the government's studies and research begins with male rodents and then to clinical trials using only male humans; women are excluded from most studies done on "people." (*New York Times*, June 26, 1990, p. 5). Women also suffer as second-class citizens because studies of breast cancer, which kills 45,000 a year, gets only $17 million for NIH basic research. Only 13 percent of NIH's $5.7 billion budget goes to study the health risks of women. Breast cancer is seen as an older woman's disease. Is it any wonder that the death rate from cancer has been unchanged for forty years?

I always say that Karen was definitely not a person with the so-called cancer personality. Her life was a testimony to the good fight against capitalism and to strong leadership in FSP/RW. She didn't like pain killers because they created a veil between herself and reality. Hurling that book against the wall was a succinct statement about that theory which blames women for almost anything negative under the sun.

A black lesbian friend and I shared the same anthroposophic doctor. She died of metastasized breast cancer, and my doctor self-righteously told me that she wanted to die because she went back to smoking and drinking alcohol. I stopped going to this doctor.

Words — like "insidious," "rapid growth," "wild," "deadly," "anti-life," "devastate," "attack" — become words recurring in my daily life and transform into fantastic images in my dreams.

Unless we have an overview of how the global situation affects you as a cancer survivor; unless we make the connection between ourselves and the system we live in, things will appear disconnected, chaotic, and we'll feel powerless, and at the mercy of these raging cancer cells.

Some Statistics

Why is it that in one year only $77 million goes to breast cancer research and over $300 million goes to the plastic surgery industry? Why do women in such huge numbers place themselves at such risk by having silicone implants? Because we are socialized, brainwashed to value appearance over health, over intellectual and emotional capabilities. Breast cancer hits at the deepest fear in a woman: that she is of no use because she has been condemned to death and that she is now ugly without the very feminine accoutrements that made her attractive. My female surgeon told me after my second mastectomy: "Whenever you get tired of your boy's body, let me know, we have great reconstructive surgeons here at Kaiser."

One in every 50 women has had breast implant surgery for cosmetic reasons alone — risking the side-effects of implant leakages, ruptures, connective tissue disease, and cancer. In 1988, 71,000 women had breast implant surgery. If a woman chooses silicone implant surgery those implants are covered with a thick layer of polyurethane foam, which begin to break down in the body immediately after insertion and release chemicals — one of which is known to cause cancer in rodents (toluene diamine or TDA).

In the U.S. one in nine women will be diagnosed with breast cancer; 25 percent of these will die within five years. Fifty percent of the original group will die in ten. Thirty years ago it was one in 20. There were 175,000 new cases in 1992 and 45,000 deaths (compared to 23,000 who died from AIDS).

Between 1965-1975 of the Vietnam war, 58,000 U.S. troops died in Vietnam. In that same period, two million Vietnamese soldiers and civilians died; 300,000 American women died from breast cancer; and more than 58,000 American workers died from job-related conditions. It's not hard to determine the priorities of American capitalism.

Black and Latina women diagnosed with cancer, although fewer in number as compared to white women, have a higher mortality rate. Among black women, breast cancer tops all other cancers. Evidence shows that because of their race and class, women of color are diagnosed later because they get less medical attention. Poverty is the major reason why African Americans have a higher cancer rate than whites. Twenty-five percent of white women and 40 percent of black women diagnosed with breast cancer will die in five years.

"[T]he rates of lung and prostate cancer are 60% to 70% higher among blacks and cervical cancer is more than twice as common. One-third of blacks have incomes below the poverty line, compared with only 12% whites" (*San Francisco Chronicle*, April 17, 1991, p. A5). Poverty, chronic unemployment, homelessness — all effectively reduce access to medical care and education.

In a racist/sexist attempt to explain the comparatively high mortality rate among women of color, some cancer experts theorize that it is from their smoking, fatty diet, and alcohol abuse (*San Franciso Chronicle*, January 17, 1990). Right. Blame the victim.

Studies show that lesbians have a two to three-fold higher risk of getting breast cancer than heterosexual women. Although homophobes would like to blame lesbian lifestyles for the higher risk — and there is evidence that lesbians as a whole may drink alcohol more, smoke more, the fact is that 1) oppression and marginalization create stress and the conditions which beg for relief; 2) smoking and drinking have not been absolutely proven to be factors which increase the risks for breast cancer. Besides more reliable studies show that lesbians get less medical attention than their straight sisters: they tend to avoid, when they think they can, a sexist, homophobic medical establishment, and heterosexual women, in order to obtain birth control, visit their OB/GYNs on a much more regular basis (*MS.*, Vol. III, No. 6, May/June, 1993, p. 44).

The Environment

We are dying of cancer because of environmental poisons, the seas "of slaughter," toxic wastes. The world around us is being laid to waste from pollution, a browning of the air, and carcinogens pumped into what we eat.

The State of California now ranks number one in the
incidence of breast cancer in the U.S. at a rate of one in seven
(one in nine elsewhere). The San Francisco Bay Area,
number one in incidence within the state, houses 26 major
radioactive material sites located along two earthquake
faults. Eleven miles offshore near the Farallon Islands,
radioactive barges from the Bikini Island atomic testing sites
were sunk in the migratory fish path in the 1950s. Since
1960 Lawrence Livermore labs in the Livermore Valley just
outside the Greater Bay Area has released 1 million curies of
radiation, 300,000 curies of which resulted from two major
accidents; the rest was released through leakage.
- Linda Reyes, *Breast Cancer Action Newsletter*, #14 (10/1992), p.4

The depth and breadth of capitalist misogyny supports the mass murder of women, while hard-selling women's bodies and their body parts. This is part and parcel of objectifying women, justifying their continued super-exploitation as free labor in the home and being underpaid at the workplace. Using women's bodies is American soldiers putting a pinup of Rita Hayworth on the war head of the nuclear test bomb that was dropped on the Bikini atoll. Hayworth was not flattered; she was devastated.

A Bit of History

As a Chinese-Korean American woman, I have felt so ambivalent about my double mastectomy. I was glad to have my right breast removed six months after the mastectomy on the left side: I felt symmetrical again and relief that I didn't have to wear a prosthesis: if one breast is gone, the survivor can throw out the alignment of the spine because of the weight of the remaining breast pulling the spine to its side.

And although I panicked because there were large cancerous tumors and knew that I could die, I rather liked having no breasts. I go back and forth on it: On one hand I feel ugly with these two asymmetrical scars slashed across my chest, and on the other, my breasts were so large, that I felt ugly with them. The image of the petite Asian woman was not ever lost on me. Nancy Kwan and France Nguyen were pencil-thin with small breasts.

As a teenager, my Auntie Helen would often say I was the next Jane Russell. I came to associate large breasts on Asian women with being a slut. Of course, Auntie Helen herself was jealous that her daughter had small breasts and so she retaliated against me. She hated that her daughter had small breasts; I hated myself because I had large ones.

I remember going to my OB/GYN in the late 60s to ask if I could have my breasts surgically made smaller. He said that I had to ask permission from my husband first.

I always hated going into lingerie shops, asking for the largest cup bra and having the clerk do a double-take.

When I went with Karen to a lingerie shop which also carried prostheses, and after Karen told the clerk what she wanted and why, the clerk carried on the whole ensuing conversation with me! Karen had disclosed that she had breast cancer, and that suddenly transformed her into a non-person.

In my all-girls Catholic high school there was a highly popular morbid joke about a man, a real roué who tries to pick up a woman in a bar. The "hilarious" conclusion is that she lets him put his hand in her blouse only to find a warm open wound.

Doctor / Patient Conflicts

I'm taking tamoxifen at the advice of my oncologist and comrade Dr. Susan. They both say it's important for someone at my stage of breast cancer to take it. It's an anti-estrogen producing drug. Medical research has shown that estrogen produced in the breast creates fertile ground for cancer cells and their proliferation. Although it can cause excess estrogen to be produced in the uterus and therefore can increase the risk of uterine cancer, I believe the positives definitely outweigh the negatives. It actually helps prevent osteoporosis and heart disease. But there is a great deal of writing against taking tamoxifen. I had an oncologist who was sexist and conservative in prescribing medication. He fought strongly against me when I asked for tamoxifen. He was conducting a study, and I was an important statistic. And when I continued to insist, bringing in medical journal articles to back up my taking of it, he gave in saying condescendingly: "Well, all right, then, since your heart is so set on it."

When Karen decided to drop her chemotherapy treatments at five months in a six-month plan, her oncologist was furious because she was part of a clinical test, a statistic. Karen would not reconsider; chemotherapy was killing her quality of life. When the doctor knew he could not win, he cruelly said to her, "Well, we might as well just lop off your other breast then."

The office visit at which Karen was to get the news that her breast cancer had metastasized was pure cruelty at its worst. The female doctor kept getting knocks on the door and leaving periodically to attend to other matters, all the while telling Karen in a distracted way that she was going to die in a few months.

The dehumanization of people with disabilities, the deferential treatment given to heterosexual couples and nuclear families by hospital staff are ubiquitous. As a lesbian, I know this to be true; I've been both the visitor and the patient.

Karen could have sued Kaiser for misdiagnosis and late diagnosis and won. She even consulted an attorney about it. But who wants to spend the rest of your precious months in a lengthy and time-consuming court case?

Just before my first mastectomy I was seen by an OB/GYN at SF Kaiser. He was incredibly arrogant, sexist, and minimized my condition. I was on guard. He said he didn't think there was anything wrong — I was drinking too much coffee (just like Karen!). When I insisted on a biopsy, he said I would have to have a consultation appointment first with the surgeons. If I hadn't already seen what happened to Karen, I would probably have acquiesced and waited for a consultation appointment for months!

Breast Cancer as a Political Issue

The connection of breast cancer to AIDS as a political movement has been part of the consciousness of breast cancer activists for at least six years. The growing militancy and publicity around breast cancer are extremely healthy signs. But it has been hampered by the leadership of liberals who do not see breast cancer as a product of capitalism, nor why and how it manifests itself, the growing numbers of women affected by it, or killed by it, the highly disproportionate way breast cancer hits women of color and poor women versus middle-class anglo women. Breast cancer has reached epidemic proportions because the ruling class has put its weight behind the global military-industrial complex. Mass murder through AIDS and breast cancer is an integral part of institutionalized sexism, and sexism is a revolutionary question.

Why is the federal government banning import of and research on RU 486? This is an anti-cancer drug and shows great promise in extending life and reducing pain at little risk. The Bush administration buckled under right-wing pressure because RU 486 is also a safe abortion-enabling drug.

Some studies in France show that RU 486 has been enormously successful in reducing cancer tumors, and similar results have been found in Canada and the Netherlands. It is one of the most successful of the anti-cancer hormonal agents, not only reducing great pain in people in the advanced stages of cancer but also reducing the usual side effects associated with chemotherapy. Yet it remains untouchable by American women because the right wing will do everything it can to prevent any effective abortifacient from being accessible. Some liberal pro-RU 486 fighters want to separate its cancer prevention proclivities from RU 486's use as an abortion agent. This is wrong! They are buckling to the right wing and should be fighting for the right to use RU 486 as both an anti-cancer hormonal agent and for safe abortions.

The Cancer Establishment

The cancer establishment is about big business: the National Cancer Institute, the American Cancer Society, and the Memorial Sloan-Kettering Cancer Center are sterling representatives. Their focus is on treatment rather than prevention because huge profits lie in selling billions of dollars worth of chemical treatment/ chemotherapy. Although the treatment hasn't improved the odds of survival in forty years, the bulk of the monies still continues to go to treatment. In 1990, the potentially critical study on diet and breast cancer was dropped.

Dr. David Korn, chair of the National Cancer Advisory Board (advisors to the NCI and the president of the U.S.) and beneficiary of contracts from the NCI, made racist and ageist remarks in rejecting the proposal to study women and diet. He said, "How accurate would their dietary memories be? Where would they be? Would half of them be in nursing homes with various kinds of senility and forgetfulness?"

He goes on to say that white middle-class women would be more reliable in keeping records of diet and fatty intake, but who could depend on a "bunch of high-school dropout black women who worry whether they can get a bottle of milk on the table for their kids, let alone whether they're eating high-fat food" (MS., Vol. III, No. 6, May-June, 1993, p. 40).

At the same time that he was chair of the President's Cancer Panel which advises the NCI, Armand Hammer was also chair of the board of Occidental Petroleum, a major manufacturer of carcinogenic materials. One of Occidental Petroleum's subsidiaries was involved in Love Canal's environmental disaster (MS., p. 57). Talk about major conflict of interests!

Conclusion

The politics of breast cancer is about changing the odds against women and breast cancer, that is, drastically lowering the incidence of breast cancer through prevention and finding a cure. We must create a humane treatment as an alternative to radiation and imposing a nuclear war within — which is what chemotherapy really is — which is painful, and has debilitating side effects. Finally, under capitalism, the politics of breast cancer must, at least, lead to nationalized quality healthcare.

Socialism is the only complete answer to the crisis in health care — Hillary R. Clinton notwithstanding. The real chronic pestilence is capitalism. And until we have an economic order that is dedicated to health and human life versus seeing only dollar signs in people's illnesses, we can at least make the following demands.

Our demands should be:

• That there be nationalized quality healthcare, free and available for all.

• That the federal government and the cancer establishment reprioritize its funding for cancer studies and make a commitment to a vast increase in funding for breast cancer: for research and prevention primarily, and secondarily to finding chemical cures.

• That the very existence of breast cancer as a growing epidemic, aided by negligence by government and modern big business and industry, be seen as an attack on women of color, lesbians, and all women workers, and that the basis of this epidemic is capitalism, in its drive for ever more profits at the expense of women's health.

• That an end to all forms of discrimination against all people with disabilities.

• That there be the right to have full control over our bodies and, in particular, full reproductive rights for all women; immediate accessibility to RU 486.

---

1 Karen Brodine was a leader in Radical Women and the Freedom Socialist Party. She died in October 1987 from metastasized breast cancer at age 40.

Donna Tsuyuko Tanigawa

I Like Beef Wit' Words

I like pound deir head into da floor. Put dem bambucha cockaroaches — da ones wit' plenty babies in da opu — into dem girls half empty soda cans. I like tell em, "Ah haole girls, you act like dis to me in Hawai'i and us local folks goin beef wit' you. You goin get karang on Kill Haole Day!" But no, I only wen look down at da floor, pretend dat I nevah hear dem guys call me one dumb local Japanee who no can talk good kine English. Shame, you know?

I T TOOK ME YEARS TO SPEAK STANDARD ENGLISH WELL. I LEARNED TO MIMIC the sounds and intonations of my haole (white) teachers. I listened to Connie Chung, repeating the way she pronounced words. I taught myself grammar and syntax. It pleased me when someone on the other end of the phone mistook me for a *haole* person.

In Hawai'i, my first language was pidgin English. Pidgin is a form of speech influenced by words from English, Hawaiian, Japanese, Chinese, and Filipino. As a student, the message was clear: Shame fo' talk Pidgin.

Why is it dat I hahdly talk in class? Not dat I one shy Japanee girl. I know, da *haoles* tink dat all us Asians are quiet. No' more tongue, li' dat. I know dem folks also tink we stupid. You nevah learn fo' talk good kine English. You nevah learn fo' write in Standard English. "Speak up, speak correct." Eh, I rather not say anyting. Let dem talk. All waha.

After years of academia, I find myself ashamed to "think" — much less speak — in my native tongue, Waiphau-kine pidgin. I grew up in a predominantly Filipino community of sugar plantation workers. Before time, I used to talk pidgin only when I was tired and my mental "guard dog" was not censoring my speech. Now, I want to learn to talk — and think — pidgin again.

As a graduate student in American Studies, I find my voice is not only drowned out by the seductive languages of the academy, but that it is also erased by the whiteness of Standard English. As a writer, it is difficult to locate any sense of self if denied the sounds of my voice. "I no shame fo' talk pidgin. Pau trying fo' act haole," as opposed to "I am ashamed to speak pidgin English. I am done pretending to be white." The self — myself — comes through and is animated by the language of pidgin English.

I find, however, that several of my local friends, people of color, are embarrassed or angered by my deliberate use of pidgin as language. It is fine to "talk story" with friends, but rules are broken when pidgin is spoken in the haole world.

It angers me that I have denied myself, and my voice. Why should the larger worlds instruct how I speak and think as a lesbian of color? It took me years to realize the subtlety of the tactics of the *haole* world.

Takes me a long time fo' feel my thoughts. Da anger is here, but. Inside my stomach. Maybe ass' why I get one ulcer. How you figgah? I used to keep everyting inside me. Hold everyting in. Take all da teaching from class and keep it in my chi-i-sa-i body. Ass' why I get stuck doo-doo. Nothing like come out. Da anger burn my okole-hole. Dis' is what my body stay telling me. Da *haole* teachers and books wen all me learn from us. Look at us. Copy us. But they nevah tell me dat I could not be like dem' folks. So now I got all of their teachings inside my stomach and nothing like come out.

I wish dat I could go back home to my small-kid days. A time wen I felt good about myself. I could talk from my stomach. My words had da power to mark my world. Dat is mine. I kapu dis. I stay struggling now. I feel like one cockaroach trapped inside day Hoy Hoy Trap-A-Roach box. I used to watch dem guys struggle fo' leave da sticky strip of glue. Struggle to deir make-die-dead. School not my roach trap. Stay da way I tink, dat's my death box. My thoughts trapped inside *haole* words.

Anuja Mendiratta

Ancient song, Indian voice
silences you quickly and with an assurity
able to stand strong through time
for kings will come and kings will go
and yet still
nothing
can be spoken
in Hindi, in Marathi, in Bengali, in Urdu.
Ney bolo. Ney!
The words of the people
cannot express
this queer life you've led in the west
and your tongue parches dry like the road in old Delhi
where you shop for mango and guava and eggplant.
The good daughter
you must be
something definite.
But love is love
remember
my breath on your neck?
A touch can say it
in your dark eyes
in your heart
I see you possess
an understanding of this.

And yet, there is purity and beauty in ritual.
The ritual of burning sandalwood incense
of offering almonds and oranges
marigolds and mums
hands folded together
in the name of Ganesh
in the name of Buddha
in the name of Sarasvati
so far away from the land which gave you birth.
These are the acts which bring you close to home.
You belong to a group of animals, of people
who call themselves by a name all their own.
Upon hearing this name you wear
your head of black hair high.

Pride.
I see what each hand holds out to you:
one, so lovingly gives strength
by familiarity and tradition
and the other
so willing to support and maintain
existing codes
silences.
Silences with looks
Silences with words.
Words heavily laced with ways of the people.
Words slither together and say:
"Don't do that, it is wrong!"

Still, the welcoming language of home is
whispering into your ear more clearly
as you prepare for the journey back.
Boxed packed and unpacked.
Old things will open up to you gracefully
as the violet opens upon seeing
the morning sun.
But what of the closures?
What of the silence?
My eyes cannot say no to the tears
when they come
as I think of it.
You speak of the lonely burden
the burden of loving me.
This, you expect to bear
without the humanity or kindness
of friendly conversation
or parental acceptance.
No red saree swirling flower day
of celebration for this love.
No *shadhi* for us, my sweet.

But, when you find that the day
is too hot and the day is too long
and this internal tension swells all hushed up
and you wait
and you wait for the giving monsoon
to settle the dust
which seems to enter your lonely mind
the dust, around these brown people
who look like you
who look like me,
remember
that there is no silence
between you and me, Dela,
even when we are quiet
with each other
Mera pyari dosth.

Ney bolo. Ney!   Don't speak. No!
Shadhi   Marriage
Mera pyari dosth   My loving friend

Lani Ka'ahumanu

Hapa Haole Wahine[1]

"In order to feel safe I need to feel known... Is visibility safety? Complex questions. Uncomfortable, uneasy answers, stirring up old hurts, old angers, old fears... Why is the possibility of `passing' so insistently viewed as a great privilege..., and not understood as a terrible degradation and denial?" Evelyn Torton Beck, *Nice Jewish Girls*.[2]

I.

I grew up
not quite fitting in
and not understanding why

I was raised
with menehunes[3]
and leprechauns
sushi and corned beef
flower leis and Ikebana
kimono and aloha shirts
chopsticks and silverware
miso and tuna casserole

Anne Helanikulani
my maternal grandmother
sold her land grant
to set up
my grandfather's business
in Japan

THE VERY INSIDE

Minerva Helani
my mother
born in Yokahama
grew up
in Kobe and Waikiki
the traditional hula
her most prideful
gift of grace to the world

Ikebana
the Japanese art
of flower arranging
my great Aunty Madge
one of thirteen Masters
in the world
(at that time)

My father, John
a proud
St. Paddy's
County Cork
Irishman
singing
too ra loo ra loo ra
whose mother, Pat
my only living grandparent
spoke a little Yiddish
and
would whisper
in my ear
"marry a nice Jewish man
they take care of their wives..."
she was sincere
and steady
in this advice

all this
growing up
in a Catholic family

I was
conceived in Hawai'i
born in Canada
October 5, 1943
during WWII
named Lani
which means heavenly

Then to Denver
for several months
where
my great Uncle Harry
a successful
California businessman
had been "sent"
to run a chicken ranch
when the relocation camps
were in full swing
he and my Aunty Madge
were the first
to give vitamins
to hens
to fortify eggs

Recently I learned
it was a cover
for a CIA radio relay station
my great Uncle Harry
proud to be
General MacArthur's right hand man
during the mid-to-late forties

common stories
while I was growing up
except for the CIA
and relocation camps

1949 St. Bruno's
first grade
Sister Theophane
told me ...
"Lani is a heathen name"
it was unacceptable
the Christian middle name Marjorie
would have to do
for eight years
in grammar school

I didn't enjoy
playing house
so I was the dad
and went outside
to "work"
to play with the boys

I didn't throw the ball
like a girl
I hit home runs
over the fence
before and after school
the only times
I was allowed
on the better fields
to play with the boys

I was told
I was lucky
to have the golden skin
it meant
I didn't have to hide
from the sun
for fear of getting too dark

for fear of being called
pic-a-ninnie
like my sister

I danced the hula
every year
in the talent show
when we studied Japan and Hawai'i
I brought nori seaweed
to eat
kimonos to try on
talked about King Kamehameha
my great great great great great uncle
told the Japanese children's story
of the "peach boy"
dombororo koko sukoko
Coming home from school
shoes all over the porch
I knew family/friends
from far away lands
had arrived
leis, poi, fresh pineapple
ukelele, muumuus, love and laughter

Friends would secretly ask
if my Aunty Madge and Uncle Harry
were really related to me
were really in my family
"Are they Chinese or what?"

I was told
never to ask
why their eyes were slanted
I knew why
and couldn't figure out
why anyone would
ask such a thing

I took pride
in my multicultural
        multiracial
            girlchild self

In high school
I talked with the girls
about the boys
we had crushes on
and
I talked with the boys
about the girls
we had crushes on

And
even though
I asked
time and again
I was never allowed
to work
because I was a girl
and
"would have a husband
to take care of me
someday"

I even
had a struggle
getting permission
to earn money
babysitting
but once convinced
it would prepare me
for my role in life
I was allowed

For me
there was no college prep
I took
typing, shorthand
business machines
so I
"would have a skill
in case
my husband died"
and I would be left
to raise the children

In my junior year
I fell in love
went steady with
the Captain of the football team
two years after high school
we were married
in the church
but
outside the communion rail
he was not Catholic

My father died of a heart attack at age 46
protecting and supporting
a wife and four daughters
that he lovingly
and conscienciously
placed on pedestals
that were built
on lost potential
his and ours

for me
the certificate would have read
underlying cause of death... sexism

Five years later
I was 26 years old
my husband taught
at the high school
where we met
we had a son, a daughter
and a home in the suburbs

I was not your everyday
full-time suburban housewife mother
following my conscience
I left the church
joined Another Mother for Peace
was an anti-VietNam, anti-nuke peace activist
collected food for the Black Panther breakfast program
supported Ceasar Chavez' UFW organizing and the grape boycott
was a Little League mom, never missed the game show *Jeopardy*
ran the art corner on Fridays, was recess lady on Wednesdays
a field trip driver, watched *Days Of Our Lives* faithfully
and was a budding gourmet cook

I began reading
about women's lib, burning bras, no makeup
my best friend stopped shaving her legs
and wore shorts in the summer
it was very radical!

I smoked marijuana
wore peasant dresses
had granny glasses
drove a VW van
picked up hitchhikers
fell in love
with "Working Class Hero"
John Lennon

read Baba Ram Dass
"Be Here Now"
spent a weekend
at an Enlightenment Intensive
asking "Who am I?"
18 hours a day

dropped acid
saw Mao Tse Tung
in my bathroom mirror
and realized
"A Separate Reality"

I grew by leaps and bounds
my consciousness raced
it was a rush to follow
u n d e r s t a n d i n g
for the first time
in my life
I had never
determined
what I wanted
what I needed
what was real for me

I was crying all the time
my husband and closest friend
figured it out
"you need to leave," he said
"you've never had a chance to explore,"
"you've never been out in the world,"
"you've never had a life of your own."
as soon as I heard it
I knew he was right
he wanted the children
saying there was no way
for me to do what I needed to do
and he didn't want to be alone
I trusted him and felt his love and support

We had grown up
fourteen years later
to be very different people
fourteen years later
we let go, and cried
remained friends and struggled
with the pain and confusion
of our two young children

I moved to San Francisco
nine months later, 1975
began to keep a journal
got involved with establishing
the Women Studies program
at San Francisco State
a hot bed of feminism
a hot bed of lesbianism
I came home to myself
as a woman
a powerful primal connection
that had been denied

I wrote papers for classes
and discovered
I was a woman loving woman
I was a feminist
I was a radical
I was a lesbian
I was a leader
I was a poet
discovered I was a writer
and came out

I spoke out publically
as a lesbian mother
marched in the
Gay Freedom Day Parade
"2-4-6-8 are you sure
your mother's straight?"
came out to my children
my ex-husband, my friends
my sister, my mother

But because I slept with men
three times in four years
I discovered I was a lesbian
who had "unfinished business"
who had "some issues" to work out
there were no bisexual
role models
women's sexuality
was
lesbian sexuality
or nothing

There was a lesbian feminist movement
with strong lesbian role models
with strong lesbian voices
with strong lesbian visions
who inspired me to be all I could be
and to trust my woman loving woman
feelings and experience

The personal was political
and fundamentally correct
unless you slept with men

I graduated with honors
travelled to Hawai'i
lived in Maui for nine months
felt my roots
grow deep into the earth
through the soles
of my feet
grounded solid
Lani my heathen name
visible everywhere
street signs, newspapers
on the tips of people's tongues
I belonged
my heart was home

In 1980
I met a kindred spirit
a soulmate
a bisexual man
who met me
eye to eye
heart to heart
politic to politic
psyche to psyche
sex to sex.

We met
as feminists
as organizers
as writers
as thinkers
as theoreticians
as lovers
as best friends.

There seemed to be
no limits or boundaries.

To deny
or keep
such an experience
hidden
in a lesbian closet
was impossible
unthinkable
to me.

When I returned to San Francisco
to my lesbian family of friends
saying I was a bisexual
saying I was in love with a man
saying I refused to be kicked out
I believed and trusted
that the personal is indeed political
even if I was with a man
I knew I wasn't the enemy
I also knew I wasn't alone
I would find others
like myself who refused
to be in the lesbian/gay closet

I travelled to Japan
with my daughter Dannielle
stepping off the plane
walking in the streets
I immediately sensed a coming home
welcomed by the
familiar ties
familiar eyes
I felt at peace
with myself, with my identity

II.

I pass for white
struggle for visibility
in a sea of white faces
a barometer for prejudice

I pass for white
self doubting my place
in the people of color
community

I passed for white
even to myself
for a while
got lost in the dominant culture
slipped over the edge
fingers barely grasping
self-acceptance

self-hate and sabotage
powerful words of denial and shame
a simmering
constant pattern
in my life

I listen to the voices
that come from my heart
and scream from my guts
I am more
than what you see

I say this only to myself
sure no one will listen
and terrified everyone will...

Sitting with
seventeen lesbians of color
in a dis-assimilation workshop
at a conference on racism
each spoke to the pain
of being invisible
erased in a white world
of trying to fit in, of trying to pass
r e a l i z i n g
they never would
they never could
l i s t e n i n g
to their anger
to their rage
r e c l a i m i n g
racial and cultural pride

I sat
i n v i s i b l e
hardly able to breathe
tears streaming down my cheeks
a lump in my throat
as big as the shame
my white skin affords me
s i l e n c e d   i n   f e a r
I could not speak
I began to cry, and cry, and cry
from a place so deep, so old, so long denied
e x p o s i n g   t h e   p a i n
of having given up, of having given in
of having been beaten down
to a white pulp
my guilt, my shame, my sense of exhaustion
my love, my pride, my sense of family connection
laid bare

With their arms around me
my words came slowly

I belong and am disowned
by one and the other

I have silenced myself
many times not speaking out
terrified of exposure
terrified people would see
                would realize
I don't belong
I am not really
who I appear to be

My voice comes
in the form
of the written word
safe on paper, in print
people "hear" but don't see me.

When I do share
my racial/cultural roots
people scoff
"you can't be!"
"you're kidding!"
"no you're not!"
then proceed to tell me
then proceed to define me
then proceed to invalidate
what is really real for me

What gives anyone
the right
to tell me who and what I am?
I never want to hear
that I don't look Hawaiian
that I don't look Japanese
that I'm lucky I don't look my age
that I can't be, that I couldn't be
Why make such a big deal about it?
Why is it so important?

I never want to hear
that I am not a bisexual
that there is no such thing
that if I haven't been with a man for a while,
I should call myself a lesbian
that I am hurting lesbians
that I am confusing
an already confusing situation for heterosexual society

Why make such a fuss?
Why don't I just keep it quiet?
Why is it so important?

Don't tell me who I am
Don't tell me what my experience is or has been
Don't tell me my personal is not political
Don't ask me why it is important or what's the big deal

I won't be silenced
I will make a fuss
and I will tell you why it is so important

but only once...

Don't talk to me
unless you are willing
to listen
Don't talk to me
unless you are willing
to face yourself

I am brown
I am yellow
I am white
I am a proud, visible and vocal mixed race multicultural woman.
I claim it all and have no shame for it is the truth.

I am a middle-aged woman. I appreciate my 50 years of experience.
This is what it looks like. My face and body are a map of my life.
I don't want to be younger. I enjoy growing older and wiser.

I am a brazen radical bisexual feminist woman.
I love women as fiercely and passionately as any woman can.
I am a woman loving women:
bisexual/lesbian/heterosexual/transsexual.
I love and trust the men who are my allies,
struggling side by side doing the necessary work
of dismantling the shame of patriarchy in their lives
and who are taking emotional responsibility for loving themselves
and each other.

VISIBLE VOCAL PROUD AND STRONG

Mixed race people threaten the core of a racist society.

VISIBLE VOCAL PROUD AND STRONG

Bisexuals jeopardize the foundation of a
monosexual heterosexist culture.

VISIBLE VOCAL PROUD AND STRONG

Aging women (no matter how old we are)
break the back of ageism.

VISIBLE VOCAL PROUD AND STRONG

Lesbians and women loving women cut to the heart of sexism.

It is time to nurture the organic radical integration[4] process.
Differences recognized and appreciated give a sense of the whole.

I am sick and tired of lesbians who love lesbians, not women.[5]
I will not allow lesbian chauvanism to silence me one more time.
I am angered by unexamined and unacknowledged internalized
misogyny, homophobia, biphobia, transphobia, and heterophobia
wherever it exists, but especially in
my bisexual, lesbian, gay and trans communities.
I am pissed at politically conscious people
who do the work of liberation but don't recognize
sexism, racism, and classism as the tap root of all oppressions.

Assimilation is a lie.
It is spiritual erasure.[6]
We must proceed with mutual responsibility and respect.
We must give words to the silence behind the lies.
We must listen to ourselves and to each other.
If we take the time to recognize the fact
that we are already in it together
this revolution is truly ours,
all of ours
and it is here, now
in our midst.
We have to be wise enough
and patient enough
to trust ourselves
and each other
and the solutions
we will create.
That is feminism.
That is revolution.

1 Hapa Haole is Hawaiian for half or mixed Hawaiian and white.
   Wahine means woman.
2 Beck, Evelyn Torton, *Nice Jewish Girls, A Lesbian Anthology*, Revised and Updated
   Edition, pp. xvi - xxvi, Beacon Press, Boston, 1989.
3 Menehune - "Legendary race of small people (in Hawaii) who worked at night
   building fishponds, roads, temples," *The Pocket Hawaiian Dictionary*, Pukui, Elbert,
   and Mookini, University of Hawaii Press, Honolulu, 1975.
4 This is a term Robin Morgan coined in "The Anatomy of Freedom, Feminism,
   Physics and Global Politics," Anchor Books/Doubleday, 1984.
5 I want to thank Hester Lox for her thinking on this point.
6 I want to thank Jane Litwoman for this concept.

Contributors' Notes

ANU was born and brought up in India. She came out during her years at Smith College. Now she is back in India and plans to settle there.

V. K. ARUNA is a nonimmigrant Black Feminist Lesbian of dual Tamil heritage, born and raised in Malaysia, currently living in the Washington, D.C. area. She writes and speaks on issues of crossracial hostility, domestic violence, and the concept of community for South Asian Lesbians living in exile outside and within their geographical "homes." Aruna's work has been published in *Sinister Wisdom* No. 47, *Our Feet Walk the Sky* (Aunt Lute, 1993) *Shamakami* Vol. 1 & 2 and is forthcoming in *Feminism Third Wave* (Kitchen Table Woman of Color Press).

LISA ASAGI lived to be enchanted by rice cookers and road trips. She was born and raised in Honolulu, but now she lives in San Francisco and is trying to deconstruct the concept of wind chill factor while working on a novel titled *Essays on the Brink of Day*.

ANA BANTIGUE FAJARDO is a Filipino lesbian currently living in Santa Cruz, California. She is a teacher/writer/athlete on the move to the Pacific. She paddles for "Akau Hana," a Hawaiian outrigger canoe club in Santa Cruz. Her writing has appeared in Cornells's *Big Red Rag*, UCSC's *Twanas* and *The Phillipine News*.

MI OK SONG BRUINING is a Korean, adopted, lesbian, poet/writer, social worker/activist. She is currently living in the Bronx with her cat and in her spare time is working on completing a book on the issues and implications of international adoptions. She has had several poems and articles published in national and local Asian American lesbian and feminist literary publications and anthologies.

DEBI RAY-CHAUDHURI is a Bengali lesbian artist living in New York City. The art work reproduced for the cover of this anthology is from the installation *Shelter/Wedding Piece* which was in fact, her wedding to her lover Mini Liu on January 14, 1992.

SUSAN Y.F. CHEN was born in Pennsylvania, is 25 years old and in the public health field. Her parents are from Taiwan and China. She loves turtles, children, and the ocean and hopes to settle down with a partner someday.

JACQUELYN CHING BLACK wants to be Bruce Lee.

MARGARET MIHEE CHOE was born in Boston, raised, and is still residing in the New York City area. She is a second-generation Korean Yankee educated at Barnard College and Columbia University. She is currently working in the field of multicultural diversity training. Her work has appeared in the APA Journal and the anthology *Closer to Home: Bisexuality and Feminism* (Seal Press).

RINI DAS was born in Calcutta, India, and lived the first 22 years of her life there. Since then she has lived in Iowa City, Stony Brook, Belgium and Minneapolis. She moved to Columbus to live with her partner.

VANESSA MARZAN DEZA is a first generation bi-Pinay immigrant from a woman-run, single-parent household and an over-extended junior at UC Berkeley double-majoring in Ethnic Studies and Economics. She also edits *Maganda* (a Filipino-American literary magazine) and performs her work at poetry readings and community events. She writes grounded in her particular context as colored and female. It is a conscious act of resistance and creative envisioning.

NEESHA DOSANJH is a luscious Libra lesbian who believes that healing from abuse, past or present, is the greatest act of resistance. She is a writer, filmmaker and publisher of *Sami Yoni*, a journal for lesbians of South Asian descent. She currently resides in Toronto.

ELSA E'DER is one of nineteen granddaughters of Ilocano and Visayan plantation workers in Hawai`i. Inspired by Gramma E'der who wrote poems and worked pineapple fields. A Taurus born in Hollywood, she loves cities, deserts, islands, and all points between.

SHARON FERNANDEZ is a South Asian artist living in Toronto, Canada.

KA YIN FONG'S favourites are garage sales, fidgeting with photographic equipment, talking to Falaful and working in the dark. She also strongly believes in soymilk. Her phobias are stale cookies and hospital washrooms.

LINDA FONG was born and raised in Toronto, but spiritually, her roots lie buried somewhere in southern China. Besides being an activist, writer, and aspiring Taiko drummer, she is also a Kung Fu movie junkie. Her future plans include going to Hong Kong and China to become the next "Asia the Invincible."

JOYOTI GRECH was born in Dhaka, Bangladesh, when it was still part of Pakistan. Her mother is a Chakma woman of the indigenous Jummu people of the Chittagong Hill Tracts of Bangladesh. Her father is from Malta. Her parents taught her the rich fluidity of culture and the changing nature of "national" boundaries. Most important to her is collective self-pride!

NAOMI GUILBERT is a biracial, bisexual, itinerant taiko player and water meter reader. She can be found either in Winnipeg, Manitoba, where she was born and raised, or in San Francisco, where she goes to escape the hot Winnipeg summers.

NILA GUPTA was born an Aries in 1961. She immigrated with her family to Toronto, Canada, from Jammu, India, in 1967. Her first collection of poems entitled *The Garden of My (Be)longing* is forthcoming. She is a founding member of *Saheli Theatre Troupe*, a South Asian feminist theatre group.

MINAL HAJRATWALA was born in San Francisco. Her mother is of Indian descent from the Fiji Islands and her father is from India. She is a recent graduate of Stanford University and a writer and journalist in Northern California.

LISA KAHALEOLE CHANG HALL is a writer, activist and doctoral candidate in Ethnic Studies at the University of California — Berkeley. Her most recent work has appeared in the anthologies *Sisters, Sexperts and Queers: Beyond the Lesbian Nation* (Dutton Press) and *Beyond a Dream Deferred: Multicultural Education and the Politics of Excellence* (University of Minnesota Press).

JU HUI "JUDY" HAN is a Queerean born in 72 in Shilimdong Seoul Korea, immigrated to California at the age of twelve, sleepwalked through schools in Los Angeles suburbs, and currently at UC Berkeley screaming obscenity all the way through the English major and the white women's studies major. She recently made a journey back to Korea, found a niche among family, Korean feminists and dykes, and feels like she's come back to the belly of the monster called "U.S. imperialism." She is a member of Korean American Women with Attitudes (KAWA).

ALICE Y. HOM was born and raised in Los Angeles by Chinese immigrant parents. She received her B.A. from Yale and her M.A. in Asian American Studies from UCLA. Currently she is on the Ph.D. road at Claremont Graduate School. Her writings focus on Asian Pacific lesbian history, Asian Pacific parents with queer kids, and whatever drama is going on in her life.

TOMIYE ISHIDA is a mixed race Asian dyke, survivor of childhood sexual abuse, former sex trade worker, university student and mother of one beautiful boy-child, currently living in passionately turbulent love with another strong Asian woman.

SUSAN ITO, who recently completed her M.F.A in writing at Mills College, is a third-generation Japanese Hapa American. She lives in

Oakland, California and runs *Rice Papers*, a writing workshop for Asian American women. Her fiction and poetry have appeared in numerous publications.

DARLENA BIRD JIMENES was born and (as of now) resides in the United States. She has a B.F.A in dance/choreography and has studied theater, visual arts, videography, costume design, and stagecraft among other academic pursuits. Her wanderlust and artistic adventure will carry her around the globe. With this project, she explores the world of literary art, which combines with all of her other avenues, and in her own timeless, ageless fashion she embarks on new creative journeys.

LANI KA'AHUMANU is a feminist writer, poet, organizer, and activist. She co-edited *Bi Any Other Name: Bisexual People Speak Out* (Alyson, 1991) and serves on the lesbian/gay/bisexual advisory committee to the San Francisco Human Rights Commission. Lani is one of six national co-coordinators of BiNET USA, is a member of Asian Pacifica Sisters, and coordinates an HIV prevention project targeting lesbian and bisexual women. She is the mother of two grown children and at 50 is enjoying growing older and wiser.

J. KEHAULANI KAUANUI is of *kānaka maoli*/Native Hawaiian ancestry with roots in Anahola Kaua'i and genealogical ties to Moloka'i and Maui. She was born and raised in Southern California and received her B.A. from the University of California at Berkeley in Women's Studies. She is currently attending graduate courses as a Fulbright student at the University of Auckland in Aotearoa (New Zealand) studying Maori and Pacific Island Studies. Her past and future plans include researching Hawaiian diasporic communities, cultural studies and decolonization and returning to Hawai'i Nei.

MINA KUMAR'S work has appeared in *Christopher Street, Kalliope, The Toronto South Asian Review, Streetlights* (Viking/Penguin), and *Women's Glib Revisited* (Crossing Press). Born in Madras, India, she now lives in New York City.

LE THI DIEM THUY was born in Phan Thiet, two hours by train to Saigon in South Vietnam. She was raised in San Diego, two hours by train to Los Angeles in southern California.

C. ALLYSON LEE writes and performs friction on the wet coast of Canada. She has a special relationship with guitars, primates and softball womyn warriors.

PATRICE LEUNG works in film production. She was born in Trinidad, lives in Vancouver, works anywhere, and remains Chinese.

BRENDA JOY LEM is a writer and mixed media artist of Toi San heritage. She is pleased to be identifying herself as bisexual publicly for the first time.

HEIDI LI is a 28-year-old adoptee from Taiwan, raised by Chinese parents in the New Jersey tri-state area. She is a writer, Asian Pacific Lesbian and Bisexual Bay area community activist, part-time law student, and generally very busy person. Her interest is to continue writing fiction and, hopefully, one day make quirky, somewhat humorous, videos and/or films. To date, she has been published in *Common Lives/Lesbian Lives* and *The Poetry of Sex: Lesbians Write the Erotic* (Banned Books).

SHARON LIM-HING was born in Kingston, Jamaica. Of Hakka (Chinese) origin, her family moved to Florida when she was twelve. She received her Doctorate in Romance Languages and Literature from Harvard University. Her creative writing has appeared in *Piece of my Heart: A Lesbian of Colour Anthology* (Sister Vision Press), *APA Journal, Unleashing Feminism* (HerBooks) and other journals and books. She is currently looking for a few quiet hours to write in.

LITTLE EARTHQUAKE is a brown, womyn-loving, vegetarian supremacist Bengali dancer. She comes from her mother's womb and worships Kali. All prem, Shanti, and Shakti to desi dykes!

LEOLANI M. is a Native Hawaiian Islander who grew up in Nanakuli. In her search for work, education and a better lifestyle, she has spent over half of her life in San Francisco.

AMI R. MATTISON is a southern born and bred, lesbian-avenging, s/m dyke of Polynesian descent. She's currently living in Atlanta, Georgia and working on a Ph.D. in Liberal Arts at Emory University.

ANUJA MENDIRATTA writes to capture the moments and movements of this crazy life on page. It is the basic things which attract her these days: touch, food, sleep, sex, spirit. More and more, she realizes that she is simply an animal with a pen.

SHANI MOOTOO is a writer, visual artist and video-maker. She lives in Vancouver. Her visual art has been exhibited in many solo and group shows including *Memory and Desire: The Voices of Elem Women of Culture* at the Vancouver Art Gallery in 1992. In the past two years she has written and directed four videos including *English Lesson* and *The Wild Woman in the Woods*. Her writing has been featured in several *Gallerie Women Artists'* Monographs in *Fuse* magazine and in *The Skin on Our Tongues*. She is also the author of a collection of short fiction Out on Main Street (Press Gang, 1993).

SUNITI NAMJOSHI has taught in the Department of English at the University of Toronto and now lives and writes in Devon, England. She has published numerous poems, fables, articles, and reviews in anthologies, collections and journals in India, Canada, the U.S., Australia, and Britain. Her latest work, *Saint Suniti and the Dragon* and a new edition of *Feminist Fables* have been published by Spinifex Press (1993) and Virago Press (1994).

MONA OIKAWA, Sansei writer, editor, student, and teacher, lives in Toronto. Her poetry, short stories, and essays have been anthologized in Canada and the United States. *All Names Spoken*, her first book was published by Sister Vision Press in 1992. She is currently working on a doctoral degree in feminist studies.

MIDI ONODERA is a Toronto-based filmmaker who has been producing films for over ten years. She has 20 short films to her credit and is currently in post-production on her first feature film, *Sadness of the Moon*. Her films are distributed by Women Make Movies, NY, Canadian Filmmaker's Distribution Centre and Full Frame, Toronto.

TRINITY A. ORDONA is a Filipino-American from a post-World War II immigrant family of 13 children. She has a 25-year history of civil rights activism in the Asian, women's, and gay communities. She was a key organizer of the 1987 West Coast Retreat and 1989 National Retreat for Asian/Pacific lesbians and bisexual women and is currently a Ph.D graduate student in the History of Consciousness Program at the University of California at Santa Cruz.

JULIANA PEGUES/PEI LU FUNG was born in the year of the rooster and is a hapa middle-class dyke. Active with lesbian of colour and Asian activist groups in Minneapolis, her ongoing goals are to fight oppression, build community, learn to pronounce her Chinese name, and have pride in who she is.

PEOU LAKHANA is a Khmer refugee, Buddhist, artist, grassroots community organizer/political activist and radical lesbian of color feminist. She seeks to find balance and peace in her crazy life and to follow the path of her soul. One of her main journeys will be returning to Cambodia to rediscover herself and her roots. Once there she will also focus on organizing around HIV/AIDS prevention and education.

LINDA C. PARECE was born in Boston and lives in Quincy, Massachusetts. She is a working-class, Catholic, mixed heritage, white, Filipino, and Chinese lesbian.

CANYON SAM is a San Francisco-based writer, performance artist, activist and educator. Her work has appeared in numerous journals and anthologies, including *Lesbian Love Stories*, (Crossing Press) *Finding Courage* (Crossing Press), *The Seattle Review*, and *New Lesbian Writing* (Grey Fox Press). She founded the first organized group of Asian lesbians in the U.S. in 1977 in the Bay area. Currently she teaches at San Francisco State University and is working on a book of oral histories of Tibetan women.

SVATI SHAH is a 23-year-old South Asian, progressive, queerly lesbian activist whose creativity primarily manifests as poetry and short prose. Her political work stresses the need for progressive movements to work in coalition to bring about the end of patriarchy and its side effects. She is committed to evolving social understanding of issues particular to people with multicultural identities.

EVELINE SHEN is a second generation Chinese American born in Colorado and now living in Oakland, California. She hopes to continue combining her writing, activism and academic pursuits in her life work (whatever that may be). She enjoys spending time with her partner Jen and their two cats: Chester and Farley. She thanks Julie and Tania for their support and encouragement.

LIHBIN SHIAO is half Taiwanese, half Hakka, bisexual, and proud.

INDIGO CHIH-LIEN SOM is a garlic-chopping, book-binding, shuttle-throwing cancer and fire horse born, raised and planning to die in the San Francisco Bay area where she belongs. She is a bi-dyke woman-of-color-identified woman of color, specifically ABC (American-born Chinese). Her work has appeared in numerous publications including the lesbian of color anthology *Piece of my Heart* (Sister Vision Press).

TERESA TAN is a lesbian of Chinese and Finnish descent. Her position on the brink of two cultures has often provoked a deep sense of alienation. Through poetry she stimulates an appreciation for the subtle connectedness in all things. Both a writer and illustrator, she will soon publish a book of her poetry titled *Intangible*. She lives in Bloomfield Hills, Michigan.

DONNA TSUYUKO TANIGAWA is from the sugar plantation town of Waipahu on the island of O'ahu. Her work has appeared in *Sinister Wisdom*, *Common Lives/Lesbian Lives*, *Hawai'i Review*, and *Heart to Heart: A Discussion of Sexual Assault* (Sex Abuse Treatment Center).

DESIREE THOMPSON is a mix plate (i.e. mixed race; multi-heritage; mixed up) Japanese, Chinese, Hawaiian, German lesbian who temporarily resides in San Francisco with her life partner, Trinity Ordona. She is a letter carrier for the postal service.

KITTY TSUI is the author of *The Words of a Woman Who Breathes Fire* (Spinster Ink.). She is also a competitive body builder who won a bronze medal at Gay Games II in 1986 and the gold medal at Gay Games III in 1990. She was the first Asian Pacific woman to grace the cover of *On Our Backs* (Summer 1988 and Nov/Dec 1990).

ANN YURI UYEDA is a Sansei (third-generation Japanese American) lesbian who lives in the San Francisco Bay area. Her writing has appeared in *Phoenix Rising; Moving The Mountains*, an Asian American women's journal; the queer issue of the Asian Pacific American Journal; and the anthology *Outrage: Dykes and Bis Resist Homophobia* (Women's Press, 1993). She is currently collecting enough of her own material for a small collection of writings and a one-woman performance. Soon, she plans to return to graduate school for her Ph.D. then teach cultural anthropology at the college level and encourage general social anarchism.

WILLY ♀ CHANG SNOW WILKINSON is a proud hapa dyke from the San Francisco Bay area. Her mother is Chinese from Hawai'i and her father is Scottish, Irish and English. She would like to see "hapa" become a household word everywhere. She strongly believes that the time is now, that the reality of mixed heritage experience be acknowledged by all.

LINDA WONG is the associate editor of *Sojourner newspaper* in Boston and is on the steering committee of Asian Sisters in Action.

MERLE WOO is a socialist feminist educator, activist and writer, and leader in the Freedom Socialist Party and Radical Women. Her works have been published in several anthologies including *Chinese American Poetry: An Anthology* (University of Washington Press), *This Bridge Called My Back* (Kitchen Table Press), *Alcatraz 3* (Alcatraz Publications), *New Worlds of Literature* (W.W. Norton) and *Yellow Woman Speaks: Selected Poems* (Radical Women Publications).

LYNNE YAMAGUCHI FLETCHER is proudly Japanese American. A poet and a writer of both fiction and nonfiction, she celebrates beauty wherever she finds it. She lives and works in Boston, but will always consider the deserts of the Southwest home.

TZE-HEI YONG was recently transported to New York state, where she is currently attempting to adjust to the ubiquitous cloudy skies and overwhelmingly lush greenery after 15 years in the sunny south-west, while also, incidentally, going to graduate school. Writing has always been a cathartic exercise that Tze-Hei does solely for her own benefit, so she is glad to know that some other people may be able to get something out of her ramblings.

ZELIE KULIAIKANU'U DUVAUCHELLE, a native Hawaiian woman, was born and raised on the island of Moloka`i in Hawai`i. She is now living between Hawai`i and San Francisco creating a bridge between cultures through her music. "Hawaiian concepts are universal concepts which I hope to share through traditional and contemporary Hawaiian music." Aloha.

AMY A. ZUKERAN is a lesbian of Okinawan descent, born and raised in Kaneohe, Hawai`i. I think it is important for our society's health that minority voices be recorded and heard. Through our lives, we prove that true intimacy transcends the cultural barriers of sexual orientation, race, and language.

Credits

The editor and the publisher would like to thank the following for their kind permission to reprint copyrighted material in this book:

Aruna, V.K. "Myth of One Closet," from *Sinister Wisdom*, No. 47, Summer/Fall 1992, was published as part of "Journey in Progress" an essay in progress about the multiple returns to geographic homelands and the psychic locations of one South Asian lesbian. Reprinted with permission of the author.

Bantigue, Ana Fajardo. "Island Dream," from *Sinister Wisdom*, No. 47, Summer 1992. Reprinted with permission of the author.

E'der, Elsa. "Family Reunion: the Longing," from *Smell This 2*, Spring 1991. Reprinted with permission of the author.

Fong, Ka Yin. photograph of "Amita and Vinita" from *NOW magazine*, May 1993 and *XTRA!*, June September 1993. Reproduced with permission of the photographer.

Hom, Alice Y. "In the Mind of An/Other" from *Amerasia Journal*, Special Edition Burning Cane, Vol. 17, No. 2, 1991. Reprinted with permission of the author.

Hom, Alice Y. "An APL's Alphabet" from *The APA Journal*, Vol. 2, No. 1, (Spring/Summer 1993). Reprinted with permission of the author.

Ito, Susan. "Yoo Hoo" from *Side Show: An Annual of Contemporary Fiction*, Somersault Press, El Cerrito, 1992. Reprinted with permission of the author.

Kaahumanu, Lani. "Hapa Haole Wahine" from *Bi Any Other Name: Bisexual People Speak Out*. ed. Loraine Hutchins and Lani Kaahumanu, published by Alyson Publications, Inc. Copyright 1991 Lani Kaahumanu. Reprinted with permission of the author.

Han, Ju Hui "Judy" and J. Kehaulani Kauanui. "'Asian Pacific Islander:' Issues of Representation and Responsibility" from *Asian American Women's Journal: Moving the Mountains*. Special Issue, 1993. Reprinted with permission of the author.

Kumar, Mina. "Jeannie" from *Christopher Street*. October 1993. Reprinted with permission of the author.

Lee, C. Allyson. "Owed to Grandmother," from *Possibilitiis*. Premiere Issue, July 1993. First Place in the First Annual Poetry Contest. Reprinted with permission of the author.

Lee, C. Allyson. "Recipe" from *West Coast Line* No. 8 (26/2) Fall 1992. Reprinted with permission of the author.

Little Earthquake. "Rati" from *Heridan: A Womanist/Feminist Journal*, Spring 1993. Reprinted with permission of the author.

Little Earthquake. "Making Love To You" from *Heridan: A Womanist/Feminist Journal*, Fall 1993. Reprinted with permission of   the author.

Mattison, Ami R. "Misplacing Alissa" from *Agnes Scott College Writers' Festival* 1993. Reprinted with permission of the author.

Mendiratta, Anuja. "Untitled," appeared as "Silence of Home" from *APAJ Journal*, Vol. 2, No. 1 (Spring/Summer 1993). Reprinted with permission of the author.

Mootoo, Shani. "A Recognition," "For Naan," and "Manahambre Road," from *Did You Know That Snow Was So Cold?* by Shani Mootoo and Sher Azad Jamal, Rungh Cultural Society, 1992. Reprinted with permission of the author.

Oikawa, Mona. "Stork Cools Wings" from *Riding Desire*. ed. Tee Corinne. Austin, Texas: Edward Williams Publishing Company, 1991. Reprinted with permission of the author.

Som, Indigo. "Internalization" from *Smell This* 2, Spring 1991. Reprinted with permission of the author.

Som, Indigo. "Just Once..." and "In My Sleep" from *APA Journal*, Vol. 2, No. 1 (Spring/Summer 1993). Reprinted with permission of the author.

Tanigawa, Donna Tsuyuko. "I Like Beef Wit' Words" from *Common Lives/Lesbian Lives*, Summer 1993. Reprinted with permission of the author.

Tsui, Kitty. "A Chinese Banquet" from *The Words Of A Woman Who Breathes Fire*, Spinsters Ink, San Francisco, 1983. Reprinted with permission of the author.

Uyeda, Ann Yuri. "Love Letters From the Movement" from *Asian American Women's Journal: Moving the Mountains*, 1993. Reprinted with permission of the author.

Anu. "Response to A Room of One's Own" from *Shamakami*, 1990-91. Reprinted with permission of the author.

Woo, Merle. "The Politics of Breast Cancer" from *FSP Discussion Bulletin* July 1993. Reprinted with permission of the author.

Woo, Merle. "Yellow Woman Speaks" from *Yellow Woman Speaks: Selected Poems*. Radical Women Publications, Seattle, 1986. Reprinted with permission of the author.

Yamaguchi, Lynne Fletcher. "Recurring Dreams" from *For Crying Out Loud: A Newsletter for Women Survivors*. Reprinted with permission of the author.

S ISTER VISION: BLACK WOMEN AND WOMEN OF COLOUR PRESS was founded by Women of Colour in 1985. Sister Vision's mandate and priority is publishing books by Black women, First Nations women, Asian women and women of mixed racial heritage.

The vision of Sister Vision Press came out of a need for autonomy, a need to determine the context and style of the work, words and images that are produced about us.

Our list features ground-breaking and provocative fiction, poetry, anthologies, oral history, theoretical writing and books for young adults and children.

A free catalogue of our books is available from:
Sister Vision Press
P. O. Box 217
Station E, Toronto
Ontario, Canada
M6H 4E2
Phone (416) 533-2184